Until He Died

by Arthur F. Clark

ISBN 0-7414-2762-1

Published by:

INFINITY
PUBLISHING.COM

1094 New DeHaven Street, Suite 100
West Conshohocken, PA 19428-2713
Info@buybooksontheweb.com
www.buybooksontheweb.com
Toll-free (877) BUY BOOK
Local Phone (610) 941-9999
Fax (610) 941-9959

Printed in the United States of America

Printed on Recycled Paper

Published April 2006

Contents

Chapter:

Photo Schedule:

Dedication

To my wife, family and friends who've given me the courage, and support to pursue my dreams.

Chapter 1

Pipe Smoke, and Rum

The boy sat there, idly tracing the outline of something hard and heavy in his mother's carry-all as it lay on the seat between them. He was bored, and tired of listening to her and his sister talk endlessly about nothing. Without thinking, he blurted out, "If you shoot someone else with this gun, does that mean we'll have to move again?"

Sarah's response was immediate. Turning on him, she shushed the boy, while at the same time throwing quick glances around the train's car to see if anyone else had heard. Her whisper came back hard and sharp. "You know better than to talk about such things in a public place! What is wrong with you today?"

Andy gave the bag a shove, and replied, "But, Ma! It's sitting right here where anyone can tell what it is!

Besides, I don't want to go to no Cape Cod! This place sounds like it's out in the sticks, with nothing but stinkin' cows and fish!"

Amy piped up, "Even cows and fish smell better than the sewer runnin' down the middle of our street! Who knows, maybe it'll be fun."

His mother suggested he withhold judgment until he knew what he was talking about, and then added, "We're almost to our stop, so be patient for a few more minutes."

Chafing against nerves frazzled by so many weary miles, the high pitched sing-song of the conductor's "Yarmouth Port, Yarmouth Pooort!" was like one of the patent medicines of the day. Bitter to swallow, but the promised cure worth any price.

Intermingled with the incessant clanging of the train's warning bell, the man's next call, "Yarmouth Port, Yarmouth Pooort, next stop Hyannis, end o'the line! Aaaaall change here for down-Cape stations!" may have been annoying for its repetition, but endured with the numb patience and toleration only a long journey's end could bring.

Adding insult, the noise and confusion seemed to build in direct opposition to the declining speed of this mechanical marvel. Tuned out like a heartbeat, the background rhythm of wheels pounding on rail-joints was dying, only to be replaced by a gathering of loud rattlings, bangs, and groans. Complaining mightily, the train's arthritic cars were shifting their weight forward in response to the steel-against-steel scream of brakes.

Those passengers who were going on, sat in studied boredom. Staring off into the distance of their minds, or out of windows through their own reflections, they waited like permanent fixtures for the next and final stop. Around these living statues, the interior of the passenger car erupted into the confusing hustle and bustle of disembarkation.

A few of the overanxious stood to don coats, hats and scarves, while those fearful of forgetting things, attempted to gather their various packages and belongings. As a result, collisions of both purpose and a physical nature were inevitable. Add to this the train's unpredictable swaying motions, plus brakings, and balance became an impossibility.

Careworn mothers delegated responsibilities and duties in their usual, time-honored, but absentminded manner. "Harry, take your sister's hand! Joannie, get out of the man's way! Don't forget your mittens!"

Their offspring responded with equally common, but questionable degrees of attention. Some having just been rudely awakened, and still half-asleep. Others, dancing and bubbling with barely restrained excitement.

Passengers of predictable occupation carried bulky display cases, and cheap cardboard luggage. Battered from countless trips and endless miles, the baggage looked like natural appendages. Salesmen for the most part, they stubbed out smelly, half-chewed cigars, and stood waiting as if this were their normal lot in life. Organic machines, wearing brown derby hats, coming from nowhere—with an equal destination—and carrying round-trip tickets to prove it.

The more affluent gentlemen, businessmen or whatever, wore their velvet-trimmed overcoats, and checked their golden, chain-bound watches against remembered schedules as they gained their feet. Others, carrying umbrellas and top hats, ducked down to squint through steamy, smoke-clouded windows into the gathering gloom.

Possibly they were checking to see if the connecting train had arrived. More likely, they hoped for the sight of a familiar buggy waiting to meet them.

Cape Cod afternoons seemed almost nonexistent on cold, dark, and blustery November days such as this. Barely past four-thirty, the light was failing quickly. The sun, hidden by a seamless gray where sky should have been, was folding its token glow into the shadows of the bony hills some referred to as pastures in this part of New England.

Stark in their nakedness, Elm trees etched their severe, brush-stroke silhouettes across a dome of depression.

There was a raw dampness, and a promise of rain or sleet in the bone-chilling air. Salty ocean, and fermenting marsh made their own presence known by penetrating the more expected odors of the train yard with a quality almost strong enough to taste. A greeting from home, and the elixir of life to some, it brought wrinkled noses and questioning looks from the uninitiated.

Smoke, dust, rust-brown leaves, and yellow, discarded newspapers whirled, chasing each other around the ash and coal cinders which passed for paving. It gave onlookers the impression this gusty, freshening nor'easter was doing its best to scrub things clean.

Massive, the black locomotive had brought its earth-shaking rumble, ringing bell, banshee whistle, and the roar of steam with it into the station area.

Tied to the hitching rail, horses stood imprisoned by assorted buggies, carriages, and delivery wagons advertising their parent companies. The animals twitched and shook nervously, trying to evaluate this newly-arrived, noisy monster. Having few alternatives, the poor creatures blew slobber, stamped hooves, tossed heads, and rolled their big, brown eyes around obstructing blinders.

Arrogantly ignoring these living engines, the train belched dark and sulfurous coal-smoke to mix with its white steam, and the wind.

The loading platform was cold and bare when Alex Matthews stepped out of the waiting room, away from the warmth of its pot-bellied stove. Backlit by the soft glow of coal-oil lamps from inside the station, the man's whiskers and hair were briefly turned into a golden halo by the light. His massive, dark bulk emphasized by the normalcy in size of the others crowding through the door behind him.

With his visored hat scrunched down on his head against any stray blows; pipe cupped in one hand, the other held to his brow as if to shade tender eyes from a summer sun; woolen sea-jacket buttoned tight, collar upturned to thwart the weather; feet wide-spread, in a sea-stance; body leaning into the wind; intense gaze squinting into the confusing waves of arriving people, freight and greeters; the man became the perfect, living caricature of how a working sea captain might mount his vessel's bridge.

It happened quickly. Like the sweep of a wand, a gust indicative of that which was to come, cleared the air of its mixture of smoke, steam and debris. Although not quite as nebulous, the hubbub of people and noise seemed to melt away in the same currents, and left Alex standing there alone.

Under these ephemeral conditions, Sarah and her two children seemed more to have materialized from the confusion, than physically arrived on the train. Standing clumped together at the foot of the passenger car's steps, right in front of the man, the new arrivals looked like so much jetsam dumped on the shore by a passing tide.

Alex greeted them with a, "Whoop!" that was going to become only too familiar. This was followed by a, "Hey, Sister!" in a volume one would consider he might reserve for hailing a distant, passing ship.

Sarah, unsteady on her feet after riding for so long, staggered in the blustery wind and grabbed at the abomination of Victorian splendor perched on her head. A mountain of black silk and ribbons, the hat partially hid blond hair done in a French-twist style. The combination stirred her brother's memory, and he looked closer.

Still pretty, in a wholesome sort of way, the woman seemed careworn beyond her years. A touch of hardness had crept in around the corners of her mouth, and with the exception of that extraordinary hat, the clothing of all three echoed a same, tired drabness.

Alex was sure it had been a long and tedious journey, but the sense of desperation read in her eyes had to come from a far deeper source than one day's travel could have wrought. Stirred by the obvious depravity before him, the man felt a need for action before he betrayed his concerns.

This large, intimidating figure scootched down onto one knee, wrapped a huge arm around Sarah's waist and tried to gather the two children in with the other.

Andy squeaked out a, "Hello, Uncle Alex!" then managed to skip back just in time to avoid the embarrassing crush.

Interrupting their greetings, a large coach-and-four came wheeling up beside the train and stopped at the last car, two behind theirs. The driver and a footman scrambled from the expensive carriage, and began to assist one of the conductors and a diminutive porter in getting an extremely portly gentleman down the narrow stairs of the private parlor car.

As if the earth had somehow stopped, all heads in the train yard turned to watch.

Resembling a humorous skit parodying a lack of dignity, and performed by a band of roving actors, the four men lifted, shoved, pushed and cajoled, finally getting their puffing, elderly passenger conveyed to his new means of transport. Breathing heavily, the man's servants scurried back to their positions, and the coach left in the same type of flurry with which it had arrived.

Show over, everyone in the area returned to their personal errands without missing a step, and the world began to turn once more.

Responding to the questioning looks, Alex replied, "Amos Otis! He's one of the directors, and owner of a good portion of the Cape Cod Branch Railroad. You must remember him Sarah! He's been one of the leaders of our community for years. Surely you've read his, *Letters from Skipper Jack to my Old Friend that Prints The Yarmouth Register?"*

Sarah frowned. "Isn't he the one who planted the elms along Hallet Street?"

Alex nodded, and added, "Back in forty-one. He, Ansel Hallet, and old man Thacher. Started the Barnstable County Insurance Company a few years before that, remember? That's where his money came from y'know! Bein' the relative of a patriot don't do diddly for a man's pocket!"

Sarah may have been tired, but she still recognized an insult when she heard one. "What do you mean, 'If I remember?' That was before I was born!"

Smiling at the anticipated rejoinder, Alex got in another bantering jab. "No wonder the poor man looks so old!" Then to ease the sting, hurriedly added, "Do you people always travel in such exclusive company?"

Amy fell for the good-humored bait. "We've never ridden on a train before! Did that man have to ride in his car all alone? He could have come into ours. We had lots of people he could have sat with. Is he rich? Does he own the station too? I didn't see any luggage, so he can't be staying long! Did he eat on the train? We did! We had a loaf of bread Ma brought along, but I'm thirsty now!"

Alex backed off, and put up his hand. "Whoa, girl! You carry on like your mother! What's the matter, didn't anyone talk to you all the way home?"

She shook her head, and answered, "They talked, they just wouldn't listen!"

The man grinned in complete understanding.

Out of the corner of his eye, Alex had noticed her brother standing beside them. Wearing a mixed look of disgust and affected boredom, Andy continued to play with the strings of his dufflebag while the salutations and small talk went on. When spoken to directly, the boy responded to Alex's inquiry as to the condition of his health with a muffled, "Fine!" and then ducked as his hair got ruffled by the older man's big, rope-hardened hand.

Greetings over, Alex made an obvious assumption. One he immediately regretted. "This can't be all of your baggage, Sarah! I'd best get over to the freight car before the train starts again, and half of your stuff ends up in Hyannis!"

Sarah, the desolation of her world now showing plainly on her face, corrected him. "What you see, is what we've got!"

"Sad isn't it? We did leave in a bit of a hurry. . . . Still, a person would think that after fourteen years of marriage, and a lifetime of work, there'd somehow be more than this to show for it."

Stunned, Alex acknowledged the unexpected admission of poverty with a shake of his head and a frown. Busying himself to hide his sister's shared embarrassment, he sat Amy on the crook of one huge arm, where she perched, clinging to her string-tied box of possessions. Grabbing Andy's dufflebag with the other hand, the man stood up and said, "Pick up your Mother's bag, Son, and c'mon! Let's git out of this weather afore it starts into rainin'." Then he turned to walk away.

Sullen, and without thought, Andy made a major blunder. Expressing the foulness of his mood as much by the tone of his voice as the words chosen, the boy muttered, "She can carry her own damn bag!" Facing the luggage, he kicked at the offending burden with a scuffed toe.

Alex continued his turning motion so smoothly an observer would have thought the action had been planned and rehearsed. Bending down, he placed Amy and the bag gently back on the ground, and still turning, by the time the captain had completed his three-hundred-sixty degree maneuver, the man was empty-handed, face to face with Andy, and on the young man's level again.

With one big fist, the man grabbed his nephew by the shirt front, and lifted him effortlessly as he stood back up. Alex held him within a cat's whisker of his own face, while the boy's holey-soled shoes dangled two feet from the ground. So close were they that, smothered by the captain's hot breath, the young man's whole world suddenly became buried in the smell of pipe tobacco and rum. Adding to the discomfort, Andy felt sure he was going to drown in his own spit with his collar pulled so tight.

Alex, eyes sparking with intensity, his neck bulging and flushed by the surge of anger, exploded in the boy's face. The tirade started as a shout, and ended barely a whisper, but every word was distinct. "Boy! Don't you 'ever' talk back to me again! I did not ask you a favor that had the option of denial, Mister! No! I 'told' you to help your mother by carrying her bag, and now by Jesus you had best do it!"

Placing the boy back on the ground as easily as he'd picked him up, the man turned again, took Amy by the hand and scoffed up the dufflebag with the other. Puffing on his pipe as if in competition with the train's steam engine, Alex grumped, "C'mon Sarah!" and stomped away toward his own buggy without as much as a backward glance.

"All abooaard! Hyannis! Next stop, Hyannis! All abooaard!" Mixed with the renewed puffing of the engine and hiss of steam, the conductor's voice was barely audible. Slowly, the wheels began to turn once more.

Stunned, Andy and Sarah looked at each other as if the sudden exchange had gone beyond human comprehension. With emotions running wild, the boy didn't know whether to cry, or shout back in his own gathering anger. This had been an unexpected, and frustrating humiliation at the hands of a virtual stranger. No matter that the man was related, or the rebuke well earned.

Turning away from his mother so she'd not see him fighting tears, the boy channeled his rage at the departing train. The shout commanded almost as much respect as his uncle's. "Bastard! I hate this God-damned town! I hate him! I ain't gonna stay in this friggin' place and take his crap, I'm goin' back to Albert. I'm goin' back to the city, where it don't stink like SHIT!"

In the act of swinging aboard, a startled conductor looked back to see if he were being hailed over the engine's noise.

Sarah, her mother's heart breaking, reached out a hand to put a protective arm around the boy, and opened her mouth to speak.

Andy brushed the hand away angrily. The last thing he wanted now was the added embarrassment of a mother's touch. Picking up the luggage, he went marching off in the direction his uncle had gone, and let the heat of his anger burn itself out slowly in the effort of carrying the heavy bag.

Hand to mouth, Sarah hid a puzzled half-smile as she followed the procession. Deep down inside, she was aware of being home. The feeling, one of comfort and security.

On a more conscious level, however, her thoughts expressed the hope all would soon be right with her world in spite of this little outburst.

Suddenly the woman's work-hardened fingers pressed into her lips, turning them white. The smile became a worried frown as new thoughts caught her off-guard.

No matter that she instantly recognized them as being more punitive Calvinistic than substantive, the fears were bothersome. *Oh God, what if these two 'stay' at each other's throats? And, if Andrew does leave, what then? Worse, what will become of us, if Alex, driven to a change of heart by the turmoil, refuses to grant refuge?*

Could he . . . would he . . . throw his own flesh and blood to the wolves?

Chapter 2

Aunt Sophia's Ghost

The nor'easter continued to build with the gathering darkness. Sleet turning to snow rattled and hissed on the canvas side-curtains of the buggy as Alex turned off the muddy mixture of sand and shells known as Hallet Street.

Clinging to pre-Revolutionary dreams, a few Tory-minded individuals still insisted on calling this thoroughfare The King's Highway, but politics mattered little to the four of them tonight. Only a mile from the station, fifteen minutes of bouncing in the cold buggy had the newcomers aware they'd misjudged the weather, and Alex's hard-packed, shell drive was gratefully accepted as timely deliverance. Getting down from his protective enclosure to open the barn door, and lead the horse inside, Alex was forced to shield his face from the biting onslaught of wind-driven pellets.

Accompanied by its familiar smells and the quiet, the inviting warmth and darkness of the barn was such a contrast from the relentless fury of the storm left behind they found themselves whispering.

Sarah suggested it was because the welcomed shelter had produced the same feeling of safety one gets upon entering a great cathedral. Protected there by the hands of

God, one was careful not to break His peace, or provoke His wrath.

With that same peace and wrath in mind, she spoke softly when she asked, "Is this a good omen, Alex? This storm?"

To poke fun at her theory, Alex feigned difficulty in hearing, but his reply was soft too. A fact not recognized by those unaccustomed to the man's gruff voice. "Eh? Omen? The storm, you say! You feel intimidated by this greeting, and want the good Lord to cease His ruminations? Well, now that you're here Sarah, I presume you'll order the rest of winter to be springlike, with bird's song and daisies too!

Good omen? Not likely, m'lady! Praying for a balanced ledger sounds a bit wishful, don't you think?"

Working in the friendly, yellow glow of kerosene lanterns, they began to get old Sandy unhitched, rubbed down and settled in for the night. Busy with their tasks, the newcomers were startled when a dark doorway erupted with life.

Adopting a stiff, formal manner, Alex introduced the late arriving, four-legged members of the family to his guests. "Sarah, Master Sears, Miss Amy, may I present Ulysses Matthews, and his older friend, George!"

Ulysses, a young, handsome, black Labrador greeted them joyfully. Eager to please, he used his wagging-tail, wriggly-body, and wet tongue to thump, bump and slobber each one individually.

Alex explained his choice of name. "Stole it from Homer's *Odyssey!* That tale's seagoing hero lived through some pretty wild adventures, and my spirited, young friend here seems inclined to run down the same path! Bullheaded, I can't for the life of me make him understand how that nose of his does not belong in everyone else's business! With little thanks, my shoretime is often spent bailing the fool out of trouble!"

He added, "This Ulysses is a sailor too, y'know!"

No one missed the affection in the man's voice, nor the captain's attempt to include the dog in his brotherhood of the sea. It was almost as if this fact might somehow explain, or excuse the animal's reported misbehavior.

George was big for a cat. A dusty-yellow tiger of many years, he left no doubt as to who's barn they were in. His regal attitude also made it obvious why he'd been named after that particular English King.

Selecting a comfortable throne in full view, he ignored his new family members as long as convention would allow. Aloof, his royal highness eventually condescended to grant his new subjects the boon of scratching his chin and neck. Mistake! Seduced on the instant, he gave in, purred noisily, curled around their legs, and got underfoot like any commoner.

During this greeting ceremony, the creature did make one distinct point. He avoided the dripping buggy. In the warmth of the barn, the accumulated slush had turned into rivulets which ran sneakily onto the wooden-plank floor.

Not that anyone's imagination gave the puddles life, but one could almost sense an inner awareness waiting there, hoping to trap an unwary foot in their mushy wetness. The cat sensed this aura long before the others, and without passing judgment on its malevolence, treated the mounded residue with the natural disdain of any feline.

Their tasks finished, the weary travelers gathered their belongings. Carrying one of the lanterns, they wound their way through the myriad doorways and halls of the connecting rooms and buildings that led into the main house.

Guarding against stragglers, Alex brought up the rear.

With apparent, malicious intent, bursts of sleet rattled against the dark windows as they passed. The wind too screamed its frustration around the corners of the building, and moaned in the Elms overhead. Menacing, taunting, threatening, the sounds evoked a feeling of evil. A sense of some venomous spirit seeking entry to get at the warmth and life hiding there.

Leading the way, Sarah asked Alex over her shoulder, "Have the packets put up for the winter? I know I'd sure hate to be at sea in this!"

Alex, his voice deep and gravely, answered amiably enough. "Most of them have stopped running altogether. It's sad, but just another sign of how hard the times are for sail. I've heard Ansel Hallet sold the *Charles B. Prindle*, now the season's run is over. She's going to the Cape's south side for the New York trade, but who knows how long that'll last. Most of the Masters have been talking about giving up, those that haven't sold already. Captain Gorham, who owns the *North*, was just saying he's not sure he'll make it through the next season as a packet, so he's looking into lumber."

No one asked, but he answered the question anyway. "Me? I'm just one of those stubborn, old diehards I guess! Resisting change until the bitter end, I'll probably hoist anchor when everything's gone, and trust God and the wind to steer me safe!"

His future plans explained, the man came back to the present. "Right now my old gal's down to bare poles, and tucked into her winter mooring over behind Sandy Neck. Her hull's so old I don't dare take a chance on its gettin' stove-in by ice, which means she's got to come out soon. Any luck, an' I'll get the topmasts unstepped tomorrow, then maybe I can get her hauled out and on blocks during this week's flood-tides."

"You are talking about the *Yarmouth*, right? She can't be that old."

"Hey, she was Commissioned back in '41. Captain Thomas Matthews built her as one of the first centerboard schooners designed just for these shallow waters.

Nat Taylor had her for a few years, then passed her on to old man Chase and his sons who sailed her on the Hyannis to New York runs. She lay idle through the war years, up 'til I bought her and brought her back to this side in '67."

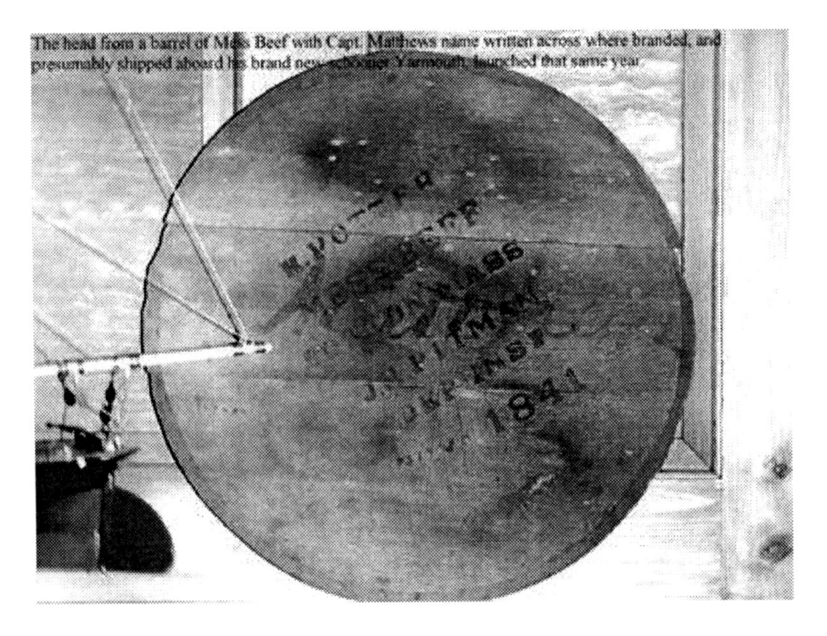

The head from a barrel of Mess Beef with Capt. Matthews name written across where branded, and presumably shipped aboard his brand new schooner Yarmouth, launched that same year

"I guess almost thirty years is old for a ship."

"Ancient, for a working vessel, but she handles so sweet it's easy to overlook the few shortcomings of age. I bought her right, but now what with the depression so bad, it's hard to justify the upkeep of an old ship. O'course, skimping there might put me in the position of the king who lost his crown for want of a nail. . . ."

"Well, why don't you sell out too?"

"Got to admit I've thought of it! The future's bleak. Cargo is scarce, expenses are getting out of hand, and I figure the competition from the railroad is here to stay. Topping that off, now I hear rumors about the salt works giving up.

Could turn to coal, but it's messy, labor intensive, and the hold gets so black no one would ever ship a 'clean' cargo with me again! Lumber on the other hand is clean, but it takes an awful toll on a boat. I'd have to cut extra hatches into the forward bow to load long pieces, and that means a weaker hull and ready-made holes for the sea.

Ice is a possibility, but people in the Southern climes can make their own these days what with steam engines, and ammonia compressors. Besides, m'schooner never was big enough to make that a paying trip.

Kinda leaves a ship with nothing left to haul, don't it? Especially trying to make the scheduled runs of a packet."

If he had seen it, the smile on Sarah's face would have troubled him deeply.

As they approached the final doorway, Alex cocked a mischievous eye at the children, and asked conversationally, "Aunt Sophia is sure making her presence known in the attic tonight, isn't she Sarah? Listen to her groan and rattle those bones up there!"

Without warning, his sister stopped dead in her tracks. Crowded into a narrow hallway, this caused numerous chain-reaction collisions throughout the procession. Even George and Ulysses, padding along quietly behind the crowd, ended up dancing and stumbling over each other.

Sputtering in the sudden flush of remembered emotion, Sarah fumed, "Alex, you stop that! You're not about to put another generation through the torture you made me endure as a child!"

"Hah!" Alex chortled and coughed. A sinister attempt at laughter, it was almost as frightening as the thoughts he'd conjured from their shared past.

The admission was difficult, but he had to agree he'd been as surprised as the others by his throat's unrequested, strangling noises. Uneasy, and somewhat embarrassed by it all, the man tried to suppress any further spontaneous outbursts. Lingering, uncontrollable heaves of his body forced a strained stiffness into his voice.

"Youngsters, for years I had your mother convinced that every time we had a hard nor'easter, your Great Aunt Sophia would come back to haunt our attic.

During little windshifts and gusts, you can hear groans from the big, old weathervane where she sits up on the barn's cupola. I'd tell your mother it was auntie, lamenting her endless fate.

The branches of the trees brushing our roof, and the house shifting and complaining about the breeze would be crazy old Sophie again. She'd make those noises rattling her long-dead bones up the stairs and on the ceiling overhead, while she searched!"

Amy fell for the bait. "Searched? What was she looking for, Uncle Alex?"

His grin was broad, and his voice booming when he answered, "Why, trying to find another child to murder, of course!"

"That's not funny, Alex!" Sarah had turned in the doorway, and was standing there blocking the way. Her hands planted on her hips in a pose of defiance.

"Hah Haaa!" This time Alex couldn't contain himself, and he convulsed in remembered glee. It had been years since he'd actually laughed out loud.

This uncle of her's was unsettling. First he was stiff, stern, almost fierce, but then he'd show a soft side over which he seemed to be quite embarrassed. Now, tales of ghosts? Amy wasn't sure if she was going to like this move to Cape Cod after all.

Looking anxiously from one adult to the other, she chanced one more question. "What happened to Aunt Sophia that she'd want to come back and haunt 'this' house?"

Trying to put on a solemn face, Alex burst out, "She hung herself in the attic, during a wild nor'easter!" The man exhaled another burst of suppressed laughter through his nose, and continued, "That was after she'd slit the throats of half the children in the neighborhood for laffin' at her, and then threw her own youngsters off the widow's walk 'cuz she caught 'em talkin' after bed-time!"

Crouching to the children's level, and whispering in that heavy, rum and tobacco flavored breath, he added, "Supposedly, according to family rumors, she'd just found out her husband had been eaten by cannibals in the South Seas! He'd been caught dallying with one of their maidens, which seemed excuse enough for them to hold a feast. Him being the guest of honor o'course, and especially since they kinda had a taste for white meat anyway!" With that the man grinned from ear to ear, licked his lips, and opened his eyes widely as if in ecstatic pleasure of a feast at hand. His hands rose, with fingers waving like flames, and he exclaimed, "Yesss!"

Continuing his tale, he added, "Well, for some reason, this drove poor old Sophia completely maaaad!"

It was hard to miss the twinkle in his eye. "Turned her right into a witch, y'know?"

The children stood there in wide-eyed amazement. The subject matter seemed hardly fit for mirth. Was this puzzling, contradictory man to be believed?

Equally disconcerting was that the tale had been told through bursts of suppressed laughter. Laughter, obviously aimed at their mother. Collectively deducing that it would take a madman to laugh in the face of such horror, they took a step backwards and bumped into their mother's blockade.

"Alex, you stop that! Family rumors, my foot! If there ever were any, you started them! Listen to the weird things that go on in the back pastures of your mind!"

Sarah, feigning anger in a poor attempt at hiding her own amusement, continued, "This clown of an uncle of yours told me tales like this every time we had a storm! After a while, all it took was a light breeze to turn me into a pile of blubbering fear.

For some reason, no one ever spoke of poor old Sophia in front of the children, so I believed him! In desperation, the morning after one especially horrible, and sleepless night, I finally got up the courage to ask Mother the truth of the matter. Well, that's when I discovered how full of horse-droppings your uncle really was.

Murder and suicide, indeed! Poor Aunt Sophia died an old maid, and her end was certainly tragic enough without any of 'his' elaboration." she said, nodding at her brother.

"One bright, summer afternoon, the poor woman was taking some air up on the widow's walk. Laying on the rail, apparently she dozed off in the sun's heat and tumbled off the roof!

Nothing but an unfortunate accident, pure and simple!"

Backing off a little, she added, "Well, rumors flew of possible suicide, and cooking sherry may have had something to do with it, but most certainly there were no storms, witch-craft, or murders associated with her death!

Mother explained how family embarrassment over this inglorious end was the probable reason for avoidance of the subject. That, plus I guess she was an extremely-bitter old woman, who enjoyed taking her hate out on anyone within reach of her tongue!"

Sarah smiled, "While we're divulging family secrets, ask your uncle what I did to get even!"

"Hah Haaa!" Alex exploded into laughter again. His face was less of a grimace now, as if getting used to the idea of what its duties were supposed to be during these episodes.

"D'you know what a June bug is? Those big, brown scarab-beetles that bumble against the window screens on a spring night? Well, your mother took a big mason-jar and filled it with 'em, then emptied it into my bed.

That night, when I crawled between the sheets, I thought every crab in Cape Cod Bay had ahold of me. Those things cling and stick like crazy! By the time I got through hollerin' and rippin' the bed apart, not to mention knocking the furniture over, and damn near tearing the hinges off the door trying to get out of my room, everybody in the family was there to see what all the hullabaloo was about.

After the candle was relit, and the deed uncovered, Sarah confessed. O'course, she had to give the reason she'd done it. . . ." The unfinished sentence being an implication his sister had broken a sacred trust.

Getting no response from the accused, he continued. "Mother thought Sarah's retaliation was such fit punishment, she gave your mother a week off from her chores to show approval. Naturally, those fell to me. The idea being that I shouldn't forget *Sarah's Justice* too soon!

Fat chance! Took me all summer, and many sleepless nights afore I was sure I'd gotten rid of the last of those bugs!"

Allowed to share this family confidence, the children began to see their uncle as more than just a figure of authority and discipline. He had, after all, been a boy once. Showing tentative approval, they joined the now easier laughter of their elders.

The family warmth was added to by a cheery, cast-iron and chrome cooking stove which greeted their entry. Turned low, a whale-oil lamp sat in the middle of the kitchen table where it illuminated place settings for four.

Smells of freshly baked bread, and a quahog chowder on the back of the stove awakened hungers long forgotten in the weariness of travel.

Stacking their collective luggage in a corner, while Alex lit another lamp, they followed the man through the adjoining rooms much like children behind a pied piper. Directing their gaze with the light of his lamp, the man proudly explained how the new arrivals would be able to use indoor facilities now, while he showed them the full-bath installed in the old birthing room. It had a real flushing toilet, a sink, and a copper-lined, wooden tub complete with running water. Hot water would still have to be lugged from the cistern attached to the stove if they wanted a warm bath, but it was better than most in the village had to offer.

Moving back in the general direction of the kitchen, Alex told the family that some day he'd show them how the windmill pumped water up into the attic tank. "Then you'll know what to do when I'm at sea, and you've run dry."

Looking at the boy, Alex suggested, "That'd be a good thing for you to learn, young man!"

Andy's scowl brought back recent memories, but no comment.

Ignoring the lack of response, the captain continued, "You young ones can have the two rooms over the kitchen. The heat goes up through those ceiling grates from the stove here, so you ought to be warm enough. Guess you can settle amongst yourselves which gets which!"

Amy and Andy threw uneasy glances at each other. The question was never voiced, but reading their faces posed no problem. Their entire lives—the years they could remember anyway—had been spent in a two-room flat, sharing the bedroom with their mother. A hand pump in the courtyard had served the whole block of factory housing for water.

Toilet facilities amounted to chamber pots dumped into an open-ditch sewer that ran into the canal. Bathing, when it couldn't be avoided, took place in a big, wash tub they'd drag out into the middle of the kitchen floor.

Misinterpreting their nervous shifting of feet, Alex's voice became a little sharp. "Those rooms were sufficient for your mother and I when we were growing up, so I assume you'll get by!"

Pulling the chowder forward to the heat and stirring it, his tone became easier. "Sarah, I guess you get the folk's room in front if you don't mind? I've been pretty well set-up in the back guest room for years now, so's I can watch the harbor and the old girl at her mooring between runs.

Your beds have all been made up fresh, but you'll have to move the furniture around to suit yourselves tomorrow, when you can see."

At least Sarah's curiosity never tired. "Alex, you didn't go to all of this work by yourself did you? I mean, that chowder, and the bread and all? Humph! Those straw flowers and the everlastings on the table look like a woman's touch to me!"

Understanding her implications, he looked a little uncomfortable as he explained. "Matter of fact I did do the cooking part, Sarah. The rest of it though, you can blame on Martha Howes and her sister Ida who came over the other day. They heard you were coming home, and insisted on making things a little more habitable. Drove me right out, with all that dust and the washing going on. Told me I could sail a mite, and cook enough to keep from starving, but when it came to housework I didn't seem to know which end of a broom to hang onto!"

This statement seemed to amuse him, but after a short reflection he changed the subject. Busying himself around the stove, he said, "Here, let's serve this up afore the youngsters start chewing on the dog's bone."

"Master Sears, if you'll open that little cupboard over there in the wall, you'll find the winter coldbox. The back end of it hangs outdoors so we don't need ice to keep things fresh when the weather's favorable. There you'll find some milk and butter."

"Amy, get the bowls off the sideboard so's your mother can fill them!"

"Myself, I'll pull the bread pudding out of the oven here, then it'll have time to cool before dessert."

Turning to his sister he asked, "Tea, Sarah?"

"Oh, I'd love some Alex, but now tell me about your lady friends!"

Alex scowled good naturedly. He'd been expecting the question. "You're as bad as the church ladies. Been here two minutes, and you're matchmaking. Don't you womenfolk ever think of anything else?

More important, I assume you'd like to know of all the eligible bachelors hereabouts too?"

Chapter 3

Take a Walk With Me M'lady

There was nothing wrong with Sarah's appetite, but it was difficult to tell whether it was food or talk she hungered for most. "Don't tease, I just want to know who your neighbors are before I meet them on the street!"

"Humph! I know better than to believe that, but if it'll buy me some peace I'll refresh your memory.

You know the Howes girls! They're both widowed. Make do as best they can with baking and whatnot. Live together in the old Chase house two doors east. Sold each of 'em a coupla shares in m'schooner t'help them make ends meet, but that's our only real tie."

The man kept pausing between sentences, as if putting his thought into words took effort.

"I've got to admit, I think they kinda' take a shine to me . . . at least they always seem to be squabbling over which one's pie I like best. Damned if I'll tell 'em! Sure as hell, they'd stop baking if it weren't a contest!"

Seeking a reprieve from Sarah's wordless inquisition, the Captain hauled off on a new tack.

"Amy, more milk?"

"No thanks, Uncle Alex."

The young girl, intent on the food before her, would not be drawn into a conversation easily. Accepting her needs as legitimate, he gave up and turned back to his sister.

"Well, neither one of the Howes girls had children, so they damn near mother-hen me to death at times! Lost both their men on the *Ida*, when she went ashore on Sandy Neck. Remember? Back in '53? Joined six or seven others that night, courtesy of a hellish gale.

C'mon Sarah, you must remember that one? That was when you were giving every boy in town fits!"

Had he made her blush, or was the heat of the stove getting to her?

Putting him off easily, she sassed, "Oh Alex, don't be telling tales!"

The man had finally found a topic of conversation he could feel comfortable with, and it had little to do with childhood romance.

"Yes'm, that was one of the worst nor'easters I can remember. Peaking on a flood-tide, the storm surge pushed five ships up into the marshes here.

The *Yarmouth* was listed among 'em, but this was long 'fore she was mine.

Coupla other schooners an' a sloop made it all the way across the marsh to the mainland without so much as a cracked rib, but it took months afore everything was back out to the harbor and seaworthy.

Central wharf got smashed to smithereens! Hawes and Taylor's General Store, out on the end, went with it. Christ, there were barrels everywhere! Two-thousand of 'em, remember that? An' that don't count the provisions an' staples washed away! Took 'em weeks to find all the sails from the loft overhead.

Betcha even now you could find enough staves an' hoops along the shore to start a cooperage.

The Hallets had lumber stacked out there too. Got some back, but a good part went with the tide, what didn't end up as chicken coops, or hog pens all along the shore."

Looking at Andy he continued, "Now, boy, those were the days of sail! You'd see six, maybe eight vessels at a time tied up to Central wharf. Two to three more out in the basin, awaitin' their turn, and another half-dozen over to Simpkin's fish pier. Comin' an' goin' all day, place was the busiest spot in town.

That storm fell a little later in the year than this'n, which was a good thing for merchants and seafarers alike. Most of the packets had hauled out, or were sheltering over in Try-yard cove behind the Neck, waitin' for the rails to be free so they could join their brethren on shore.

Couldn't say what loss of life resulted Capewide, but this town lost seven, countin' those missing or unknown."

Sarah flowed along as easily as a cork floating on the tide. "That's so sad! So many of our people have lost family to the sea. I'll bet every house in town has lost at least one or two of their own."

Looking at him directly, she set what at first seemed an innocent hook. "Why do you keep going back to it?"

Intuitively, Alex sensed a trap. Doing his best to sidestep the abyss, he bounced back to his earlier dodge.

"Boy, have another biscuit, and pass that beach-plum jelly!"

Spotting a favorable wind to ease him off this new shoal, he turned back to Sarah. "Might as well tell you before you ask. 'No', I did not make the jelly! I was hauling sugar, and Isabelle Gorham traded me some of the finished product for one of its main ingredients."

Giving her a quick glance, he added, "Woman's eighty if she's a day, so don't get any funny ideas about her and me, Lady!"

Sarah, however, had found the spot she'd been looking for, and dropped anchor. "Alex, don't change the subject! I'm being serious. Why are you still going to sea?"

Caught like a guilty child, he squirmed visibly. Not sure of the answer himself, the man settled on drowning her with facts.

"God, woman, where to begin?

Sarah, everyone knows most of the menfolk hereabouts have gone down to the sea at one time or another in their lives! Must be thirty or forty Captains living presently here on Yarmouth's Hallet Street, not counting other officers, the able seamen, or those who've gone beyond.

The village itself only stretches a couple of miles from Barnstable's town line to White's Brook, so of course it's reasonable to assume a few would be lost out of that many in any occupation!"

He grasped at a thought. "That reminds me! I'll bet Amos Otis came in on today's train for the funeral! His sister Maria's husband, Captain Howes, died three days past. Good man! Good solid man, he was!

In spite of your misgivings about the profession, this man lived a long and productive life. Wearing down over the years, the poor fellow finally gave in to his wife's urging and insistence, quit the sea and retired.

Suddenly, with no purpose to any of his endeavors, the sorry fellow had little rhyme or reason to live by. Man set his affairs in order; sold his instruments of navigation; gave away his clamming skiff; settled into his rocking chair . . . and died!"

Alex hadn't really stretched the truth too much. The man had retired a short while ago, and he did die.

The captain kept a discreet eye on his sister as he related this information. Fully aware of his point, she chose to ignore it, so Alex returned to his original course.

"It wasn't many years ago, a Cape mother could sit at the kitchen table with her four boys knowing for a fact three would go to sea, and be just as sure two would never return! There was, literally, no other way to make a living around here. Land on the Cape was so poor, a hand to mouth existence was all one could expect. People were forced to harvest the ocean to insure survival.

Well, it may have been a harder life then, but neither the clock, nor man's ingenuity stands still for long."

Alex was beginning to rise to the occasion. He tipped his chair back against the wall, lit his pipe, and made an attempt to settle in.

The familiar actions brought little comfort tonight. A nagging, uneasy feeling floated in the back of his mind. A sensation he could only compare to sailing fog-blind on a channel tack. That not being his usual manner of conducting business, he luffed sail and began to search for a marker. Like an itch just out of reach, the man's brow furrowed with effort, and similarly, the thought refused to be ignored.

Sorting through the evening's topics took time, and the answer, when it came, left him buried.

Sarah! A woman! She was actually pressuring him! Sister or not, arguing points, let alone questioning answers, was not done by a female in his world. Wondering if his authority was being challenged, the smoke from his pipe began to form layers.

It was a defeat of sorts, but the man finally decided he was just being teased into parting with philosophical knowledge that he alone could put into words. A rationalized fiction of his own mind, it was flattering enough to void further reservations. Oblivious to the passage of time, the captain picked up the conversation right where he'd left off.

"There's more land-side work now. More industries to support a family. Farmers have discovered they can grow turnips, spinach, and those damned sour-cranberries in this sand.

Look at Tom Matthews! How many years was he Master of the *Commodore Hull*? Talk about going over to the enemy. Now the man's station agent for the railroad here in Yarmouth Port!"

Relighting his pipe, he talked through its smoke. "Sea itself is getting to be a safer place to work too, though that's balanced by a scarcity of cargo.

Aids to navigation are getting better. The Humane Society is setting up surf stations along most of the coast for those of us who still venture. Every harbor has a steam tug or boat for hire to help the sail craft in and out, and haul the unfortunate—or stupid—off an occasional bar . . . .

Reminds me, Ansel Hallett's father! Would you say he died on land, or the sea? Remember? He was crushed when his sloop, *Messenger* rolled over on him while he was trying to dig her off the bar at low tide!"

Sarah hadn't lost focus. "I don't care about what others do, or how they died, it's you I'm concerned with! Why do you still go? I'm sure it's not a lack of money!"

The remark sounded blunt, even to her ears. Add this to the fact that Alex had just settled a similar matter in his own mind, and it did much to explain his sudden flush. Here again, women were not supposed to know, let alone talk of money matters.

Embarrassed at her own lack of tact, Sarah tried to take some of the edge off. "I'm sorry Alex, I guess the long day is beginning to show! It's just . . . I know you're not rich, but

I'm sure you've got enough invested and squirreled away so worries about starving would be baseless if you never went to sea again!"

His frown and tone of voice had somehow lost their mellowness.

"Aren't you the pushy sister I remember?"

Not only was Alex getting pressure, but the irritation was obvious. "Well, I'm not sure what concerns you about my affairs, m'lady, nor why you're making it your business to meddle in them? 'I' am the one person responsible for my follies, and like it or not, that fact shall not change to please the likes of you!"

Hearing these position statements voiced, Alex too became aware of how uncompromisingly gruff he must sound. Torn between righteous indignity, and his new family attachments, the man surprised himself. He weakened.

Embarrassed at these unaccustomed feelings, he plunged on as if further conversation might flush the whole incident away. "I guess my remarks haven't answered your question about the why of it all, have they?

Damn, woman, you know a seafaring person has a queer partnership with the sea! A desire to go, but a pull almost as strong to stay home! A paradox, m'lady, but also a challenge to last a man his lifetime.

What else do you want? Want me to admit there's danger?

Back, summer 'fore this'n . . . six youngsters . . . children really . . . borrowed a new boat without permission. Boys and girls mixed, they struck off on a moon-lit cruise.

Never took into account the boat was so new she hadn't been ballasted proper.

Flipped-over out by the Neck.

Long flowing dresses, an' walking shoes 'stead of seaboots easily kicked off, every single one aboard drowned before anyone could respond to their cries!

Whether for business or pleasure, anyone who steps foot on a deck sails in the knowledge that he works, sleeps, and eats the thickness of the hull, or a missed step from death! A fact tied to the profession as closely as my keel to the sea!

I hate to sound profound, but this gives a fullness and meaning to life. The tease that gives everything its spice and reason."

Brightening a little, he remarked, "Say, I'll have to bring this up to the Parson! Sounds like a fine topic for a sermon, and his could use a little help of late!"

Not much got by Sarah. Aware of Alex's shift away from their confrontation, she mistook the resulting easing of tension as a sign of capitulation. Yes, victory was in her grasp.

"You're wandering off the subject again, Alex. You've admitted there isn't much money in the business anymore. Well, come home! Give up the sea before it claims another life. Before it takes everything back!

Showing more patience than recent memory would allow, Alex wondered if he'd be able to handle this new life thrust upon him. The end to his monastic peace. This instant chaos.

His male friends had warned him. Needling him to the point of distraction, they'd questioned an old goat like him putting up with a woman and family, even if she was his sister! Well, maybe they were right! Old dogs and new tricks, or some such nonsense.

With these thoughts in mind, he responded to Sarah's prodding grumpily. "Damn, you can be a nag, woman!

All right, listen!"

Take a walk with me m'lady,

and I will show the sea to thee.

Take a walk with me m'lady,

and the sea will show you me.

"They're lines from an old sailing ditty, and no truer have ever been sung. Written by a humble, forgotten seaman, no poet of renown could have put it more eloquently.

The sea, it is indeed a part of me, and I a part of it! We've all heard, the longer a person lives with someone, or something, the more they grow alike. Well, when the sea is wild and white underfoot, and the wind's aroarin' through my riggin', I feel alert, alive, and part of all creation!

Then too, when the air is flat-calm and the ocean smooth, I find my own demeanor to be equally calm and at ease. The world is free out there, Sarah, with only God and nature to answer to! I find it damned exciting at times, plain boring at others, but it matters not which for I'll take her any way she comes! It is me! It is my life! It is my soul!"

Having said about all he could on the subject, Alex redirected his attention to the table. "Amy, would you serve the pudding, please? Watch out for that pot, it might still be hot to the hand!"

Once more Sarah misjudged her brother's mood. In her intensity, she was blind to his attempt at pleasant table conversation, and blurted out, "It's a game to you, isn't it? Is this some private club I don't know about? You, shipping off to Boston every week with your card-playing, rum-drinking cronies, so you can thrill them all with your derring-do?

Well, I guess it's fortunate the tugs can find the dock for you! Then what? Do you carouse around the town like drunken sailors? Come Sunday, I suppose you return home to the pious life you all portray, then do it again the next week as if life had no purpose other than to satisfy your base desires! Stupid, stupid men!

It was your very own uncle who used to say, 'Any man who'd sail for pleasure, would go to hell for a pastime!' Humph! I think you've found it, and I can see I'm wasting my breath trying to make sense with your likes!"

No matter that Sarah was his sister, Alex had put up with just about all he could stand. His reply came closer to a shout than a conversational tone.

"God-dammit woman, stop preaching to me! You're like a dog worryin' a bone. I happen to like it out there. I like the whole way of life. The danger, the constant challenge, the peace it gives my soul. Everything! D'ya hear that? EVERYTHING!"

Sarah would not give an inch, and her snappy retort did little for any peace he'd find this night. "You've been out there so long, your mind has filled with dry-rot!"

This caused Alex so much emotion and turmoil he could no longer trust his tongue to be civil. The man sat there bolt upright, his face a stern mask of authoritarian control.

Full minutes passed. Slowly he refilled and lit his pipe. More minutes slipped by. The man puffed furiously. Deep in thought, his smoke cloud's size suggested more than tobacco was burning.

The man was not accustomed to confrontation within his own household. Worse, deep discussions with a woman were anathema to his world. His very purpose in life was being questioned by this creature.

The same self-discipline used to gain his Captaincy at the age of twenty, came to his rescue. Adopting an objective point of view, he concluded the whole argument was absurd. The man had to admit his way of life probably made little sense to Sarah, but that was no one's business other than his own.

Deeper inside, he knew part of the reason he sailed would never be shared. Not even with his sister. It had to do with loneliness.

There was a curious contradiction here. With the house empty, he sought human companionship. Now the house was full, and he found himself in the position of longing for the peace and quiet of his schooner. Preferably, miles at sea.

Reaching an accord he could live with, the man decided he enjoyed the mental stimulation, if not the topic or source in particular. With this in mind, he settled on a different tack. Taking a deep breath while regaining his composure, the captain adopted a quiet tone and felt his way along, sounding the shoals as he floated in with the tide.

"After losing your husband, I'm sure you weigh things a little more carefully now, but tell me, why does a bird fly? It might get caught by a hawk!

My answer to all of your questioning is that we do what is in our nature, ordained by God! I sail with His blessing, to this date!

Life is for the living, Sarah! You? You went off with your man to get away from the poverty and the country ways around here. As memory serves me, after John came back from the war, you sought a better way of life. Your children were to be exposed to the excitement, culture, and technology of a modern city. To find schooling and chances for advancement beyond that which the Cape could offer.

An admirable goal, which no one could deny.

Course, John didn't think he could be of much use around here with only one leg, so that might have added weight to your decision!"

Sensing the conversation had shifted, with herself as the new focus, Sarah stood up and began to clear the table.

Alex in turn, aware that he had now gained the upper hand and was about to have it stolen from him, burst back into his shout of authority. "For Christ's sake, woman, you've harped at me long enough to get under my skin! Now that I'm about to make a point, what gives you the right to just stand up and walk off?

I suggest you'd best sit right back down in that chair until I'm finished, or by all that is holy. . . . "

Startled by the suddenness of her brother's attack, Sarah took a step backwards. Her chair, still in place from where she'd risen, caught her behind the knees, and she fell right back into it as if at the captain's bidding.

The children sat there in amazed silence.

Alex smiled slightly at his sister's involuntary compliance, and picked up the conversation as if nothing had happened.

"Guess the two of you thought there'd be more opportunities elsewhere. Well, maybe things didn't work out, but it wasn't because you didn't try.

You have an inborn courage, Sarah. Hell, look at today's trip! You and your children traveled over a hundred-miles by yourselves. What do you suppose Father would have made of this? A woman, traveling alone? Questioned your sanity, I imagine, and possibly your moral convictions as well!

Do you realize most people don't make a single overland journey of that length in their entire lifetimes?

You, are a gutsy lady! You may not be challenging the sea, but you've taken charge of your own life. I only ask that you allow me the same courtesy, and let me live mine!"

Regaining her composure, Sarah knew she'd lost the argument. Her crusade would have to rest for a while. Appealing to his reason hadn't worked, so she'd just have to think of another way to get this lump of a brother off the sea.

Patience. . . . Patience is the game to play.

"Alex, calm down! My, but you've grown testy since I've been gone! I have no intention what-so-ever of interfering with your life!" The, *for now!* was added silently.

Acquiring a tone of humility, she added, "As for comparing our different paths, they're hardly the same, but thank you for the vote of confidence, and thank you for taking us in!"

This last was said quietly. As if there were more feeling behind the simple statement than she knew how to voice.

With his destiny no longer an issue, Alex mellowed. "Hell, that's what family's for! Things'll work out. God knows there's chores enough to keep ten-pairs of hands busy 'round here, just ask Martha and Ida!"

With that in mind, the man suggested enrolling the children in the Academy over on the corner of Hawes' Lane as a place to start, then began to assign tasks they could fit in around those hours. "Master Sears, you can be in charge of keeping the wood-box full, and plenty of kindling chopped. I also expect the ashes to be hauled out to the leaching barrel behind the shed on a regular basis. We'll use 'em for soap come spring, what we don't spread on the garden. Tomorrow, I'll show you about the animals in the barn."

Stimulated by the heated conversation of the adults, Andy probably reacted with more emphasis than intended.

"No God-damned way! I ain't your nigger-slave! And I ain't gonna go to school no more, neither!"

Alex hesitated just long enough to take in a deep breath, then stood abruptly. Bumped as he gained his feet, the table full of dishes jumped and clattered, adding a sense of violence to his action.

Every living creature in the room jumped in unison. Ulysses managed a scrambling, deep-throated, "Whuff?", while George melted off his chair discretely, and disappeared into the darkened hallway leading back to the barn.

The Captain's bulk was threatening, his reputation for vocal power well earned. Tonight he vied with the storm in rattling windows. "Master Sears, 'I' am a Sea Captain! 'I' am accustomed to having my orders obeyed without question! This matter of back-talk has already been explained to you once, and I shan't break a habit of long-standing to speak twice on topics of this nature! I assure you Mister, it will not happen again!"

His tongue was sharp enough so that jabbing his finger had not really been needed to emphasize the point he was making, but it was there anyway. Big and blunt as a club, it carried the scars of too many wet ropes, and years of juggling men and ships.

Regaining his self-control somewhat, Alex continued at a slightly lowered volume. "You seem to have a habit of spittin' inta the wind, boy! Don'tcha ever get tired of it comin' back in ya face?" Not meant as a question, no answer would have been allowed if offered.

He continued, "While I'm spouting off on things comin' home to roost. . . . If ever, I hear you curse in front of ladies again, I shall personally wash your mouth out with lye-soap! A person would'a had t'a been deaf and dumb, not to hear what you was a hollerin' at the top a'your lungs at that train station today! My suggestion is, you button that lip afore it gets ya inta the kinda trouble no mortal can save you from!"

Lighting his pipe to give the last message time to sink in, the man considered a few other irritations. It needed little thought. Turning to his nephew like a compass back to North, he added, "You hear-me well, boy, just so there's no misunderstanding! As long as you continue to live under my roof, you will do as you're told! I also expect you do that share of the work considered equal to your keep! These are not options, nor will I consider anything different until such time as I decide you competent to think for yourself!"

Andy was on his feet with as much controlled violence as Alex had displayed. Facing his mother, he exploded in a staccato burst, "Ma, I ain't stayin' here! I'm goin' home! He's not my father! He can't tell me what to do! Ain't no way I'm gonna do his dirt-work, and I ain't goin' back to no school neither!"

Sarah was tired. Tired from the trip just completed. Tired of living in poverty. Tired of the drudgery her life had become. Her guard down, she lashed out at the closest target. "Andy, I'm ashamed of you! Who do you think you are? I believe you owe your uncle an apology! He's taken us in when we had no place to turn, and out of the blue you take it into your head that you don't have to do your share?

As for school, do you want to spend the rest of your life in the mills with that damned Irish trash? Hiding behind their holier-than-thou lace curtains, you'd think they had the personal blessings of their Pope, and the Lord Almighty too.

They killed your father, because he wasn't one of them! The bastards hated him! He was a Protestant, and a foreman, and he made a dollar a week more than they did. Mill accident, my foot, it was those God-damned Irish tempers. Loving their tankards of ale and undrinkable whiskey, someone crawled out of a pub and shoved him into that machine out of thick-headed hate!

N.I.N.A. No Irish Need Apply. You know why that was always tacked onto every help wanted poster? Those people are so hot-headed and emotional they can't work for anyone else. Drunk or sober, they're stubborn as a watersoaked knot, and do as they damned well please, instead of what they're told. To their minds, they were born to give orders not take 'em!

Besides, they stick together like thieves. It wasn't your father's fault the mill laid off all those people, it was just his job to tell them."

Tears began to ease down her cheeks, and her voice got thick at the memory of her loss. "The bastards killed him for it, and not a single son-of-a-bitch in that room saw a thing!"

Wiping her face dry with an angry swipe, she focused on her son once more. "Don't get an education! If you don't like the mills, maybe you can ship out as a cabin boy. You're old enough! Ask the Captain here! From what I've heard, some of his peers are especially fond of pretty, young boys! You know, like sticky-sweet, and friendly Mr. Saul over on Canal Street? Want to be one of his boys?"

Andy, unable to get a word in edgewise, shifted from foot to foot and gave his mother a blank stare of boredom. This was a mistake. Misinterpreted, it drew even more of his mother's ire. "And don't you give me that wide-eyed, innocent look, Mister, because I'm sure you know exactly what I mean!

Maybe if you live long enough, and the life suits you, some ship will offer you a deck hand's berth. Boy, that'll make you rich! Well, that's as high as you'll ever get, unless you learn how to read and cipher!"

She paused to catch her breath, and Andy managed to squeeze in a sullen response. "I can read and cipher!"

Again, it was his tone of voice more than what he said, but this was all it took to rewind his mother's spring. "You're a fool! A damned, fool! I'm not talking about counting on your fingers, and moving your lips to sound things out! I'm talking about deeper learning! An education!"

Alex, sitting on the sidelines, could no longer contain himself. "Sarah, that's enough! I don't mean to interfere in your family discussion, but talk such as this will not be tolerated in this house! What kind of people have you been associating with, anyway? I don't mean to berate you in front of your family, but the language you're using would blister paint! And, tell me, since when are degenerate morals a subject for discussion with children?

This is Cape Cod! Mind your barmaid's tongue, woman, and remember where you are. The natives hear that, they'll be heating a pot of tar and plucking chickens in your honor!"

Making sure his point was understood, Alex added, "In other words, conduct yourself in the manner these hypocrites around here do. Pretend you're pure as the driven snow, and keep the doors shut if your neighbor's about."

His usage of that term made him suddenly aware of the seeming hypocrisy of his own statements. Remembering a few possible indiscretions he might have made in the heat of this evening's debate, the captain was annoyed. Managing to impale himself on a sword of his own manufacture was embarrassing. The man's voice sputtered back to life. "I'll admit I curse and swear a mite myself, but I'm supposed to! I've worked hard to gain my reputation as a humble, honest man of the sea!"

It was a lame excuse, and far from justification for his colorful language. Caught in a stiff-breeze on a lee-shore, he now found himself trying to include the errors of his own doing within the hard and fast rules he'd just laid down.

"Like I just said, what goes on behind closed doors is anybody's guess, but in public, or in front of strangers, we should all be blameless. The family as a whole had best not bring shame, one-upon-the-other, from a mere slip of the tongue! Prissy, my lads. That's it, we shall all become prissy, so as not to offend the sensitive or tasteful ear!"

Damn, but a person had to think fast around here! Family life was a bit more complicated than he remembered, and a lot different than the bachelorhood of which, until now, he hadn't been aware he'd been enjoying.

With Sarah around, humble-pie wasn't far behind. "Phht! You, prissy? Oh, really now! Since when have you ever considered a delicate ear when something was troubling you? I suspect there are few in the village who haven't heard your gentle voice carry clear across the harbor, and whatever was on your mind as well!

Alex, I admit our language and manners aren't what they should be, but where we've just come from a person would be ostracized if they didn't curse a mite!

Like you were just suggesting, 'When in Rome. . . . '

As for my use of inappropriate examples, don't forget I've had to raise these children by myself. If we didn't discuss the dangers to be faced in our own neighborhood, where would you have them learn? When they reached the street? A bit late then, don't you think? That's barely a step above the gutter!"

Sarah sighed deeply. She seemed to be running out of the energy to fight. "I readily admit the Academy we've come from is lacking in good graces. I also have to admit that I'm as guilty as either of my off-spring in abusing proper etiquette. Strange . . . I'd almost forgotten there was such a thing as polite-society."

"Children, Alex is right. We're going to have to bite our tongues from time to time, and put on a good act if we want to be accepted into this village!"

Hiding her fatigue, the woman's voice turned sharp again. "However, as for 'you' telling me what to do, Alex, and about my cursing, all I can say is that old habits are hard to break. John gave up on telling me how to behave years ago. I do promise we'll make an effort not to offend anyone in this town, but you know my temper as I know yours. It might happen, and right now I'm too tired to worry about that bridge until I get there!"

Alex was not sure if he should be angry, or proud of her rebellious spirit. The easiest way was just to ignore it.

Visibly relieved by this decision, he passed from an embarrassing topic to something more comfortable, at least to him.

"Whew! Now that's been cleared, we can get back to the subject at hand."

"Master Sears!" The Captain commanded the boy's attention en-route to establishing his own authority. "Idle hands do the devil's work! I assure you Sir, that will not be a problem around here, nor will your education!"

Andy had no intention of backing down. "You got no right to tell me nothin'! I'm goin' back to the city and work the streets with my friend, Albert! He always had plenty of money, and he never had to get no job neither."

Alex struggled to ignore the hatred pouring out of the boy. Keeping his voice calm, and the tone conversational, he remarked, "From what I'm hearin', he sounds like a real nice fella, Son. The kind who'd probably sell his mother, if the price were right.

Would you dare turn 'your' back on him in a dark alley?"

The response, "I'm not your 'son'!" was spit out as if the mere thought were distasteful.

Amy could no longer stand her self-imposed silence. She chose this moment to dive in, and express her own sympathies. "Andy, why are you so bitter with Uncle Alex? I like it here!

Besides, I'm tired of working in the Mills. We've got our very own rooms, and 'I' want to go back to school. We'll meet lots of new friends, and think of the fun!"

Getting leaned on from a new source, Andy made no distinction. He just dipped into the same bucket of anger.

"You stay out of this, Amy! You never liked Albert anyway."

Amy snapped right back. "I didn't trust him! You know the way he used to look at me! It didn't take many brains to tell what he was scheming, and I had no intention of becoming one of his 'girls'. Remember. . . . "

Her own memory triggered at the suggestion, and the result focused building emotions. "In fact, you were there! That's when Ma walked in! He was teasing and stuff, and then actually tried to kiss me!

A lotta help you were. You thought it was funny!"

A head taller than Andy, she stood and reached out toward him. "Playing that stupid harmonica, and laughing, I otta break your head right now just to get even!"

Alex felt the time had come to re-established order. "Whoa! I think maybe we'd all better simmer down a mite!

What scupper did this reptile slither out of, anyway? Where the hell did you meet someone like this, Sarah?"

"He's one of the reasons I had to ask if we could come home! Albert Antonelli, Rosie's brother-in-law. I've written to you about her many times. She was the one true-friend I had in the world.

When Jonathan was killed, Rose helped with the kids and confusion while we tried to get our lives back together. Albert was always hanging around, trying to be helpful and sympathetic to the poor new widow, if you know what I mean?"

"I'm not sure I care for the implications!"

Her brother's expression of concern made Sarah realize her statement carried the stigma of self-incrimination. Hurrying, she corrected the oversight. "Alex, give me credit for some sense! I thought of him as harmless and amusing. Really more of a bother, than a threat to be taken seriously. . . . Well, that is until I caught him with Amy!

It was then I realized what an influence he'd become on all of us. Andy, while Amy and I worked, and my innocent little girl whenever he got the chance. Always hanging in the shadows, he was a vulture waiting to reap the harvest should one of us stumble."

Alex frowned. "I guess that explains the telegram of two-days past?"

"No, that's when I grabbed Jonathon's gun and shot the bastard! The telegraph came later. When it dawned on me the seriousness of what I'd done, and we had to get away!"

"YOU WHAT?"

Alex was completely stunned! His sister, a murderer? And she'd come to him, neither asking his complicity, nor explaining the trouble she carried until now! The audacity of the whole thing left him momentarily speechless. Blood was thick, but could he hide someone who had committed such an act, and still answer to his own conscience?

His first thoughts may have been to distance himself and his precious reputation from this woman, yet under the surface he knew he had no choice but to help her. Wondering if he had time to reprovision the *Yarmouth* before spiriting them all away, she broke into his mental processes one more time.

"Oh, it wasn't anything serious! I didn't kill him, for God's sake, though now I wish maybe I had! I'd pulled the pistol out of a drawer as a threat to scare him away. He wasn't fooled, so I tried to cock it to show I meant business, and he made a grab for it. The stupid thing went off, and blew a hole right through his foot.

Served him right, but he screamed and whined so you'd a thought he'd been gut-shot! I threw a rag at him to wrap it in, and he left limping, vowing to get even."

Despair swept across her face, darkening it. "I couldn't stand the thought of what was happening to my children!

Andy was only a few months from turning twelve. The age when supposedly he could come into the mill to work. Work at wages so poor it forces whole families into virtual slavery just to put food on the table.

Ourselves, we had started out more fortunate than most, what with John's income as a floor manager, and his disability check, but after he died things changed quickly. Without his position, we were forced into cheaper housing. Bills began to pile up.

I had so wanted Andy to finish school, but it was getting crazy. The work was hard, the hours long, and I could see little hope for change. Doomed to life in a limbo of endless drudgery, or succumb to the temptations of Albert's kind and live in hell forever. I walked out on it. Call it quitting if you must, but I felt John's memory and our children deserved a better fate!"

Visibly relieved, Alex found many points to admonish his sister about. In a perfect display of his double-standard, he sputtered, "There you go with the damned cuss words again! A gunshot wound to the foot may not be serious to you, lady, but the authorities might feel otherwise!

Tell me, why in hell did you wait so long before you came home?"

Sarah noticed his *faux pas*, but other than a smile, chose to ignore it. Taking his concerns in the order he'd raised them, she replied, "I warned you a habit of years might prove hard to break. As for Albert, we may not have heard the last of him, but I doubt he'd ever turn to the law for help. They'd be more interested in what he'd been up to, than why he'd been shot!

Your last question is more difficult to answer. I am a proud woman, Alex. Begging does not come easy."

With an empathy born of the same blood, Alex understood. Seeking a diplomatic way to put and end to the conversation, he stood and announced, "All right people, dishes time, then bed! It's been a long day, and morning comes early here on the Cape. Tomorrow we'll get organized. Holidays are coming up, with a lot on the calendar. A church fair; some social obligations we've all been invited to; a Christmas Ball at The Yarmouth Society's Lyceum Hall to show you people off at, and that's not counting the personal entertaining we'll do now that you're here to celebrate the season with me!"

Sarah put a hand to her mouth. "Alex, you're teasing again! Are we really expected to attend all of those events?

Amy and I have nothing to wear! The dry goods store? Is it near?"

The man grinned at his sister. "Hah! I thought that would get your attention. There's Payne's, down in Yarmouth; Crocker's, that's in the other direction; and, old man Knowles of course. He's got a nice big one, right down the street! You 'must' remember James Knowles' store, Sarah?"

Deciding this might be the right spot to offer a peace-branch, and so avoid a long, cold winter, Alex added, "While you're busy with patterns and cloth, maybe your son and I can get one more batch of sea clams afore the winter ice. Barring it coming on this storm, that is."

Looking at Andy, he continued talking to see if any signs of interest had been kindled. "S'posed to be a good moon-tide for the next few days. If the wind don't favor sea clams, we'll turn our hands to quahogs and the soft shell variety instead. Course, then again if we're real lucky, this storm may drive some bay scallops in out of the channels.

We'll have to check that at first light, or we'll never beat the gulls to 'em, boy!"

Andy colored a little under his scrutiny. Not wanting to sound too interested, the boy's reply was noncommittal. "I don't know nothin' 'bout sea clams, or quags. . . qauks. . . them other things!"

"You'll learn!" Alex replied. "I'll show you how to live off the land just like an Indian. Might even take you hunting and teach you how to shoot, if things work out between us."

Amy made her contribution. "See, Andy? I told you it would be fun here!"

Andy's retort was predictable. "How do you know? Have you ever been to a Ball? Women, humph! All they ever think about are clothes and men."

Alex acknowledged their first, recognizably common ground with, "Sounds like you and I do see some things the same way, boy."

Sarah joined in. "Go ahead, side with him Alex! We'll get even, won't we, Amy?"

It was Alex's turn in the banter again. "If you girls get down to Knowles' before we get back from the shore, introduce yourselves, and put your purchases on my tab. Not much hard cash around these days so we all barter a little, and he still owes me freight from the last haul.

Smile and flirt like you used to, Sarah, and who knows, maybe we'll own the store by Christmas!"

"Alex! Now I'm shocked." Pleased by the turn of this evening, her spirits had lifted. She almost chirped, when she said, "Come children, bed-time! We'll go together, and I'll get you settled in."

There was no warning. The door just slammed and banged a couple of times, then burst open. Wrapped in oilskins, a figure flew into the room. Slush and snow sprayed in all directions. The room's candles and lamps jumped, then flickered in unison to the blast of moving air.

This strange apparition had brought chaos with him. Turning to face the onslaught which had seemingly thrust him through their door, the creature's hood flew back to reveal a comical, gray furball. Staggering against the gale, the man began a ferocious tug of war over control of the outer, wooden-slat, storm door. Victory was announced by a loud bang, and the storm's human offering turned to face the stunned family. His eyes and nose were both red and wet from exposure to the elements.

Breathless from his battle, yet excited to the point of near witlessness, the sodden man began a frustrating attempt at communication. A mouth, its position obvious from years of tobacco stains in the beard around it, began working in an agitated manner.

"A A AAlex, s s sorry ab b bbout bout b bbustin' ininin . . . likethis, b b b but we wee weee gottawreck!"

Chapter 4

Dead Men Don't Bleed

As if angry at losing the tug-of-war, the storm slammed and tore at the door with a vengeful fury. Screaming its frustration through the cracks, the wind made it easy for Amy to understand how her mother had been led into believing those tales about Aunt Sophia's ghost.

The howls of lost souls proving an ineffective ploy to gain re-entry, the gale turned its mindless energies to a more annoying venture. It overrode the voice of the stutterer by rattling and banging the door-latch, timing its rhythm to the exact cadence of the poor man's speech.

Alex's movements became slow and deliberate. Showing complete control of the situation, he used one of his rough, flannel sleeves to wipe the freshly applied, melting snow from his face. This discomfort removed, the man next reached out and shut the inner door firmly, thereby silencing the wind's threat. Now, everything back to near normal, he chose his words carefully, and addressed their surprise guest softly.

Ignoring the urgency of the man's message, Alex nodded in the direction of each member of his family, and introduced everyone around. "Sam Thacher, I'd like you to meet my sister Sarah Sears, her daughter Amy, and son Andrew."

Still speaking in that deliberate, even voice, it was obvious to all that Alex was making an effort to calm the poor fellow. "Sammy, slow down a little until you catch your breath! I'm sure a few minutes one way or t'other won't hold back tonight's storm, nor the tide either for that matter.

Now, you say there's been a wreck?"

Sammy bobbed his head in acknowledgment. His mouth, failing him, sputtered in silent frustration. What little face the listeners could see through the man's wild whiskers became more and more flushed, and his eyes began to bulge. The words, bottled up inside, seemed to be creating a pressure designed to test human limits.

Taking a deep breath, the man finally managed to stammer, "B B BBad one! B B BBodies comin' comin' a sh sh sh shshore all r r ready, w w wwiththewreckage!"

The release of words was indeed a release of pressure, and his demeanor returned to as near a normal state as it ever attained.

Alex prodded him a little. "Did you get the word out on the way over here?"

Sam bobbed his head again, his mouth going through a series of strained grimaces, though never uttering a sound. This produced another flushed face, and the man's eyes began to widen in building exasperation.

Alarmed at this reaction, Amy wanted to tell her uncle not to ask him anymore questions for fear the poor creature would bust something in his attempts to vocalize.

Sammy's physical motions, quick, jerky, nervous and perpetual, passed on his frenzied state of mind to those around him. Again, to Amy it was as if she could see him tightening up like the strings of a violin, and she didn't want to be around when the conductor lifted his baton.

Alex's voice assumed the tone of command when he spoke this time. "All right Sam, you know where I keep the wreck-gear in the barn. Take that lantern over there with you, and get the stuff loaded into the surf wagon! I'll be out to help you with Sandy's hitch as soon as I get my foul-weather gear on."

Settling into a chair to remove his shoes, he added, "Throw her blanket on, if you get time! Means we'll have to loosen things so we can put her harness on over top, but with this wind the blanket'd blow right off again otherwise. Poor horse, she's going to need everything we can do for her tonight."

As he turned away, Sam bobbed his head once more in acknowledgment and picked up the bull's-eye lantern indicated. After firing it off from one of the night candles which had been lit just before his dramatic entry, the man disappeared through the endless doorways in the direction of the barn, dripping all the way.

Noticing the boy watching him as he moved toward the hall closet, Alex wondered how much of his nephew's sass might be real backbone, and how much just cocky, city talk. Smiling with sudden inspiration, he lifted one eyebrow and looked at the young man.

"What have you got for gear, boy?"

Andy, startled at the thought of being included, jumped toward his duffle bag. Looking wide-eyed at his mother, as he tore at the strings, the young man's expression was asking, "Can I go?" The words, stuck in boyhood pride, never reached his lips.

"Oh Alex, please be careful!" Sarah pleaded. All present easily translated these words into, "You've got my permission, but I'm not too happy about it!" And its second interpretation, "Alex, I'm trusting my son to your care! You'd damned well better not let anything happen to him!"

In borrowed sea-boots two sizes too big, and miss-matched foul weather gear from the ditty-box buried deep in Alex's same closet, Andy clomped along behind his uncle toward the barn. Somewhere in the maze of doorways, almost as an afterthought, one more chilling exchange passed between the two. Alex asked the young man bluntly, "Can you swim, boy?"

The reply was just as curt. "Yes, Sir!"

The question, seemingly out of context, set the boy's mind spinning. He became aware of a sinking feeling creeping into his throat. Was his uncle crazy? Who, in his right mind, would go swimming on a night like this?

Almost as alarming, another thought chased the first. Had his mother heard this exchange, just by implication she'd have canceled any hopes he might have had of tagging along on this night's adventure.

The barn no longer held the air of a chapel. In the short time they'd been away, the building had taken on more sinister feelings. Alarmed, Andy fought to ignore the things he recognized as everyday objects, but it came down to a battle of wits. His own mortal intelligence against an imagination being fed limitless ammunition.

The two men huffed, grunted, and worked at a feverish pace as they lifted heavy, nameless objects into the high-sided wagon. Little was spoken. Their effort directed by the familiarity of a well-practiced routine.

Sandy, standing there in her traces and knowing she was going back to work, puffed, blew, and shook her head. Pawing nervously at the straw covered planks, it was almost as if she couldn't wait for the ordeal to begin.

Ulysses had also been invited along to partake of this evenings work. He paced around the confusing scene, panting in anticipation of things only imagined in the boy's mind.

Silhouetted by the harsh light of the bull's-eye lantern, the moving shapes threw menacing, black shadows against the walls of the barn. Lock-stepped in a ghoulish dance with their living partners, the phantoms whirled and kicked to a rhythm beyond measure, their size dictated by the owner's proximity to the light source.

This same light, reflected from depths immeasurable, made the animals eyes burn with a demonic fire.

A loose shingle rattled somewhere to a cadence of its own in the gale.

True to what Alex had described, his weather-vane moaned up there on the cupola, in the little wind-shifts between gusts.

Andy could barely measure his relief when the door finally slid open to allow men, beasts, and their wagon of mercy to escape into the storm.

Wrapped in tarpaulins, the lot of them were hardly recognizable one from the other. The boy soon realized the wisdom of this foul smelling gear when he discovered the snow, instead of falling, was flying horizontally. Any and everything in its path was quickly plastered with the sticky wet heaviness. The smell of naphtha from these canvas tarps mixed with the pungent aroma of linseed oil from his oilskins and became almost comforting.

Their wagon lurched dangerously as it pulled off Central Street, and shaking violently in the wind, for an instant, threatened to tip over. In hindsight, this again could have been taken as an ominous sign of things to come. Unfortunately, it wouldn't be the last time Andy would question his wisdom at tagging along on tonight's rescue party.

Climbing down off the seat, Alex and Sam joined a few others gathered in the lee of Simpkin's Storage and Ship's Chandlery building. Located at the base of the fish wharf, it was a natural assembly point for any concerns along the shore.

Alex, shouting to be heard above the roar of the wind, greeted them with, "Hey boys, we've got one on the bar have we?"

A solitary voice answered for the group. "Aye, Cap'n! Had to be there, from the spread of flotsam we got!"

"Have ye named her yet?"

A chorus of negative murmurs came from the group.

"Anybody organized a search for survivors?"

The same sounds issued forth, with a little more foot shuffling to hide their collective guilt.

"All right, times awastin' lads!"

Alex didn't condemn their foot dragging, he understood. Family men all, with responsibilities no one else would shoulder if they themselves were lost this night, they held priorities beyond mercy.

The Captain took charge as if this were his right, with no alternatives considered, nor would he have condoned one if offered. As commander, he split his crew into workable units and sent some of the men over to Harbor Point on the Barnstable side of Mill Creek.

At low tide, this waterway held a mere trace flowing out of what had once been known as Stony Cove. Years earlier, Hallet's Mill and dam had been built at a narrow spot in the cove's inlet, resulting in a rather unique mill pond. Instead of depending on a stream, or fickle rain storms to replenish its waters, the endless tide performed the service twice a day.

Under normal circumstances, the sea flowed back and forth through this channel in a peaceful, orderly manner. Tonight, the conditions were anything but. Pushed by a northeast gale, the storm obscured creek had become a formidable expanse of wave-tossed water. Not even a crossing at the dam site was to be taken lightly.

The Captain commanded these men with the subtlety of suggestion. After all, being volunteers, they were not bound to him in any tangible way. It was the way he asked, and his manner of treating them as equals which seemed to get their cooperation.

Unlike many others in his position, the man was not afraid to explain his reasons for doing things in a certain way. Such as, "Maybe a couple of you boys otta go out to the end of Central Wharf and stand watch. That way, in case either we or the other party gets into trouble and sends up a rocket, you might be able to direct some help our way. . . . God willing!"

He went on, "Another thing, with the wind out of this quarter and the tide acomin', anything with life still left in it has got to fetch-up on one of the three places we're going to man, so keep a sharp eye!"

Weary in body and soul, his mind drifting with the storm, Andy heard, but didn't really listen to what was being said. Mention of his own name changed this instantly. Coming to with a start, the boy was left straining, trying to decipher past and present conversations at the same time.

Out of context, the meaning of Alex's proclamation was barely grasped. "I do not wish to cause alarm, but hear me well, friends! Sammy, my newly-arrived nephew, Master Sears, and of course myself, will be taking our surf wagon over to Baker's Island. My intent is we'll cross the marsh on the old hay road, where she goes behind Hornbeam Island."

This part sounded fine to Andy, but then the man added, "I'm laying out our course so you people will have someplace to start looking, if, come mornin', we ain't back!"

The boy frowned in the darkness. *"If, come mornin', we ain't back?"* He tried not to think of the alternatives, but now his uncle's seemingly pointless question about swimming came back to taunt him. The young man shivered.

Alex knew, if he had the tide figured right, they should have just about enough time to get the wagon over the bridge on Lone Tree Creek before the marsh flooded. Baker's Island, little more than a raised hump of sand between marsh and flat, and their intended destination, would truly become an island, isolated until the tide receded once more. With this thought in mind, the man's voice took on a quality of urgency.

"Eben, why don't you and your brother Nathaniel come with us. You seem to be dressed the warmest, and God knows that'll be needed where we're goin'. We'll be there 'til the tide gits out again, probably 'round three or four o'clock in the mornin' with this wind ahowlin' like she is. Better give us an hour or two's travel time on top o' that!"

This piece of information told the others when to expect their return. The intent was plain enough so the captain hadn't felt the need for such specific orders as, "If we haven't shown up by daylight, start the search parties!"

Wrapped in a tarp, Andy and Ulysses sat in the wagon sharing each others warmth. Listening to the plans being mapped out, Andy didn't understand any more than the dog what they implied. All he knew for sure was that he was shivering and yawning, and even in this he couldn't tell if it was the cold or the excitement as a root cause.

Catching the boy's attention, lantern beams shot out between the arms and legs of the men. The light's presence revealed by the snow driving around the corners of the building. In Andy's imagination, the white flakes became summer fireflies. Dancing and twirling through the sudden calm and eddies behind the big building, they blinked on and off as they passed through the moving shafts of brightness. Daydreaming again, he noticed the flakes disappear back into their black shadow of nothingness with a deathlike finality. Others taking their place reminded him of the endless stream of life.

Alex brought him back to the conscious world abruptly. Swinging up onto the seat, as other men climbed into the wagon bed, Alex yelled to him over the wind, "Master Sears! You can ride in the wagon until we get to the bridge, unless the cart-path is under water. If it is, then we'll all walk, and feel for the edges of the trail with our feet while we lead the horse. That way, maybe we won't lose wagon, horse-and-all, into a tidal creek."

Jouncing and joggling over the rutted path down onto the marsh with these strange men around him, Andy began to experience his first real doubts about coming along with his uncle tonight. Holding a hand up to shield his face from the sharp sting of the snow, now that they'd turned into the blast of unbroken wind, he could just make out the serious, deadly-silent faces of the others in the reflected glow of the lantern.

Suddenly chilled to the bone, the boy was reminded of his father's funeral procession. That somber day; the cold, windblown rain; the wearied, stoic expressions on the faces; the haunting seriousness of the moment; his own tumbled emotions; all brought back in this one instantaneous flash of recognition. Riding in on the feeling's coat-tails came the same overwhelming flood of panic, and he fought the urge to run just as he'd done then.

The flickering thoughts choked off his breath. He coughed. Snow hid the tears. At that moment he'd have given anything to be back with his mother in the warmth and security of Alex's kitchen. His mind was spinning. With no conscious intent, the boy hugged Ulysses.

A big, warm tongue rewarded his efforts.

The spell was broken. Again Andy became aware of the wind and snow whirling about them, and discovered a new rhythm developing in the motion of the wagon.

With nothing solid to build on, the path across the marsh had been built as a corduroy road. A simple construction, it was made up of cut logs laid side by side, crosswise, like very close railroad ties. Put together in sections called rafts, saplings had been nailed across the ends to hold everything together. Twenty or so feet long, the rafts were anchored in place by posts driven into the bottomless muck.

This may have been a great idea to support a wagonload of salt-marsh hay, but Andy had never ridden on anything like it in his life. He jiggled up and down so fast his eyes wouldn't focus properly. Suddenly, everything had a twin.

A lot of colorful, sea-worthy exclamations came from his fellow passengers as they too shifted around, trying to ease the abusive motion.

Too much for Ulysses, he refused to endure this in a sitting position. Freeing himself from the tarp he and Andy were sharing, the dog stood grumpily, squinting into the snow. Every few minutes he'd shake his head, making sure everyone knew his ears were getting wet now that he had to stand, and to inform them how he felt about the whole mess.

Glancing down, Andy thought it was rather strange that their ice and snow covered path was silhouetted by a black nothingness. He couldn't reason why snow on the marsh should be any different than snow on solid ground. Everything should be white! It took a cake of snow-ice drifting by for him to realize the darkness was water, lapping at the edges of their log road.

Remembering Alex's words of caution, the boy kept an anxious eye on his uncle to see when they were going to stop.

The sharp contrast made it easier for the captain to navigate in the dark, but he found himself on the bridge before he was ready for it. Other than a slight upward thrust, there had been nothing to distinguish the span from other parts of the road in the limited visibility of driving snow. Everyone piled off the wagon.

Andy, in his eagerness to jump ship, was saved from a frozen bath by the same hard grasp which had lifted him so easily from the train platform earlier in the day. To his uncle, this action on the boy's part showed an alarming lack of awareness. He sputtered to himself, *Damned young-un can't even get off a wagon without finding trouble!*

The logs and bridge were coated with a mixture of condensed, frozen sea-fog, and salt-spray ice. "Rime", Alex called it.

Slipping and sliding, Andy figured whale-oil on a pitching deck couldn't be any worse, and said so.

Leading Sandy by the bridle, and leaning into the gale, Alex shouted over the storm. "You think this is bad, Son, you should try clambering a hundred-feet up into a ship's rigging coated with this stuff. Climbing on the weather side, so's the wind'l blow you inboard toward the sails and ropes iffen ya slip, a man has to fight for his life all the way. Then, if and when you do make it into the fore-top, a frozen sail'l be waiting there to swat you off the foot-rope at the least sign of weakness, or keep you working with its stubbornness until your hands are too numb to hold on any longer.

The weather's almost always foul traversing the Cape of Good Hope at the tip of Africa, or rounding the Horn, trying to slip by Tierra del Fuego in the Straits of Magellan.

Sailing men have good reason to label that part of the world the roaring forties. Storm piles upon storm at that latitude, and a lot of good seamen have been known to climb the shrouds right into heaven when it gets like this."

The man paused to check the status of his crew and wagon. Satisfied nothing was missing, he turned back into the wind and continued. "Putting things in perspective, I suggest you keep one thing in mind. Bad as you might think it is here, those poor souls we're trying to reach tonight would trade places with you in an instant!

That is, if there's any life left in them to wish for such things."

"Do you really think we'll find anyone, Uncle Alex? Could anyone be alive out there in the water, with it so stormy and cold?"

The older man's reply didn't carry much hope. "It's fall, and the sea is still pretty warm compared to deep winter. If they could grab a piece of wreckage to keep their heads above water, then ride it in to shore, anything's possible. We've gotta look anyway, in the off chance some survived. After all, someday it might be you or me out there, and I'd sure like to think there'd be help ta the le'ward if we made it that far."

Andy shivered at the thought. "I ain't never goin' to be out there, if it's stormin' like this!"

Alex just smiled to himself at the innocence of this youth. Where the hell did the boy think he was he going to get off, if he was out there when it started?

They'd crossed the main stream, but Alex thought better of any more riding in the wagon. Hardly pausing for breath, the man bellowed, "We'd best keep ta walkin', Boys!"

Skating and splashing, he added, "You hear me now! Forget that saw about one hand for the ship, and the other for you! You hang on to the wagon with both hands! And if she goes over, to hell with her, let her go!"

"What about Sandy, Uncle Alex?"

Irritated that someone with no proven worth would dare question his judgment, he grumped, "Much as I love my horse, she's not worth a human life, boy!" Then giving it some thought, he added in a softer tone, "We could probably save her after the fact! Creeks left to cross ain't that wide anyway."

The wind carried his voice back to the other men. "Only a little further, Boys! We're just going to make it! Now the waters breaking over the path, another ten minutes and we'd be fumbling like blind-men out here."

"Uncle Alex, how come the snow stings my face so much out here? The wind blowin' that much harder?"

"Didn't notice it crunches between your teeth too, boy? Mixed with beach sand and salt spray, this close to the shore. Keep your mitt over your face, or pull the brim of your hat down 'til we get on the weather side of the dunes. Damned stuff'll take the hide right off your bones if you let it. Out yonder, she might be blowin' a dight harder, and carryin' half a wave in each gust, but at least the beach'll be underfoot instead of in your mouth."

A sudden upturn slowed their procession, and Andy knew without asking they'd made landfall because everything around them had turned white again.

Coming to a halt behind a clump of brush, Alex said, "We'll hitch Sandy behind these beachplum bushes to break the wind and sand. She'll be more comfortable here than out in the spray anyway."

Raising his voice to include all, Alex shouted, "Fix this spot to mind, gentlemen, so if anyone needs the gear we brought, you'll know where to find it!"

Gathering in the lee of the wagon, Alex addressed his crew with words of caution while laying out plans for the search.

"Mind you, it was less than a year ago Barnstable's Captain Bursley wrecked his ship *Minnehaha* on this shore. He salvaged her remains, but the stern was still laying to the north'ard last I knew, so don't confuse her with the new wreck if she's shifted in this blow!

I s'pect we'll be here awhile, gentlemen! With this wind and cold, don't get your tails wet or you may never live to see sun up!"

A dark form shifted with nervous energy. The captain had no problem addressing the man by name. "What do you say Sammy, shall we have at it?"

"AAAye, C C Cap'n!" Andy knew the head was bobbing, although it was more imagined in his mind's eye than actually seen in the darkness.

"Nate, Eben, wanna light your lanterns from ours here in the lee?"

"Aye, Captain! That makes it. We're ready!"

"All right lads, lets head out to the beach. I'll place a life ring on a stake where we come out, so's you can get a bearing to Sandy here.

You Hallets lay off ta the east'ard, and we'll head west. When you get to land's end, come about and sweep the high ground on your return. If nothing's found, everyone should meet about here again and we'll swap directions. If we don't meet, chances are the other party's working something."

An alternative thought prompted him to advise, "Take care, trouble's not what we seek out here tonight!"

Back to his original course, he barked, "The party who's not engaged gets the wagon and brings it down the beach 'til they find the other, clear?"

The man was much too impatient to waste time waiting for obvious answers, so he kept right on talking. "Of course, if it seems like too much time's gone by, maybe we've both made a discovery. In that case one of you come along the beach, and I'll send someone, and we'll fight over who gets the wagon first."

"Aye, Captain! Sounds like a good plan. See you in about an hour, God willin'!"

"Amen to that, Nathaniel."

As they made last minute adjustments to their personal gear, Alex spoke directly to his nephew. "Master Sears, you stick by me! If trouble should find you, yelling your lungs inside out wouldn't do much good over this wind and poundin' surf unless you're close to hand!"

"Yes, Sir! What are we lookin' for?"

"Anything that doesn't seem to belong where you find it!"

Tromping single-file out through the last dunes, each man carried a coil of rope over his shoulder and a narrow-beamed bull's-eye lantern in his mittened hand. They would have preferred search lanterns, but cold snow against hot glass would have shattered the fragile chimneys. A short pause by Alex, to mark their wagon's location with the life ring on a stake driven into the sand, was enough for the two parties to lose visual contact.

Directing his dog to follow, as their group turned westward along the beach, Alex shouted, "C'mon Ulysses! Good dog. Lets see if your nose works in salt spray."

The boy swallowed, and curiously felt tenderness in his vocal cords. Suddenly he understood why his uncle's voice always sounded gravely. After years of command, Alex made certain he was heard the first time he spoke, no matter what the conditions.

Aware he was probably going to lose his own voice from this unaccustomed shouting to be heard over the storm, Andy still couldn't restrain the urge. There was so much to wonder about out here.

"Where do you think the wreck is, Uncle Alex? Is it on the beach? Those waves are huge, so the water must be real deep!"

"Looks are deceiving, Mister. At low tide, you can walk for a nautical mile straight out from this beach, afore you'd reach water. Normal rise of tide on this part of the coast is about eight to nine foot. That would put it a foot less than where it is now, but this is a moon-tide. They come along over a two or three day period a coupl'a times a month. That's gonna add another three and a half feet to it tonight. Plus, with this wind piling it on shore, you can add another three or four feet on top of that! In other words, we'll have a double-tide 'fore she peaks about three hours from now."

"Isn't nine feet of water enough to float a boat in?" Andy asked as he looked up into the wind, trying to picture how deep that would be.

Surprising himself with his patience, Alex explained to this bothersome appendage he had so unwisely invited along, "Normally, four feet would float a coastal packet like mine on a calm day, what with the centerboard you could pull up.

O'course, we don't know what kind of ship she is out there yet, but even a centerboard schooner would'a been only ankle deep when this one struck.

She must have hit a couple of hours ago. Maybe an hour after dark, on the outer bar beyond the edge of the flat.

Out there tonight, the waves are probably twenty feet high. Running up the flat takes the steam out of them, so these are only about ten-footers we got here. Two hours ago, the trough between those twenty-footers would have left maybe two feet over that bar.

My guess is, every tenth heartbeat that ship would be gettin' picked up twelve to fifteen feet by the surge of the wave, then slammed down onto the flat like a kid tryin' to crack a coconut. Ain't no ship ever built, could take that kind of a poundin'!

In a coupl'a minutes, when she stopped floatin', every wave breaking over the bar would smash into her with all of the weight and power of that train you rode in on this afternoon. Come mornin', don't think anyone will ever know there was a wreck out there 'ceptin those poor souls who rode in on her."

"A A A AA!" Sam was waving his arms, bobbing his head, and pointing into the foamy sea. Grabbing Alex's arm, he willed as much as directed the man's gaze to the proper spot.

A small section of the violent turbulence seemed to have substance. It moved in a rhythm all its own, counter to that of the storm-driven waves.

Ulysses spotted the object at the same time Alex did, and added his voice to the din.

In the following excitement, Alex became all Captain again. His commands flowed out of him in staccato bursts interspersed with exhilarated chatter. "I see, Sam, I see it! You got yourself a Blackfish! Men aren't the only creatures of God dying out here tonight!"

"Let's see if we can get a rope around her flukes, and tied off to a stake!"

"Mister Sears, step lively and look for a small post, or piece of driftwood about three feet long! Sharp on one end, so we can drive it into the sand!"

"Damn, these things are heavy, and hard to handle. That's it Sam, get the tail up the beach so I can throw on a couple of hitches!"

"Ulysses! Get outta here dog afore you get stepped on!"

"Look out, Sam! Get slapped by that tail and you won't wake up 'til next week."

"Mister Sears, take this block of driftwood and drive that stake you found into the sand, about fifty paces up the beach! Tip it away from the water a little!"

"I appreciate your help ahaulin' on this rope Ulysses, but if you bite it through I'll kick your butt all the way to Sandy Neck! Damn fool dog!"

"There, boy, I'll bend this line onto your stake, down close to the sand, and maybe it'll hold. We'll kedge the whale up the beach with the tide, every time we come by."

Andy was puzzled. "I thought you said it was a Blackfish?"

"Blackfish, Pilot whale, same thing!" By the shortness of his answers, one could tell the man's patience was wearing thin. Undaunted, the boy kept at him.

"Is a bend the same thing as a knot, Uncle Alex?"

The reply was an affirmative grunt, but this time its tone was warning enough for Andy to leave his uncle alone.

Aware this man had called him 'Master Sears' for the most part, and now that they were out in public, a more formal 'Mister', Andy wondered if his uncle had any feelings for him at all. That is, other than the anger and resentment which he himself had precipitated.

In defense, he reminded himself that he really didn't give a damn what the old goat called him, because he wasn't going to stay here more than a couple of more days anyway. Just long enough to figure out a way back to Boston!

Grabbing the dog to keep him out of harm's way, Andy looked up and frowned. His personal vow of silence forgotten, the boy yelled, "What's Sam doing to the whale?"

Squinting face-on into the spray and snow, the boy could just make out what appeared to be a knife in Sam's hand.

Alex, finishing his hitches on the stake, glanced towards the thrashing creature. "Making his mark! He's carving his initials in it, so if anybody else finds the carcass, Sam has first claim."

"But . . . it's still alive! Can't we let it go?"

Taken aback by the naiveté of the boy, Alex growled a reply. "That little whales got enough oil in him to light Sam's lamps all winter. Gotta be worth fifty, sixty dollars. Hell, Sam don't make that much in five, six months work, and you want me to tell him to let it go?"

Frowning at the boy he added, "You tell him!" And he paraphrased the old saw, "It's an ill-wind that doesn't blow somebody some good, boy!"

Impatient at their delay, Alex shouted, "Let's go! Unless we shake a leg, the other lads will be catching up before we even get started!"

The four of them staggered down the beach like drunken sailors. In addition to the soft sand, cakes of slippery salt-ice, and slushy snow, the wind gusts threatened to topple them over at each step.

To Andy, the gale seemed to be playing a malicious game. First, it would force them to lean into it because it blew so hard, then it would stop momentarily, as if pausing for a fresh breath. They'd end up fighting to keep their balance from the sudden loss of support until the next gust started the process over.

The boy's sharp eyesight caught a shadowy-dark mass at the edge of their lantern's light. "Wow, look at that pile of stuff! Did it come from the wreck, Uncle Alex? Look at all the ropes, and everything all wound up in 'em! Reminds me of Ma's knittin' basket after the cat got to it."

Ulysses began barking at a corner of the debris just as Sam grabbed Alex's arm again. The man waved and pointed, his eyes bulging alarmingly and his feet almost dancing.

Andy began to realize this was normal for poor Sam when he became excited, but it was still a little unnerving.

When he finally spotted what Sammy and the dog had been trying to point out, Alex sprang into sudden motion.

"Oh Jesus! Boy, come help us cut this poor fellow out of the tangle! Oh God!"

"Look out, Ulysses! Good dog! Good dog."

"He ain't only drowned, he's busted up pretty bad too. On second thought, Mister Sears, let's anchor this pile to the beach. Take one of these broken spars, and drive it into the sand like you did for the whale! While your going up the beach, take this line with you and tie it off down close to the sand the way you were shown!"

"We'd better look for survivors, and cut this dead fellow out later. He ain't in no hurry to get loose."

"Sam, take the lantern and climb up on the mass! See if there's any bodies up there with life left in 'em."

The pile of debris surged with a big wave.

"Watch it, this stuff's in motion! She still belongs to the sea! Wait up! Luff your sails a minute there Sam, let me bend on a lifeline. I don't want to lose you too."

Out of breath after his exertions, Andy puffed back to the pile in the surf's edge, and watched his uncle pay out the line to a disappearing Sam.

"Uncle Alex, Ulysses won't leave this sail alone. Want me to cut it loose?"

"Aye! I can't leave Sam's lifeline. No tellin' what it holds, so be careful!"

His warning was almost drowned out by a, "HOLY JESUS!" from Andy.

Alex's immediate thought was, *Christ, now what's that boy gotten into? Don't he know I got my hands full with Sammy's line?*

"What's the matter, boy? You all right? You need help?"

Andy's sheepish reply brought relief with it.

"Rats! Four or five of 'em! Hiding in the sail, and damn near as big as George, they scared the shit out of me! How come they lived, and the sailor didn't?"

Before his uncle could answer, the boy paused a moment and then added a slightly embarrassed, "Uuuh, sorry about the cuss words, Uncle Alex!"

Smiling to himself as he kept Sammy's line tight, the captain answered, "Boy, there are times when nothing else but a cuss word will fit. It takes a gentleman to know the difference though. Your learning, Mister! At least you knew you said one.

Now as for rats, I've seen 'em come ashore from a wreck twenty miles at sea, and swam every inch of the way. Guess it's up to God what each of his creatures will live through!"

The man started moving quickly again, taking in line. "Ropes gettin' slack. Here comes Sam."

The one-eyed stare of Sammy's lantern slashed and stabbed in wild gyrations, as the big, bear-shaped mass slid off the pile to the wave-washed sand beside them.

"N N NNothin Cap'n!" the man reported.

"Grab the lantern, Mister Sears!"

Showing genuine concern, Alex fussed over the other man, making sure everything was as it should be. "You all right, Sam? Let me get you untied. Glad to have you back on solid ground, my friend."

There was obvious relief in his small talk. "Ulysses found the boy some rats, but I guess that's all for this pile. Lets check the rest of the beach, and we'll get the body out on the way back."

Andy had another question. "How come we can see in the dark tonight, Uncle Alex?"

Again, his uncle wondered to himself why he'd brought this extra bother along. The boy was turning out to be as pesky and noisy as a Jay-bird after a cat.

A long sigh preceded his answer. "There's a full moon above these storm clouds; a little phosphorescence in the water; white sand, lots of foam, and a fair measure of snow to reflect what light there is."

They staggered on. The wind, snow, sand, sleet, and spray howling from their backs over their right shoulders turned that side of their faces a bright red, and numb.

Still carrying his uncle's lantern, Andy asked, "Is that a log floating out there, Uncle Alex? By that pile of waves?" The boy prayed he was right, but knew the answer before he'd asked.

Correcting the boy's terminology, Alex replied, "Waves don't make a pile, Mister, that's a rip! I see the place you mean though. It's a body, for certain."

"See it, Sam? Out near the rip at the mouth of Lone Tree Creek. Can't get it from here, that's for sure. No point in worrying about it though. The wind and tide'll carry it down to the boys at Central Wharf, or if they miss it he's gonna end up in Mill Creek or Stony Cove."

"Swing that lantern over here, Mister Sears. Let's see what the time is gettin' to be." The captain dug a big pocket watch out from under his foul weather gear, then sheltered it as best he could with his back to the gale.

"Ten thirty. That makes it another hour and a half, maybe two hours before the tide changes. I figure the body ought to make the wharf in about a half hour, so they've got plenty of time to snag it 'fore the water roughens up."

Putting his watch away again, he informed them, "This is the turnaround point. You boys warm enough? The wind and snow will be hard on the face, but the work it'll take to walk back against this stuff will keep your boiler stoked.

C'mon Ulysses, back this way! Don't like the weather do ya, fella? Don't blame you dog, neither do I. Any damn fool out on a night like this deserves to get wet, but you didn't ask to come, did you ol'boy?"

Leaning into the wind, Andy asked, "Did you say the water was going to get rougher, Uncle Alex?"

Alex groaned inwardly and wondered to himself if the lad would ever run down. Deciding he'd answered enough questions for a while he said, "I'm about out of shoutin' power in this wind, boy. Wait'll we get back to the lee of the pile with the body in it!"

Disappointed, Andy had to admit it was hard to talk and fight his way into the wind and snow at the same time. Head down, and settling into the task at hand, a new voice out of the dark startled him into looking up.

"Ahoy there, Cap'n! Find anything further down-wind?"

"Hello Nathaniel. Glad to see you, and we're all glad to see you've brought Sandy too. One body beyond the point, drifting down towards the wharf, and one back at the big pile just east of here. How 'bout you?"

"We picked up two other pilot whales about a hundred yards east of Sam's, but that was all. Didn't even see any wreckage 'til we got to the pile you was jus' talkin' 'bout. Eben's cuttin' the body out now, whilst I came lookin' for you.

Near's we can figure it, the ship must'a hit on the inner end of the bar next to the channel, judgin' the wind and where that tangle ended up. 'Nother coupl'a hundred feet, and she mighta made it."

As they led Sandy and the wagon back up the beach, Alex speculated, "That poor lad in the pile was probably in the tops. I s'pect he was trying see above the spray and spume, to locate the light on the Neck.

It's hard to judge, with all the sail they was acarryin'—even though they'd shortened it considerable—if they knew where they was agoin' or not. If they were running scared, trying to beat the gale into safe-harbor before dark, it was a poor judgment on the Master's part!"

Nathaniel added, "We figger it must have been that vessel what's been sailing in fits and starts off the shore for the last day or two. She never put up a distress signal, but she appeared disabled. Don't know why they'd have crowded on sail in this wind, unless her anchor chains parted and they was makin' one, last, desperate attempt to slide inta harbor. Had to have been close! S'pose they had too much head, and fell away from the channel?"

Alex's voice carried a tinge of contempt. "The man had to have known he was almost on the bar from the noise of the breakers. Crowding that much sail in a wind like this is pretty foolhardy, unless you're driving a Clipper designed to run, and you've got plenty of room to stretch your wings. But, here? On a lee shore? Man had to be crazy!"

He was obviously questioning the doomed Master's competency.

Andy had no idea how his uncle could tell what the ship had been carrying for sails anyway, the mess on the beach was so confusing. Especially in the dark.

Alex continued to grump. "Wouldn't surprise me if she lost her gear before she even reached shore, and if not, I'll bet her masts were cleaned right down to the deck when she first struck. That boy Eben's working on was probably on the beach before they even missed him."

Nathaniel joined in. "I found a life ring in the pile, Cap'n. I'm sure you knew her. The schooner *Granite*, out of Quincy. Probably haulin' her last load of cobblestone out of Rockport due this season, bound by way of Barnstable for Hyannis.

Carryin' heavy like that means she hit real hard. Bet she blew all apart as soon as she found the bar."

Alex began to fume. "Yeah, I knew her! Knew her Captain by reputation, too! Torrey's the man's name. Rumor said he had a taste for whiskey, and a nasty disposition when his supply ran short. Maybe this trip he was well provisioned, an' forgot where he was agoin'!

It's one thing to be courageous, another to be foolheaded. Might of been heading for Plymouth when the barometer started to fall. Be just like him to get a late start ahead of the storm, found he couldn't make it to Pilgrim country, then ran for his life toward Barnstable. Hauling all that ballast, and running down wind, the man would've crowded on as much sail as he could find room for, then fought to shorten as the gale built. She'd of been counter-down from the weight, and green water over the deck all the way.

May have even rolled on her beam-ends, comin' about for the last reach into harbor! And, like you said—loaded heavy like that—once she touched bottom even God would have been hard put to keep her together."

His body heaved a sigh of sadness. "Damned shame! She had a good crew. . . ."

"Hello, Captain!"

Eben had completed his work and followed Nathaniel down the beach. "I got the body out, and hauled him up to the top of the dune. Wrapped it in a sail-cloth cut from the pile, to keep the sand out of him."

"Aye, Eben! Good job done."

Eben was the more talkative of the Hallet brothers.

"Hey Cap'n, d'you think we'll run out of beach afore the tide changes? I ain't got much taste for joinin' those whales tonight, and y'know my wife would never forgive me if'n I died out here instead of home in bed! She'd wanna give me hell for not finishing the fence first!"

"We've got over an hour to go, maybe an hour and a quarter. How much freeboard d'ya reckon 'til flood?" Was Alex's questioning reply.

"Vertical feet, I figure a couple, maybe three at most. Hard to tell, but we're up against the base of the dunes now, and they're pretty low on this island."

The alarm in Alex's voice was hard to disguise. "Damn, Eben, was that to the highest point?"

"Yessir!" That's just above Sam's whale."

There was no need to drive anyone now. "C'mon men, we ain't got time to stand here and jam! Get the body on the wagon, and lets get back t' the east'ard. I knew we were gettin' short of beach, but I'd forgotten the wind had knocked the tops off the dunes too. With this surf arunnin', who knows how much more sand we'll lose 'fore things peak."

Everything was business, and Alex laid the course.

"I know the dune you mean, Eben. It's got the little one that's almost as tall just behind it, where we tied Sandy. If we can get back in time to build that one up a dight with our shovels, we ought to be able to park the wagon right there again. The front dune should break the force of the waves, and if we're lucky, spray is all we'll get."

Sammy volunteered to lead the wagon, and the rest of them fell in behind to help Sandy by pushing.

Almost trotting to keep up, Andy still had a question which seemed to have pertinent implications. "Uncle Alex, is that when the waves are supposed to get rougher?"

Here we go again, his uncle thought, chafing at the bother.

"Don't let that be of any concern, Mister Sears! In these shallow waters, the waves will only build where there's a current. When the tide changes, 'round midnight, the flow will be in the opposite direction to the wind. Wind against tide, pits one of God's mighty forces shoving against another. With no give to the bottom, only place left for the water to go is up!

Sometimes I've seen waves get as big as a barn in a storm like this, but only where there was a channel or creek to give 'em body. That's where the water is deeper, and it can run real strong to push against the breeze.

Off the beach, like here, there ain't no real flow so all that can happen is the waves will break a little sharper and quicker.

Another thing you'll notice about these kinda blows, if you hang around here long enough, is that quite often the storm will peak at high water. If that happens tonight, the wind'll shift to the nor'west and drop with the tide.

Time an' tide, my boy, time an' tide. All we can do is wait and see."

Then in a more confidential tone, he added, "You know don'tcha, Eben ain't the only one who's gonna be in trouble if'n we die out here tonight?"

That same mischievous look caught Andy's eye that he'd seen when Alex was teasing his mother about Aunt Sophie's ghost. His immediate thought was to wonder if this stiff old grump was trying to be mean, or if he was he just trying to scare him, but then the light dawned. *How can we get in trouble if we're dead?*

In spite of the damp, wind-driven cold of the storm, and the apparent danger still to be faced, Andy suddenly felt curiously warm inside.

Rough hands grabbing him under the arms brought his mind back to the night, the wind, snow and sand.

"C'mon boy, let me hoist ya up on the tailgate. Ol' Sandy ain't agoin' to notice your piddly weight, an you been takin' three steps to every one of the Captain's and Sam's all night."

"Thanks, Mister . . . uhhh." This was embarrassing. No one had bothered to introduce a mere boy to these men, and he couldn't be sure who was who, just overhearing them.

"Name's Hallet, Andy. You can jus' call me Eben iffen you want to though."

Jerking his head toward the man beside him he added, "This tall, skinny fella here's my brother."

The other dark shadow leaned closer, "My name's Nathaniel, young fella, and like my brother said, after a night like this all the Misters and Sirs you're s'posed to call a person don't amount to as much as a pile of this here snow under an April sun. Jus' call me Nate!"

Fifteen minutes, and a half mile down the beach, they reached their point of sanctuary. The water was chasing them now. Each wave, as it stretched out at the peak of its dying surge, trickled through the spokes on the port-side wheels. Thwarting its greed, they made a sharp right-turn, up and over the first dune.

In a totally unrelated train of thought, Andy wondered on seeing this naked crown topped by its thinning fuzz of beach grass, if sand-dunes went bald for the same reasons men did.

Alex's voice of command came through sharp and clear again. "Watch it boys, don't let the wagon tip over! Grab the wheels and help Sandy git it up on this hump! That's pretty good right there, iffen we add a little insurance on her weather-side with the shovels.

Mister Sears, break out some of those small tarps again. We can wrap up in them while we wait the tide out."

Still carrying his uncle's lantern, Andy scrambled further up into the wagon and stopped dead. He hesitated a moment, and then almost in a whisper said, "The body's laying on them!"

Waiting at the tail-gate, Alex's patience was wearing as thin as the beach grass. "Well move it! He ain't goin' to bite you, Boy!"

There was another slight hesitation, while Andy sat the lantern down, and then came the reply, "I ain't never touched a dead man before."

You could almost hear the young man screw his courage up a notch with each word.

Alex's voice was gruff and unsympathetic. "Everything that's ever happened, had to start with the first wave down someone's wake!"

Then he bent a little. "Look, all of us have had to do things from time to time that we didn't think too much of! Now, you got his shoulders up at that end, so I'll grab his feet, an' we'll just roll him over easy. He won't mind a bit!"

In the mixture of light and shadows, there was motion on the boy's part, and some rustling as he tried to slide his hands in under the sailor, then there was another pause.

Without warning, the boy leapt to his feet fighting for breath. "Yuck! I got blood on me, Uncle Alex!"

The man's startled reply was a shout. "You What?"

"I got blood on me! Warm blood!" Fighting panic, the boy kept trying to wipe the sticky redness off onto his wet, oil-skin pants.

"Jesus Christ, boy, dead men don't bleed!"

Alex's orders came fast and furious again. "Sam, throw a tarp around the wind'ard side of the wagon!"

"Eben, help me get him down offa here!"

The effort of removing the injured sailor caused no interruption to his stream of commands. "Nate, dig a little fire pit, and pile the sand on the lee side to make a reflector! Then stick all our kerosene fire signals in it, and get them agoin'!"

"Mister Sears, get those tarps and that horse blanket out of the rescue gear! Somehow, we've gotta get some warmth back into this sailor."

After Andy had passed these down to his uncle, the man said, "Now son, get down here, and help me strip him down! We've gotta get these wet clothes off the poor fella, and wrap him in the blanket. After that, we'll snuggle him up close to the fire."

"Nathaniel, you'd better get a tarp or something up on the landside of that fire quick, or some other well-meaning fool will be risking his life to come to 'our' rescue!"

"Sam, pile a little more sand on the bottom of the wind-break on Sandy's end! She's still a'whistling through there pretty good."

Kneeling beside his nephew on a spread out tarp, they undressed the seaman hurriedly. Alex, keeping the boy's mind occupied, spoke to him in a conversational tone. "Now, Son, I've got to ask you to do something else you might find a little difficult."

"What's that, Uncle Alex?" Reluctance began creeping into the young man's voice before he even knew what was in store.

"When we get set, I want you to lay down on the ground-cloth next to this lad, on the side away from the fire. We're going to pull this canvas up behind you, and out towards the flames to help trap the heat. Your purpose will be to keep our sailor here from having a cold side. In other words, you're going to have to open your coat and wool shirt, then huddle tight up against him."

The boy said nothing, as his mind whirled around the idea.

His uncle continued. "You'll probably feel like you've crawled right into the coffin with him!"

Still nothing came from the boy.

"Do you think you can handle it, or ain't you got the guts?" Alex thought a little challenge wouldn't hurt, knowing his nephew's usual set of mind.

Andy took a deep breath, and shivered inside. He knew he shouldn't have come on this trip. Another deep breath was followed by a quiet, "What are the rest of you going to do?"

Taking Andy's question as an affirmative answer, the harsh edge was gone from Alex's voice when he answered this time.

"We're going to be right here, son. Hell, we couldn't go anywhere if we had to for a couple hours or so. If you hadn't noticed, our little island is only about a hundred feet across right now, and it'll be down to less than half that before the tide turns."

Talking now to keep Andy's mind off the duty he faced, Alex rambled on. "If it wasn't for the dune to the wind'ard, we'd be in a heap of trouble. As it is, we're going to be busy keeping the gale from blowing our shelter away. First, we've gotta put a spray shield over the wagon, you, and the fire, to keep everything from gettin' drowned out, and then comes some shovel work."

Alex was pleased his nephew had responded in a manner he considered 'proper'. It showed the boy could put some things above his own selfish interests.

Still talking, the older man made the last tucks of canvas and blanket around the sailor's motionless form. "Bet half this beach is missing come morning. Probably build up again before winter's done though, from the stuff coming down to it from Gray's beach to the east'ard. Dunes are kinda like giant, slow-moving waves, don'tcha think?"

Details completed, he looked toward his nephew. "All right Mister, everything else is ready. You all set?"

"Don't go 'way too far!" Was Andy's quiet reply, as he slid into the small opening.

"That's it," Alex encouraged him, "get right up against the fella's backside! After we get this canvas set, we'll put the lanterns at your head and feet to give you both a little more heat."

The captain's next statement brought up mind pictures that hadn't occurred to the boy until now, and his heart crept back into his throat. It was put gently, but it might as well have been a shout for the end result. "If you should hear our poor sailor groan, or think you feel movement, yell real loud! We'll come see what's goin' on!"

Alarmed, the boy called out, "Uncle Alex?"

"Right here, Son!"

Andy tried to stall the man's departure without sounding too much like a frightened child. The boy didn't think very highly of being left here alone, wrapped up with this strange man to begin with. Now, thoughts of listening for what might be agonized screams, or moans, were almost more than he could bear.

"When you get time, will you come back and talk to me?"

"I'll do that son, but right now we've got some fast shoveling to do or your tail'll be gettin' wet. Ulysses will keep you company for a few minutes, won't you boy? He's already crawled in out of the weather behind you, lad!"

Andy lay there sharing the warmth, and by his presence, added his spark of life to the nurturing womb of the shelter. He could feel the earth shake under his body from the tremendous power of waves crashing on the nearby shore. Their rhythm a hypnotic beat, like some gigantic heart pulsing life into the world. Wind and waves blended to a constant roar. The boy's weary senses numbed. An occasional clank as two shovels met, gave him a reassuring attachment to his uncle, and the men close by. Thoughts began to blur. This had been the longest day Andy could ever remember. Drifting off, the youngster's mind questioned if it was really only this morning when he and his family had stepped off the front stoop of their tenement. . . .

Removing the sailor's dead, cold, and now stiff body, the men paused momentarily before putting it in the wagon. Glancing down at the sleeping boy in the flickering light and small warmth of the fire, they more closely resembled a band of benevolent, conspiratorial elves than the hard men of the sea they truly felt themselves to be.

Alex's smile was one of satisfaction. To his way of thinking, the boy would do. Any questions about backbone, and how his new charge would react under pressure, answered. More paternal than he'd ever care to admit, the man tucked the remaining canvas in around his sister's son.

Huddled together, deep in their own thoughts, the men shared their meager shelter and waited the tide out.

Chapter 5

Of Stars and Men

It seemed strange to Andy that weather could change so quickly. The wind-driven snow of the night just past had moved on. In its wake, an unforgiving nor'wester pumped the first arctic cold of the season into the marshes, while scrubbing the sky clean. From the feel, the boy was sure the wind had blown across an iceberg along the way, and he was glad they were going home.

As they dragged the last few feet up off the cord-road, Alex and company entered a world of white. Their early season storm had dumped six inches of wet sticky snow on the upland shore.

"All out boys! We've got to help ol' Sandy one more time!" Following the older man down off the wagon, Andy decided the storm hadn't taken much out of his uncle's voice. He trudged beside him as they led Sandy up the snow covered path by her bridle.

Weary, but talkative, Alex maintained his usual habit of letting those around him know his course of action. "It'll be easier once we've gotten through the ruts and up this hill, Mister Sears. The Hallet boys'll get off down the road, while we continue on to the storage building. That's where the wreck party'll be awaitin' us with any other bodies they've found. We'll leave Sammy and our poor lad with them, then head for home ourselves."

After a moment's pause, he added in a questioning tone, "I imagine your mother's beside herself with worry by now?"

Choosing not to think of what lay ahead, Andy ignored the inflection and instead asked, "Where does Sam live?"

Not being a stupid man, his uncle read the change of subject for what it was. Realizing there was little either he or the boy could do about Sarah at the moment, the man went along with his nephew's reasoning and answered, "Don't suppose you noticed in the darkness last night, but there's a big warehouse at the foot of Central wharf, right next to the storage building. Sammy's got a little cubbyhole upstairs in the corner of the sail loft there, where nobody bothers him."

"Does he own the warehouse?" The long night had done little to quench the boy's curiosity.

"No, no! He kinda keeps watch on the place in exchange for the space. The man lives off the shore, clammin' and fishin' to eat, then sells some of his take and anything else he might find of value beachcombing for his few other needs. It's a simple life, but he seems happy enough!"

"Don't he get lonesome?"

Alex paused a moment to give this inquiry some extra thought. The boy could ask the damnedest questions. Finding nothing wrong with the truth, he asked one of his own. "Tell me, son, do ya notice how he stutters?"

"Yup!" Feeling patronized, Andy considered this a stupid question. Didn't this man give him credit for any sense at all? A person would have to be both mindless and deaf not to notice something that obvious!

Alex, oblivious to it all, rambled on. "Poor Sam's one of those people who get real nervous with others around. Especially if he don't know 'em too good! In fact, if everybody's watchin' him, like in a crowd or sumpin', his talkin' gets so bad you can't understand a single word. As such, avoidin' people has gotten to be second nature to the poor fellow. So, to answer your question, I guess he must not miss 'em much anymore.

Real shame, he's a good man!"

Giving Sam's way of life more thought, the captain added, "You know, I wouldn't be surprised if that might be the main reason he can't bring himself to sail with me! Cooped up with a bunch of people not of his own choosing, on a dinky little boat an' no place to get away from them? Yessir, probably drive the man crazy!"

Sam's plight had never consciously crossed Alex's mind before. He'd always taken the man at face value, without questioning the why of his limitations.

Coming full circle, Alex admitted, "Thinking about it, now that you've brought the subject to mind, I don't really know if he gets lonesome or not. I've never asked."

"I 'spect I would!" Andy confessed. The boy cranked his head around in his foul-weather gear to steal a peek at the dark shape, puffing, and putting its back into the weight of the wagon.

Alex interrupted his thoughts. "That's it boys! All aboard. Sandy ought ta be able to handle it from here, unless we hit some big drifts."

Watching the men climb into the back of the wagon, the long dark shape laying there caught Andy's attention again. "Uncle Alex, why did the sailor die?"

The older man sighed, indicating a reluctance for this topic, but he answered anyway. "I told you he was pretty bad stove-up, when we found him! After you and I stripped him, to get him into the blanket, I could see that most of his ribs on one side was broke. Don't think he could have made it if he'd had a doctor sittin' beside him in a surgery.

We did the best we could for him, and I think in the end he knew he'd been rescued. Five minutes after we left him with you, I came back to see how things were goin'. His eyes had opened. He looked at me, blinked a couple of times, squeezed my hand, and then just sorta faded away. . . .

After we finished shoveling, we got him outta there.

Didn't see much sense to wake you just to wait for the tide, so I letcha sleep a few hours."

This gave the boy something to think about for a minute, and the muffled silence of their white world enveloped them again. Only the squeak of snow under the wheels, and the muted rattles of the wagon, assured them of progress.

Alex reined the horse to a stop. To Andy, they were still in the middle of nowhere. Nothing was visible in the half-darkness but the same snow-bent field cedars, and half-buried scrub brush he'd been seeing since they'd left the marsh.

The captain's voice broke the quiet. "Eben, Nathaniel, this is about the best I can do for you under these conditions. Thank you for joining us tonight. I imagine you'll want to sleep a while after this night's work, so I'll tell the men at the wharf to watch out for your whales on the chance they've come ashore near here."

As the men clambered down out of the wagon, it was Eben's voice that responded. "Thank you Cap'n. I'm glad it was you leadin' this party. I don't think we'd a been comfortable out there with anyone else on a night like this. Oh, and thank you for the offer about telling the men, but I think we'll prob'ly grab a bite to eat, then get down to the shore by first light. Can't afford to lose those whales iffen there's a chance to find 'em!

We'll look for yours too Sam, iffen you want?"

"N N Nnothanks. I'll I'll b b bbethere."

Used to Sam's ways, Eben supplied most of the words and let Sam respond in monosyllables. "Why don't we all work together? We'll help you haul yours into shore, and try it out, iffen you help us with ours. Deal?"

"D d d dd. . . . Yup!"

Sammy was bobbing his head again. This shook the wagon so much it reminded Andy of the cord-road they'd just left.

Their shapes little more than shadow against shadow, melted into the dim, predawn light. A voice drifted back. "Take care Andy! We'll see you around."

Pleased, the boy responded, "Aye, Sir! Bye Nathaniel, bye Eben. . . . See ya!"

Alex flicked the reins, "Giddap, Sandy!"

For some reason, Alex still felt talkative. It might have been his fatigue, or maybe the boy had hit a responsive chord somehow. Both of them were vaguely aware of the fact, but neither was willing to acknowledge, nor admit to anything.

"You know the stars, boy?"

"Nope!"

"You see those right up there, shaped kinda like a water dipper?"

Squinting up into the cold, dark sky, Andy answered, "Yup, I think so."

Waving his arm around, Alex was pointing heavenward. "Those two on the lip, they point over there to another star. See that bright one? The one at the end of the handle of that little dipper?"

"Yup!"

"That one's the pole star. Polaris! The north star! The first one you've got to learn if you're going to navigate. Yessir, sits right on top of the north pole. Don't hardly move a dight from night to night, nor year to year, so it's always there. Think you can remember that one, boy?"

"Yup! How 'bout that little bunch over there. Do they have a name?"

Getting this kind of response encouraged Alex to pursue the matter further. "Every star up there has a name, son. Over on that side of the sky, they're just getting ready to set. That bunch you're looking at are the Pleiades, or seven sisters. Next to them, d'you see that vee-shaped bunch? That's Taurus the bull. The orange star's Aldebaran, one of his eyes. Then comes Orion the hunter. See the sword hanging off his belt?"

"Yup, but if Polaris stays put, does that mean the rest of them ain't always in the same spot?"

"They rise and set every night, boy, just like the sun does during the day. Don't know if you realize it, but there are stars in the sky all day too. Just can't see 'em is all, 'cuz the sun's so bright it drowns 'em out. Fortunately, the two march to a different rhythm, so the night sky changes with the seasons. That way, over the course of a year, we get to see all the stars."

"Wow! And they've all got names? Maybe I'll remember the ones you taught me tonight, Uncle Alex, but I don't think I'll ever be able to keep track of 'em all!"

His uncle smiled to himself. "I've got an idea you'll remember lots of things, Mister. The way you ask questions, you probably know enough already to show them teachers a thing or two when you see 'em next week."

Andy took this as a compliment, and responded with his usual, "Yup!"

The Captain smiled, "Lord help them!"

Alex was feeling pretty smug. He'd just gotten Andy to consent that school was in his future without going through another big row. Figuratively speaking, he almost wore his arm out patting himself on the back. Indulging his ego a little further, the man decided if he was patient, he might be able to put up with this combative, little monster long enough to find him a new home. Taking it a step further, he wagered with himself that if he really set his mind to it, he was sure he'd be able to tame and house-break this scamp in no time! All it would take is the proper approach and a keen mind. . . . *Who said I'd never get the hang of this family business thing?*

"Ahoy there, chandlery! Anyone aboard?" Alex shouted, as they pulled up in front of the storage building's doors.

Showing the ravages of a cold night, the man almost creaked with the effort of climbing down off his wagon seat.

Sam slid off the tailgate and came around to Andy's side of the wagon just as one of the big barn doors opened, and a cloud of steam and light spilled out into the yard.

Squinting from the sudden brightness, Sam turned towards Andy and his hood blew back revealing that comical ball of fuzz again. His mouth working like mad, Sam grabbed the boy's hand and shook it as fast as he normally bobbed his head.

"S S SSolong, A A AAndyfriendamine?"

Andy, a little puzzled at first, finally grasped the meaning. Returning the handshake with a grin, he said, "So long Sam. I'm glad I met you, and I'd be honored to be your friend."

Beaming and bobbing, Sam returned to the back of the wagon to help the others unload the sailor's body. Carrying the poor dead boy inside, they laid him beside those of his shipmates who'd been found, to await their final voyage . . . by train.

Swinging back up onto the wagon seat, Alex shook his head in amusement. There sat Andy and Ulysses, leaning against each other much as they had nine or ten hours ago on the opposite end of a very long night.

They made quite a pair.

Chapter 6

Home are the Weary

Sarah and Amy slid the door open, as the worn group squeaked and lurched into the drive, off Hallet Street. Pleased at the gesture, the adventurers rode their wagon right into the barn.

A few wisps of hair had slipped out of place on one side of his sister's hairdo, and it was quite apparent she'd been perspiring. Alex remembered this woman well enough to know she'd never have gone to bed with the two of them out in a storm, so he wondered what kind of mischief she'd been up to while the endless night dragged into dawn.

She may have opened the door for them, but Sarah's first words were not those of a joyous welcome. "You can pardon my language, or not as you see fit, but where in 'hell' have you two been all night?"

She stood holding Sandy's bridle in one hand; the other was planted firmly on her hip.

Alex seemed to be paying much more attention to detail than usual. With studied deliberation, he climbed down out of the wagon, helped Ulysses down, removed and folded his oilskins, lit his pipe, then finally gave what was to him a complete answer. "Down to the shore!"

With that, he began unhitching his horse.

Sarah could hardly be expected to settle for this crumb. "Alex! Is that all you've got to say? Leave us here to worry ourselves sick all night, and all you can say is, 'down to the shore!'?"

"Ain't been out there for pleasure on a night like this, Woman! Didn't git back 'til just now! You asked where we been, and I toldja!" Not seeing any future in pursuing the subject further, Alex turned his attention elsewhere.

"Mister Sears, afore you climb down, you wanta throw all them wet tarps and the blanket outta the wagon? And toss out any lines, or other gear that's left in there too!"

"Sure, Uncle Alex!"

"Hi Mom! Hi Amy!" Andy was tickled to see someone else on the receiving end of his mother's only too familiar inquisition for a change. He was also a little amused to hear the same kind of responses coming from his uncle that he himself used when he was on the defensive.

"Men! Humph!" Her anger, a thinly disguised release of pent-up worry, and emotion not completely expressed, Sarah nonetheless threw herself into helping put things in order. She grumped and bossed Amy, Ulysses, Sandy, and even George into doing her bidding, but curiously not the men. As a mother, she did sneak a big hug on Andy when she bumped into him behind the wagon, but aside from that the woman did not again mention the worries borne through the stormy night.

Amy, chatting merrily about how she'd never stayed up all night before, helped Andy string the ropes across the barn, and then hang the tarps, blankets, and other pieces of gear and clothing out to dry. Weary, they finally trouped through the connecting doors into the house.

The aroma of hot coffee and fresh doughnuts greeted the travelers. A tablecloth had found its way to the kitchen table. Furniture had been rearranged. A picture Andy had never seen before, hung on the wall over the fireplace as if it belonged there. And, somehow, a big, heavy, braided rug had materialized on the floor under the table.

Alex looked at his sister, grinned and asked politely, "What have you two been up to tonight, Sarah?"

"Women's work!" she snapped back. Fighting back a smile, she walked over to the sideboard to get cups for the coffee. No words were necessary. Her bustle flipped with a little sass that told her thoughts. *That'll teach you to give 'Me' a smart answer, Buster!*

After eggs and ham were prepared to go along with the doughnuts, a more complete, and better-humored discussion of the night's escapades was held by both parties during the meal. Then they climbed the stairs, with an incredulous Amy still asking Andy if he'd really slept with a dead man.

Alex was not just a little proud of his sister as well. That is, after he discovered she and Amy had ventured out into the attic, by themselves, to get things during a wild nor'easter that even Aunt Sophia would have had pause with.

Alex's figure departing down the hall was followed by one last shot from Andy. "Hey, Uncle Alex! We goin' scallopin' this mornin'?"

Smiling to himself, Alex replied, "Nope! Missed the tide. Hafta have a go at 'em tomorrow, iffen the weather holds." Then added to himself, *Well if nothing else, the kid's got spunk.*

Chapter 7

Preparations

It was about noon, when a tremendous banging and commotion at the kitchen door woke everyone. Alex, his night-shirt tucked into hastily grabbed trousers, pushed a growling Ulysses out of the way and swung the door wide.

There stood the Reverend John Dodge. Next to him, Town Father/Selectman Braddock Mathews gripped a coat collar tightly against the breeze. Bringing up the rear, the Honorable Charles Swift, Editor of the Yarmouth Register as well as past State Senator, stamped his cold feet in a futile attempt at restoring circulation.

Blinking reddened eyes against the brightness of sun on fresh snow, and clearing his throat to find a lost voice, Alex finally coughed out, "Gentlemen! To what do I owe this visit from such an illustrious group?"

Full of his own importance, pompous Mr. Mathews used any opportunity he could wheedle to display what he considered his splendid oratory. "Captain Matthews. The word has passed around the village of the commendable, if somewhat hazardous actions you took last night, in attempting to rescue the crew of the ship *Granite*.

The agents of the vessel were wired immediately, and notified of her ill fate. This morning, we received a return telegraph which we felt duty-bound to bring to your step.

In this missive, the owners and families of the crew have expressed in your behalf their heartfelt thanks and gratitude, and I also thought you'd like to know that yourself, your nephew Andrew Sears, Eben and Nathaniel Hallet, and Sam Thatcher are going to be recommended to the Massachusetts Humane Society for honors as a result of your bravery, tenacity, and efforts under conditions of extreme hardship far beyond those one would normally expect."

Alex, tried to stifle a yawn. Rubbing one eye, he asked, "Did any of the *Granite's* crew survive?"

"Unfortunately, no!" The Reverend Dodge replied.

Alex frowned. "Then I see no reason for a commendation!

Thank you gentlemen, for your kind thoughts. I will pass them, along with those of the families and the owners, to the other men."

Lack of sleep did little to enhance the man's graciousness, but passenger carrying coastal captains could little afford the luxury of being rude. He did the best he could under the circumstances. "I must beg your forgiveness for not being more prepared to receive you, but as you can see I have just risen. Normally, my friends, I'd invite you in for a bite of lunch, but to be honest I'm not too sure if there's anything left in the larder.

With the quadrupling of my family, things haven't quite gotten settled out yet."

The Reverend Dodge spoke quickly, not wanting his long-winded companion to get wound up again. "No, forgive us Captain, for not being more thoughtful of your own recovery. You must be quite exhausted after the night just past.

Please, extend our good wishes to your sister and her children. We shall expect to see them tomorrow night, and again at the church fair Saturday next."

"Thank you, Reverend, but we need no further prodding after a night such as last. Be assured, your Wednesday eve Thanksgiving service shall be well attended, and the fair as well."

Seizing this opportunity to end things, he closed out the conversation before anyone else could speak. "Come again, so I may make amends for today's lack of hospitality, and thank you all for your kind thoughts. Now, a good afternoon to you!" With that, he shut the door.

A voice broke the stillness behind him. "Alex, you went to the door dressed like that?"

Visibly startled, Alex sputtered, "Jesus, Sarah! You might as well shoot a person, as scare him to death!"

Embarrassed, the man felt compelled to explain. "I'm used to living alone! When someone sneaks up behind me, then speaks to me in my own house without warning, it takes a moment or two to remember.

Of course I went to the door dressed like this! Iffen anyone wants to be met formal, they should send out invitations, or appointment notices.

What have we got left around here for lunch?"

Sarah smiled. "A little chowder, some ham, and I'm sure the hens have been busy. Aside from that, you'll have to tell me."

"Guess we'll have to make do with what we've got for now. I'll make up a little scrapple for tonight." was Alex's response. Then began a long recitation of inventory, while he fried up potatoes and onions to go with their eggs.

"The corn meal is in a barrel next to the barrel of flour, and just above that there's a ten pound box of salt and a fifty pound sack of cane sugar. A keg of molasses, and a keg of rum are in the cupboard next to them, along with the preserves and the vegetables I canned last summer between runs."

Lighting his pipe he said, "Iffen you ever need it, there's bully beef in the root cellar, and a few pickled herring. They're kinda smelly, so I keep 'em out there, along with the potatoes, turnips, carrots, and a few winter squash. Got a barrel of apples in the barn cellar, a barrel of vinegar and a crock of pickled eggs. There's a keg of cider there too, but it might be gettin' a little hard now. Onions are hanging in the back room next to the cheese, a few sausage, some smoked cod, beef, bacon, and ham. Tub of lard's there too.

The spices and condiments are in the cupboard over the stove, but I guess you found them seein' as how you put saleratus, nutmeg, and cinnamon in the doughnuts.

If you're still hungry after that, you'll have to poke around on your own, and see what I forgot to tell you about."

Remembering one more item, he added, "Oh yeah, I keep a bucket of quahogs next to the apples, should your taste run to pie or chowder."

Sarah wasn't sure she could believe what she'd just heard. "I realize you were stocking up for the winter, but if we weren't here, who was going to eat all that food?"

Her brother grinned at her. "I told you I like to cook a might! Why do you think Ulysses is so happy?"

"Alex, you can't be serious?"

"No, I just wanted to see what you'd say! A lot of the staples are provisions left over from the sailing season. I hauled them back from the *Yarmouth* yesterday for storage, what won't go bad."

He hesitated as if unsure how to continue, then showing some unease, settled on a course. "I ain't lookin' for no praise or nothin' from nobody, but hell, what I can't eat I give away to them as needs it!"

Suddenly thrust into the land of plenty, Sarah wondered who could possibly be considered needy around here, but it was Alex's discomfort that caught her interest as much as anything. Being a natural-born skeptic, and intuitively sensing a door had been opened, she inquired, "Like who?"

Snow removal at try-yard anchorage.
(Note Rear ship down to standing rigging)

Surprisingly, Alex didn't take offense at her sarcastic tone. Instead, he rambled on. "Let's see, there's Lester Chase, lives in the wreck of the *Benny Gorham.*

Remember her? She's sitting high-and-dry down by the landing, and you must remember Lester too! He's as foolish as ever. Can't really take care of himself too good now. Man's too proud to go to the poor farm, but I can't say as I blame him for that either."

The old names were bringing faces and memories back to Sarah. "You don't mean the fellow with the bad arm and limp, do you? I thought he must have died years ago."

"Yep, that's the one. He got twisted up like that when he was hit in the head by that broken rigging-block back in '54. Course, if the truth be known, I s'pose he weren't too right even before he got hit. . . .

As I recall, he was sailing under Captain Bacon on the *Paul Jones* when it happened. They never thought he'd live long enough to make it home, but the tough old coot fooled all of 'em. Outlived most of his shipmates to boot, them goin' down in a Java Sea typhoon a coupla years later.

Good thing you reminded me about him, seein' as how the tide came up pretty good last night. I'd better stop by and see how he's doing, when I go down to check m'schooner.

Another fellow I help from time to time would be the one we call the Mayor of Yarmouth. Name's Harry Hollidge, but being the town drunk, and not really native to these parts, I don't think you'll remember him. He stops by maybe once a week, and I'll trade him some food in exchange for splittin' firewood.

There's a few others. The Howes girls get some of the extras to help 'em over the hard times, and as part of their share-out, and o'course I drop stuff off at the almshouse once in a while too."

A little ashamed of her doubting insinuations, Sarah came close to a conciliatory tone. "Well aren't you the village do-gooder!"

"Just tryin' to do my Christian duty for those less fortunate. Besides, I can't stand to throw things away iffen somebody else can use 'em."

This hit a responsive chord in Sarah. "Speaking of throwing things away, Alex, I hope you didn't mind me getting this stuff out of the attic?" Her sweeping hand taking in the newly placed furnishings. "I thought I remembered a trunk I'd stored out there when John and I moved. Then when Amy and I got up our courage to face Aunt Sophie, I saw all of these other things as well. To tell the truth, I'd forgotten how much we'd stashed away, and there's still more."

Admitting it had taken courage to enter the attic, she now gave the real reasons for their endeavor. "Besides, on a stormy night like that, I couldn't just sit here and worry about you people, could I?

We never did get the trunk open, you know. Amy and I went looking for it, because I remembered packing away a pretty, green-velvet dress. Our main hope was that, with a few alterations for style, it might fit 'her' now."

Getting a sort of dreamy quality to her voice, Sarah added, "Green velvet . . . it used to be my favorite. . . ."

Reminding him of the difference in their fortunes made Alex feel uneasy again. "Sarah, iffen it makes you feel more comfortable to have these things around, go to it. This was the family home, so I think you should consider the use of it rightfully yours 'til such time as you're ready to move on again.

Myself, I kept things rather Spartan because that made less junk to collect dirt." Adding, "Place needed a woman's touch anyway." he then changed the subject to something more comfortable. "Now, Thanksgiving is day after tomorrow. Lot of baking and cooking to be done, and I don't mind sharing the kitchen one bit iffen you let me do the pies?"

Sarah glowed at her brother's lame request. "Alex, what can I say? Of course I'll help."

He continued, "Always have turkey. Gotta pick it up in the mornin' at Gray's farm. S'posed to be all ready for the oven, but I usually have to singe the pin-feathers off and clean out the brights myself. Humph! You don't think the Gray's would eat 'em that way, pin-feathers and all, do you?"

Not waiting for an answer, he continued. "Then there's the ice cream to mix, freeze, and pack." He paused, "Tell me, have the kids ever turned an ice cream freezer crank?"

Sarah smiled at the memory this produced. "Not that I know of, but it's time they learned how."

Alex continued his recitation. "Fruit cake's already made, and soaking in brandy, but o'course the vegetables need to be done up fresh the day we serve them." He listed the menu. "Carrots for slicing, winter squash, turnip, onions, and potatoes to be mashed."

"Got some cranberries, and made up a sauce for garnish the other day." In a half-whisper he added, "Splurged a little on my last run to Boston, and laid in a bushel of tropical fruit from Cuba. We got some special treats this year. Oranges, grapefruit, and a couple of them pineapples!"

Sarah's voice picked up that slightly haughty tone again. "I thought you said there was a depression? I've never heard of such largesse. Even President Grant won't be dining as well as this! Don't you feel guilty about all that food?"

Alex was in a good mood this morning, and he wasn't about to raise to any of her baiting. "Food is my weakness, Sarah. Not quantity, mind you, just variety. I'm hungry now just athinkin' about all them things we're gonna be havin'. Going to be a busy day tomorrow, gettin' ready!

Guilty? Hell, no! I've already told you, nothin' goes to waste around here. We've got six more people comin' to dinner to help us eat it, ya know!"

"What?" The spark in Sarah's eye this time wasn't indicative of good-humored bantering.

In fake embarrassment, Alex raised his hands to his face. "Oops! I didn't get around to tellin' you about them yet, did I? Lester, Sam, Harry, the Howes girls? You know, jus' them people we was discussin' a minute ago!"

"You, 'didn't get around to telling me about, yet?' Six extra people? When were you planning to let me know, when we set the table Thursday noon? No wonder you want help in the kitchen!"

Suspicions aroused, she asked, "What other surprises have you got hiding back there behind that pipe?"

Pleased with himself at getting Sarah's dander-up without letting her get to him first, Alex grinned and assumed a thoughtful posture. "Hmmm! Oh yes, Reverend Dodge just reminded me; Church service tomorrow night, and the Christmas fair on Saturday."

He puffed a couple of times on his pipe. "Got some other things penciled in on the calendar over there."

As if his memory needed refreshing, the man wandered over to peruse the scratchings. "A dinner party to celebrate your return, with Prudence and her brother Elijah Crowell." Looking at her he added, "I think they said there'd be a few other invited guests, and that'll be next week at their home down the street in Yarmouth."

Turning to read again, he continued, "Some of our more prominent families are throwing a gala Christmas Ball, which I've mentioned before. That's going to be at the Lyceum Society's hall in about two weeks, the fourteenth I believe, and of course we've all been invited to that." Why the date should be a puzzle was curious, because he was reading it directly from the calendar.

Straightening up, he finished with, "Then there are various and sundry open-houses, carol sings and church celebrations."

Running out of ways to stall, Alex finally got around to the subject he'd been trying to find a delicate way to broach. Striking a thoughtful pose he began with a, "Hmmm! I don't think it's realistic to assume you can stretch one velvet dress between the two of you that many times, do you?"

Not waiting for an answer he continued. "Maybe you should wake the children, and I'll drop you off at Knowles'. From there you can travel up to Crocker's store by shank's mare."

"Shank's mare? On foot? Alex, I haven't heard that term in years. That's one Father used to use."

Alex just smiled and never even paused for breath. "I have to go to Loring's Feed and Grain. Need a bag of oats for Sandy. After that, Isaiah Bray next door at the lumber yard, was supposed to be getting a delivery of fancy black-walnut. I thought I'd pick up a piece, and attempt a jewelry box for Amy as a Christmas remembrance. Next, I gotta go over to Harbor Point, just to eyeball my ship and her moorings, and check on Lester. And, if you're still at one of the stores when I come back through town, I'll give you a ride home."

"Alex, I really feel like I have come home!"

He was embarrassed again. "You have, Sarah, you have!" Continuing on the same subject, he added, "Tell you what, Friday we'll ride to Hyannis on the early train. They've got four or five stores over there offering readymades, plus all kinds of fancy cloth and gew'gaws that come in from the southern ports.

The town is booming for these times, ya know. Real busy, with its protected harbor attracting ships from the south, and now rail connections to the rest of New England. Probably be a city some day!"

It was Sarah's turn to frown and show embarrassment. "I'm sorry! It's a nice thought, but we can't go.

I sold as much of our stuff as I could before we left Lawrence, but after settling our debts, we have nothing. I can barely afford plain yard-goods, let alone anything fancy. Readymade clothes are out of the question."

Alex puffed on his pipe a little harder although it had gone out some time back. This conversation was getting dicy. Not wanting to read the shame of her poverty, it took a conscious effort for him to keep his eyes on his sister's face. "The children need proper clothes, Sarah! With school and all . . . certainly more than they've brought with them.

Now, it is not my intent to blame or bring shame upon you. I understand both your financial hardship and pride, so I have a suggestion. Allow me to purchase a Christmas outfit for each of you as a present.

Beyond that, I will loan you whatever other monies you feel are necessary to restore your own and your children's wardrobes to an acceptable level. Of course, after an investment of this size I will have to be assured of your survival, therefore it is my intent to feed and house you as long as it remains mutually agreeable.

Repayment, we can discuss whenever you happen to come into reasonable sums of money."

Hand to mouth, Sarah was speechless. Tears began to trickle down her cheeks. "Alex, your generosity is so overwhelming, I don't know what to say! You have put more meaning into this Thanksgiving than you will ever know."

Alex, almost as emotionally overwhelmed as she, relit his pipe and puffed furiously until he could speak. "Madam, I have a family again! I will remember this Thanksgiving of 1869 as the most heartfelt I have ever known."

Sarah was almost dancing as she turned her face up toward the ceiling grates that led to the children's rooms. "Amy! Andy! Time to get up! We have a lot to get done today, and you've already slept it half-through!"

"Aw Ma, do we have to?" Twin echoes filtered back down to the adults from above.

She sassed them back. "If you don't, you won't be able to sleep tonight. What do you want to eat, eggs, or eggs?"

"If they're hen's eggs, I guess they'll do." Came the equally spirited reply from her son.

Sarah had begun breaking the main menu-item into the ever-present, black-iron skillet when she glanced at her brother. "Alex, it just dawned on me! You're not trying to dress the peacock are you?" A little smirk crinkled the corners of her mouth.

Alex feigned complete innocence as he continued the tone set by her son. "Don't know what in hell you're talking about, woman!"

It was a flippant response, the tone uncalled for.

Not much got by his sister. "You know perfectly well what I mean! You probably think the one good dress I brought is too gaudy for your stuffy little town, right? Or . . . could you have another, more ulterior motive?"

Her glance may have appeared casual, but it lingered a split-second longer than innocence would have dictated.

Continuing, she asked, "But then, what obscure reason could you have for not telling me about something this intriguing? A dress-up occasion? Come now Captain, I smell a secret! What big mystery have you got up your sleeve?" Her eyes narrowed in concentration, as the sound of her last inquiry faded into the sizzle of frying bacon. Frowning, she realized her tongue had run ahead of her thoughts.

The captain's face had not changed one iota, but it might as well have been Andrew's she read it so easily. Tauntingly, it told her 'yes' to something! Mentally cursing her own stupidity, she wished she'd had the presence of mind to limit her questions to one at a time.

"Why Sarah, are these suspicions how you show gratitude?"

The reply was blustery, which only helped to confirm her feelings. She'd tipped her hand, and getting any more out of him would be pure luck. Her choice of progressively colorful, mental adjectives reflected a growing frustration, but with no alternatives she blundered along. "I've never known a man yet that would willingly take a woman shopping! Not even his sister! You know I can't stand to wait for things, Alex, what are you keeping from me?"

"Curiosity killed the cat, Sarah!"

"What's Uncle Alex teasing you about now, Mom?"

To Alex, Amy's arrival couldn't have been more timely. He disguised the sigh of relief behind his pipe smoke.

"Would you believe this man is taking us clothes shopping, and he won't tell me why?"

"Time and tide wait for no man, girls. I noticed when I greeted our early delegation that the roads have been rolled, so I'm going out to the barn to tend the animals and hitch up Sandy again. Think maybe I'll break out the sleigh! Dress warm, and c'mon out when you're ready."

Turning to slip into his jacket, Alex caught movement out of the corner of his eye. "Why if it isn't the late Mister Sears! Good afternoon, Sir."

Andy, still half asleep, scratched his head and mumbled a, "Hi, Uncle Alex."

Amy was bubbling. "Andy! Uncle Alex is taking you, Mom, and me clothes shopping. Isn't that exciting? Aren't you just thrilled?"

This interrupted a stretch, abruptly. "Yuck! Ma, do I hafta go?"

Chapter 8

Courtin' Time

What a perfect time of year to have arrived on Cape Cod. The bustle of activities preparing for winter were still going on, but at a more leisurely pace than the frenzied, hard work of harvest. For the most part, the coasting schooners had been laid up for the season. Their gear removed and stored, to be refurbished over the course of a long winter.

Cape Cod, renown for its open, relatively snowless winters, contrarily proved these features to be a liability. Lack of a snow blanket in such a cold climate allowed the frost to penetrate the ground to a depth of four feet or so, most years. Consequently, stonewalls tumbled regularly from the heaves created by this constant motion of the earth underfoot.

Homes, built with granite block and field stone foundations, had to have their underpinnings banked with salt-marsh hay for the same reason. Not only did it slow the infiltration of winter gales through open cracks, but it prevented the earth from freezing underneath. A happenstance guaranteed to put foundation-house-and-all out of alignment as easily as the stone walls.

This marsh hay gave each house the appearance of sitting in its own, cozy bird's nest.

Waste not/want not, being an adage born of this hardscrabble life, the rough grass was given a second function come spring by being used as food and bedding for the livestock. So enriched, it was then plowed into their gardens to enhance the soil.

Wood piles were topped off. Trees for the following year's fuel were felled in wood-lots, to be dragged home on the sledges of winter. Later, the logs would be stacked to season properly.

Ice houses were being cleaned, and prepared to receive another supply of the cold, blue solid. Hay and sawdust were stockpiled nearby to provide the necessary insulation.

Cut from local ponds, the product, who's only cost was labor, was shipped, literally, all over the world. The advance of technology and its steam driven ammonia-compressors made it possible for many countries to freeze their own, but with the high cost of fuel it was still marginally cheaper to import the finished product.

The holidays themselves, Thanksgiving and Christmas, aside from their religious significance, could be construed to represent a celebration of, and maybe a pause to reflect upon these efforts to survive. A gathering in to themselves of the communities dotting the shores of the Cape, and looked forward to annually as the period during which her fishermen, farmers and sailors became reacquainted with their families and neighbors. Also known as that specific interval during which one could build, or re-establish friendships postponed by those requisite labors of the other seasons.

Some called it courtin' time.

Chapter 9

The Artist's Fee

"Alex, did you have any special reason for not telling me about Chris Gardner coming to dinner on Thanksgiving?"

"Reason? What reason could I possibly have to keep something like that from you? It just slipped my mind, is all. We were talking about those with no family who've been joining me on the holiday for four or five years now, and I just assumed you knew he was among them. Don't tell me he's got you lookin' to the wind'ard?"

A voice piped up from the jump seat. "Uncle Alex, you talk funny!"

He reached back to tug on her bonnet playfully, and asked, "Are you picking on me, Amy?"

"Yes! I'm not always sure I know what your talking about."

Alex smiled. He was feeling quite jocular tonight. Maybe the festivities of the season were getting to him.

"A sailor always keeps an eye off to the wind'ard, or upwind, to make sure another boat or a squall line isn't bearing down on him. In other words, I was asking your mother if this gentleman had caught her attention."

"Did he, Ma?"

"Don't be ridiculous, Amy! This conversation is none of your business anyway, I was talking to your uncle!"

Not to be out-teased, Andy decided a sing-song chorus was in order. "Maa's got a fellaaa! Maa's got a fellaaa! Maa's got a fellaaa!"

Any boy worth his salt knew instinctively that to be done right, it had to be chanted loud and long. His efforts were rewarded with a sputtering explosion.

"You children stop it! I've only met the man that once at dinner! That's certainly not enough to know if I even like him, let alone if I'm interested. Besides, who says he likes me?"

It didn't take much intuition to tell Andy he'd found a tender spot. He eased off a bit, but he wasn't about to let go. "We can tell you're sweet on him! Ma's got a fellaa! Ma's got a fellaa!"

"Children should be seen, but not heard!" Hoping to divert attention, she lashed out at a convenient target.

"Now look at what you've started, Alex, with all of your stupid nautical talk."

Alex needed no help with his defense. "Sarah, all I did was answer your question!" But then he added, "He's going to be there tonight you know." Out of the corner of his eye the captain noticed her stiffen on the buggy seat beside him. A fact followed by a short, inward struggle to keep his smile from showing.

Sarah turned her head slowly and stared at the man, as if by studying his too-innocent face long enough, it might give her an insight into a possible plot . . . with his stamp all over it.

Except for a giggle or two from the whispering children, the silence of thought reigned for a while.

Oblivious to the chatter, Sandy, clip-clopped her way down towards the Crowell's home, and their dinner party.

The night was mild. All of the snow from last week's storm, long gone. A clammy sea-fog made halos around the warm lights streaming from the windows of the houses they passed. Fragrant wood smoke, hanging in layers in the still, damp air, whirled into eddies and left a visible wake behind them.

Amy was not one to be quiet for long. "What's that bell I can hear every once in a while, Uncle Alex?"

"That's the bell buoy out at the mouth of the channel. If you can hear it in the village, it means the drift of the wind is out of the north. It's got to be almost flat calm though to hear anything that far away. Must be two or three nautical miles from here."

Andy's tongue and curiosity were never still for long either. "Is that why we could hear the surf on Thanksgiving day? I didn't hear the bell that day, though."

"No, not really, boy! Ya see, around these parts, when it starts t'blow from the northeast it's usually a sign of a storm way out over the open Atlantic. That means the wind's got a long fetch, afore it hits land."

Amy took her turn. "What's 'fetch' mean, Uncle Alex?"

"Amy, I'm going t'hafta get you a book on nautical terms, I can see that. Either that or I'll have to stop talking! You interrupt so often, I forget what it is I'm trying to say."

What better spot for a sarcastic rejoinder from Sarah. "You, stop talking? Hah! That'll be the day! However, you could stop talking like a heathen sailor, and start using the King's English you were taught!"

Alex flared immediately. "Woman, you've got two-cents for everyone don'tcha?"

"Well it's true, Alex! How do you expect these children to know what you're talking about if they can't understand what you're saying?"

Still speaking with emotion, although it was more embarrassment that he'd let his sister get to him than anger now, he sassed back at her. "I do not choose to compare our beautiful surroundings to Lawrence, but just as that city had its dangers, so do we. If these two are going to live by the sea, they've got to know its secrets. As a start, it would be best if they understood the terms and language used by seamen."

Alex was fond of parable and metaphor. "Iffen one of Amy's classmates was to tell her she reminded him of a Gordian knot, the girl wouldn't know whether to tell the head-master on him, or say thank you, now would she?"

"You just love to be right, don't you?"

"No gain in being wrong! It would take years before I'd hear the end of it from the likes of you. Of course, if the truth were to be known, I do try to stack the deck in my favor every chance I get, and I don't mean a card deck!"

"What's a Gordian knot?" The younger lady in his life had spoken up again.

"Amy, tomorrow we look for that book! A Gordian knot is mostly just for decoration, or to show off a sailors skill. It's a very intricate, very delicate, and most difficult knot to master. That's why it's often compared to a woman."

This statement was accompanied by an obvious glance toward Sarah, and a "Humph!" from her in response.

Alex let it slide in order continue addressing Amy's question. "According to the Classics, some oracle in Ancient Greece told Alexander the Great that the man who could undo one of these knots would conquer Asia. The way the story goes, Alexander turned and severed the knot with one blow of his sword."

Amy frowned, "That was cheating, wasn't it?"

"Don't know, but he conquered Asia. Of course, maybe he was able to figure out how to do both because he could see how there is almost always more than one solution to a problem."

"Wow! How do you know all this stuff, Uncle Alex?"

"I read a mite, Amy."

Sarah got in a jab. "Children, don't make his head any bigger than it is! He's hard enough to live with now. Next thing you know, he'll think he can walk on water."

"Can, in the winter!"

"See what I mean? You 'are' pleased with yourself tonight, aren't you? You're also impossible!"

Amy wasn't about to give up. "You still didn't tell us about the storm that could 'fetch' a long way, or 'stacking the deck'."

"All I meant by fetch, was that like a boat on a long straight course, or reach, the wind that whirls around a storm out over the open ocean can travel a long distance with nothing getting in the way to slow it down. This gives it a chance to pile the waves nice and tall, and get them moving. Once these ocean swells, or storm swells, get marching, they can travel hundreds of miles looking for a coastline to smash against.

Around here, a nor'easter'll usually blow for three days before the storm gets far enough away for the wind to shift to a different quarter. After piling the waves up for that long, you've got a lot of water movin' out there. That's why, on a north facing shoreline, the swells keep comin' ashore, pounding the beach for days after the wind has died."

Now directing his conversation back to Andy, he said, "So, to answer your question, boy, with little or no wind blowing in the pines to cover the sound, you had no problem hearin' the waves smashin' themselves to bits against the sand. Now in turn, they made so much noise you wouldn't have heard the bell buoy if it was aringing in your ear.

Another thing about all this business is, being a sailing man, this knowledge is valuable. If you, as Captain, could hear the waves pounding, you'd know the wind was dying and it might alter your plans to set sail, or on the other hand, a dangerous situation, with a leeward shore close by."

While Andy thought about his uncle's implications of a future captaincy, Amy took a turn.

"You mean, 'a long fetch' is just another name for a long distance? Like fetching a log from the woodpile?" If she was going to learn a new language, Amy wanted to be sure.

Sarah couldn't resist. "Yes, and Alex is another name for a long wind."

Alex gave her a false laugh. "Haw, Haw, Sister! Think your funny don'tcha?"

"Hey Uncle Alex, was that some 'Sarah's Justice'?"

"No, Mister Sears, that was just her sweet disposition showing through. In fact, I'd call it just plain old sass.

'Sarah's Justice', humph! Now that takes malice aforethought. Something that requires extensive planning, with the questionable intent of getting your undivided attention, and creating lasting memories. Boy, I want to tell ya, iffen you ever see it, you won't have to ask. It's as pointed as the skewer the pig gets at a pork roast!"

Sarah added nothing but a smile to the proceedings.

Not getting a rise out of her, Alex continued. "I do have to agree with your mother about one thing though. There are times indeed when children should be seen but not heard. Especially if the topic could be considered embarrassing to your elders, or if you're pestering your uncle!"

Amy was as stubborn as her mother. Ignoring the insinuation to be quiet, she plunged on. "What about, 'stacking the deck'? And, where's north, and which side of north is northeast?"

It was plain by his tone, Alex's good humor was fading. "Amy, are you asking these questions because you really want to know, or are you just testing my knowledge and patience?"

Not expecting an answer, he continued. "Listen, if a Captain thinks the wind is going to blow from one direction for most of his voyage, he might take a chance and stack the cargo on his freight deck so that the weight of the load will work against the pressure of the wind on the sails. Then maybe he can crowd on a little more canvas, and make better time, to say nothing about a drier, easier trip for his passengers.

Your other questions involve the points of the compass. That's something that will take a little effort on your part, but they're not too difficult to learn. It's called boxing a compass, however I don't have the time tonight to teach you navigation too.

Now, that's enough! No more questions from either of you 'til I say so!" The edge in his voice said he meant it.

"But, I didn't get a chance to ask if the Captain of the *Granite* had stacked his deck, and how do you tell port from starboard?" Andy's protests for equal time were ignored.

Sarah smiled. It was nice to have help. Her children balanced Alex's overbearing nature, and Alex shared the load of the children's insatiable curiosity.

Still testy, Alex grumped, "Thank Christ, we're here! You children behave yourselves now, and no cuss words!"

Amy was quick. "Don't worry, Uncle Alex, she's our teacher. She'll box our ears if we do or say anything wrong."

"Hmmm, know about that already, do you girl?"

A guilty conscience got Andy in trouble. "Amy, I told you not to tell!"

Amy, never at a loss for words, retorted, "I didn't say anything! You're the dumb one who just stuck your foot in your mouth!"

That was enough for their uncle. Alex was standing next to the buggy, helping his sister down with his right hand. Holding the other aloft in a threatening manner, he grumped, "Stop the squabbling you two! Do you both see this hand? It is my left hand! It happens to be the weaker of my two, but not by much. If you will think about it, the word left has fewer letters than the word right. The word 'port', has fewer letters than the word 'starboard'. And if you don't choose to feel the wrath of my starboard hand, you'd both best be quiet and behave as you were told!

We'll talk about your school problems at a more appropriate time, Mister Sears!"

Not sure if their uncle's threat of physical violence was actual, or only for the theatrics of teaching, the children settled their own differences with a couple of well hidden rib-pokes.

Still sputtering in mock anger, the captain knocked on the outer storm door of their host's home, and then stepped out of the way as it swung open.

Affording his family a narrow glance at an Alex they'd never seen before, the man waxed eloquent. "Hello, Prudence. Hello, Elijah. Prudence you look stunning this evening. That green satin is a perfect match to your eyes, and the contrast of your lace is beautiful. And your hair? What have you done to your hair? It's so cleverly entwined with ribbons tonight, it must have taken hours."

"Oh Alex! Stop it!", Prudence reprimanded him, but at the same time she was squirming with delight.

A handsome, wholesome woman, she was never-the-less one of those people who always looked dusty. Meticulously groomed, her graying blond hair and the fair complexion of a face covered with soft, fine, baby-like fuzz gave her the illusion of having no crisp, clear outline.

Another thing that became obvious rather quickly, was how easily she blushed. Alex delighted in exploiting this fact, and he did his best to embarrass the woman at every opportunity. For some reason it amused him to see such an uncontrollable response in an otherwise cool, constrained, prim and proper individual. Of course, it's just possible his interest went even deeper, but that fact he'd never admit to any earth-bound soul.

Elijah was definitely her brother. He matched the woman's appearance, her word inflections, and her response to emotions. Beyond physical similarities, they were even more alike, because he had also adopted her effeminate mannerisms to the point of making those who didn't know them, feel extremely uncomfortable. A fact the Crowells themselves were well aware of, and on occasion, one they employed to their personal advantage.

Performing the introductions, Alex rambled on. "I'm sure you remember Sarah, and these are her two children, Amy and Andrew. I know you've met them in school Pru', but now's your chance to find out how bad they really are."

Prudence was bubbling. While her guests removed their outergarb, she monopolized the conversation. "Alex, how nice of you to come. Now don't you go intimidating the children. This has got to be hard enough as it is, coming to their teacher's house to eat dinner."

Turning to the children she added, "Don't you listen to him, Amy and Andrew. I'm not going to judge you, or pick on your manners one bit tonight. You're guests in my home, and you make yourselves comfortable."

Never missing a beat, she turned to their mother next. "Sarah, it's been such a long time. I've missed you, and your sharp wit.

Children, we used to be good friends, your mother and I. Then came the war, and we all went off in different directions.

Sarah, you're back to stay, I understand? Well, I don't think things around here ever change, but I'm sure after being away for so long, to your eyes everything is different."

Alex butted in, "My goodness, Pru', don't you ever stop for breath, or to let someone answer?"

"Alex, if you weren't such a tease I'd be offended by that remark."

"Pru', I've been trying to offend or insult you for years, and I haven't succeeded yet!"

"Oh stop that, you big pest!"

Alex shifted targets as he drifted towards the parlor. "Elijah, how are you? What projects have you got going now? Back to your battle scenes, or are you working on a commission?"

Elijah picked right up where Pru' left off, hardly stopping to draw his own breath. "Oh Alex, I'm all through with that Civil War, blood and gore. That was just a phase I was going through. One of my desperate, black periods, artists are supposed to have these days.

I now have two commissions from Captain Baxter of Hyannis, for his ships, *The American Belle*, and *The Flying Scud*.

Isn't that a dreadful name for such a beautiful ship? Oh dear, I certainly wouldn't dare tell him what I thought. He's so excitable, and become such a religious man, it makes him difficult to talk to without adding controversy to our conversation. It's just terrible! I have to watch every word, so as not to offend the man. You know, he's always quoting the bible, and, well, that interrupts my thinking, and I have to stop and listen, then try to pick up where I left off.

Speaking of which, I've been trying to talk Christopher here into letting me do his boat, *The Jezebel*. Silly thing! He says all he'll pay me for is if I paint the hull, and he doesn't mean in a picture. And do you know, just like Captain Baxter, the words he used to accent his sweet offer were religious in nature too? Although, for some reason I don't think he quite meant them that way. . . ."

Alex shook his head at the non-stop monologue. It spurred thoughts as to whether or not Elijah and his sister ever talked to the other. He decided the two must become so frustrated by each other's dominating conversation that when they had a captive audience of their own, the dam broke.

Whatever the explanation, the captain figured he'd better get his oar in the water while he had the chance. "Hello, Chris! Don't tell me you've been blasphemous to poor Elijah here? He and Captain Baxter are like two peas in a pod you know? That is, when it comes to faith in the Almighty, and the way they threaten everlasting hell and damnation to those of us who don't measure-up!"

Chris nodded his greetings as the Captain continued. "I think your offer of letting him paint your hull for a dollar a day is an excellent idea. Course, no tellin' what color you'd end up with. Probably the dark, blood-red puce of Royal velvets, or a sicky green chartreuse, like the silks I used to haul back from the far east. Not only does that color remind me of a tomato-bug's innards, but then I suspect your painter would want to have mermaids swimming around in it, seeing as how Jezebel persecuted Elijah so badly in the bible. Ever think of changing her name? You know, just to remove the temptation, so's he don't set fire to her to get even for his namesake!"

Chris fell in with Alex's playful mood. "Hello, Alex. Who mentioned money? Of course if I could talk Elijah into doing swordfish instead of mermaids . . . well, maybe. . . ."

"Maybe? What do you say, Elijah? If I were you, I'd take him up on it. I think he's a little more dependable than your Cap'n Baxter. Your Hyannis man talks awful big, and likes to show off a might too much for me.

Just think of the reputation for eccentricities he's dragging in his wake, what with that round house he built on South Street!

I don't know as I care too much for the way he likes to prance around with those four white horses of his either! Remember the time he almost killed President Grant? There he was, ashowin' off his fancy rig on the Hyannis pier to make himself feel more important, and to hell with the safety of others. So what if the President happened to be aboard?

Damned old fool!"

Elijah frowned. This was serious talk. "True, Alex, true. Until his silver crosses my palm, I won't be sure of the sale. He's such a religious man though, I can't believe he'd renege on an agreement with a fellow Christian."

Alex did nothing to mollify Elijah's fears. "Humph! Don't trust the man. If I were you, I'd take payment in advance. Otherwise, he'll probably give the commission to the church of his choice—in your name, and you can't eat hymnals."

The expression on the artist's face concerned Alex. He immediately tacked away from this conversation, afraid the evening's conviviality might have been dampened beyond repair. "You know, after thinking about Christopher here, if you ever did decide to work for him you'd probably be better off getting paid in advance for that too. Otherwise he'll want a dollar and a half's work for his dollar a day wages, and then try to pay you off in fish to boot."

Elijah was willing to change subjects. "I can defend myself when it comes to the likes of Mister Gardner here. He follows in the path, and sports the name of the greatest fisherman the world has ever known. The man couldn't be truly bad, no matter how hard he tried."

There was a little twinkle in Elijah's eye when he added, "Although, come to think of it, he is somewhat of a backslider!" Cupping his hand around his mouth and speaking in a loud whisper, Elijah pretended to confide to Alex, "He wasn't in church Sunday!"

Christopher, an interested spectator to this bantering match, was a little uneasy at being thrust onto center stage. His self-conscious answer was blunt and to the point.

"Boat sprung a leak! Had to bail her out, and get her beached afore she sank!"

Elijah came back with, "There was a time when you'd be jailed for working on the Sabbath, you know?"

Poor Christopher, now being attacked directly, bristled and sputtered, "Elijah, I figure it was the Lord's doin' that my boat was leaking in the first place! Took quite a beating in the storm last week.

Iffen my cradle hadn't been buried under all that snow He brung us, I would have hauled her out on the next tide. Don't think He wanted me in church on Sunday, is all."

The response from Elijah was just as quick and pointed. "The Lord moves in strange and mysterious ways. Maybe He was punishing you for being lazy, and not hauling your boat out a week earlier."

Christopher's face now began to flush as bright as his host's. "Had my boat in, so's I could haul His quahogs to His Christmas fair! That was so His parishioners could make a chowder to sell, and make money for His church!"

With things beginning to overheat, Alex mercifully intervened. "Elijah, I think you'd best let the Lord handle

Christopher in His own way, before you lose Him a disciple."

"I was just demonstrating to you Alex, how with the help of the Lord us gentler folk need not fear persecution." With a pointed glance at Christopher, he added, "The meek shall inherit the earth!"

"Anybody ever calls you meek, they'd better duck!", came Christopher's return salvo.

The air had gotten quite thick when Prudence's question cut the tension. "Gentlemen, did I hear voices raised in here?" She melted into the room, followed by Sarah and the children.

Alex welcomed the diversion with relief. "Don't go lookin' at me like that, Pru'! It wasn't me, I swear! Your brother was apickin' on Chris here for not comin' to church on Sunday, just because he was afraid he'd have to sit next to Sarah.

Hell, Elijah even offered to move his pew, iffen that was the problem, but Chris said, 'No! He'd rather skip.'"

Christopher found himself still on the defensive. "Alex, you're a troublemaker! My boat sprung a leak, is all. I'd sit next to Sarah any chance I'd . . . get."

Timing can be so important, and Sarah wasted none. She picked right up on the poor man's blunder. "Well, thank you Christopher. I wouldn't mind that a bit either, even if my brother did trick you into saying it."

Alex was enjoying this. "Sarah, where have you girls been? I thought for a minute Pru' here had gone formal on me. Showing off for company, I was afraid she was going to leave us gentlemen to smoke and talk politics in the parlor all by ourselves."

"Alex, you're terrible!" was Pru's response.

Alex kept it going, "Oh, been conspiring over who's going to be at the Ball I suppose?"

Sarah wasn't going to be left out completely. "No we haven't, Mr. Know-it-all! Pru's been catching me up on eight or nine years of gossip."

"I had *The Register* sent to you every week, Sarah. You mean they missed something?"

"Oh Alex, this is just women talk. You know what I mean! It may take us all winter, but I intend to hear every juicy tid-bit!"

"When it comes to talk, you two could set new standards for endurance, if that's what you mean."

Elijah had been still long enough. The man used his hands as expressively as his voice. Waving one, he interrupted, "Eight or nine years? It couldn't have been that long, Sarah! You don't look a minute older. You're as beautiful as the day you left. I mean it! That's an interested, professional eye speaking, I might add. A little deeper, a little warmer, but just as gorgeous as ever."

Turning to Amy, he continued his flattery. "And this younger woman! Ah, such beauty. She is her mother's daughter in every way. An ingénue to be sure, but the promise of so much to come. So many hearts yet to be broken by this epitome of God's creation."

Completely flustered, Amy began to turn pink around the edges.

Prudence, feigning surprise, sputtered, "Elijah, stop it! Now you're embarrassing our guests."

"All right, but some day Alex, a painting. The two of them. Before much more time passes. Such a fleeting thing as beauty like this should be captured for all time."

Alex knew the times had been hard for the Crowells lately, and he'd often wondered how he could help without offending their sensibilities.

"Should have been a missionary, Elijah. You could talk Eskimos into buying ice. All right, I'll make a deal. . . ."

Before he could continue with his proposition, another country was heard from.

"I'll commission the painting, Elijah!"

Elijah, turned to the new voice. "Christopher?"

"I . . . I . . . I'll commission the painting."

Alex shook his head again, and fought with a smile. He didn't want to show how pleased this evening was making him. No one could possibly have planned anything like this.

Intervening in the name of propriety, Alex said, "Now wait a minute, Chris! Not only are you starting to sound like poor Sam, you're jumping the gun a might here. You know that would not be at all proper. What would people think, if word of the likes of this should get out?"

While he was talking, Alex kept his attention on Prudence, as if addressing her. Insinuating without words that she might be the one to pass on the nights gossip. The woman blushed under his close scrutiny.

"I tell you what, my good man," he went on, "I myself will commission the painting, on one condition."

"And that is?" Christopher's face colored up again, as if he were a member of the host's family.

Watching Prudence, Alex continued, "My condition, simply stated, is that Elijah here take on the tutoring of two somewhat rough-edged savages. Teach them of the finer things in life. Art, Music, Poetry. Things Pru' here can barely find time to touch upon during their regular classes.

Now, if you can find it in your Christian heart to donate to the education of heathen natives by a true missionary, I'd be honored to accept. Purely for the betterment of these poor unfortunate children, of course."

Alex winked at Pru' as if gathering her into the conspiracy, and at the same time taking the edge off his non-verbalized accusations.

"Done!" was Christopher's immediate reply.

Smiling all the way down to his toes, Alex wondered how he'd ever gotten the frugal Christopher Gardner to part with a dollar. Stroking the whiskers on his chin, he momentarily pondered the wisdom of what had been started here tonight.

Deciding the fates would have their way with or without his help, he left the thoughts in his wake.

Turning to the artist, he asked, "Elijah?"

"Oh, I get a voice in this, Alex?"

The man was flushed and animated. "To be honest, I'm spellbound. Imagine, two handsome gentlemen fighting over which one is going to pay for a painting of two of the most beautiful women on Cape Cod. And to think, the creation of which was a bare suggestion a moment ago. An inspiration in the throes of conception! Fascinating!

And then, the opportunity to implant culture as paint upon a naked palate? I'm overwhelmed! Of course I accept!

That is, if the other principles involved are in agreement?" His questioning look enveloped all three.

"Well?" Christopher was still a little blunt due to his embarrassment over this woman.

Sarah answered first. "Alex! Christopher! I don't know what to say. I'm so flattered and flustered I could cry. Children?"

"If this means I gotta go to more school after school the answer's NO!" Andy's reply, surly and adamant, was predictable.

Afraid he might lose this opportunity to be gainfully employed, Elijah was quick to soothe the boy's feelings. "Andrew, the day I don't make things interesting and challenging for you, is the day you may take your leave with my blessings."

"Promise?"

"You have my word on it!"

Alex wondered if this man knew what he was letting himself in for.

Turning to Amy, Elijah asked, "And how do you feel about this arrangement, Mistress Amy?"

"How could anyone say no to something as wonderful as this? It's so exciting! Of course! Yes! Yes! Yes!"

Prudence was aroused and flustered by the emotional charges ricocheting around the room. Ones that still somehow managed to miss her. Unable to contain herself, she sputtered, "Well, after all that, I think we should raise a toast to a wonderful winter. Let me get the sherry."

As much to herself as to the others, she added, "I think I need some."

Alex, immensely pleased with himself, asked as she turned away, "What will the Brays think if we're tippling without them? They are still coming, aren't they Pru'?"

"They should be here on time if they don't want to miss any of the festivities! Tonight, I think it's just as well they were late though, wouldn't you say, Captain?" She turned a meaningful glance his way.

Ignoring her implications, he answered with a smile and sassed her again. "I hope the wine isn't from the same bottle we had last Christmas!"

"There you go teasing again, Alex. Of course not! I used that for cooking, after the fuss you put up last year totally embarrassed me. This is what you brought us in September, remember? You said it was imported, and you got it from a friend in Boston.

So, my dear Captain, if it's not to your taste this year it's your own fault!"

"See Mister Sears?" Alex turned to Andy as Pru' faded from the room. "That's what I was referring to earlier about 'stacking the deck'!

Look to the future. Plan on the wind. If you've figured right, the voyage can be most pleasant, with extra returns. Course if you're wrong, you'll have to work a little harder to re-arrange your load. Not an easy task at sea. Worth the gamble in my book though! Anyway, I think it's a safe bet that at two dollars a bottle, this wine won't taste like her cooking sherry."

The Brays arrived in time to join them, but wondered for days what had gotten their fellow celebrant's holiday spirits off to such a good start.

After an evening spent in lively conversation spurred on by good food, wine, and companionship, they sang a few popular melodies and Christmas carols around the piano. To please Elijah, they ended their festivities with the hymn, *Amazing Grace*.

Andy, displaying a talent few were aware of, raised some eyebrows with his mouth organ accompaniment. He was rewarded by a round of applause.

Chapter 10

Mumbley-peg

Having an excellent memory for things others might wish him to forget, Alex broached the subject of his nephew's school problems at breakfast the next morning. Sarah and Amy sat there like spectators at the coliseum of gladiators. This was indeed entertainment to dine by.

As related by the boy on the hot-seat, a little scuffle had broken out in the schoolyard. Proclaiming personal innocence, Andrew explained how a simple game of mumbley-peg turned into a bloody-nosed free-for-all.

Apparently starting with a few minor discussions about the boy's skill being related to cheating, the real heat developed when one of Andy's new schoolmates picked on his jack-knife, proclaiming it a mongrel and therefore illegal. Naturally this was an affront to the boy's pride.

Backing up a little, Andy explained that instead of the story he'd told his mother—of how he'd picked the knife out of a trash barrel in Lawrence, and when found, an inch of blade had been missing—in truth it had been found stuck through his hand and into a door jamb after a similar altercation as that on the school grounds. The blade broke when his assailant had tried to remove it rather hurriedly, while the short club in Andy's hand was raising welts on his skull.

Sarah began to rise out of her chair—spurred along by some heat—upon hearing of the fib this child had passed off on her, but Alex raised his hand to halt the storm until the boy's new story had been told.

With an apologetic look at his mother, Andrew went on to tell how it had taken weeks, or almost as long as the stab wound took to heal, to reshape and sharpen the steel with his only grindstone being the closest cement step, or granite curb, while lounging and talking with friends.

To complete the project, he'd dipped the worn, blood-stained, wooden handle into a bottle of red ink someone had delivered to the back of the printer's shop. A place he was forced to avoid for weeks, until the color had worn off his hands. Surprisingly, that particular shade of red also just happened to match the splashes all over the unhappy printer's back steps and door.

Pulling the offending instrument out of a deep pocket to show his uncle, even Andrew had to admit the big handle and stubby blade seemed out of proportion. Possibly seeing it for the first time through objective eyes, the boy became aware its true beauty and value had to be measured by the hours of labor he'd invested in its resuscitation. Defensive, and slightly embarrassed, he finally made the statement that, in his opinion, it was no-one else's business what it looked like anyway, it was his knife!

Unfortunately, the boys on the playground had thought otherwise. They took it upon themselves to instruct him in the proper etiquette of who carried what kind of knife in this village. Questioning his intelligence, they explained how if he were a member of the landed gentry he'd know enough to carry a more discrete, genteel pocket-knife. Maybe one with a bone handle.

Now if he were a townie, the knife could be bigger like his, but probably have a lot of blades, a screwdriver, and maybe even a can-opener. If from a sea-faring family, he'd wear a sheath-knife on his belt. Handy for filleting fish, or cutting something free should the other hand be busy hanging on to the boat.

Obviously, the abomination Andrew was carrying didn't fall into any of these categories. Observing its strange shape, the boys went so far as to suggest an accident at conception, or birth. They went on to express certainty, if one could trace its lineage, the ugly beast should most likely be referred to as a bastard!

This statement also reflected a pointed insinuation about its owner, however instead of retaliating, Andy merely tallied the insult for future reference.

Mistaking his lack of response for a weak backbone, the boys began to get more personal. They moved on to their victim's strange mix of clothing, and unfamiliar colloquialisms as fair targets. The final insult came when he was referred to as jetsam, or a wash-a-shore.

Having had enough, Andy took it upon himself to discuss the mental capacity, heritage, and more immediate, hairy, tail-wearing ancestors of his adversaries. Naturally, certain colorful adjectives more common to the back alleys and alehouses of Lawrence were employed to further illustrate his point.

Altogether a rather loud confrontation precipitated, with Andrew steadily losing ground, blood, and skin, but not giving in.

After the headmaster separated the combatants, and lined them up for discipline, the crux of the matter surfaced. Andy, because he had been born in Yarmouth, felt he was as much a Cape Codder as any of those he opposed. In fact, he figured he was probably better, because he'd seen more of the world than they had.

The headmaster, somewhat tongue in cheek, did his best to explain to the boy it would take more than birthrights to be accepted by his fellow peers. Andrew could not just be born a Cape Codder, it took hard work to become one. He was told he'd have to learn the skills and mores of his new friends, and come to realize their ways and experiences, although different, were the equal of his own.

To achieve this goal, he was instructed to participate in church and community activities, respect his elders, and apply his energies to more productive ends than fighting.

After a strong reprimand to the other participants about tolerance, and a stiff warning about the consequences of a repeat performance, they were all dismissed.

Alex did his best to look stern and un-amused by this almost word-for-word recitation. The man considered his nephew's response admirable, but was wise enough to realize telling the boy this might create a larger problem of future, less-justified aggression. Instead, he fulfilled his self-imposed authority-figure duties by promising severe punishment should anything more be heard about fights, particularly ones with or about knives, and then undid it all by asking Andy if he'd like to go duck hunting with him after school that day. Such discipline a boy could only dream of.

This brought an anxious glance from Sarah, but surprisingly no verbal objections. She merely mentioned the fact that now Alex could see for his own eyes where their life in Lawrence had been leading to. "Lies, and knife fights! Rather obvious why we had to come home, isn't it?"

Alex steered the conversation back to his nephew as a less stressful destination. "Might as well get a heading on this 'learnin' how to be a Cape Codder' bit, if you're ever agoin' to be one, and duck hunting is as good a place to start as any!"

The man put up a good pretense of imposition at the sudden burden thrust upon him, but in truth he'd been looking for a way to get around the tight reins Sarah'd put on the boy after their rescue mission. To Alex, nature had many lessons to teach, and although the boy could apparently handle himself in a street fight, the sooner he learned how to take care of himself around here the better. No matter that Andrew had an infectious energy, and a *joie de vivre* which fed the man's own pleasures.

Poor Andrew! He got himself reprimanded a number of times during the more formal schooling of that day. Daydreaming about his after-hours teaching to come seemed to be the major offense, but being so excited he could hardly sit still in anticipation came in a close second.

Chapter 11

The Captain's Soul

A few days later, after dinner, Amy asked her uncle about the picture she and her mother had found in the attic during the night of the storm. The one of the ship, which they'd hung over the fireplace in the dining room.

Alex studied the formal rendering for many minutes before finally responding, "Like it, do you Amy?"

"I love it! The ship looks so real. Is she the *Yarmouth*?"

Alex tipped his chair back against the wall, the way he did when he was full, happy, and about to embark on a tale. Next, he lit his pipe. Then, after what seemed to be a lot of deliberate thought, answered. "No missy. This painting's of a blue-water ship named *The Four Winds*. A square-rigged half-clipper I sailed in the deep-ocean trades a number of years ago.

By half-clipper, I mean her masts weren't as tall, nor were they raked back as severely as a full clipper's. Built more for short, moderately-fast trips with a big payload, instead of the long, racehorse runs of the bigger ships. She wasn't quite as long and lean either. This made the old gal more economical to sail, 'cuz with less canvas to manage she didn't need as big a crew.

My present ship, the *Yarmouth*, is a two-masted schooner. Her sails are fore and aft rigged, and instead of a big, heavy, fixed-keel, or tons of ballast, she's got a centerboard which can be raised or lowered to suit the depth of water. One of only a handful designed specifically for these waters, she'll slide over the bars at low tide, and maneuver very nicely in the tight little harbors along my route. I couldn't ask for a better ship for the Yarmouth Port to Boston runs in my coastal packet trade."

Waving his pipe in the direction of the picture again, he told them with some pride, "Elijah's the one who painted this for me. *The Four Winds*. She was my ship in the China trades."

Pausing for a minute, his tone became more melancholy. "Lost her in a gale, Lisbon bound from India, back in '62. Old girl wasn't the fastest ship in the world, but she was kind to the end. Hung together long enough to ride out the worst of it, and all hands to make the boats."

"You mean your boat sank?" Amy felt herself being carried along on a rising wave of emotion, with tears not too far behind.

"Oh, she went down all right, but we never lost a man!"

Sarah saw the alarm on Amy's face, and stepped in quickly. "Don't look so concerned, Amy! By now you should know, from what you hear around here, ships sink all the time. Have you ever looked at the marine disaster column in *The Yarmouth Register*! The last three years running, over a hundred ships have been wrecked or sunk during each one of them, and that's just here on Cape Cod!

The important thing to remember about your uncle's ship is like he was telling you, everyone was saved."

"But Mom, it's such a shame! She was a beautiful ship! She looks so safe and strong in that picture I can't imagine any storm sinking her.

Didn't you cry, Uncle Alex?"

"No Master likes to lose a ship! Thank God for the insurance companies. Many an owner, including yours truly, would be wiped out if they hadn't sprung up a few years back. Yes, I cried! I loved that old girl like she was a part of me. She made my fortunes, Amy."

He paused again, and when he continued this time there was obvious distress in the man's voice. "That was the hardest voyage I'll ever make!

I didn't run a ship the way a lot of other Masters do. They'll scrounge up a new crew of scalawags in every port, only to lose them in the next. Myself, I shipped mostly local boys. Men I knew and trusted, and would sign on for the whole voyage. As you see, it made me doubly glad not to lose a single man, although in retrospect my motives were not so noble. I know now my true reasons for recruiting a homegrown crew were based in arrogance and darkness.

Hard to believe, after sailing across countless empty oceans, and thousands upon thousands of miles in fair weather and foul, she sank within sight of land rounding the Cape of Good Hope, off Africa.

Working in her lee before she went down, we had time to lash the boats together, then rode the tail end of the storm out in darkness. We sailed when we had wind, and hauled on the oars in shifts when we didn't. After a number of days following the coast, we made port at Cape Town."

Alex pulled on his pipe, making little fog banks. They drifted away slowly, to reveal a face turned solemn. He began with a weighted sigh, then settled back into his tale. "Fate, is such a strange beast! As luck, or whatever Gods there be would have it, approaching the anchorage we spoke a ship newly arrived from Boston.

Had one of the Crocker boys from Cummaquid aboard."

Sarah, her eyes widening in recognition, put her hand to her mouth. "Oh Alex! That's when you heard. . . ."

"Mmm!" Alex had a thoughtful expression on his face. He nodded slowly. "Captain was a sensitive man! Hailed us aboard, then asked Jamie Crocker and I into his cabin so's Jamie could tell me in private.

Captain Stewart, was the man's name. A good man. Saved my life, you know?"

"What, Uncle Alex? What'd Jamie tell you?"

Sarah was quick. "Hush up, Andy! Don't go prying!"

Alex sighed again. "No, no, that's all right Sarah. It's no secret, and after seven or eight years, I'm about as over it as I'll ever be."

Looking at his nephew, he stated matter-of-factly, "Jamie Crocker told me that my wife Isabelle, and my son of six months, Joshua, had died of scarlet fever while I'd been at sea."

The man shut his eyes, drew on his pipe, and reflected on a tragic instant in his life. One he hadn't visited for some time.

It took a moment for the meaning behind the words to sink in. Suddenly everything became deathly still. Even the wind, whispering in the Elms above the roof, seemed to pause for breath.

Unexpected, the statement caught Amy off guard. She shut her own eyes, and the waves of feeling she'd been fighting, crested. Tears slipped out from between the long lashes, and trickled slowly down her cheeks.

Alex continued, "Never got to see the lad, let alone heft him and measure his worth!" He puffed another little fog bank. "I too died in that moment, certain God had abandoned me. First my ship, then my family . . . I had nothing left to live for."

Pausing for a moment, the man seemed to gather himself. Steering slightly away from the grief just exposed, he changed course. "In those days I was a hard, driving man, with ambition and greed in my heart. As a reflection of my own feelings of importance, I wore a fresh, white shirt every day at sea. No matter the weather, or length of trip, I wore them to distinguish myself from the common seamen under my command. Men from my own village. Men I could drive to exhaustion, and know they'd dare not jump ship because I'd be there if they ever came home!

Returning from my final trip, I was going to own the finest house in the village. My son would be sent to the best schools in the world, and then I'd buy him the fastest clipper on the sea in which to make his own fortune.

Fool! What good was money now? Everything that had ever really mattered was gone.

I sent a letter home with my first mate, notifying my agents and consignees of our misfortune. I then begged Captain Stewart his indulgence, requesting to sail with him a while as passenger 'til I'd regained my footing.

The man felt for me, and consented. At that time he was short-hauling, as I'd been doing. Many ports of call, with small cargoes for each, and the opportunity to engage in whatever other commercial ventures he could arrange around the Indian Ocean and down through the South Seas. Canton was to be his last stop before heading home again."

"Is that in China?"

"Canton? Yes Amy, China, but let me tell my tale!"

The man's intent was not to be rude, but this journey was painful, and interruptions only served to drag things out. He took a moment to remember his place, then continued.

"I am now certain the man would never have allowed me aboard had he the slightest inkling of the trouble and grief I was going to bring him.

Pretty much keeping to my cabin the first few weeks out, my only ventures were to go ashore when we touched port. In my folly, I sought those things which allowed me a brief respite from the misery, instead of absolution for my soul.

Showing his concern, Captain Stewart assigned a man to watch over me.

The poor fellow was quite inept at the task. Soon I began chasing the Dragon. It was a long, arduous trip, with pirate chases, fire, and storm. Bombay, Ceylon, Calcutta fell astern. Through the Mallaca Straits to Singapore, and the China Sea beyond. Macao, Hong Kong and Canton. True to his word, the Captain made port within a week or two of his original estimate, but by then the Dragon was chasing me."

"You mean they have real, live dragons in China, Uncle Alex?"

"No, no, Amy! I was just using that as a figure of speech! A euphemism! I'd been smoking opium to lose myself in its beautiful, endless dreams, and that's what 'Chasing the Dragon' means!

Both memories and mountains are smoothed by time, and fortunately all I've been able to retain from those first, dim, oriental clouds is the euphoria. I've heard tell that after continued exposure I reached a point where I couldn't bear a waking moment without them, but mercifully this I do not remember. The smoke and dreams had become Master, I their slave, and it was the Dragon who was doing the chasing now!

Everything from that point forward has become a jumbled mess in my brain. No order, no reason. The dreams became chaotic and more terrifying than anyone can imagine, but there was nothing at all if I couldn't reach that pipe to smoke and dream.

The little dens have attendants to light the pipes, and place them in a customer's mouth when they reach a state where they can no longer perform that function for themselves. Life became a living twilight, drifting back and forth between heaven and hell on a boat built from smoke. No course, no destination, no reason to exist, and no means to return."

Andy always seemed to come up with the questions no one else thought of, or dared ask. "When did you eat, or go to the bathroom?"

"Food quickly lost its appeal, son. It didn't exist in the dream world I'd found. When one does not eat, the other's not a major factor, and if it was, who was there to care? You just lay there in your own filth, and someday, if you're lucky, your spirit will drift off with the smoke before your body rots away."

The boy wrinkled his nose at this thought, but it didn't still his tongue. "If, like you say, there was no means to return, how did you get back?" Andy was troubled. How could a man, as big, strong, and smart as his uncle, have any trouble doing whatever he pleased?

"Captain Stewart, to the rescue! When we arrived in Canton I eluded his man, then headed straight for a small, out-of-the-way den I'd become aware of on an earlier venture. One I myself had had difficulty finding the first time around.

Strange, when you consider my mission at that time had been to retrieve a fellow Captain in like straights. A kindred spirit, blazing a path for me to follow as it were. The poor man had lost a goodly portion of his relative's fortunes on a misguided attempt to export beef to China. Delayed by storm and misfortune, the shipment had spoiled long before arrival. Ashamed to return home, the Captain found another way to loose himself of guilt.

Aware of his failures, the man's family became alarmed when he chose not to report them in person, and instead dropped out of sight. As it had been an equal venture, they bore the man no ill will, and in fact had little personal loss involved after a healthy insurance settlement.

Mine was the next scheduled sail for Canton out of Boston, and therefore was solicited by the family to locate their loved one and bring him home.

Getting back to my own tale, Captain Stewart, upon completing his business, refused to leave without me. Feeling somewhat responsible for having allowed the situation to develop in the first place, the man vowed to find me if he had to turn the entire city inside out. Noting my depressed state of mind, and taste for opium when last seen, he felt quite sure of where to look.

This, mind you, was a huge undertaking. Canton had many millions of beings within its confines, and a proportional number of liars, cheats and temptations.

He laid over an extra month, which stretched into two, and hired trusted agents to search the literally, thousands upon thousands of dens scattered throughout the city. True to his word, it seemed he'd leave no stone unturned in his quest.

Thank God, the man's zeal was finally rewarded. They found me at the last hour. Cooped up in a tiny wooden cage at one of the market places, I was about to be sold into slavery to pay off the debts I'd run up."

"You mean they buy and sell 'people' in China?"

"China? Amy, what do you think part of the war we've just fought in this country was all about? Do you not consider the Negro a person? The war may have included its share of commerce and greed, but it was mostly fought over the ignorant pride of a people objecting to being told what they could or could not do with their invested property. Just because that property happened to be human was incidental.

Our fellow countrymen either forgot to read, or never took to heart, their own Constitution and Bill of Rights. For the most part, these people considered their slaves to be no better than livestock, and often treated them worse. And, thinking about it, I've seen a good many sailing ships, the crews of which are treated no better. Captives 'til the next port of call, or journey's end."

Looking at Andy, he spoke to him directly. "You keep that in mind, Mister Sears, and choose your vessel wisely should you ever decide to sail before the mast!"

Sarah opened her mouth to speak, but gave up as her brother continued. "Yes, they buy and sell people in China! And a few years ago, they bought and sold them right here in the United States. The morals of a society are not dictated by where you are in the world, young lady, nor should you judge theirs by your own. What is right for you and I, may be completely wrong in another culture. My advice has always been, live by the word of your own God. Others will live by theirs. Maybe it's all one God anyway, with different names and rituals to satisfy the needs of the people who serve Him!

Alex, a little embarrassed, realized he'd let his tongue get away from him. "I'm sorry children! I do tend to get wound up when I'm talking about the whys and wherefores of what other people should or shouldn't do!"

"Preaching is more like it!" Sarah never could resist an opening. "According to the Gospel of Alex!"

"Hey Sarah, I may not be an ordained minister, but I've held a religious service aboard ship every Sunday I've spent at sea. Counting summers in the coastal trade, I've left thousands of sermons behind in my wake. As for their content, or my affiliation, I lay somewhere between a conservative Unitarian and a Congregationalist, with a step toward the Methodist's liberalism.

I feel a person's relationship with God is his own matter. All I've ever tried to do was point out the obvious temptations laid before us mortals, and suggest alternate courses to my listeners.

I tell you, that philosophy is as good as some I've seen with the variety to choose from these days. A new church is going up on every corner. One-family projects like the Simpkin's Church of New Jerusalem—just down the street—to huge campgrounds for the Methodists. Those people have built one on Willow Street, another to the west'ard of Hyannis, in Craigville, and I here tell the place rising on Martha's Vineyard has become so over-run, the island defies recognition in-season.

Thousands of people congregate in those enclaves every summer. Some, to renew their faith. Others, I'm sure, to enjoy our weather."

More interested in the real-life drama of her uncle than the failure or success of any particular religious group, Amy piped up again. "What happened when Captain Stewart found you, Uncle Alex?"

Recognizing Amy's unspoken motive, Alex picked up his story without missing a beat. "Well, Amy, he bought me, and they carried my worthless carcass aboard on a litter.

On the voyage home, the good Captain and his crew nursed me back through three weeks of pure hell.

An ocean voyage affords much time to a passenger. Once I could eat on my own again, I was given a Bible and all the time in the world to think my problems through. Interesting, how this simple application of common sense worked. To my surprise, I discovered the sorrow I had allowed myself to indulge in was not really for my dear wife and son, but merely self-pity because my own dreams had failed.

That was also when I decided the good Lord must have had something in mind when he allowed the Captain to find me. I vowed at that moment, instead of looking out for my own selfish interests, I would do what I could to help those less fortunate.

I have never been a pious man, but from the wisdom of my years I was sure that sooner or later He would lay out a course, and point out the stars to follow.

Then again, neither am I an idle man! From the start, I had no intention of just sitting on my backside 'til the Lord opened the sky and drew me a picture of what to do. No, so attuned, I had a strong feeling the old homestead was where I belonged.

A stop in Boston to settle my affairs with Captain Stewart and those who had looked out for my best interests while I'd been away delayed my journey but moments, though they seemed endless. Now running in my eagerness, I shipped aboard Captain Doane's *Enterprise*, and never missed a tide.

Cape Cod from the sea shows a bare sliver, but no mountain could have beckoned more true. I was coming home.

Within days I'd bought the old *Yarmouth*, then spent countless weeks—actually months—rebuilding her. I found the labor good for my soul, and the time well-spent, getting re-acquainted with my neighbors as they came by to help.

Nowadays, I sail my ship as much for the physical and social pleasure it brings, as the monetary reward. Often I've waived the passage fee in exchange for a pair of hands, or a simple, home-cooked meal.

My hands! Have you ever seen a Captain with hands such as these? I like the feel of a halyard fighting my will, and the wheel responding to my touch.

As a blue-water skipper, I had soft, white hands and manicured nails. My cabin, treated almost as a throne room, housed an expansive wardrobe. Now, I share my meals and modest accommodations with the passengers, and have been known to sleep with the crew when overburdened."

The man heaved a sigh, and as if becoming suddenly aware of how long he'd rambled on, ended his story with a simple statement. "So here, my family, you see me! And here I shall remain until such time as directed to do otherwise!"

Sarah and her children realized, in that moment, Alex had just shared his soul. He knew, in turn, they would never betray his trust.

The captain's sister picked up the conversation gently. "So that explains why you do so much for other people now? Things beyond consideration for the Alex I remember."

She paused, and then finished her thoughts with, "Including the kindness and security you've shown us in our hour of need, I might add."

Chapter 12

The Gift

Alex, dressed in his best attire and carrying an armful of mysterious packages, was gone for three or four days in early December. Grumbling about train travel being like drifting on a choppy river, his visible excitement belied the truth of the complaint, and no one felt he considered the trip to be in the least bit distasteful.

The man never actually told his sister these trips would become a pattern, but she put two and two together when he mentioned he was planning another around the first of the year which would last a full week.

Ostensibly, the Captain was off to Boston to confer with his agents and investors, and to renew his lease of dock space on Long Wharf. This reasoning however, peaked Sarah's curiosity and another minor confrontation was the result. "How can there be that much to do, that it would take days? I should think you'd be better advised to conduct these things by mail, or even telegraph. That way you'd have a record of the transaction, and save yourself all that money wasted on transportation, lodging, and meals every month! Besides, you won't need the dock space until late March or April, so why reserve it now?"

Momentarily flustered by her logic, a defensive Alex over-reacted. He cxplained how he preferred to conduct affairs of business in person, and then insisted—a little too emphatically—that whether she liked it or not, this was what he'd always done, and he saw no reason to change his ways just to please her.

Such protective touchiness about the subject puzzled her more than what the man professed he was going to do when he got to Boston. Not having much choice, Sarah accepted his headstrong decision with a few rather large reservations filed away in her memory of questioning thoughts.

Alex, had no one to blame but himself. After all, it was a rather unusual idiosyncrasy in a person who was always priding himself on the efficient use of his time. And when one considers how a solitary penny could drive him to days of frustrating distraction in search of the error in his ledger book, this pointless expenditure seemed totally out of character.

Christmas arrived, marked by the usual anticipation, excitement, preparation, then let-down afterwards. To Andy, the church services and functions seemed never-ending, but even he had to admit the season as a whole was better than any in memory. The formalities, barely tolerated, became an excuse to see his friends, and if not, an opportunity to tease the girls in attendance. Something else he enjoyed was getting Christmas day off from school.

This was the first year the children had ever experienced the novelty of a Christmas tree, and adopted the relatively new custom with enthusiasm. A bit old to be overly excited about Saint Nicholas, they nonethcless hung stockings to sustain the myth, then happily reaped the sweets and trinkets left by his ghost.

More directly, family gifts were exchanged. Presents requiring days stretching into weeks, with the various stages of planning and the actual construction or manufacture thereof.

In spite of Alex's stiff and grumpy facade, everyone could tell he was tickled beyond words at receiving something personal from each of them.

Amy knitted him a scarf with his initials embroidered ever so neatly on one end, and taking advantage of his city absence, Sarah made up a special box of his favorite caramels with nuts.

These were wonderful gifts, but it was Andy's that was somehow special to the man. Having attempted the craft himself, he could appreciate the effort involved.

Done under Sam's tutelage, Andy had spent hours carving a scrimshaw watch fob, with a reasonable likeness of the schooner *Yarmouth* on its side. Getting it just right, a tooth from his mentor's pilot whale was transformed into a thing of beauty, and the accomplishment became a matter of well-deserved pride.

For a week afterwards, the family caught their hardhearted, old captain humming under his breath, and by reflection this pleased them all.

The gifts which Sarah received were similar in nature, and just as intriguing.

A beautiful cameo brooch Alex had carried home from one of his travels to the other side of the world, got rave reviews.

From Andy, came a pretty little box. Meant to hold potpourri, he'd decorated it with shells. Apparently some of these may not have bleached quite long enough in the sun, so she was also grateful it was filled with fragrant petals scrounged from some neighbor's lingering rose garden.

Amy too had spent hours laboring. She'd worked on a cross-stitch, picture sampler in school. Filled with sea gulls and shells, it displayed a map of Cape Cod in the background. Although not finished in time for the holiday, the promise of completion came with the gift.

On receiving the beautiful, hand-rubbed, velvet-lined, jewelry box that her uncle had done, Amy danced into his lap and planted an enthusiastic kiss on the man's cheek. Embarrassed beyond words, it was difficult to tell who was most pleased by the whole thing.

Not to be neglected, but somehow losing importance in comparison, she was presented with a pretty, hand-sewn chemise from Mother, and scented note paper from Andy.

Completely lacking in the funds department, the boy remembered his uncle's earlier suggestion about bartering. It didn't take much talking to convince Mr. Knowles that a bushel of clams and quahogs were the equal of a five-cent box of paper.

Andy, in turn, was the recipient of a fishing-tackle box. Made of wood, his uncle had personalized the gift by carving the boys initials into the lid.

A handsome leather belt came from Amy. Alex had shown her how to tool a design into the smooth leather, using a wooden mallet and odd scraps of metal.

His mother gave him an elegant, but discreet, little pocket knife. Its bone handle and two blades would make any gentleman proud to be the owner.

Plain to all, however, there was one gift the boy cherished above everything else. Maybe it was because it came totally unexpected, but then again. . . .

Sammy, his self-appointed friend and teacher, had fashioned him a small but beautifully proportioned and finely balanced sheath knife. The blade had come from a discarded, metal-working file. A piece of metal on which the man had obviously spent countless hours with a foot-operated grinding wheel to shape and get smooth, and then re-tempered in a smithy's fire. Surprisingly, using sail needles and a piece of oil-cured leather, the sheath was also made by those same coarse hands. To give it even more a feeling of being something special, Sam had burned the unmistakable outline of a swordfish into the rich, dark leather.

Sarah seemed impressed by the thoughtfulness, and even the craftsmanship of this present—not knowing fully Sam's capabilities—except that, remembering Andy's references to what these things stood for at the time of his school-fight, she wasn't too pleased about the association with the sea this gift implied. And besides, not only was it a direct affront to her own presentation, but the boy's preference was thinly disguised.

Chapter 13

Sandpipers and Eels

By now the Sears family was at least recognized throughout the village, if not totally accepted.

Everyone had become aware of Sarah's sharp mind and wholesome good looks. It was said she was everything a "Southern Gentleman" supposedly avoided in a woman. Qualities, which in New England were both acknowledged and admired.

Southern ladies were thought of as being pampered, spoiled, and helpless, whereas Sarah displayed the ability to take care of herself and family, as widows of the sea had always been forced to do. Industrious and productive, it was unfortunate her quick tongue could make those around her feel so uncomfortable at times. On the other hand, her no-nonsense, stand-on-her-own-two-feet approach to life, and the way she refused to condone a woman's subservient role branded her not only a tolerated, but esteemed rebel among her female peers.

In light of this attitude, some of the men felt sorry for Alex. Furthermore, they questioned Christopher's sanity, as few in the village were unaware of his fascination with the woman.

As for Sarah and Christopher, their visible courtship was conducted according to the rules laid out by the strict Victorian Society they lived in. Aside from formal, chaperoned visits, other socializing was limited to public or church functions. Titillating their curiosity, and spicing the gossip of a few of the more meddlesome ladies, a rumor floated around about a painting of some sort, but no-one was able to come up with the details.

Rumors aside, Christopher made such a fool of himself whenever Sarah was in the vicinity, he might as well have painted his intentions on the sail of his work boat.

Amy had become the delight of her newly acquired friends. Her mother's tutelage had given her the confidence to speak her mind when challenged, much to the surprise and consternation of her teachers, and in chain-effect, Alex.

There were boys too, among her increasing circle of friends. Infatuated by her beauty—and the fact she was the new girl in town—they learned quickly it was best to give her a wide berth and not crowd on too much sail.

Schools of this era were sexually segregated. Above the sixth grade, separate doors and separate classrooms supposedly kept the boy's minds on their lessons. Basically, all it did was create the illusion of keeping the few girls who pursued a higher education isolated to their mostly domestic studies. And, naturally too, this policy instead had the reverse effect by concentrating the attention of both sexes on that which was forbidden, at least until after school hours. As a result, both boys and girls became adept at the art of flirtation, innocent love-poems, whispers, coy looks and an occasional wink.

Boys fought over the privilege of carrying a particular girl's books to or from school, and often the price was dear. Instigated no doubt by sore losers, it wasn't so much the black eyes and bloody noses, as the public chastisement of getting caught associating with girls. Driven into hiding, the intrigue of secret romances and stolen rendezvous became the norm. In truth, with disapproving adults, and jealous spies everywhere, these relationships had as much romance or secrecy as a handshake, and less physical contact.

Andy couldn't be bothered with all that nonsense. He had more important things to pursue.

Ice-fishing on the ponds with one of the Hallet men was one favorite pastime, although even he'd admit he probably spent as much time teasing their daughters as fishing.

The boy's faithful companion, Ulysses, tagged along no matter what the adventure. If Andy wasn't sledding or skating with his new friends, he was exploring the swamps and marshes, or clamming the flats with Sammy. Ulysses was always there, in the way, under foot, or competing.

Sam, self-appointed authority of all things Cape Cod, had become as much peer as mentor. Much to Andy's surprise, having accepted the boy as a true friend, and feeling at ease in his company, Sam lost his stutter. It was under this man's watchful eye that the boy truly learned the ways of nature and the shore.

Andy couldn't get enough of what was offered. Like a glutton filled to capacity, he still reached for just one more piece of cake, or a candied sweet, secure in the knowledge that somehow mother nature would make room. A fact which amused Sam enough so that if the tide was right, or if this private person had a special adventure in mind, he and Ulysses would often brave exposure to others of the human race to wait for Andy at the school door. The household benefited too, as the effort was seldom without some fruits of these endeavors, although admittedly they were not always welcomed with open arms.

One time, the boy staggered home with a burlap bag containing forty-some-odd sandpipers. A person might think it unusual for a healthy twelve year old to 'stagger' under the weight of four pounds of feathers, but there were extenuating circumstances.

The small shore birds, about the size of a large sparrow, had apparently been migrating. Too exhausted to seek better shelter when they arrived, they made the mistake of landing on a weather shore to rest. There, huddled together for warmth, they never realized the salt spray from the nearby waves was freezing on their feathers and anchoring them to the sand. By the time Andy and Sam found these strange lumps, they had attained the size of grapefruit. A little hole in each one, where the bird kept moving its bill to maintain an airway, was what first attracted their attention.

What in the world Andy thought his mother was going to do with such tiny, feathered morsels only the Lord knew. Adding insult to injury, Sarah discovered, as she picked up the first ice ball, that the bird inside was still alive. It peeped, and wiggled its bill through the hole. Of course this opening happened to be in the palm of her hand at the time. The action was automatic, instantaneous, and most pleasing to Andy. His mother shrieked, and let go of the strange, frightening object.

Following nature's laws, the ice ball shattered on the floor, which in turn released the bird.

The poor thing, suddenly released from its ice-egg prison, must have thought it had been re-born into a circus. It flew in a frenzied panic from room to room, as Andy, Ulysses, George, and even Amy whooped and thundered after it. With knickknacks spraying from every window sill they visited, a frazzled Sarah threw all of them outside, birds included. There, at their mother's insistence, the children released the rest of the pitiful little feather balls from their icy enclosures so that nature could point them south to the warmer climes they'd been seeking.

Two days later, the eels he brought home to his mother weren't received with much more enthusiasm. They too were still alive, and squirmed around in the bucket like so many slimy snakes.

Gruff, no-nonsense Alex, came to the rescue this time. He showed Andy how to nail the heads to a board, then skin the creatures with a pair of pliers. Next, the captain cut them up into pieces about two-inches long, which he dipped in egg, flour and spices.

Fried in butter with a diced onion, the aroma was enticing. On the other hand, Andy was delighted to point out to his mother and sister how the chunks of eel were still alive enough to jump and quiver when first placed in the hot skillet. After that, it took much cajoling and persuasion by a perturbed Alex to convince them the flesh was indeed fit for human consumption. Finally, after the first few tentative bites, the end result was very popular.

This was as close to heaven as a twelve year old could get. Andy had all day, or at least that part which wasn't spent in school and on chores, to pursue those things which brought him nothing but pleasure. All of this done in the company of his best friends. And then to top it off, he received praise for dragging home the boyhood treasures and plunder his efforts produced.

Lawrence vanished so completely from even the most hidden pockets of the boy's mind, it was almost as if it were someone else who had lived that other life.

Chapter 14

No Trouble Fishin'

Many social events took place in the depths of these Cape Cod winters. Lectures were held on instructive topics by the Yarmouth Institute, a Lyceum Society. One, a presentation by the Honorable William Sturgis of Boston on, *The Aborigines of North Western America*, and advertised as, "A racy and valuable account, drawn from my own experience." packed the building. The Institute's Hall, built as a gathering place for the village on a bend of Hallet Street across from Summer Street, or Hawes Lane, was a busy place. Other entertainment included literary and poetry readings by respected members of the community. Even famous orators such as Oliver Wendell Holmes, and Horace Greeley were drawn by the twenty-five dollar fee offered to men of such renown.

To Andy, the spectacle which created the liveliest time that winter was the minstrel show. One of the more positive aspects which surprised him was the month of rehearsals, as these occupied most of the doldrums of winter.

A semiprofessional troupe was invited into the village to organize the affair. These people provided the basic scripts and somewhat knowledgeable direction for the show, whereas the community itself produced the talent, and would-be thespians to act out the parts.

A wide spectrum of the village was represented, and the shared experience created bridges across usually impassable chasms of social, political, and financial differences.

For example, as unlikely an individual as anyone could pick, Mr. Seth Crowell—the rather stuffy and quite aloof president of the bank—consented to play the part of Mr. Interlocutor, or master of ceremonies.

Nathaniel Hallet had been tapped to play his fiddle. Then someone leaked word that Andy's harmonica hardly ever left his hip pocket. This same individual related how, when the boy played Camptown Races, his mouth-organ had been known to get so hot it had to be held with a pot-holder. To those in charge, it seemed only natural the two musicians should be teamed up to form a tall and short of it for a comical medley of Stephen Foster.

Once in production, these two interspersed some banter between their numbers which referred to a certain packet boat Captain. They claimed he was known to be so engrossed in saving time that it had even been rumored he'd sailed his schooner to Boston stern first, thereby avoiding the loss of the few minutes it would take to turn it around when he got there.

Another made reference to all the fish that must be piling up around his house. Obviously he was receiving a lot of deliveries, reflected by the many comings and goings of a certain catboat Master. Now picking on Chris Gardner, they suggested it was quite remarkable how, in spite of the man's vessel being high and dry in its cradle on the shore, he seemed to be having no trouble at all fishing for what he wanted. It was also noted that catching some prizes was often more difficult than the fishing, and they advised a change of bait to bring him luck.

This latter reference brought a flush to Sarah's cheeks along with smiling nods and sly glances from her neighbors in the audience.

The act received much applause, which led indirectly to the boy being completely humbled. Encouraged to do an encore, Nathaniel and Andy held a hurried conference on stage, after which the boy reheated his harmonica and began an inspired, solo version of, *The Battle Hymn of the Republic.*

So much for innocent improvisation. Nathaniel let the boy get through the main body of the piece, then beckoned for the rest of the crew to sing backup during the chorus. The man started them off very softly, and then allowed their voices to rise to the occasion.

The second verse continued with the voices as soft backup, followed by the entire audience asked to join the chorus. The third and last verse was sung by all, until they got to the chorus again. Here, Nathaniel cut off everyone except Andy. Somewhat embarrassed by the attention focusing on him, Andrew finished the poignant, moving piece by himself. Without conscious intent, it came out as a haunting, plaintive cry, reminiscent of *Taps* from some distant, hill-top bugle.

Only a short time after the Civil War had ended, this piece brought the audience to their feet in a foot-stomping, hand-clapping, whistling round of applause. From that night forward it became the closing act.

Unexpected, the reaction startled the boy at first, and a wave of goose-bumps swept over him. He was aware of the drama created by the piece, but it wasn't until Andy saw some in the audience who had actually been brought to tears that he realized how truly moving it had been. Memories kindled by the hymn were fresh. . . . Too fresh.

Suddenly, the boy wished he'd picked *Little Brown Jug*, or something else. Anything else. Even *Dixie*!

The Hamblins were there. It was their son, Brevet Major General Joseph E. Hamblin, who had been Yarmouth's highest ranking hero in the war, but there were many other families as well. Many, who's children had gone off to serve their country. Many the brave young sons who would never again taste the fresh salt-air on their tongues; welcome the soft, cool breezes from the bay on their faces; or feel the white sands of Cape Cod under their feet.

It took many minutes for the standing round of applause to die down, and the audience to regain their seats. There was no point in a second encore, for nothing could top this.

Alex frowned. In the captain's opinion this response would undoubtedly, and unnecessarily, go to his nephew's head. He was equally certain it was going to be the family who would eventually pay the final bill when the whole thing was over.

Deep down inside, he glowed with a pride he'd never admit.

In total, forty-some-odd persons were chosen for parts, and each brought their own peculiar talents and points of view to the show. Naturally, their families and a string of relatives came along to watch. The performance, a guaranteed success before the curtain ever went up.

It was a grand time. With the actors all made up in blackface to hide behind, they could poke fun at the idiosyncrasies of everyone else in the village with relative impunity. That, of course, was the appeal of the show. With no one spared, it insured all would attend. Who would dare miss that which was to be said about them, supposedly in jest, when in fact it was perceived as more of an insult to be left out of the pointed barbs than selected as the chosen target?

Chapter 15

Ice Cakes and Brant

Just as the dog days of August can be the hottest and most summery of a season almost past, February days can be the coldest, and her snows the deepest of winter.

Alex tried to tell his nephew how a lot of this white stuff wasn't really snow, but just the stuff they had in the Arctic. With the barometer rising when it happened, one could not rightly call it a storm so the only answer that made sense was frozen fog, or what they called sea-smoke in those colder climes.

To Andy, snow was snow whatever name his uncle wanted to put on it. The air was cold and crisp enough to chew on too, and yet Alex claimed the sun was swinging further north with each passing day. Increasingly warm, and dazzling bright, it reflected off the Captain's melting white stuff in a teasing hint of those better days to come, and like a crocus in spring, the boy's energy rose right along with it.

It was on a bright day such as this when Andy, flushed with excitement and out of breath, came running into the yard. Ulysses bounced around him, trying to figure out which door he was headed for so that he could be the first one there. Pausing in a cloud of steamy exuberance to unlatch the storm door into the kitchen, Andy reached up into the late-winter sun and broke off an icicle from the eves of the pantry roof. The snow, melting briefly in a patch of sunny warmth, froze again in the shade where it became these long icy stalactites. They created pictures in Andy's mind of whale harpoons, or possibly a knight's broadsword. The shorter ones, he figured, could be used for spearheads or even a pirate's dagger.

As Andy picked the weapon of his choice, Ulysses buried his nose in the snow to retrieve an errant piece that had fallen. The dog came up with the black wetness of this part of his anatomy frosted high with white. A lopsided-grin showed where the chunk of ice hung precariously from a corner of his mouth. Immediately challenging his companion to a game of keep away, Andy disappointed him by suddenly remembering the focus of his headlong rush.

Bursting into the kitchen, the boy yelled for his uncle. The door slammed shut behind them, encouraging the dog to suck his tail in out of harm's way. Dropping his chunk of ice, the ever-faithful one stood over the treasure expectantly, guarding it with the hope of challenge in his eyes.

Alex poked his head through a doorway, spectacles on the end of his nose and a ledger book in his hand. "Don't you two ever come into the house quietly?" His curt, admonishing response held no welcome.

Andy ignored both the question and tone of his uncle's reply. First, he pulled the icicle out of his mouth, and wiped the latter on his sleeve. Then, in between desperate attempts to breathe and talk at the same time, the boy managed to communicate his message. "Uncle Alex!" Puff, puff. "There's little geese all over the flats!" Puff. "Let's go get 'em!"

Alex straightened up. His eyebrows raised from the frown of his greeting to a wide-eyed, but questioning look. Methodically, he took the little half-glasses off his nose, folded them carefully, then tapped his pursed lips with the end result while he thought. The studied slowness was not helping to diminish Andy's excitement. Like a shortened sail with too much wind, the boy looked like he was about to burst a gasket as his cheeks reddened in the heat of the cook stove.

Alex, knowing full well what was going on in Andy's mind, paused and dragged everything out just that teasing little bit longer. "Hmmm! Brant must be back! Heading north to the breeding grounds, I presume."

He looked at the boy, and still tapping his glasses on his lips, asked, "On the flats, you say?"

Andy, shifting from foot to foot, was getting a little perturbed at the delay. Clearing his throat, he replied, "Yep! On the outer edge, next to the channel. Can we go get 'em?"

With no visible response from his uncle, the boy was beginning to anticipate a negative answer. After the long run, he was finally catching his breath, but now despair began to creep between the words.

Alex still chose to ignore the question, and instead, strung things out even further. Seeming to be talking almost more to himself than Andy, he muttered, "Brant always get here about now. Middle of February. Thousands of 'em. First sign, winter's loosing its grip. Looks like I'm going to have to shake-a-leg pretty soon, and get m'schooner back in the water. Almost time to get her standing-rigging back on too."

Pausing to ponder, he continued his musings aloud. More or less directing them at Andy now, the man began to list numerous reasons why they shouldn't venture onto the flats this particular afternoon. "Tides about to turn, boy! She'll be coming fast today, with no wind to hold her out. Bet it's gettin' cold too, now that the sun's on its way down. Besides, no time left to hunt after you figure out how long it'd take to get out there and back!"

Now leaning in the doorway with his spectacles back on, and apparently looking at the columns of figures again, he was instead watching the boy slowly melt in disappointment.

Looking up suddenly, Alex announced, "Time and tide waits for no-man, son! If we're going, you'd better get movin'. You know you can't hunt in them clothes, and after you change, someone's got to clean up your friend's puddle afore we can leave the house!"

Grinning from ear to ear, Andy's "Yes, Sir!" came over his shoulder as he scooped up Ulysses's melting ice. Heaving it, along with his own out the door, the boy had to dance in the opening to avoid the dog following in hot pursuit.

The two of them crept across the flats, dressed in old white sails to help them blend into the background. On the way, they hid behind ice cakes so numerous they looked like apples sitting on the lawn after a late summer windstorm. These apples were three to six feet thick however, and often so large the hunters had to climb over them instead of going around. Pausing for breath once, they watched and listened as the afternoon train smoked and wailed its snaky course along the upland edge of the Barnstable marshes, telling one and all it was on its way.

Alex, carrying his big, double-barreled, ten-gauge shotgun, let Andy choose the course across the flats, but as they crept from one lump of ice to the next the man seemed to have no time, nor room in his heart to enjoy the moment. In his usual turmoil, he was wondering why he'd agreed to this adventure, while at the same time he weighed those very real reasons listed earlier for not coming out here today. Grumpy and gruff it also annoyed him, that hard as he tried not to let it show, watching this little pest of a nephew did indeed give him pleasure.

Schooner Harwood Palmer locked in ice on Yarmouth flat, 1905
(photo courtesy of Matthews C. Hallett, Yarmouth Port, Ma)

Staying out of sight, Andy peeked around the corners and over the tops of the giant ice cakes. Crawling like an Indian, the boy flattened himself out as if he were trying to blend into the ice itself. He, at least, was approaching this day's hunt in deadly seriousness.

Ulysses, on the other hand, thought the trip was just for his amusement. The puddles trapped by the ice were right up his alley. He splashed into and out of them as if he had seal blood in his veins. Stopping to sniff and investigate every stone, ice cake, and piece of driftwood they came across, the dog was oblivious to Andy's urgings to keep up and stay out of sight.

The ice field ended abruptly at the tide's edge. Andy's chosen flock of Brant sat right there in about six inches of water, feeding on eelgrass and yodeling their hellos back and forth between other family groups.

Alex patted Ulysses to keep him quiet, and crouched beside the boy. They were hiding behind a three-foot thick ice cake. As if in thought, the captain paused for a brief moment, carefully loaded the paper cartridges into the breach, closed the weapon, half-cocked the hammers and installed the percussion caps on the nipples, smiled, then passed his nephew the gun.

Andy had accompanied his uncle a half-dozen times this winter, on similar hunting expeditions into the marshes after ducks and geese. Occasionally he'd been granted the boon of carrying this sacred behemoth on the return trips, if they'd been successful, while Alex carried the fruits of the hunt.

Alex always had Andy make sure for himself that the gun was unloaded. He also made a point of showing his nephew how best to carry this weapon safely, and how to lead a flying bird, should the day ever arrive when he'd be allowed to try his hand at shooting.

The last couple of times, Andy had been permitted to clean the gun after their hunt too. A tedious task involving ramrods, oil-soaked cloths, and care not to leave fingerprints on either the gun or his mothers furnishings.

As an unintentional side effect, this mixture of burnt gunpowder and the oil combined to produce a unique, pungent odor. Little did he know that years later the smell would return like an old friend, bringing with it flash-backs and fond memories of hunts, and days along the winter shore. Today, however, was the first time Andy had ever held a loaded gun with the anticipation of using it, and the boy's sparkling eyes said it all. His breath seemed to come in short gasps as he fought for control.

Alex noticed, but just attributed it to equal parts excitement of the moment, and the exertion of clambering over and around the thick, up and down, mile-wide mixture of sand and ice they'd just crossed.

The boy had been painstakingly warned how much a ten-gauge could kick. He had also been instructed to hold the stock tight against his cheek and shoulder as he aimed, so that when the gun went off, the recoil would translate more into a shove than a punch.

Unfortunately, that part faded into a blur with the boy's eagerness.

Alex went over the most important points with him one more time, telling him not to bring the hammers to full cock until he was going up on the birds, so no one else would get shot by mistake. He then told Andy to rest the arm that was going to hold the weight of the gun on the ice cake in front of them. This, he suggested, would steady the boy's aim, though both knew there was no way the young man could have supported the full weight of Old Betsy in one hand with his arm extended anyway.

Lastly, Andy was told to shoot the birds in the water.

Not very sporting maybe, but a more probable way to show results for a first-time shot.

After all of the instructions had been rehearsed, and the boy appeared settled and ready, Alex took one last peek to ascertain the birds hadn't wandered away. Easing back into his place, he told his nephew right where to look when he went up.

The moment having finally arrived, Alex simply said, "Have at it, boy!" The excitement building in the older man's throat was barely outdone by Andrew's own heartbeat.

Ulysses could sense that something was about to happen, but Alex kept the dog from dancing by straddling him, pinning him with his legs.

The captain stood up to see, as Andy, in one motion, threw the cannon on top of the ice cake, cocked the hammers, took aim, and pulled the trigger. The boy's technique couldn't have been improved by any number of hours rehearsing. The click of the hammer brought its familiar, slightly-delayed, thunderous explosion. Immediately, a dense cloud of impenetrable white smoke enveloped them, signaling the black powder had functioned properly. It was the last thing to happen as expected.

Following that gunshot, chaos became the order of the day. The first shot was followed almost instantly by a second explosion, the gun pointing in the general direction of the setting sun. A second, reinforcing, fog bank of gun smoke blotted out their world. Between these two shots, with no measurable elapsed time, Andy had slammed back into Alex from the recoil of the first. The second shot was accidentally triggered by a mix up of fingers not doing exactly as they were intended, aided by this impact with his uncle.

Alex, anticipating the first shot, but not what was about to follow, had his arms up to catch the boy. With his legs tangled in a bolting Ulysses, and not expecting the second discharge, Alex lost his balance too. Over they all went, dog, boy, man, and gun, splashing into the frigid, ankle-deep soup of slush and salt water.

Ulysses, annoyed by the restraint and now free, erupted from the tangled mess successfully. In reaction, the others foundered once more.

The dog tore around the ice cake, intent on retrieving whatever had been shot. Used as a launching platform, his human companions never rated so much as a backward glance to see how they were making out in that slippery cauldron. A very wet Alex eventually found his footing after this second dunking, and dragged an even wetter Andy up out of the water by his collar.

This grip was becoming all too familiar to the boy. Andy, in turn, still had the gun cradled in his arms.

Looking at his nephew, sad, bedraggled and droopy, Alex figured the boy would have preferred to drown than let go of that shotgun. The last straw was when water began pouring out of the twin barrels as Andy adjusted his uncle's beloved cannon in his arms.

Alex let out a "Whoop!", and began laughing so loud and unexpectedly that it startled the boy. With tears of laughter mixing with the ocean salt they were wearing, the two of them turned as one to look for Ulysses through the now dissipated smoke.

The dog's jaws were already full of bird and feathers, but he was trying to crowd a second one in as he pushed it toward shore. A third Brant, belly-up and surrounded by floating down, bounced like a cork on the rippling water nearby.

Forgetting his stiff, authoritative image in the heat of the moment, Alex became so excited he was practically dancing. He shouted, "Three, boy! You got three of them!"

Andy, still dazed from the kick of the gun and the sudden dousing, was becoming aware of a dull ache. It seemed to emanate from the shoulder and then radiate downward, deep into his body. Like a weight getting heavier, and heavier, he found himself fighting to breathe again. Afraid he'd drop the gun, the boy moved to place it back on the ice cake, and at the same time opened his mouth to tell Alex that something was wrong.

Without warning, the pain exploded and grabbed him like a closing fist. The boy's eyes went out of focus, and as he slowly began to melt back into the water, he felt Alex's rough grasp around his chest. Unable to catch his breath against the pain, Andy's ears roared with the noise of storm driven surf, then everything went black.

Afterwards he could remember vague mind-pictures, as if through a dense fog. Ice cakes and sand, with a surreal, orange winter-sunset splashing its color over all. As he thought about it, he could see the sun strike fiery bursts of gold and silver from the frozen, diamond-like crystals of snow and ice. Mercifully, little else came back to him.

Alex, surprised by the sudden collapse of his nephew, stood there holding the boy in his arms. With building apprehension, he yelled and shook the lad, trying to get some response of life, his mind racing, looking for possible causes. The boy's earlier shortness of breath came to mind, but it made no sense.

A coming tide; approaching night; the increasing cold now that the sun was going down; all concerns he'd thought of earlier, were coming back to haunt him. Taking full responsibility, he punished himself with a one-sided conversation. "Why did I let the boy's disappointment cloud my judgment? More important, how in hell am I going to get this burden back to the shore over that hellishly slippery, up and down ice-field before the tide? Damn! I knew I shouldn't have given in! It was too late in the day before we even got started!"

Trying to think logically between his condemning, self-incrimination, the man started at the bottom of his cares and decided to leave the gun and Brant on a big ice cake. With luck, he could retrieve them the following day. Two seconds later he had dashed that thought, when he realized the gun might be needed to signal for help in case someone happened by.

Forcing his mind to a solution was difficult, when each point raised needled his psyche with guilt.

Another wave found his voice. "Why in hell didn't I leave word with someone, telling them where we were going?"

Taking stock of the physical conditions around them, he acknowledged the building offshore breeze. It would take most of the ice on this outer-edge to sea tonight.

With time running out, he was quite certain he'd never make shore carrying the boy before darkness and the tide caught them.

Waiting it out on an inshore ice-floe until the flats bared again was a possibility, but there was no guarantee the wind wouldn't freshen enough to take all the ice, and that was not a manner in which he chose to put to sea.

Adding pressure, an icy rivulet trickled down his back reminding him that both he and Andy were soaking wet. Aware of the implication, he understood without conscious thought that if they didn't drown, exposure would claim them long before morning brought first light and help.

Laying Andy out on his gun-rest ice cake, the captain's first thought was to climb up and survey their predicament from the advantage of height. Working to place the lad in a comfortable position, he must have done something instead to cause pain. This brought forth a moan, and the boy's eyes fluttered briefly.

Encouraged, Alex spoke, then yelled into the young man's face.

Nothing happened.

Following up on the actions which had produced the first groan, he moved the lad's arms down to a more natural position. Another grunt of pain resulted, and even Alex's unskilled hands could detect a strange looseness of the boy's right arm.

A wave of relief swept through the man's chest. He now had a possible answer to the lad's problem, and some certainty that, if right, it might not be too serious. With difficulty, he slipped a thick, heavy hand under Andy's outer clothing, and felt along the top of the boy's cold, wet shoulder.

The man's stomach almost turned over. His touch revealed a horribly deformed area, although nothing sharp. Angry again, he wondered why something as simple as a dislocated shoulder should bother his own viscera. He'd amputated a man's leg on the high seas once, and never batted an eye.

Now he understood the 'why' of Andy's fainting, anyway. After doing its damage of dislocation, the gun's weight had splinted the joint more or less in place. Unfortunately, when the boy put that heavy monster down, his muscles contracted and this pulled the bone completely out of its normal position.

Standing there, the Captain debated whether or not to feel out the collarbone to see if this might be broken too, but decided it was of little consequence compared to solving their more immediate problem. Remembering what the last probing had done for his insides, he buttoned the boy's collar and clambered up onto the ice cake instead.

Ulysses, the three Brant piled neatly on a small piece of floating ice in front of him, stood nearby and looked up at Alex expectantly.

Glancing down from his perch, Alex acknowledged his faithful friend's accomplishment with a, "Good dog, Ulysses!"

Their dilemma was getting his full attention so this minor interruption hardly broke the man's concentration, but it mattered little. Somewhere in the remote distances of his mind, all things received dutiful processing with or without assistance.

Suddenly the captain's face twisted into a surprised expression. Looking back down at the dog, he bellowed out another "Whoop!"

With no thought for personal safety, the man leaped from his perch, back into that icy cauldron where their troubles had begun. Water and slush splashed to gratifying heights, while Ulysses got paid back in the same coin he'd visited upon his masters.

Alex reached out with a fond pat to congratulate his startled dog, but the creature learned fast and wanted no part of this idiot. Once wet was enough for him, and he danced away, not quite sure what to expect next.

Grabbing the Brant out from under the nervous dog's puzzled nose, and the gun off the ice cake, Alex sloshed out to a small floe of pan-ice moving by in the tide. Returning, he scooped up Andy, called to Ulysses, then caught up with the moving ice again. Being careful not to add insult to injury, the man placed the boy gently on the cold, white surface. Helping the dog aboard next, Alex picked out a particular spot and sat himself on the edge of the floe.

Allowing his booted feet to hang into the water, he steered the ice somewhat, and helped it over its occasional hang-ups by pushing on the sandy flat below. Drifting with the tide, they floated in along the edge of the channel as easily as if they'd been aboard one of those stink-pot, steam boats he hated so.

Smiling now, and looking toward the docks, Alex could make out Sammy's familiar, jerky, body motions moving among the fading shadows. The man was using a boat hook to pole a borrowed skiff out between the floating ice cakes.

The captain's smile widened. He should have known somebody would be keeping their eye on any activity out here. Thinking pleasant thoughts now, Alex guessed it was that old, cracked spyglass he'd given Sammy a few years back. A treasured gift coming home to thank him.

Speaking to the comatose Andy, he remarked, "You're a lucky boy, you know? Between your dog's bright idea of floating the Brant on an ice cake, and Sammy's ever watchful eye, it shows how much they care! Yep, I'd feel pretty safe if I was you. Sure brings home the fact they ain't never gonna let much happen to you if it's within their earthly power to prevent it!" A curious feeling. One that Alex, suddenly, became uncomfortably aware of sharing.

The man slammed this gate shut as soon as it broke his plane of thought. It irritated him that he was unable to control these feelings. The spark of anger returned, dragging along an even blacker cloud, and his mind churned on. *"I don't need human ties, or at least those that are this close! Don't want them for that matter!"*

Un-asked for, the rationale behind this reasoning thundered in right behind the other thoughts. *"They hurt too much when they end. . . ."*

Grounding the ice cake in the shallows where they met, Alex explained to a worried Sammy what had happened. The two men stripped and cut Andy's clothes off of him carefully, right there on the ice, then pulled his shoulder back into place while he was still unconscious. This produced an enormous groan from the boy.

Giving their spirits a mixed lift, the young man woke with a torrent of complaints about the agonizing pain. Never skipping a beat to sympathize, the two of them bound the arm to his scrawny body with what was left of his shirt.

Sammy stripped his own rough-wool shirt-jacket off, and covered the boy's shivering frame. Alex's clothing wouldn't have helped if offered. Soaking wet, the man was beginning to ice over from the cold himself.

Across the boat basin, a small group of men had gathered on the end of the pier to observe. After Sammy poled the skiff over to where they waited, these gentlemen aided the two men in getting the boy topside. Then they helped bundle him up, lay him in a borrowed wagon, and covered him completely with a canvas tarp to help trap what little body heat he had left.

"Understand you've got a guest at your place, Cap'n." one of the men informed Alex.

"Came in on the afternoon train, then had to hire a carriage to take him to where Mrs. Sears was staying, 'cause he didn't know the way himself!" another added, stating this last as more of a question than fact.

Damned, meddlesome gossips! Alex thought, as he wondered whom could be calling on Sarah unannounced.

Snapping the reins to get the horse moving, he realized there could only be one answer. This in turn stimulated another burst of anger, and he could feel his neck and cheeks flush.

Cursing under his breath, the man squeezed water out of a sweater cuff with his free hand, and shivered. Immediate creature needs having been brought to mind, the captain passed the reins to Abel, the boy who was going to return the wagon to the wharf. Cupping his hands, he blew heat into their puffy, wet, redness, and knew chilblains were a certainty tonight.

Already in some pain, the captain could not still his mind. It gave silent voice to feelings never considered until now. *Will these family crises never end? A man could drown just traveling from crest to crest on waves such as these!*

Chapter 16

The Uninvited Guest

Alex cradled his shotgun in one arm, while he helped Sarah get Andy out of the wagon with the other. In the midst of this, he vented the pressure which had been building all the way home. "Albert Antonelli? Who in hell invited that scum to Cape Cod? Don't we have enough low-life of our own around here? Christ, this is as bad as coming home to a skunk under the outhouse.

My God Sarah, I'd have thought you had more sense than that!"

The man looked towards the door. "I will not have the likes of him under my roof!

Get out of my way woman, I intend to tell that dastardly creature to vacate these premises immediately!" The captain had a premonition about whom to expect when he'd left the wharf.

This bluster was exactly the way Sarah was sure the man would react to this particular guest upon his arrival. The fact that Alex seemed to know someone was here long before he got home himself puzzled her some, but what she really hadn't expected was the manner in which her men had returned.

Sarah met them in the driveway, standing there bare-headed and without a coat, just the way she'd run from the house. Entangled in her apron, the woman's hands were clasped together, pressing the cloth against her mouth to hold in a building scream of anguish.

All she'd known was that Andy had left her a barely legible note. Obviously written in a hurry, it said they were going hunting, with no time of departure, no destination, no time of return.

Worriedly looking out the darkened window a few minutes ago, she'd barely made out her ice-covered brother arriving home from God knows where.

Being driven to his door in a strange wagon, filled her with apprehension enough, but then to spot her son's apparently dead body, wrapped-up and stretched out on the wagon-bed under a tarp fulfilled the nightmare that haunts and terrifies every mother.

Her relief upon seeing Andy sit up when the wagon creaked to a stop, was totally overwhelming. The woman was so engrossed with her son's well-being she wasn't even conscious of the others around her, let alone that she'd blurted out Albert's name in response to her brother's surly inquiry.

Torn between tears of relief; anger at Alex's accusing insinuations; and the fright that these idiots had instilled in her; Sarah had trouble settling her feelings and thoughts onto any certain course. "No! Alex, wait! I told him you'd be upset . . . and myself too!"

Muddling through barely restrained emotions to her main focus, she sputtered, "What happened to you two? Where have you been?"

Putting her arms carefully around Andy, she held his cold, wet, disheveled form against her bosom. This led to the discovery of strange lumps under what was obviously Sam's smelly shirt. Exploring the bindings around her son's chest, she found they were keeping his arm immobile. Leaning against the wagon to help support Andy's weight she looked toward Alex, questioningly.

Her own anger beginning to flash now, the corners of her mouth tightened as she thought, *For your own sake, this had best not be just another of your, 'down to the shore!' blankets, my Captain!*

The very idea that her brother might have been careless enough to let something happen to this boy shook the woman to her foundations. Questioning her own judgment as well, she realized continued trust in this man had to be stupid when at every turn he showed how completely undependable he could be.

Still on the wagon, Ulysses took advantage of his new-found height. Even though he knew all the answers, the dog stuck his big, black, wet nose in Andy's ear to show his concern.

Alex, annoyed and scowling at the delay of his eagerly anticipated confrontation with a certain labeled scoundrel, turned back to her. The quick intensity of the movement displayed his animosity. Reacting, she took a step backwards as he began to spout off. "That damned-fool son of yours wasn't content to shoot half the Brant on the Yarmouth flats with one shot! No, no, he had to pull the trigger a second time and knock the three of us ass-over-teakettle into the drink! Then he had the nerve to compound this insult by feigning injury so he wouldn't have to lug his share of the load home!"

With that tongue-in-cheek explanation, he turned again and stomped toward the house. Ice, flaking off his garments like last November's leaves in a wind storm, crunched to the ground with every violent step.

Sarah glanced at the boy who had driven her menfolk home. To her relief, the grin on his face confirmed that it wasn't just to her ears, Alex's colorful response had sounded more humorous than angry. Apparently, the man's ferocious, physical appearance and noise had been just that, noise.

Nodding to the boy, she said, "Thank you for bringing the boys home, Abel!"

Without question, it was stated as a dismissal.

The boy, through no fault of his own, had been trapped in the middle of a family squabble. Discovered at his eaves-dropping, Abel responded with immediate industry. The young man nodded his head in reply to Sarah, shook the reins and clucked to the horse, all in one motion. Turning the wagon around in the confines of their drive was time consuming. The boy kicked at a clod of mud frozen to the offside wheel, which gave him an added excuse to dally, and hide his still red cheeks over the embarrassment of being caught.

Even to Sarah's eye, it was apparent the fellow was being quite slow and deliberate about his maneuvering.

The boy wouldn't tell her of course, but Abel had his reasons for delay. After all, he didn't want to miss what might precipitate from the captain's dramatic entry into the house, carrying that shotgun.

Albert hadn't gotten the label of 'slippery' by standing still. Having watched and listened to the commotion in the yard through the open door Sarah had burst out of in her haste, he was ready and waiting for Alex's entrance. "Captain Matthews! My dear Sarah's benefactor, and a personage I'd like to consider my own very good friend!"

It was a high-pitched, nasal voice. Along with the man's unfortunate intonation, the sound came out carrying the quality of a dog's whine. Alex had expected no less.

The little man stood there, arms spread half-wide and hands even with his shoulders in a surrender type posture. Then curling these appendages inward, spider-like, he clasped his hands together and wrung them a couple of times, making Alex think of a miser counting his money. Finally, the creature thrust one grubby paw forward to shake hands, and announced, "How fortunate we are! I was hoping you'd return before I moved on to my lodgings. After hearing about you and your grand exploits for so many years, I have been eager to meet the man who commands such fame, wealth, and stature."

Met with this pompous bombast of noise and flattery, Alex never even flared a nostril while he waited for his eyes to adjust to the gloom of the darkening room. Effectively blocking the door, he wondered about the 'We' this worm had referred to. Sarah hadn't mentioned any other guests, and Alex certainly didn't consider himself among the fortunate today. Ignoring the extended gesture of greeting, the captain stared at this outlandish apparition who, uninvited, had invaded his kitchen.

There stood a scrawny, little fellow, attached to a pot belly so large and grotesque it could have filled a bushel basket. He was wearing a green and white, striped shirt. A dirty, stained collar, red suspenders, and a string-tie that may at one time have been a red ribbon, made up the accessories. Thin, greasy hair parted in the middle echoed an enormous, handlebar mustache. The mustache itself was complimented by a very pointy nose which cantilevered over it like the prow of a ship.

Protruding, cleft, gold-capped teeth coated with enough green scum around the edges to carry out the color scheme, provided the basic foundation which held all the rest off the man's shoulders. There was no chin.

"A damned rat!", was Alex's immediate thought. He shuddered visibly. Not in fear, but a minor reaction to the attempt to control his self-induced rage, and rekindled memories.

His mind's eye pictured the poor Chinese in Canton's anchorage. Starving, they scavenged the dead roaches and rats thrown overboard after every ship was fumigated. A harvest he still had problems accepting. This specimen in front of him would make a meal large enough to feed a hundred of those skinny coolies, with some left over for lunch the next day.

As the extended hand wilted under the Captain's glare, Albert instinctively kept one nervous eye on the relative brightness from the open doorway which peeked around the bulky figure blocking it. Not expecting to be trapped like this, the fellow seemed to be developing a seizure of fidgets. His babbling monologue became choppier, and he coughed and cleared his throat repeatedly.

Shifting from foot to foot, the poor man's darting eyes kept coming back to that teasing glimpse of daylight, but there was no way they'd dare rest on that fierce continence barring his way.

Panic was setting in. He began to dwell on his chances of keeping this threatening hulk off balance and distracted until Sarah came back to save him. Seeking other baskets to put some of his eggs in, the man furtively sought out avenues of escape should flight become the only alternative.

Wiping cold sweat from his forehead, he whined, "Sarah wanted me to stay with you kind people! Said she'd have the kids double-up, to make room!

Well, much as I know she'd like me to, I told her it was out of the question. At my insistence, she sent word down to some friends of hers who might have space available. The Crowells? I'm sure you must know them! She told them she had a personal friend she needed lodgings for. . . ."

Now Albert was visibly squirming under the heat of Alex's silent, barely-controlled intensity. "So, I'll be on my way as soon as she gets back in here and tells me where this place is. You couldn't tell me could you, friend?"

Still getting nothing in return, the man tried a different approach. "Say, are you soaking wet, or is that ice just on the outside? Where's your whiskey, my good fellow? I'll get it for you, and maybe we can share a dab or two while you thaw out."

With only silence to respond to, the man was becoming apoplectic. He croaked out a weak little, "Sarah?"

Sarah and Andy came through the still-open doorway just as Alex, in all his stuffy, puritanical, self-righteous glory, pulled himself up a little taller and expanded his shoulders and chest. You could even hear the man getting larger.

The noise as he inhaled, long, drawn-out, and ominous, sounded like the tell-tale hiss a falling topmast-spar or boom might make in that last instant, just before it hit the deck. In turn, this brought to mind the thought that something of this nature would crush anything which might be unfortunate enough to lay beneath it.

Then, as Andy watched, Alex unobtrusively stuck his elbows out a little further and widened his stance. This visibly increased his already-sizable bulk one more notch. Still a little dazed, but standing in the doorway, Andy couldn't help thinking, in a manner surprisingly objective for him that this uncle of his looked like an oversized, Bantam rooster. One who had just been challenged by a new arrival in his own hen yard.

Still in complete character, Alex cleared his throat loudly to assure all attention was focused where he wanted it, and finally broke his menacing silence. "Don't drink whiskey! As for you, you're not anyone's 'friend' around here! And lastly, by the time I get back from changin' m'clothes, not only will you be gone, but I do not expect to find a single trace of your ever having been in this house!"

The captain had exploded in his typically loud, intimidating, vintage-Alex gruffness. While the shock-wave from this eruption was in the process of expanding, he added impetus to it by his next action. Throwing his body around violently, the man pointed it at the dining room door like a cannon, and stomped noisily out of the room.

Ice flew from his clothes, and Sarah's china rattled on the sideboard to the beat of every step.

The shotgun he'd carried was never intended as a threat by Alex. He had no need for something that minuscule.

Albert had staggered backward from the force of Alex's outburst. Now flailing his arms like a drowning man grasping for support, the man fumbled for the greasy derby and topcoat shed on his way in. Grabbing these and the carpetbag left by the door, he bolted from the house in a good imitation of a lover being pursued by a jealous husband. His one-time-white spats got splattered by yet another layer of mud from the freezing puddles in his haste.

"Boy, waitup!" Spotting the loitering Abel's wagon as a vehicle of salvation, his utterings became a squeal. "Haeey, boy! Heyboy, gimme-a-lift, willya?"

Saved, he turned slightly and shouted back to Sarah in that same, high-pitched, nasal twang. "Sarah, I'll send word, and maybe we can meet for . . . tea!"

Sarah waved from the door, and then began to laugh.

Hurrying along, Albert had been struggling into his coat at the same time he was yelling his parting words. Too busy to watch where he was going, the man tripped over an equally surprised Ulysses. Not weighing much more than the dog, he became airborne, and flew headfirst into a pile of snow freshly shoveled from the path.

Albert never missed a beat, apparently feeling it was all forward motion. Picking himself up, he hustled onto the wagon without so much as a pause to brush the cold wetness from his clothing.

Closing the door, Sarah could still hear his demanding tenor. "Let's go, Boy! Ya do know where the Crowells live, don'cha?"

The poor, unfortunate creature might have been less eager had he known what Sarah had forewarned in the note sent down to her dear friends. More than a request for lodging, it was a plea for help, and related her intense dislike of this fellow. She mentioned the man's complete lack of moral principles as a reason, and she also expressed concern about the possibility of his presence in the village becoming an embarrassment to all.

The Crowells, understanding full well her implications, prepared a memorable welcome for their guest. One guaranteed to be far stranger than anything he could have ever imagined or anticipated.

Warmer and dryer, Alex returned to the kitchen at about the same time the rest of the family was settling down around the black iron, cook stove. Waiting for it to heat extra water for a warming, therapeutic bath, Andy was disputing this remedy's worth rather vehemently.

He'd mellowed out some, but the captain's mood was still a little sharp. He took to rummaging around in his pantry, and came up with a bottle of rum. Declaring this to be more dear to a seaman's heart than any whiskey could ever be, he poured out a generous, medicinal measure for his wide-eyed nephew, and another for himself. "Proportioned," as he explained, "based on age and body weight."

Triggered by his first swig of the potent nectar, Andy shuddered violently.

After smiling to himself over the boy's reaction, Alex began to ask some rather pointed questions. He learned from Sarah that Albert had arrived uninvited, and she had no knowledge of how he'd found them. She also added, from what their unwelcome guest had insinuated, she thought he might even be fleeing the authorities.

Feeling a touch of guilt, Sarah explained to Alex what she'd passed on to Prudence and Elijah.

At this her brother grumped how she should have left their friends out of family matters, and sent the scum to the Yarmouth Inn instead.

Her retort carried a valid explanation. She claimed to know this gutter-rat well enough that if she'd done as Alex proposed, the man would have spent the night in the ordinary, drinking and talking to one and all. By morning, everyone in the village would think he was practically a member of the family. Sarah ended with, "What do you think that would do for the Matthews and Sears family reputations in this town? We'd be lucky not to get tarred, feathered, and run out on a rail!"

Amy, upset that she'd missed all the excitement because she'd been at a friend's house, was trying to ask as many questions as Alex. He was about to silence her when she asked Andy, "Did you ever send that letter to your friend, Jessie? The one you fought about with Mother, the night she told us we were leaving?"

The girl turned to her uncle and announced, "Mother didn't want anyone to know where we'd gone, because she owed a lot of money!"

Alex, taken aback by this piece of news, wondered what other secrets they might have brought in their baggage. "Sarah, Is this true?"

Flustered for a moment, his sister threw a black look Amy's way, then heaved a disturbed sigh. "Yes, partly! At the time we did owe a few people, but the reason we left had more to do with the situation and Albert, than any monetary considerations. Since that time, Jonathan's check has come from the government, by way of Rose, but I'm sure she'd never tell Albert where we'd gone. Granted, he is her brother, but she understood the man and his ways!

"You're talking about the compensation check for Jonathan's war injuries, I presume?" Alex had his pipe out, and was engrossed in one of his perpetual attempts to light the thing.

"Jonathan received eight dollars a month, twice a year, for the wounds he received in battle. As his widow, I am blessed with half the amount to raise his children on, and at that we are more fortunate than most. My debtors were aware of this, and it was against this fund they would allow credit. I have now sent a change of address to the proper authorities, so Rose should never again have to be involved toward my benefit.

I assure you, with the exception of what I owe you, my brother, our debts in this world are now paid in full!" This statement was directed to her daughter as much as Alex.

Enshrouded by a cloud of smoke, Alex grumbled, "Good thing! Your worries about what Albert could do for your reputation ain't got nothin' on what debtor's prison would wreak!"

"Mis-ter Sears!" Alex's enunciation was deliberately distinct. "Considering your obvious silence, would you care to contribute any cerebral theories as to how Mr. Antonelli might have come across your wake?"

Distracted by pain, Andy had no fight left in him. He confessed that he'd left a note in the door for his friend, and the only address he'd known to give for mailing purposes was in care of Captain Alexander Matthews, Yarmouth Port.

It was obvious to all that someone else had found the letter first. Alex felt relieved. Certain now that no one had invited this disgusting leech to the Cape—for God knows what purpose—the trust placed in his new family had been re-affirmed.

Now all they had to do was get rid of this intruder quickly, before his sordid past made enough ripples to draw attention.

Chapter 17

Madhouse

Albert climbed down off the wagon, still looking over his shoulder in the gathering darkness. This was more out of habit than anticipated pursuit, or fear of Alex. Flipping the boy a copper ha'penny, he grabbed his bag and headed for the Crowells' door.

Abel sat there looking at the worn coin in his hand with disappointment. He'd expected at least a nickel after listening to this braggart for the fifteen or twenty minutes it had taken to travel the long mile.

He asked Albert's retreating form if he could spare it.

Spinning in mid-stride, Albert took out his earlier humiliations on the innocent lad. In a rather colorful tirade, he screamed that the boy was lucky he'd been paid anything, and should probably have been whipped instead.

It wasn't often Albert found an individual of lesser physical attributes than his own. Taking advantage of the present opportunity, he ranted on about how the horse was so slow and the wagon in such a state of disrepair, he was ashamed he'd had to ride in it. The man added that his backside would probably ache for a week because the boy, in his inexperience, had hit so many bumps.

To Abel's ear, this loudmouth's choice of nouns and adjectives would have made a seaman blush. The boy decided he could get that kind of an education anytime, and left with a few choice words of his own, muttered at the part of the horse to which he was comparing his passenger.

Albert barely brushed the door with his knuckles when it flew open. The suddenness caused him to jump back, as much in fear of getting hit as reaction to the unexpected. Still a little worked up over his encounter with Abel, the incident probably added to his normal skittishness and saved his shins from getting barked.

The man was drawn in to the relatively bright light of the parlor's kerosene lamps. There, grasping, grouping, eager hands took his money for the night's room and board, submitted a blank ledger for his signature, and relieved him of his hat and coat. A short tug of war ensued over the bag, but the guest would not release his grip on this.

Under a torrent of words expressing flattery, welcome and introduction, the man was floated in to a formal, candle-lit, dining room. Albert, sensitive to such matters, got the uneasy feeling he might not be in the right house. This was no pub and lodgings! *Could Sarah's message have told these people to expect royalty of some sort?*

Yessir! Good girl, that Sarah!

Seated at the head of the table while being waited upon, coddled, and fawned over by these people, he began to realize the gentleman of the house was having a problem keeping his hands to himself. Flaunting his effeminate mannerisms, the host seemed to be conveying the message that he was quite taken with Albert's physical attributes.

This suggestion came as quite a surprise to Albert, for he knew few found him attractive. Admitting to some rather strange and prurient tastes for women, such a liaison as this had never occurred to the man. For some reason, the mere thought struck him as not only threatening, but terrifying.

On guard once more, his eyes flitted over to the woman. She seemed oddly dressed to be the proprietor of a lodging house. Her shoes didn't match for one thing. Studying her in the gloom, he could make out three, separate, entirely different aprons, everyone of which appeared soiled beyond mere kitchen work.

Then there was the matter of her hair. Long, straight, but tangled and graying, it hung down to hide her face completely. The occasional flash of an eye could be seen, but nothing else.

He became aware of a noise. Coming from the woman, it was most bothersome. An incessant humming and giggling, the sound went on, and on, and on. . . .

Scurrying around like a roach, the woman served him plates of food. Apparently meat, buried under heavy, brown gravy. A loaf of bread, possibly rye, or oatmeal from its mottled look under the suppressed light of his single candle. Cheese, and a glass of amber wine to complete the offerings. Giggling again, she scuttled back to the doorway of her kitchen.

Still standing by the table, Elijah explained apologetically that his poor sister wasn't quite right, but that Albert needn't worry. He went on to suggest, "In fact, it might be better if you pay her no heed at all. It seems the last time she took a strong liking to someone, they found it impossible to rid themselves of her.

I finally had to lock the poor soul in her room until they'd left. If she'd followed them off into the night, who knows what mischief might have been wrought to one or the other?"

Albert shot a nervous glance in the general direction of where the woman stood. "Why do you let her hang around where the guests can see her? Keep the slut away from me, I got no time for coo-coos! Be a good idea to chain her in the cellar anyway, if she's not safe to the public!"

Elijah bit the anger from his tongue, and maintaining his usual habit of relating everything to his religion, phrased a prophecy. "The good Lord will take care of all of us in His own way, and at a pace that suits His own stride, I might add."

The inflection of this statement seemed to imply more than the words literal aversion to Prudence, but it was too subtle for Albert. The man wasted little effort on things that were not within his physical grasp.

Suddenly aware of how close Elijah was standing, he brushed the man's hand off of his shoulder, and exploded into a tirade of expletives straight from the gutter. Completely oblivious to the presence of a woman, or more likely, insensitive and uncaring, his litany was unique enough to have been poetry were it in a more appropriate form.

As he expressed his opinion of these strange innkeepers, the man's voice rose in volume, becoming a full-blown squeal. Neighbors came to their windows to ascertain the location of this animal in torment, and dogs started barking.

Simply put, the thrust of Albert's main complaint was for Elijah to keep his fondling hands to himself, and that he had no interest in a tryst of this nature. Next, he suggested 'the Woman' had best be locked up, or he'd take a cane to her head, and finish what Elijah's 'Lord' obviously had no stomach for.

Prudence had been standing there with her hands over her ears, to no avail. After this offensive outburst, a fire burned from eyes that seldom expressed anger. Emotionally involved, her part in this charade would be played with much more insight and vigor now.

Glancing her way, Albert noticed a tongue sticking out through the hair. Bemused, he watched the childlike woman place her thumbs in her ears, then proceed to wave her fingers at him. This was a challenge. Picking up the little braided chair-pad from his seat, Albert heaved it in her general direction, accompanied by an extra curse word or two.

This action forced Prudence to duck back into the kitchen. Smiling at the insults she'd pulled off, it ran through her mind that a barmaid could probably expect better treatment, then blushed at the absurdity of comparing herself to one of such low character.

Not having eaten all day, Albert could wait no longer. He grabbed the utensils and dove into the food, albeit keeping one eye on the doorway.

Prudence re-appeared. Standing in the opening, she swayed from side-to-side to the rhythm of her own tuneless hum. Wearing a stupid grin on her face, the woman watched him intently. Her constant giggles and mumblings were as bothersome as ever, becoming audible hiccups in the song.

Unnerved, Albert whined, "For Christ's sake, get her out of here! Don't like to be watched while I eat! And, God damn-it, don't you stand so close to me neither! Already told you I ain't interested in your kind! Get on back to the kitchen, the two of you, and I'll call if I need somethin' else!"

Ignoring him, Elijah leered back, "The lady of the house just wants to see if you like what she's prepared for your dinner, Sir. After you've made your peace with God, and thanked Him for your repast, she'll wait out the first bite or two, then depart.

No Sir, no need for thanks, take my word for it! Your reaction is the reward she seeks!"

Between the first few, huge bites shoveled in, sans the grace Elijah suggested, Albert managed to spray a few words out. "She made this slop?"

Not trusting his voice at the moment, Elijah, smiling widely, nodded in response.

"Better not be poisoned, or I'll sue you for every cent you've got!"

This exchange must have triggered a second thought in what served Albert for a mind. Suddenly it occurred to the man it might not be a bad idea if he tasted that which was being devoured whole. This considered, he paused to chew the next fork-full.

It had taken Prudence and Elijah an hour just to round up the hot spices and peppers available in the neighborhood. These contributions, mixed mischievously with castor-oil and molasses, made a beautiful, hot, brown gravy. Poured over rancid slabs of lamb fat from the tallow barrel, it hid their foulness long enough for the victim to swallow a number of bites.

"Ptahh!" Spitting the current mouthful out forcibly, Albert shoved a fist-sized chunk of bread into the ugly hole. The intent was logical. He wanted to soak up the fiery grease now coating his mouth.

In due course, it dawned on the man that he might have made a second mistake. That portion of the bread remaining in his hand moved with a life of its own. Crawling with weevils, it could have walked to the table unassisted.

This mouthful followed the entree back onto the table after which a mad grab for the glass of wine produced its own spray. Pure vinegar, the acid willingly mixed with the rest of the half-chewed mess while a strangled scream issued from Albert.

Finally catching his breath, a long string of expletives supported the words, "You're trying to kill me! I'm sending for the Constable! You're both crazy! I'll not stay the night in this madhouse with the likes of you!"

Elijah trailed him into the kitchen where the man's search for drinking water—to put out his internal volcano—had led him.

The first thing Albert found on the other side of that doorway was a wet mop. Hitting him in the face, it was followed immediately by a startling scream. The mad-woman began flailing at him with this weapon, all the while shouting, "Unclean! Unclean!"

In the fashion of upper-caste children from India chasing beggars for sport, she drove him right on through the kitchen, and out into the freezing snow.

Still following the poor, bewildered, and now battered creature, Elijah had thoughtfully brought along the man's hat, coat and bag. Displaying a degree of willpower beyond anything he thought himself capable of, the Innkeeper begged Albert's forgiveness. He explained that Prudence had a taste for spicy food, and had perhaps overdone it a touch. The wine, he suggested, had merely spoiled, probably from a poorly sized cork.

What he neglected to mention was the castor oil, which Elijah figured Albert should have gotten a very healthy dose of in the first two or three bites he'd swallowed. A matter that should come back to haunt their guest as surely as the sun follows the moon.

Helping Albert on with his coat, he pawed and patted ostensibly at the wrinkles, which made Albert dance away from him again.

Asking the Lord's forgiveness under his breath for this night's work, Elijah suggested that the man wait a moment or two, and he'd hitch up his horse and take him down to the old Yarmouth Inn for the night. There Albert could meet the relatives, this place just being an overflow of their family business. An out and out lie for which Elijah promised penance later, it did the trick.

Albert, completely confused now, waved in negative protest. He wanted nothing more to do with this lot.

The last Elijah saw of the poor fellow, he was stuffing snow in his mouth as he disappeared into the night, and cursing the circumstances which had driven him to this God forsaken armpit of the world.

Never a scholar, Albert's mindpicture actually had it located a little further south.

Elijah and Prudence were so delighted with their handiwork, they immediately dressed for the cold night and did indeed hitch up their wagon. Keeping a weather-eye out for their 'guest', they set a course for the Matthews' residence.

Upon arrival, the two of them related and pantomimed their night's activities. Regaling in the laughter, praise, and applause of their dear, indebted friends the Crowells felt well rewarded.

Albert, it was later determined, must have headed straight back to the depot. There, he hoped to catch a train to anywhere, as long as it was away from this asylum.

It must have done wonders for his consternation when he heard one leaving as he neared the station. Once inside, the man discovered a couple of heavy set, no-neck type gentlemen waiting there. They had obviously just gotten off the now departed train. Chomping on cheap cigars, they were asking the agent if this was the stop that had responded to their telegraphed inquiry.

Keeping out of sight while he listened, to Albert it sounded like they were seeking a person matching his own description. Someone who had ridden in on the afternoon train.

Flashing Railroad Detective Agency badges, the two said the man they were looking for was wanted for questioning concerning a robbery at the train station in Attleboro. According to witnesses, the man performed his dirty deed while a train discharged and re-boarded passengers. In the confusion, he'd been able to leap on the moving train as it pulled out of the station. This happened to be the afternoon train to the Cape.

Enough heard, their presence sent the terrified city-rat flying back into the cold night air again. Tripping over a spittoon on his way out, he now had the commotion-alerted, intense gentlemen in hot pursuit. Shouts of, "Stop! Police! Halt or I'll shoot!" did little to retard the pursued one's progress.

Albert probably theorized that, in the dark, those fat fools couldn't hit a barn door with a shovel, let alone a running man.

A few trail markers were left, showing his general direction and the haste with which he'd fled. The man's well-greased derby lay about three steps down Central Street, toward the wharves. Next came a glove, and then another. His bag was the last, and the detectives theorized this to be intentional, possibly abandoned to lighten his load. Especially since it was found out on the end of the fisherman's wharf. Surmising their fugitive may have stolen a skiff to make his getaway, they thought it more likely the man would be trying to save his skin instead of worrying about worldly possessions.

The gentlemen poked around some, but gave up after a short-while, figuring dawn would provide more of an advantage than any number of hours in the dark. Besides, after opening the bag, they realized they had their money back.

They laughed and joked about the rabbit sitting out there in the cold marshes. He'd be listening, and trying to elude non-existent pursuit, while they got a good night's sleep under their belts. It was only logical that a fresh start in the morning, with the sun to see by—along with whatever local folk they could round up to help—should produce results, and they'd most likely be home for supper.

Confident about this reasoning, the men bedded down on the hard, wooden benches of the depot to guard the only fast and relatively untraceable way out of town.

Early the next morning, about daybreak, a gentleman inadvertently woke them when he came in to ask the station agent to telegraph the Sheriff up in Barnstable.

It seems that a body had been found floating next to the fish wharf.

"Apparently a city slicker, from the way he was dressed!" The man said in response to questions from the detectives. "Definitely a stranger anyway! Not knowing the lay of the land, he evidently took a long walk on the wrong pier. This one being only a hundred feet long, while next to it, Central Wharf is over a thousand." It may have been early, but the ghoulish humor produced a few guffaws.

A scurrilous event of this magnitude didn't take long to spread. It even rivaled some of the scandalous stories in Alex's Police Gazette magazines. Periodicals Alex had thought well hidden, until Andy stumbled over them while helping his mother move the attic trunk.

This was another little episode which had tickled Sarah at the time, although she'd kept her mirth private. To think that her holier-than-thou brother was mortal after all. . . . *Sketches of barely clothed women, and the language of the street! Where does he get off, telling us how we should behave in his little kingdom?*

Humbled and chagrined by the discovery, Alex convinced himself how that incident had produced as much, or possibly more, embarrassment to the principles involved—mainly himself—as this mess did now.

Considering which side of that particular issue he was on, he may have been right.

Chapter 18

One of These Days

Sammy carried the news of Albert's demise when he came to the house that morning. The excuse for the visit, to bring Andy his Brant—all plucked and dressed for the oven—but everyone knew the real reason was to check on the status of his boy's health.

After seeing Albert through eyes that had taken on new values, thoughts of him did not linger long, nor was he mourned by any of the Sears family. Sarah did write her good friend Rose, to inform the woman of the details surrounding her brother's loss, but that completed any and all moral obligations felt.

Unimpressed with the village hubbub and excitement over the death of a robber, the 'Great Hunter' was not a very happy boy that morning. Having discovered the only position which offered him any relief at all was sitting up, Andy had spent a night of agony in a chair padded with horsehair. Blankets provided plenty of warmth, and his mother sleeping nearby gave him comfort, but every time the boy dozed and his head slipped, or he sagged to one side, a fiery pain brought him bolt-upright again and wet with perspiration.

By morning, his shoulder had stiffened up so badly it even hurt to move his fingers. Temporarily, neither duck or goose hunting held much interest for him, let alone food. His attitude did not improve much as the day wore on, and then as if to annoy him even further, the Brant tasted delicious. A day this black was indeed a rare occurrence.

Fortunately for his family, injuries heal quite rapidly in the young. Within a matter of a week or two he'd cast off his sling, and resumed his normal position at the center of the universe.

A flurry of gossip spun through the village following the city-slicker episode. It seemed everyone knew this man had paid a visit to Sarah, at the Matthew's residence, before moving on to the Crowells. Abel himself vouched for that fact, having transferred the gentleman between the two homes personally. Of course, when the Sheriff arrived to investigate, his visits to the homes of these principals added further grist to the mill.

Much prodding and prying went on, but other than false rumors about the possibility of the death being less than accidental, it remained a mystery. Nothing official was ever made public, nor any charges filed. Fortunately, with the advent and preparation for the spring sailing and planting seasons upon them, people had precious little time to waste on such nonsense anyway. Much to Alex's relief, they soon lost interest, and the whole thing faded away like just another winter sunset.

Being frugal in nature, the captain preferred to do his own ship related repairs. The man's espoused reasoning was that he saw no advantage in paying out good money for things he could do better himself. Especially with the safety of his vessel on the line, and considering shipyard flunkies had nothing to lose in the venture.

Other opinions held that it was a labor of love, and the truth lay closer to the fact he just didn't want anyone else touching the one thing he held most dear.

Whatever the reason, Alex hired the Hallet boys to help, and they began the refurbishing process, which included all of the *Yarmouth's* standing and running gear. It was a little early to think about launching the old girl, so on good days—with the schooner still high and dry on her blocking—the men refastened planking, caulked seams, and painted her inside and out.

Preperations for a new season

On rainy days, when Andy joined them after school, Alex's barn floor and the half-empty hay loft were strewn with assorted ropes, cordage, lines, blocks and pulleys. The captain made sure each and every piece was tested, and if found wanting in either condition or apparent strength, repaired or replaced.

Eschewing sail lofts for the same reason he avoided shipyards, these mountains of canvas were also spread out, patches sewn on, grommets replaced, and points of strain reinforced.

Working alongside, Andy learned his sailing nomenclature from three ardent teachers. By the time the season got under way, he could rattle off the name of any sail in a square-rigged clipper's sixty-three, to the simple gaff-rigged cat's single rag. The cordage gave him more problems, as he couldn't quite grasp the need for so many names for ropes, when basically they all did the same thing. But, he struggled on, from the painter—for holding a ship's dingy close—to a fore-top halyard used to haul a sail aloft. More names, such as mast stays, dead-eyes, gang-blocks, chafing gear, boom-throats, came at him. And knots! So many, it was hard to believe such things even existed. He went to sleep many nights dreaming he was buried under coils of naphtha-smelling, twisted hemp, and sun-bleached sail cloth, only to wake tangled in blankets and pillows, with the odor from his own tar-stained hands adding a mental fog to blur the reality of his bed.

Alex returned from his first of March visit to Boston, and seemed in a chipper mood for days. One afternoon Sarah even caught him humming.

To a woman this meant but one thing, and answered many nagging questions. *It would appear the Captain must have himself a lady-friend!* Chuckling at the discovery, she murmured, "One of these days, Captain Matthews, I suspect this information will come home to rest. Yes Sir, just like having money in the bank!"

Startling the man, Sarah hummed an accompaniment to his tune.

Chapter 19

A Member of the Crew

The afternoon of March thirteenth was anything but pleasant. It started with a freshening, easterly breeze and a falling barometer. The temperature, hovering in the low thirties, made it feel raw and blustery. A lowering blanket of gray clouds painted their depressing color on the moods of every living creature. Even the chipper chic-a-dees stopped tending the feeder, preferring the shelter offered by deep woods over free food.

Alex had launched the *Yarmouth,* and had just finished her standing rigging. Eyeing the weather, he doubled up on his mooring lines as a precaution, the old ones having survived a whole, previous season and getting tired.

Much to the Captain's pleasure, Andy was becoming more aware of the world around him. When he came home from school that afternoon, the boy remarked to his uncle about another nor'easter coming in. Alex confirmed the forecast, then the two of them stood in front of the ship's barometer hanging on the wall, as if by watching they could see the mercury fall.

The older man informed his student that when a storm started to build-in at this time of day it was apt to be a bad one, and suggested that Andy'd better bring in another load of wood before dark.

The wind continued to rise throughout the night, and from time to time an extra strong blast would shake the house to its foundation. Between shrieking, window-rattling gusts, the boy could hear the hiss of snow on his window panes. Laying there in the secure warmth of his bed, Andy gave the storm the benefit of doubt by declaring it lonely, and suggested it kept waking him merely to keep it company. Understanding the feeling only too well, he listened to the sad, continuously-moaning sigh.

A wooden groan somewhere reminded him of Aunt Sophie. Alarmed, the boy scrambled to find another avenue for his thoughts. Concentrating, he wondered if this was what the wind would sound like in the *Yarmouth's* rigging. With that in mind, he fell into a troubled sleep of wave-tossed water, with himself climbing endless ratlines into a dark void of flapping sail-shards, and blowing snow above.

Tangled in his bedding once more, and exhausted, the boy clawed fretfully back to the conscious world. He gained nothing. Here he was drawn to his first evening on the Cape, and the storm which greeted their arrival. The sailors who died with the *Granite* because of it, and the heart-pounding wildness of that weather during their rescue attempt. From this it was a short hop to those who might be at sea in this current misery. He pictured the white, rime-coated rigging his uncle had told him about, and waves breaking green over the deck.

Somewhat puzzled, the boy felt pride in the realization of how he'd become aware of others who could be in danger. Most of them, perfect strangers.

Aside from his uncle's hauled-out schooner, he'd never actually set foot on a ship's deck, but he could feel a growing kinship with these rough men. Drawn like filings to a magnet, old and bent men retired from the sea, or those waiting for a berth, seemed to think the *Yarmouth* had been installed right where it was just to provide them with a place to congregate, smoke their pipes, and jam. Sitting in a sunny spot on deck, or in the main cabin when weather was foul, these men paid their rent by splicing rope or scraping paint, and even they'd admit it was as much for the companionship of like fellows as keeping idle hands busy. Pleasant to work around and listen to, the boy couldn't stay away.

Now, laying here and listening to the wind, he knew that some of those very men were out there somewhere, their ship plowing along in heavy seas, or laying-to under storm sail. Humbled by these new-found concerns, Andy graciously whispered the Seaman's Prayer for men he'd barely met, and others he'd never see. The Reverend Dodge usually worked it into his service, and Andy repeated it as best he could remember. Asking for fair winds, a sound ship, and safe passage, this time he fell into an easy sleep. His dreams now giving him the warmth of a summer sun splashing off bright, white sails, and underfoot, matching wave-caps of a marching sea.

Dawn did not break that morning. The sky got a shade or two lighter, but even that difference was subtle. Instead, the day's energies were being diverted and expended by a wildness beyond man's reasoning. A force of nature that left precious little for the human element within its grasp.

Starting out much like that fateful night in November, a banging crash at the kitchen door was followed by excited voices drifting up through the floor grates. Sammy's excited, chopped, unintelligible staccato, and Nathaniel Hallet's out of breath baritone wove themselves into Uncle Alex's deep rumble. The boy knew instinctively that something out of the ordinary was going on, but his bed felt too good after the restless night to bother investigating. What did threaten to tease him fully awake were the familiar breakfast smells from the kitchen below.

Suddenly aware that he'd heard the word 'wreck' Andy leaped out of bed. Straining to hear those disembodied voices clearly now, in case anything pertinent were said, the boy dressed hurriedly. His actions resembled the dance of an Indian dervish, as he threw on every warm thing he could find in the near dark, and bolted for the stairs.

On his way by, the boy blew a hole in the frost on the window pane and strained to see what the shore might have to offer. Not wanting to take the time to stop and really look, all he could make out in the faint light was a dark mass. It seemed to be way out in the edge of the surf delineating the bar. The surf-line confirmed his memory of the tide anyway, telling him it had to be an hour or so from dead low.

Surprisingly, the kitchen was all but deserted as Andy came thundering in. Only his uncle remained, huffing and puffing as he pulled on boots and foul-weather gear.

"Where's the wreck?" Andy's first words were quite predictable.

Without pausing to look up, Alex sat there and shook his head. He continued to methodically weatherproof his massive bulk while he grumped, "Don't think there'd be much use for you out there this morning, boy!"

"But, where is it?" Andy repeated the question, though now his voice carried a touch of disappointment.

Alex sighed. "On the outer bar again, only this time a little to the east'ard. She's breaking up pretty fast. Bodies and wreckage come ashore already."

"Do you know her?"

Alex knew that giving in to the questioning was a mistake, but couldn't resist the flattery implied in this one. "Knew of her! The boys told of one man, the Captain, who was still alive when they got to 'im. Managed to pass on some information 'fore he collapsed. Near's we can tell, she's the Provincetown schooner *Electric Light*, home-bound from Boston with five passengers and five crew.

Lost all her rigging but the foremast in the first squall yesterday. Anchors went by the way after a few hours. Been runnin' under storm-sails all night, jury rigged as best they could, and ran out of sea before they ran out of darkness. Guess they found the bar just afore first light."

Alex paused a moment, then decided he was too far into the story to stop now. "Worst part, is what Captain Victorine told the boys!"

Andy rose to the bait. "What? What'd he say?"

The older man sighed, as if this part was difficult to tell. "Hearing the roar of the surf, the captain knew they were bearing down on a lee shore. A lee shore in this wind and weather meaning almost certain death, the man took his young son into the rigging, and lashed him in where the fore-topmast was stepped. I assume he remembered the wreck of the English brig, Margaret in '52, off Eastham. Her cabin boy, John Fulcher, was 12 years old at the time. Someone tied him to the mast in a similar fashion. Boy ended up the only survivor, and still lives in Eastham. So today's gamble certainly took courage, but our Captain probably figured this was the only chance his boy would ever have too."

"Ya mean, he's still out there?"

"Hope so! Me an' the boys thought we'd try and get a dory out to the wreck, to see if we can save him, iffen it ain't too late already. Most likely dead of the cold an wet by now anyway!"

Excitement pushing his voice, Andy asked, "How come they're not launching the surf boat from the Neck station?"

Alex was about dressed to his satisfaction, and as he started to get up, paused. "Signals have been exchanged across the harbor between Central wharf and the station light. They say they can't see any signs of life from over there, but then, it's still too damned dark to see much at all.

They're out of use to us at the moment anyway. Wind's against the tide over there. Trying to run down the channel would put them up against waves bigger'n a circus tent, and a capsized boat would serve no one well. Once clear of that mess they'd have to skirt the bar, which is too far and too rough, sliding sideways with the breakers. They'd never be able to keep even a surf boat from swamping under those conditions. Low tide in a little while, so there's not enough water to float that heavy scow across the flats, but too deep to walk it un-manned in the waves.

The boys an' me were hopin' that just before low water there'll be enough tide held in by the wind to walk a dory out there on this side of the channel. Then, in the lee of the wreck, it'll just be a short pull to see what we shall see."

"What if there's not enough water to float the dory?" Some things never changed. Andy's questions were both pointed and endless.

Alex became a little impatient, which was the usual result of the young man's inquisitions. Plopping his hat down onto his head abruptly, the Captain puffed, "Damn it boy, I ain't got time to stand here and argue every point! Time and tide! You'll learn someday that time and tide'll wait for no man, Mister Sears. If we can't get out there, we can't do it, that's all! The boy's most likely dead by now anyway, and it would be unforgivable to lose others in an attempt to retrieve his body!"

They both knew he was more angry at the thought of failure, than at Andy.

After a winter spent in the man's company, the boy wasn't cowed by his uncle's bluster. The questions kept flowing from his tongue as quickly as they formed. "But what if he's 'not' dead? Can't wc use a skiff? That'd be light enough to carry over the flats, makin' the distance shorter, and therefore quicker. Leaving room for the boy, you and me could still make it out to the ship, if it ain't too rough in the lee!"

Alex, who had just gained the first of those many connecting doorways leading toward the barn, stopped in mid-stride. Turning back to his nephew, he pulled the just fastened chin-strap loose, and scratched his head under his sou'wester. Finally he spoke, but it was in a softer, more conciliatory tone. "Boy, you've just talked yourself into a place on this crew! I hope you ain't sorry for it. Getcha gear on, and meet us in the barn!"

Andy let out a "Whoop!" A cry which sounded naggingly a little too familiar to the departing Alex. This produced an angry flush. Continuing on his way, the man was left with the burning impression that he'd just been mocked, and as usual, the weight of his footsteps reflected the man's emotion.

Andy, for his part, never noticed what had escaped his own lips, nor the subtle change in his uncle's demeanor. He was too busy tearing into the closet's ditty box. Burrowing in, the boy pulled out and threw everything in his way onto the hall floor.

Sarah, awakened by the commotion, stomped grumpily into the room while Andy was putting the finishing touches on his own apparel. "Andrew? Just where do you think you're going at this ungodly hour? And what's all the noise? Your uncle must have had a hand in it, for I can't believe you'd make that much ruckus by yourself!"

Dancing from foot to foot, Andy was trying to pull rain pants up over his boots and didn't want to take the time to explain the whole thing to his mother. About all she got from him was that he and his uncle were on the way to a shipwreck, and to look out the back window of the upper hall. With that the boy grabbed a chunk of bread off the sideboard, dipped it in his uncle's still-warm bacon grease laying there in the pan, picked up a couple of boiled eggs where they'd been left to cool in the sink, and disappeared after Alex.

The ever-present Ulysses bounced after him looking for scraps, or a windfall.

Sarah stood in the kitchen, still just half-awake. She held a high-button shoe from the pile in front of the closet in one hand, and with the other pushed a strand of hair back away from her face. Andy barely heard her quiet, "Bye! Be careful!" as it drifted ghost-like down the passage-ways behind him.

Chapter 20

Blind to the End

There is an energy to a storm that interacts with a man's soul. Something which fascinates and draws him out of his warm cave to experience and defy the elements. A magnet, pulling him, staggering along at the edge of fear and awe at the power of his God. This feeling can fill a person with a love and excitement for life, but at the same time drive him to efforts beyond comprehension in the name of compassion and empathy for another. Often as not, it serves to blind the individual to his own danger . . . up to the instant of death.

The wind this morning was blowing a full gale out of the north east. The small group found snow drifted waist deep in spots, as they fought their way down to the shore.

Sandy was lucky. It was determined she'd be more of a liability than help under the circumstances, so she got to stay home in her warm barn with Ulysses, George, and the chickens to keep her company.

The dog was not so pleased with this lot, and Andy could hear his lament fading slowly out with the distance until it too was eventually lost in the storm.

What gear the men felt essential they wore or wrapped around their bodies. Things such as coils of rope, small tarpaulins, and the bulky, cork-and-canvas life-preservers.

Andy thought staggering along in this gusty breeze out onto Central wharf, with rime-ice greasing every step was challenging enough. But he found swinging out over the edge, wearing that cumbersome, awkward life-preserver, and then trying to clamber down an equally icy, straight ladder was almost his undoing.

He felt his Uncle Alex's usual iron-grip on his collar, and for a change bore no resentment in his heart. Unnecessary, it was still a welcomed comfort as the boy looked down into that waiting malevolence of black water next to the dock.

From there the men walked along a narrow catwalk which had been cantilevered out over the water, and anchored to the edge of the marsh-bank by waist-thick pilings driven into the mud.

At last they arrived at the spot where a small floating dock used to set. Pushed up onto the walkway by the force of wind and waves, it had been joined by knee-high windrows of ice and straw colored, salt-marsh hay. The men located the skiff and oars which had originally been tied upside down to the float's deck, but it required a precarious trip across part of the ice-covered marsh to retrieve them.

Andy had been warned that to the lone traveler this muddy salt-marsh was fiendishly treacherous. Its myriad, bottomless, water-filled potholes—some only as big around as one of the pilings they'd just come by—could swallow a man. Gory details were supplied to impress upon the boy the need for caution, and he could recite them word for word. "With the pothole, not even a tell-tale blood stain will remain, nor anytime given for a scream to echo across the marsh. The mud holds its victims like quicksand, until the salt and peat-tannin seep in to embalm them. Men have been found—through accident—where they've lain for a thousand years. Mouths still open in soundless screams of death, eyes preserved forever, staring into the mud they'd become a part of."

Today these man-eaters were covered by thin sheets of salt-water ice. Snow covered, like the marsh around them, they were completely hidden, and virtual death-traps to the unwary. The boy waited on his wooden walk, and watched the others help each other out of hidden, muddy sloughs.

Finally, dragging the boat with them, the men angled their way down off of this mess onto the bare sand of the tidal flats, swept clean by the still raging storm.

Plodding along, Andy was curious as to whether it was always the same men who accompanied his uncle on these rescue parties. The Hallets were there, along with Sammy, and a couple of others he remembered from the ship's chandler on the night the *Granite* had foundered. Ansel Gorham, and a mister Cahoon, he thought their names were. They seemed to be as eager to be with the Captain as he was.

Trying to answer the question for himself, he wondered if it was that these men trusted his uncle's judgment, or if they just liked the adventures he led them on.

Only a mile and a half, in the early morning light and through the blowing snow, it looked more like ten out to the breakers. Tiny silhouettes revealed others who had ventured out to the site ahead of them. Some for the macabre thrill of being on the scene of a wreck, and others eager to salvage what the dead no longer had use for.

Little was said among Andy's group, with everyone saving their energy to lean into the force of the gale instead. Carrying the skiff, they paused only to shift off every now and then to ease tired muscles, and kept on plodding.

This particular craft was chosen for its lightness. A product of Chris Gardner's cleverness, it had been constructed of native, white cedar. Because his jointing had been done so carefully, the hull remained tight without the need to soak up a lot of heavy water to swell the wood.

Subtle at first, the closer they got to the edge of the pounding surf, the more its noise dominated their world. The skiff may have been light, but the rescuers were weary when they grounded their little boat at a spot directly downwind from the wreck. Pausing for breath, Alex pointed out to all how the tide must have just turned. Now with both wind and water traveling in the same direction, the waves were starting to flatten out.

Not that the change needed additional confirmation, but each new wave surge seemed to push a little further up the flat than the last. Seeing this, the Captain reminded those who were to remain on shore to keep a weather-eye out so they wouldn't get trapped by tide-water filling the low spots behind them. All knew if this should happen, they'd have to abandon the rescue effort in favor of saving themselves. Also aware of the change, the ranks of spectators had thinned considerably by the time the salvors arrived.

Andy squinted out toward the ship, a little intimidated by the sheer violence of all this water in motion. Black against the sea and sky, she lay there on her side, much like Sammy's dying whale in that other storm.

While the men set about getting the little skiff ready for its perilous journey of mercy, Andy tried to pick out anything that might be the boy, still clinging to life.

The impact of waves hitting the hull on the weather-side sent spray and water flying fifty feet into the air. Torn and shredded by the gale, there was little left to fall back to the sea.

Studying the wreck, the boy could see it coming apart little by little, with the ship shuddering visibly with every massive blow. Like the shafts of broken harpoons, the stump of her main-mast stood protruding from the remains, and still stepped, her shattered fore-mast—with fore-top attached—

reached for the shore. The last vestiges of torn storm-sails, rigging, broken spars, hatch covers, and splintered wood from the hull trailed away from the wreck, to spread along the edge of the tide-line where he stood.

Here in the shallows, the diminutive little boat was set to go. The belly knocked out of them by the shore, what was left of the huge waves insisted on slopping aboard the tiny craft as if to whet their appetite for the feast to come. Refusing to be intimidated, the rescuers climbed into the skiff, with big, burly Alex at the oars facing the stern, and Andy behind his back in the prow. The rest of the men walked them out to a point just inside the breakers, and held their little craft steady while they got set.

Even before they started, the walls of water seemed so insurmountable, and the distance so far, any chance of success was deemed all but impossible. A discussion broke out, but having come this far, the decision was made to try anyway.

No one asked Andy.

The others made ready to shove them off, trying to get the timing of the waves right so the boat wouldn't capsize upon launch, when the boy thumped his uncle on the back, halting everything. Speech being difficult over the noise, he merely pointed to the wreck.

The black mass had started to shift. The coming tide was adding its weight to the efforts of the storm, and in minutes the stern had twisted closer. Not only did this expose more of the bow to the brunt of the waves, but it also let them slip around the ship easier. Immediately, the cresting surges made further tumult in the expanse the two had to cross.

Already wearing life-preservers, Alex now became even more conservative and insisted that in addition they should each wear lifelines tended by those on shore. Finally launched, and trailing their lines behind—along with the words, "God speed, Captain!" Alex began the arduous effort to gain the dark bulk a hundred some odd yards away.

Hardly three boat lengths into the trial, a wave broke over the skiff. Alex struggled to keep her head into the waves and upright, while Andy bailed in earnest desperation to keep her from swamping. By the time they had gained the half-way point, both of them were soaking wet from the energy expended, and breathing heavily. This brought into play another serious worry as they fought on. Doubt about the amount of strength they actually had left to complete their mission.

It was Andy who noticed the lines laying in the water. Streaming down the wind and tide from the ship, they were only half-floating. Picking one off the top of a wave that seemed intent on burying them, the boy pulled it aboard and began hauling.

Alerted by the changing rhythm, and the fact that Andy had stopped bailing momentarily, the captain looked over his shoulder to make sure he still had a crew. Cradling his oars as he caught his breath, a relieved Alex coughed out, "Good work Mister Sears! Haul away!"

Alex's intent had been to try for the stern, which was closer to shore. Then when they had gained the lee of the wreck, he was going to work their way up toward the foremast in the relatively calm seas.

So much for plans. As Andy hauled in hand over hand, and Alex bailed, the rope was leading them directly to the fore-topmast. In the vicinity of their eventual destination, this route also took them out into the full fury of the gale. The dying ship kept shifting around more and more into the wind, and like an attached fishing pole, the mast pulled the skiff out into line with all of the waves now sweeping around the bow.

Andy had learned the rhythm. He'd hang on to the rope desperately, while the mountains of water surged and lifted them almost as high as the exposed parts of the ship, then released by the wave, he'd haul like mad. They slid so fast down the backside of these sickening, never-ending roller coaster rides that it made him feel giddy, but he made grand progress.

Fatigue toying with his mind in the midst of this effort couldn't hide the thoughts that if their purpose hadn't been so deadly serious, and the water so frighteningly cold, he might have even considered this undertaking to be fun.

The captain held the oars locked together at-the-ready with one hand, should the rope break, and tried to keep ahead of the waves sloshing aboard by bailing with the other.

It seemed a torturously long journey that finally brought them to the cascade of lines which tied the mast to the waves. Alex tried to keep one eye on the tumultuous sea, while he picked out what had to be the precious cargo they were seeking.

Still lashed into the top, right at the shoulder where topmast and fore-mast joined, lay a bundle of sailcloth. The man heaved a sigh of relief.

Preoccupied with this search overhead, he felt the skiff leaping upward long before he actually saw the monstrous roller that swept them toward the sky. Reacting to the motion by instinct, he pulled on the oars to stabilize their little boat, and promptly parted ways with his seat—the little twigs having grabbed nothing but air instead of the anticipated resistance of water. Over the confusion he heard his nephew shouting, "Jump, Uncle Alex! Jump!" but it was too late. Everything had become total chaos.

Airborne by the endeavors of the furious sea instead of his own, pictures froze in Alex's mind of the skiff half on its side, three feet above the wave-top, as if in suspended motion. The oars tumbled in mid-air above this, and became tangled in what had to be Andy's rope. The bailer, fluttering like a bird of prey about to stoop to its quarry, was silhouetted against the sky above everything. Lastly, the dark mass of the slowly disintegrating hull hung beside him like the shadow of doom.

White foam streaming off of it reminded him in that instant of mountain cataracts in spring, and he wondered why something laying there in death should make him think of the season when all life began. Ending this tableau, the debris laden sea welcomed the captain eagerly. It closed its tangled covers over his head before he had time to realize he'd entered its breathlessly cold embrace.

Andy, seeing the wave coming from his vantage point in the prow, and feeling its power as it lifted them effortlessly, knew from the premonition in his gut the end result of this mad upward rush. Heaving himself forward, he placed one foot on the stem of their little boat, and using the full thrust of the wave like a springboard, pushed against it. The wave's energy now channeled in the direction he wanted to go, threw his body toward the tangled mass of rope.

Standing there at a cock-eyed angle, and just fingertips out of reach, the mast teasingly challenged him. Missing it cleanly, the boy had barely enough time to react before falling headfirst into the ropes dangling below. Clinging like a cat, he mentally thanked his God for deliverance before scrambling above the reach of the passing sea. The hull of the wreck, rocking in the surge of the powerful waves, passed this motion on to the mast. Plunging up and down, it in turn hauled on the ropes, and lifted him upward with each thrust. Again using this power of the ocean to his advantage, he reached the mast.

It had been a wild climb, but Andy dragged his body on top of the greased-smooth wood, twisted around and sat up, straddling the one-time tree with his back to the wind.

Pausing for breath he looked around, wondering how his uncle had fared.

The boy's heart sank, pulling the moisture from his throat after it. There in front of him lay the capsized skiff, twirling slowly in the churning, debris-clogged sea and drifting off down-wind toward shore. Alex was nowhere in sight.

Looking back to the relative safety of the flat, Andy's breath came out in a coughing sigh of relief. Through a snow squall, he could make out the activity of the men on shore. They were hauling his uncle's life-line in hand over hand, with what had to be Alex submerging and porpoising after it.

He could also see Sam crouching there, squinting into the wind and snow. One hand was shielding the man's eyes, and running seaward from the other there appeared to be a rope which Andy assumed was his own life-line.

Good old Sammy!

Pulling on the rope from his end, Andy sought to free it from the sea, and thereby make sure it wasn't tangled on anything. The return tugs he got from shore were an unexpected but reassuring contact with humanity. The boy's wavc was answered by what might have been cheers, could he have heard them.

Turning to the task at hand, Andy swung around and began hitching himself forward into the torrent.

Because of the way the ship had twisted, each wave that broke on the bow now seemed to heave its formidable remains in his direction. The larger ones threatened to knock him from the mast, so again timing his movements to nature's dictate, the boy inched his way toward his target in spurts.

In the little time between scrambling and hanging on, he tried to make some sense out of the odd lump ahead. Able to withstand the punishment, it had obviously been tied securely. Wrapped in a piece of sail, the mass appeared to have been lashed into the doubling of the foretop.

Unkindly, another wave hit the boy, forcing him to hold his breath and hang on, literally, for dear life. Feeling as if he were riding this heaving, bucking pine-horse through a shower of ice straight from hell, self-doubts about stamina began to creep in again, but he ignored them.

One minute stretched agonizingly into the next, and the one that followed seemed even longer. Finally reaching his goal, Andy strained toward the wrapped body, putting his hand on what looked like it should have been the child's shoulder. Getting no response, he hitched a little closer, leaned forward and reluctantly lifted a corner of the sail, not sure what would greet him.

There, staring straight into his heart, were a pair of the darkest brown eyes Andy had ever seen. Stark against the deathly foam-white skin, they appeared to have no pupils. The youngster's lips, blue with the cold, moved slightly.

Andy locked his legs around the mast, so he could lean closer to the lad, and thought he heard a whispered, "Thank you!" against the roar of the sea. Now sitting back up, he could see the words being formed over and over again.

Tears from both boys mixed with the salt spray, and the brown eyes closed.

Andy looked toward shore, and waved to reassure them all was well.

Alarmed, he was a little taken aback to see how much the flat had shrunk since the last time he'd looked. Pushed by the wind, the tide was coming fast. Sammy was in water to his knees, restrained by the length of Andy's safety line.

Two of the men had followed the drifting skiff along the shore, where they were waiting for it to come within reach.

Uncle Alex was easy to spot. The black, wet bulk was staggering around like a sailor who'd found the keys to the spirits locker. He kept falling down, then he'd regain his feet, wave his arms like a bird, and stumble again.

One of the other men was trying to help, but only seemed to be getting in his uncle's way. There was no question in Andy's mind, but what Alex was in trouble. He finally decided the man must be stomping his feet, and beating his arms against his body in a futile attempt to restore circulation.

The boy frowned about thoughts of a similar cold bath ahead for himself.

Removing his mitten, he studied the ropes, while digging under layers of bulky foul-weather gear for his sheath knife.

Feeding on fatigue, the boy's mind began to play tricks on him again. His fingers touched the handle of this most-cherished treasure, and he was overwhelmed by a flashback of the Christmas just passed. Hesitating for only a moment, it was as if he had been recharged by the warmth of those memories. Withdrawing the shiny blade, he began to saw on the tough rope with a new-found strength, intensity and purpose.

Cutting the youngster's legs free first, he then wrapped an arm around the boy's chest and started chawing on the top rope. The freezing salt-spray made his fingers go numb, but he needed the assurance his bare hand gave him, cutting near both of their faces.

Without warning, the rope parted. Surprised, Andy fought to hold on. The full heft of the young boy, added to his own, was just too much for his drained energies. Rather than let go, he slid with the weight, trying desperately to control their progress.

Truly, the battle was lost before it had even begun. Accepting the inevitable, he sputtered a few curse words from the past, and the two of them slipped away.

Everything happened so fast, Andy had little time to act and none to think, as they fell toward the sea. Severed from the mast, he dropped the knife, wrapped his second arm and legs around his burden, then locked bare fingers onto his other wrist.

Dropping twenty feet, they plunged deep beneath water so cold it burned.

Their dive seemed to last forever, but with the help of the life-jacket the two of them finally surfaced to a world Andy had no way of preparing for. He chokingly discovered that at this level, there was no clear demarcation between sea and air. Ripped off the wave-tops by the wind, ice, spray, and foam filled the space just above what he had thought would be the ocean's surface. This confusing zone of frigid nothingness was exhausting, and tried to smother any effort to breath.

To add to the discomfort of mind-numbing cold was the turbulence of the ocean itself. It gave him no true sense of up or down, or in which direction safety may lay. In these pulling, dragging, pounding gray waves, only the endless struggle to draw in the next breath remained terrifyingly real, and even that was fading.

Andy became conscious of pain. The life-line pinched and cut into his flesh, right through all the heavy gear. At the same time, his chest was being squeezed fiendishly. This made it all the more difficult to suck in the few gulps of air available to him, but in the back of his mind he knew the pain and surging motion were to prove his deliverance. He was being hauled ashore to safety.

Slamming into other objects and debris along the way brought more pain, and under better circumstances these blows alone could have caused tears, but he found himself becoming strangely detached and beyond caring. Unable to help either himself or the youngster in his arms, all the boy could do was pray and try to hang on, and then he remembered who was on the other end of the rope. Finding a scrap of comfort and security in the thought, Andy squeezed the child tighter to his chest. He knew Sammy would probably die himself before he'd give them over to the elements.

The seemingly eternal voyage finally ended when he felt the rough slam of sand meeting his back. Rough hands picked him out of the surf, and he was conscious of being pried loose from the object of his ordeal.

Sammy was there, holding him in his arms.

Through his clenched, chattering teeth, Andy sobbed, "I lost the knife, Sammy! I lost your knife!" Then the boy's world mercifully closed in on him, and thought became as confusing a whirl as the maelstrom he'd just left behind.

Andy had no feeling in his arms or legs. On the edge of consciousness, he wondered without really caring, if they might be frozen. Through a cloud of memories, he pictured his uncle thrashing around on the flats. Now he understood why, and wondered if he too would be under such duress.

The men picked the boy up, and turning him upside down to achieve their purpose, dumped his boots out without removing them. Then they placed him in the skiff next to Alex, with the rescued boy on the other side, and tucked them all in with the tarps they'd brought.

After retrieving the little boat, the men had kicked the middle seat out. This gave them a vehicle in which to transport their incapacitated captain and the boys back to shore. To all appearances it could have doubled for an oversized, multiple coffin.

The captain had warned the men to watch behind them, so if the water filled in, they wouldn't get trapped. Now his premonition of danger appeared to be coming true.

Pulling their heavy load along in the shallows of the coming tide, the men ran at times, fighting against time. On the way back to shore, they had to follow the water's edge in order to float the skiff full of bodies, so the distance they had to cover was a lot longer than the direct route across the flats they'd taken on the way out.

All were exhausted by the time they reached the last deep spot they needed to cross. The water where Lone Tree Creek had carved its shallow channel into the sand of the flat was up to Nathaniel's armpits, and he was their tallest member. Floating in their life-jackets, facing a turbulent sea, with deep-water waves and a wild wind, the men clung to their skiff to keep from being swept away, and let the gale push them across.

Fortunately they were close to the docks now. Some of the spectators, who in spite of the elements had remained to watch the dramatic event unfold, came out to help.

The boys were actually carried and passed from hand to hand along the walkway, then up the ladder to Central Wharf. There they were loaded into a covered delivery wagon, wrapped in blankets, and taken home to Sarah. The frozen crew were also helped up onto the wharf, and dispatched to their respective dwellings.

Alex was too disabled and heavy for this treatment. He remained in the skiff while it was floated around the end and down the length of the dock. Brought right to shore at the base of the wharf, the man was helped out of the little boat by many hands. Wrapped up, he was placed into a waiting carriage which in turn followed the boys home.

Chapter 21

Wild Horses

Both Sarah's men and the boy from the ship were bedded down under the care of old Doctor Parker. Instructed to stay put for a week, Andy wasn't sure he'd be warm by then. Bed-warmers—consisting of heated bricks wrapped in toweling—hot soup, and much motherly attention were administered with varying degrees of success.

Her men at least, responded to the efforts.

Adding to Sarah's burden, she wasn't the only one worried about them. Showing their concern, Ulysses refused to leave Andy's bedside, and Sammy did everything in his power to become a royal pain.

The man always seemed to be underfoot. He brought in so many buckets of sea clams, soft shelled clams, and quahogs that Sarah ran out of places to put them, but within a few days she found reason to forgive the man completely.

Evidently touched by the reality of his own mortality, Andy's spirits, usually so high as to be annoying, had lagged since the episode. The boy lost his appetite, and when he wasn't sleeping, lay there withdrawn and tearful.

Sammy brought his boy a present which made up for every inconvenience the youngster's mother had been forced to endure. Lovingly, the man made a replacement for the knife Andy lost during the rescue. Patterning it as closely after the first one as he could remember, it turned out even more handsome than the original. More important to Sarah, the man's gift triggered the response she'd been praying for. When he held that knife in his hands, Andrew's interest in this life seemed to be rekindled, and from that point forward he made rapid progress.

Even before their rescue party had reached shore with the young boy, the lad's father, who was also Captain of the wrecked ship, had succumbed. It was generally thought the man died from a heart attack, likely brought on by over-exertion, exposure, and worries for the safety of his child.

The ship's owners were contacted by telegraph as soon as the wreck was identified. In Provincetown, they fearfully awaited follow-up messages, with details going out to them as soon as they became available. This was a tremendous loss to their village. All ten aboard, five crew and five passengers, had come from the town itself.

To the surprise of all, the boy's distraught mother and aunt arrived on the afternoon train. Their parish priest, and a delegation to claim the bodies, accompanied them. When they appeared, the deceased Captain's widow and sister were shown in to Alex's home where they were offered every hospitality.

The young boy, not really conscious, had been put to bed in Sarah's room a little earlier. Unfortunately, his anxious family spoke mostly Portuguese, but the language of mothers concerned for their young is universal. Sarah intuitively understood their needs and concerns without interpretation.

Provincetown, a fishing village, was somewhat hardened to tragedy from the sea, but seldom did the loss of one ship claim this many natives. Isolated out on the end of the Cape, it was a fairly closed society. Because almost everyone was related by either blood or marriage, this wreck was particularly unsparing in that it touched three-quarters of the families living there in one way or another.

The priest was overwhelmed by such a catastrophe within his flock, but he did his best to console the women in their grief. Visibly shaken, and torn between loyalties, the poor fellow knew he was probably needed at home even more than here.

In Provincetown, the shock of what had taken place still echoed from the sand dunes out back to the fish shanties on the ends of her piers.

With great reluctance, the man unintentionally, but ominously prophesied the future by giving their boy the last rights of the Church, then left the three of them in Sarah and God's care. Sarah felt an empathy toward the man, and in spite of the vexing load dumped in her lap, found his concerns troubling as well. She knew the trip home on the funeral train would be one of the saddest journeys he would ever make.

In shock over the loss of her husband, the mother clung to her boy with desperate hope, yet tempered by despair. Her son's spirit did little to help. Erratic as a weather pennant, it fluttered between life and death for days. Sometimes he was conscious, sometimes not, but his womenfolk fussed over him, spoon fed their child, and took turns sleeping exhausted on the floor beside his bed in the off chance he'd need them.

Sarah and Amy prepared food, and provided a sympathetic though not always completely understanding ear to their guests. Making them as welcome and comfortable as possible under the circumstances, the ordeal was shared.

During one of the long afternoons, young Mister Sears had a visitor who was different from his usual parade of friends. The young boy's mother came in to thank him for what he'd done. The woman tried to keep her composure, but upon seeing Andy and his improved condition, broke down sobbing. From there it built into an uncontrollable wailing, which reflected the woman's old-world mannerisms carried into her new country.

Andy, embarrassed by the raw emotion displayed so openly, leaped out of bed and ran smack into his mother.

Alarmed at the noise herself, Sarah inadvertently met him in the doorway, surprising both.

Sarah got him back into bed, and then calmed the woman down enough so that she could complete her mission. Finally, between blessings and prayers, the mother thanked him for the life of her son. In her broken English, she somehow conferred to Andy that he too was her son now, and that he had a second home any time he would like to come visit. After this, she said another prayer over him, kissed and patted him profusely, then, much to Andy's relief, went sobbing back to the long vigil at her own son's bedside.

The young boy died of pneumonia in his mother's arms the next day. At least she'd had him back with her long enough to say goodbye.

Alex had only spent one day in bed before the idleness cramped his restless spirit. Over protests from Sarah and the doctor, he got up, dressed, and spent the rest of his recovery out in the barn with the Hallet boys, putting the final touches on his running gear.

The next afternoon, after Sarah got through with him, he may have wished he'd stayed in bed awhile longer.

The woman lit into him full tilt. She felt that if he could work, he'd recovered enough to take the what-for he deserved. Besides, she could no longer contain herself anyway.

Not being especially known for tact, her first question came right to the point. "What right did you have to endanger the life of my son? I didn't know you were going to be so stupid as to go out on the water in that storm!"

She went on to question his sanity and his competence to have men in his command, let alone a boy, and especially her boy. She informed him, "You no longer need to consider taking Andrew on as a crew member for the summer sailing-season! The answer is, NO!"

This was a topic she'd ignored for lack of an excuse when mentioned earlier, but now. . . . "Over my dead body, will a son of mine become a sailor under your command! To drown out there, cold and alone? Absolutely not! An impossible request. How could I ever allow you to lead him into your shiftless way of life, only to end up lying like a beggar in that same, unmarked, bottomless grave you seem to be in search of?"

As she ranted on, Alex began to see why, when this woman had first arrived, she'd been so adamant about him giving up the profession. Maybe too, this explained why it was taking Christopher so long to convince the woman that he was the right man to love and provide for her, being a man of the sea himself.

Her outburst had finally triggered his memory. The captain recalled the fear his sister had harbored in her own childhood here on the Cape. Although she'd hidden it well, Sarah had seen so many friends and relatives of friends perish out there on the ocean, she had become deathly afraid of it herself. Strange, for the daughter of a Sea Captain, but it also accounted for the trip by train. She could as easily have met his ship in Boston, on the last run of the season.

Because of this phobia, Alex realized that naturally she would be terrified of losing her only son to that same, unforgiving mistress. It was small wonder the woman was behaving like a mother bear protecting her cub. Trying to insulate the boy from what she feared most, Sarah was ready to fight those who might tempt him away from her.

At last, and in tears, she began to wind down and Alex was able to get a word in edgewise. "Sarah!" he began,

"What makes you think that you, me, or anyone else can convince that son of yours not to do something he's got his mind set on? I could tell from that first night, he was at home around the water. The boy has a way about him that says he has a love for that world out there, not fear. The other morning, he proved not only his worth under pressure, but his courage as well!

You do know he's going to get a medal for his efforts this time, don't you? Thanks to our selectman Mr. Mathews, and our past and probably future State Senator, the Honorable Mr. Swift from the Register.

No one told your son what to do out on that wreck, he was alone out there! He could have just as easily jumped into the water with me, and been hauled to shore . . . with no question remaining about his bravery. A fact, I might add, he was well aware of. Not only that, but it was his idea of how to go after the boy to begin with. And he had a one-set mind about that too!

My portion of the rescue had been completed when the boat flipped over. With the help of God, I'd gotten him out there. Then, your son did what he considered his part.

I guess what I'm trying to say is, from what I can tell, if the boy's got his gumption made up to go to sea, wild horses won't keep him ashore. You trying to do it will only drive him that much harder to seek his goal, and separate the two of you to boot. The lad's got a will of his own, and come hell or high-water he'll do what he damned well pleases. He's his mother's son!"

Softening his tone a little, Alex added, "If it makes you any happier, Sarah, I will make one concession to you. I'll respect your wishes, and not ask him to join my crew as I had intended. However, if the boy asks me for the position, I shan't turn him down!" With that the man got to his feet, and as was his wont when he was emotionally aroused, stomped back out to the barn, leaving her to smolder and stew.

SILVER MEDAL AWARDED ANDREW J. SEARS BY THE HUMANE SOCIETY OF MASSACHUSETTS

After 1849 it was the custom of the Humane Society to present their new Silver Medal, as the equivalent of the Gold Medal of former times, when the rescuer showed uncommon courage and perseverance in saving human life at the risk of his own.

Sarah didn't know it, but Alex had been fighting with his conscience over this very dilemma. He went back to his tasks feeling that the good Lord had rescued him one more time. The captain hadn't been too happy with a decision he'd made earlier, to take the lad aboard come summer. True, the boy had proved his worth out in the storm, but Alex wasn't sure he could put up with Andy's headstrong and disruptive presence day after day. Now he wouldn't have to.

Why is it, he wondered, *that anything which involves my nephew, tears my own world apart so?* He was still shaking his head as he got back down onto his knees next to a pile of rope.

Alex was wrong. At least in the part about the direction in which he thought his particular God was pushing him. Andy, laying in his bed above the kitchen, had been awakened by the rise of his uncle's gruff, crew-hardened voice. The boy just caught the tail-end of the conversation, and it was enough for him to decide right then and there to ask his uncle for the job, not yet, nor now likely to be, proffered.

Chapter 22

Fireflies, Whip-poor-wills, and Love

Ah, springtime! What a frustrating joy it can be. Another whole facet of this world was opening up for Andy to explore. So many new things to do and learn. . . .

On the Cape, the frost retreated like the British from the guns of Concord, leaving its contested ground under the heat of an early spring sun.

The first or second week in April brought out the long awaited tree-frogs, or peepers, to sing their sweet, shrill, siren songs from every freshwater swamp and pothole on the peninsula. A sound guaranteed to uplift the spirit, and fill the soul of those wearied of a long winter's gray skies and howling gales.

Andy and Ulysses chased these elusive little creatures until dark, and usually brought home buckets filled with frog and salamander eggs instead. Not being allowed to bring these treasures into the house, Andy threw them in the farm pond to see if they'd hatch.

Once boys arrived on earth, nature had no problem achieving genetic diversity. That pond had so many tadpoles in it by summer, there was no room for the poor creatures to swim. Soft-hearted, the boy ended up hauling the same buckets filled with a mixed-bag of this next stage of their existence, back to the swamps he'd originally gotten the eggs from.

Between pickup baseball games, the boy helped his uncle get the schooner provisioned and ready for her summer trade. Of course the best and most exciting part was when Andy was allowed to ride along on some of her trial runs. Runs that somehow always seemed to get scheduled after school had let out. That's when Uncle Alex, crowding on every sail he could find room for, tested the gear to its limits.

Now Andy could see what each block, rope, and line he'd helped with, was meant to do, and learned by the sweat of his brow and the blisters on his hands how they worked.

The biggest thrill came when he was given a turn at the wheel, and could feel for himself the power of the wind, and how it gave life to something he already considered the most beautiful thing ever built by man. His uncle, standing by in case a firm hand was needed to ease the strain, pointed out how to steer a compass bearing, and bring her head back on course when she fell off line.

To be honest, Alex felt a little guilty about sharing something he knew was addictive. But, the joy of a pounding sea and a stiff breeze was almost visceral, and in truth he could not deny the boy something he himself considered a basic birthright of any Cape Codder worth his salt.

Still a little early for spring planting, the Hallet men were usually there, along with Mr. Cahoon, and a Mr. John Silva.

When Andy first spotted this last man, it triggered thoughts in the boy's mind of pirates, broadswords and buried treasure. Besides the fellow's name, he wore an eye-patch, just like the evil character in his new book, *Treasure Island* that Elijah was having him read. Fortunately, Mr. Silva's kind nature soon altered that impression.

According to Sam, when dandelions began to bloom on the lawn it meant the tautog and sea bass were biting out around the wrecks and rock piles just off shore. Much to Andy's delight, when the weather was right, he and Sammy would row out and catch these fish by the basketful. Typical of the boy's new appreciation of all things Cape Cod, he found almost as much fun in digging the fiddler-crabs they used for bait out of their holes on the edge of the tidal flats, as he did fishing.

On bright spring days, the sun warmed the bottom mud and flounder would come out to test the new season's offerings. Once caught on the clam-baited, tiniest of hooks they had, the funny one-sided fish provided the most delicious suppers Andy could remember.

By mid-April, herring started their up-stream spawning runs in every little brook and freshet. This triggered another industry, and the first real cash flow of the new year on the Cape. During the daylight hours, those who rented or owned the fishing rights to these waters would dip thousands upon thousands of the bony, oily fish out of basins and pens that had been fashioned in the streams to trap them for this purpose. This left the dark hours to the completion of nature's course.

After acquiring these wriggling masses, they were stripped of their eggs, which in turn were canned and sold as a product similar to caviar. To those who had access to it, the fresh roe was dipped in egg and flour, fried in butter, and eaten as a delicacy even more rare. The remaining carcasses, and the male fish—which of course lacked roe—were corned or pickled in brine to be eaten whole once the bones had softened. Many of these were also stored to be used later for lobster bait, with the surplus sent by rail to inland cities, and by sailing vessel to off Cape ports.

The in-shore cod started biting around the first of May, which was about the same time the striped bass arrived. By the middle of that month came the voracious blue fish.

These could make the water boil, and stain it with clouds of blood when they were feeding on schools of herring. If squid were the fish's *entré du jour*, momentary puffs of inky blackness would be left silhouetted against the sandy bottom, where one life was traded for another's sustenance.

Poor Sam's companionship began to suffer once Andy started to accompany Mr. Gardner on his work boat. Here, the young man discovered first-hand how to set pots for lobster. A smelly, muscle-straining job that had its own delicious rewards.

In fact, Christopher taught the boy many of the secrets of his inshore fisheries trade.

The tell-tale odor of watermelon drifting down the wind would pinpoint where oil slicks floated, quieting the ripples above schools of fish feeding in the depths below. Why fish oil should smell like watermelon was one of those questions that Mr. Gardner said only God knew the answer to.

By watching the terns wheel and dive, chasing food, Andy learned how to spot other catchable fish beneath the water. Driven to the surface by blues or bass, these small bait-fish betrayed their pursuer's presence even as they were plucked off the wave tops by the birds above.

Seeing this cruelty of nature, Andy felt a touch of sympathy toward the masses of poor little sperling and sand-eels. Somehow it just didn't seem fair. At the same time though, he realized if someone didn't eat these zillions of little fish, pretty soon Cape Cod Bay would look like what he'd done to the farm pond with the tadpoles.

He did his best to even the odds a little—and soothe his own feelings of injustice—by catching as many of the bigger fish as he could. At a penny a pound, Christopher didn't care about the reasons, it was the end result which pleased him.

School became an inconvenience barely tolerated. That is, until Andy became aware of sweet Temperance.

It happened one evening after supper.

He and Amy had gone over to one of their neighborhood friends, where they planned to shoot marbles and play Fox and Hounds in the long evening twilight. As luck would have it, a large group congregated. Marbles seemed too tame for this many people and such a magic time of day, so they moved on to the other game.

Fox and Hounds was something like hide-and-seek in reverse, with one person, the Fox, being given a head start from the den. All the rest, called Hounds, split up into packs and tried to catch him before he could sneak back to his hole.

After the usual laughing and squabbling over who was going to be in who's pack, and who was going to be the Fox, Amy settled the matter by taking charge. She split the group up into packs of fours, which allowed her the liberty of selecting who was in whose pack. Now organized, the game commenced.

Things seemed to be going quite well, until one of the girls in Andy's group sprained her ankle. Unfortunately for Andy, the two older members thought they had seen the Fox disappear into a clump of bushes across the field. Ignoring his protests, they left him to get the injured member back to the house on his own.

Disappointed at the turn of events, Andy accepted his assigned duty and turned to the girl. Reading his face, she apologized and acted sad too. Not wanting to make her feel any worse for what happened, he teased the young lady a little, and gave her some sass. Taking her wrist, he drew it across behind his neck, then giggling and fooling, tucked his shoulder up under Temperance's arm.

She smelled nice. Clean, with a hint of lilacs or something. He put his other arm around her waist to support her, and they started to hobble back toward the den.

Laughing and staggering like a pair of drunken sailors, they stumbled and fell from time to time. Sometimes, not even on purpose. Within sight of the house, the two of them paused to catch their breath in a shaded glen, and Andy threw himself down on his back in the relatively cool, knee-deep grass. Pulling out a long stem, he stuck the sweet, moist end in his mouth. Around them the grass, or green, Timothy hay actually, released its stored heat and tender fragrance into the evening twilight. Crickets chirped, peepers sang their chorus in a nearby swamp, and a robin took up scolding a cat somewhere in the next yard.

He'd known Tempy all winter. They'd often played together in groups, skating, or playing snow-fort and king of the hill, and he'd treated her just like any other member of the gang. She—a real tomboy at her age—had played along, giving tit-for-tat in the rough and tumble that often ensued.

Sitting there beside him this evening, she seemed preoccupied as she rubbed her ankle through the high-button shoe. They talked quietly about the summer to come, while the pleasant warmth of the evening settled around them. Fireflies were starting to appear, and created a new topic as they wondered to each other what made them glow.

Andy, refreshed, started to sit up and playfully poked her in the ribs. She in turn put her hand on his chest, and shoved him back down. Grabbing the other end of his piece of grass, she put it in her mouth. This began a squealing but gentle tug-of-war. The grass broke a few times, and was retrieved by whichever one had bitten it off to resume their game.

All at once Andy stopped tugging and froze. It had suddenly occurred to him the stem had gotten much shorter. Tempy's face was only inches from his own.

He looked, or maybe it should be said he tumbled, into her soft blue eyes, as she too paused for a moment, half on top of him now, pinning him down. Her wide-eyes stared back, locked into his in mutual recognition of what was happening, then they acquired a mischievous glint.

Holding him frozen with the power of her gaze, like a predator about to pounce, she began to nibble on the grass once more. It was a deliberate, tantalizingly slow, bit of teasing, as she drew it into her mouth rabbit fashion. Almost as an anticlimax, their lips finally met. With his eyes closed, Andy's arms went around her instinctively and he held her close.

The kiss lingered. It was as soft and warm as the early spring sun, and as innocent as their youth, but the promise it held whispered so much more.

She rolled away from him abruptly, bounced to her feet, and ran skipping and dancing towards the house.

Andy's heart was still pounding in his throat. He scrambled up, and puzzled, called after her. "Tempy? Your ankle!"

She glanced toward him, and her soft laughter drifted back over her shoulder. Even from that distance he could see some of the grass still tangled in her hair. The poor boy's thoughts were in complete turmoil.

Tempy disappeared around the corner of the building with a thoroughly confused Andy in hot pursuit. By the time he reached the spot where he'd seen her last, she'd vanished completely. His sister and a couple of her friends, having gotten tired of the Fox chase, were sitting there playing jacks.

They looked up at a flushed and out of breath Andy as he inquired, "Where's . . ." then, thinking better of his original question, lamely rephrased it in mid-stream to, "everybody gone?"

The girls smiled, tee-heed, and whispered among themselves as they exchanged knowing looks.

This unnerved Andy a little more. He could feel his ears starting to burn, and his face getting red.

Amy sassed at him, "Tempy had to go home, if that's who you mean? She had a sore ankle."

The girls twittered again.

Andy knew Tempy couldn't have gone home that quickly. Even if she'd run, she'd still be in sight from here. Obviously, she had to be hiding nearby, spying on this little exchange.

All right, he could play the game. Sounding indignant now, he said, "Pfhh! What do I care about her?" Making a face of disgust, he pretended that she was the last thing on his mind. Next, he tried to convince the rest that his sister must be crazy to ask such a dumb question. "I mean all the rest of the gang, and you know it, so quit trying to twist things around! Did they catch the Fox yet?"

By the mere fact he was concentrating more on the foundation plantings than his sister's group, told all where his true feelings lay. What he got for his trouble was more spirited whispering, and a slightly nasty sing-song, "I don't know!" from his sister.

Understanding from the tone of her answer it was a lost cause, he turned and stomped off toward home. His hands in his pockets, and his ears still burning.

Out came the harmonica, but it never quite made it to his lips.

In retrospect, the kiss was twice as sweet, and his soul sang songs to him that he'd never heard before.

Let them laugh, he told himself. *I don't care!*

Unharnessed, his mind wandered on to prove the boy could even lie to himself. Andy didn't understand why

Tempy had run away, or hidden, nor if she had really turned her ankle, or had just faked it for the specific purpose of being alone with him. For that matter, he wasn't sure if it had just been luck that put the two of them together this evening, or if his sister had done it on purpose. *I wonder if she's trying to be a matchmaker, like Uncle Alex?*

Did Tempy ask her to make this arrangement? That was a pleasant thought.

Are they in cahoots? Why are girls always so hard to figure out?

In spite of all this heavy thinking, he could never remember being so happy.

Just wait 'til I get my hands on that sister of mine! Boy is she gonna pay for setting me up, and embarrassing me in front of everyone!

"Girls!"

Vocalizing this last thought, poor Andy didn't know if he meant it as a noun, adjective, or epithet.

In the slowly fading, soft, evening twilight, a Whip-poor-will began its own haunting serenade of love and longing.

Spring had truly come to Cape Cod.

Chapter 23

Sarah's Justice

Alex was back at his trade, happily plying the routes around Cape Cod Bay, and north as far as Boston.

The early spring cargoes were large and plentiful this year. All Captains agreed it was purely a result of fewer packets running, and the backlog of freight stored up over a long winter, but none complained. Fortunately for the sailing craft, there still seemed to be a number of shippers and manufacturers willing to waive the immediacy of shipping by rail in exchange for their less expensive services.

After the initial surge, things slowed to a more comfortable level, and Captain Matthews' trips came as close to a schedule as any sailing vessel could ever keep. His published sailing days allowed sufficient leeway for the vagaries of weather and fate, and he settled into the pleasant routine of a Packet Master.

Sarah soon began to notice an oddity in the clothing Alex requested for his ventures. At least those that called him to Boston. They were not what she expected a sailing man to need in the course of his normal business ventures, nor what a businessman would wear for that matter. Why would a sailing man ever need a top hat, or brightly colored ribbons to tie at the throat of his stiff, white shirts, when black was considered standard attire? And, to what use could he put white gloves and an ivory-topped cane? Beyond his many idiosyncrasies—which she had begun to accept as normal—these were quite remarkable.

Knowing better than to make an issue of the matter if she truly wanted to find out what was going on, the woman prepared everything on his list, thought a lot, and said nothing.

A Grand Peace-Jubilee was to be held in Boston this spring. Advertisements and hand bills went out across New England, calling for a chorus of ten-thousand voices. A number of the ladies in the church were all-a-twitter, having been invited to join such a splendid gathering. About ten of them decided to make the trip en-masse, and laid plans to that effect. Much energy, letter exchanges, and preparation went into the venture, which expanded to include a short trip to Middleboro for a joint rehearsal the week before the event. Their final schedule called for the ladies to travel by train, and spend the required nights with families of a sister church in the Boston area. After rehearsals, and performing in the Grand Chorus through the week, they were to return home again on the late train Sunday.

Although Sarah had no plans to attend, she lent her welcomed efforts to the good of all. Alex, on the other hand, had every intent of being in Boston during the period of this glorious occasion. A fact Sarah had been made well aware of, when she made a fuss about him being away on his birthday.

The man became defensive, then went into such detail about the demands of his business, his sister couldn't help but know this trip was more than just another run to Boston.

He explained how his published schedule called for him to make one trip a week, with Thursday being his sailing day—Yarmouth Port to Boston. Friday and Saturday were layover days to exchange cargo there. Sunday was his return trip—Yarmouth Port bound, from Boston. Monday was a layover day here to offload, and then short hauls took him to neighboring ports such as Brewster and Orleans, gathering cargo headed off Cape. Wednesday he reloaded and the cycle would repeat, Thursday to Boston, and so forth.

Much depended on the weather, but if it was fair and the wind held, his schedule left enough time for such variables as a quick turnaround when a shipper was willing to pay the price, or a slow trip if forced to beat into the wind.

So much for schedules. He didn't fool Sarah, because even this early in the season she'd seen him scrambling to get off on Thursday's tide. Although more profitable, the length of his manifest seemed to carry less weight than pleasing a passenger, and he'd been known to leave heavy items on the dock in favor of a fast trip, if that was the person's wish.

Supposedly careful with a dollar, the man reserved his dock space in Boston on a long term lease, albeit at a cut-rate. As such, he was obligated to every Friday through Sunday, from the first of April through the last of October.

Not convinced his sister grasped the significance of this, he went against his better judgment of discussing such things with a woman, and dipped into some of the intricacies of his business. He explained how it was common to write penalties into an agreement of this sort, and consequently his own contained a covenant calling for payment of three dollars for every day he ran over. "And, woman, money once spent can never be spent again!"

Sarah was not a stupid person, but her brother wouldn't let up. He kept hammering on the same things over and over, until she was sick of hearing them.

"In order to attract cargoes and passengers, I have to maintain some semblance of a schedule don't I? The very word 'Packet' indicates an agreement with the public to sail on a certain day. Failing that, my customers will take the train, and soon I'll be hauling lumber from the Maritimes for a living."

Having explained the importance of his routine from every perspective he could think of, the man backed off, hoping his sister had lost the desire to meddle.

This was fine with Sarah, with the exception of sputtering about him running a hoity-toity yachting service, instead of being the mere, menial deliverer of goods that he was trying to paint. Anything to shut him up . . . until she heard him humming to himself as he wandered away. Obviously the man was quite happy with the fact he'd be somewhere else on his birthday. A detail he was hoping she'd forgotten under his verbiage of facts.

Remembering the last time he was so musically inclined, Sarah got that smug look and nodded her head in secret acknowledgment. Yes sir, Captain Matthews had found a new way to put his foot in his mouth—sideways.

It was a beautiful Saturday in late spring, that birthday day. Running into head winds the whole way, it had taken Alex until Friday afternoon to reach Long Wharf. A tow into the docks by an inexperienced tug Captain didn't help his mood much either. The man almost brought them both to ruin, when—to avoid a collision at the last moment—he turned so quickly the *Yarmouth* heeled almost onto her beam ends. A heated discussion followed, with the man settling for half his normal three-dollar fee.

Alex grumped about a near swamping, but it was obvious who'd gotten the better end of the bargain when he wished the tug captain better luck on his next tow.

Concerned about his freight after such an experience, the man elected to personally supervise the unloading. Eggs, shipped directly from the Yarmouth Port docks to Boston, found a ready market because of the Jubilee, and the Captain a share of the profits for suggesting the idea to local farmers. Of course, no one on Cape Cod had been able to buy fresh hen-fruit for the whole previous week.

In a move completely out of character for Captain Matthews, the man disappeared into his cabin, leaving his crew to clean out the packing straw and ice from the hold. Emerging a short while later dressed like a dandy, the captain set off on what appeared at first to be an urgent, late-afternoon mission into the city. Just by his pace, it was obvious to any who observed, the man had something important on his mind.

This was the last week of the spring school-session, and therefore Andy had not yet joined his uncle's crew. A fact which pleased the man enough to bring forth a muttered, "Thank God!"

With his ship well astern, the man slowed to luxuriate in the spring warmth. Wandering up Long Wharf onto State Street, he took stock of the construction project.

Fill was being dumped behind the old Barricado, and they'd changed the name of the rutted, wagon road along the top of the dike to Atlantic Avenue, as someone's idea of a more tasteful label. Musing to himself, he decided if they kept filling in behind the wharves, pretty soon the Charles River was going to be a pond, and the harbor covered with buildings all the way across to Charlestown. The amount of soil coming from nearby Fort Hill left him wondering if that too had been leveled under the guise of progress.

After such an urgent departure from his ship, it seemed odd to see the captain pause for a moment, as if undecided just what his course should be. Making up his mind, he took a right at Merchants Row and then strolled up by the Faneuil Hall market place. The immediacy gone from his step, the man now appeared to be looking for an excuse to stall.

The streets were crowded with all the extra people in town to attend the Jubilee. Scanning a few of the Boston press supplements in passing, the man read with interest where President Grant, Admiral Farragut, and many other distinguished visitors had attended the event on Wednesday past, to hear the celebrated Johann Strauss conduct.

Confronted, and accused of being a cheapskate by the street-urchin hawker—for reading his wares without paying for the privilege—he winked at the boy's aggressiveness, tossed him a copper and left the paper too.

Pausing again, he withdrew his big, gold, pocket watch, and compared its time to the nearby clock tower on the Custom House. Unhappy with the result, the man drifted along with the other aimless wanderers. Being no stranger to the area, he nodded to many casual acquaintances along the way, and began searching the faces of those he passed.

It was almost with relief that he spotted a commanding figure in the crowd, and hailed the man, a fellow Captain with whom he'd shared a few ports of call. They shook hands like long lost friends, slapping each other on the back, and swapping remember-whens.

Getting jostled by the crowd, Alex suggested they step into The Bite, a tavern on the west side of Market Square. Over a nickel-tankard of beer, and food proffered at the bar courtesy of the house, they passed on to discuss the new arrival's long winter voyage, with Alex seemingly deeply engrossed.

The man had circumnavigated the Atlantic, or sailed round the pond as they called it, picking up whatever stray cargo he could for a port in the general direction he wanted to go. A rather risky way to conduct business, but one which afforded the fellow a little leeway to express his personal will upon this earthly course. A thought Alex could empathize with, and even envy, now that his own world had suddenly become somewhat restrictive.

Andrew came to mind, a clam-rake in one hand, the other resting on Ulysses' head. Fuming, the captain wondered how the boy could intrude on his private thoughts and world at will, while he himself had no recourse.

Breathing deeply, he forced his attention back to the other man, and wondered if he'd missed anything of import.

A pointless exercise. The spell had been broken. Restless again, and now with the edge taken off of his hunger, Alex bid the other Captain a friendly if somewhat abrupt adieu.

Darkness was gathering when they stepped back out onto Change Avenue. Lighting his pipe, Alex waited for a little distance to develop between he and his just departed friend, and then wandered across the square, still apparently rudderless, with no set place to go. This man, usually so single-minded and purposeful, was definitely procrastinating over some major decision tonight.

Nervously looking over his shoulder, like a petty thief afraid of being caught, he stopped at a flower peddlers. A nosegay of violets caught his fancy. The purchase complete, packed into a box, and tucked under his arm, Alex meandered on into Dock Square.

To observe the fellow, tacking first one way and then another, you'd think he was lost to the whimsies of the wind, but the drift of his course was always uphill.

Leaving the crowds of the dock and market place behind, the captain's steps suddenly quickened. He headed up Elm Street to Hanover, just as the gaslights were being lit. Not aware the brick and cobbled streets had gotten so dark, he welcomed their friendly, mellow glows.

Turning right on Hanover, he took the next left onto Portland, and left again. By his pace, one would think he'd finally made up his mind about where he was going, when he stopped abruptly. Overhead, Bullfinch's golden-domed state house loomed, gracing Beacon Hill with its dominating majesty.

The captain had navigated himself into a neighborhood of importance. Businessmen were among those who lived here, climbing to their lofty positions on the backs of immigrant laborers.

Hacks and statesmen occupied some of the other multi-floored brick townhouses, where they were handy to meddle in the welfare and politics of Massachusetts when it was convenient, or meant a personal profit.

Landlords, wealthy enough to own half the city's real estate—including her slums—chose this enclave above all others for their personal nests.

No question the seat of Boston's society and power, but to Alex, a neighborhood whose powerful tenants bore watching more closely than the thieves and pinchpockets of the docks.

The brownstone he'd stopped in front of was handsome, but indistinguishable from those on either side. The captain adjusted his collar and accompanying satin ribbon, brushed his hair back with one of those rope-hardened, callused hands, and reset his hat at a cocky angle. Standing tall, he tugged on the lapels of his coat to make it settle onto his shoulders more comfortably, and almost dropped the box of flowers. Juggling to make them set level once again, he held the box in front, prominently, like the cast-iron prow of a steam tug used to breakup winter ice in the rivers. Finally, looking both ways as if to make sure no one had followed him, he strode purposefully up to the door.

A graying, colored servant answered his knock, grinned irreverently, nodded and greeted him with a, "Good evening, Captain!"

Tossing his hat to the man, Alex boomed in his usual, gruff voice, "Hello Thomas! How's the 'Old Goat' doing tonight?"

The man's grin broadened into an open smile, his head bobbing almost as fast as Sammy's. "Jus' fine, Sir! I be getting along jus' fine."

Putting his arm around the servant's shoulders, they turned to walk down the broad, carpeted hallway, and Alex asked in a more confidential tone, "And, m'lady?"

"She's doing jus' fine too, Sir! Yessir, Mrs. Lowell's in the parlor, awaitin' your arrival, an' doin' jus' fine." Still wearing his smile, Thomas showed Alex into the room where the object of this visit waited patiently in the gathering dusk.

She was sitting at the piano. As the captain entered, the woman stood, smiled, turned coquettishly, and extended long, provocative arms toward him.

The gaslights from the hall spilled their sighing iridescence into the room ahead of Alex, and held the woman as if in a glow created solely for her existence. Struck by the vision, the man was forced to wonder why he'd vacillated so. A self-indulgent question he'd answered many times before.

That the woman was beautiful went without saying, but he knew the feelings he held for her went much deeper than any mere, base, physical attraction of the flesh. Worse, lately they'd become compulsive.

Few things bothered Captain Matthews, but this one had caused many a sleepless night until just recently. Now, what restless slumber he got had become tormented by dreams. Good dreams. Bad dreams. Conflicting dreams of both rapture . . . and terror. Nights, no longer welcome, had come to represent exhausting experiences.

Pausing momentarily to admire the woman before him, all fears of involvement faded in the joy of her presence. She was tall, and apparently thin. A fact difficult to ascertain with the fashion of the day calling for whalebone corsets pulled hour-glass tight, and a bustle over the stern to hide any real shape a woman might have.

She'd gathered some of her long brown hair in back, where it was captured by a ribbon. The rest fell in soft curls and ringlets. The woman's long, graceful neck was not any less seductive for the lace she wore to cover it, but it was her eyes that truly captured his heart. Wide, sparkling, and blue as a tropical sea, they told him more plainly than words how much a woman she could be if given the chance.

Alex felt like the proverbial man with a bear by the tail. Afraid to hang on, and even more so to let go, he had no need of a falling barometer to tell him he was in for one hell of a stormy ride on this trip. His ship, or even his life might founder in such a sea, but that mattered little to him anymore because his heart was already lost.

Setting the flowers on a table, Alex reached forward and grasped her fingertips at arm's length, then sassed her to hide his true feelings. "I didn't hear the piano when I came in!"

Her smile became a playful pout. "Of course not, Captain! If I made a lot of noise, I wouldn't be able to hear who was at the door. Then how could I tell which one of my handsome gentleman friends had come to call?" It was a teasing, impish reply. Stepping forward to embrace him, she continued, "Where have you been, you scoundrel? I thought you'd be here this afternoon! Elizabeth told me you docked around two."

Returning her embrace he mumbled into her hair, "Got your spies out, have you?

We were carrying eggs, of all things, and I had to remain aboard until we'd offloaded. Wanted to be sure my dumb tow-operator hadn't scrambled 'em! Might have left me with an omelet below decks, big enough to feed half the city."

"I know that too." She snuggled against his chest.

The aroma of pipe smoke and bay-rum filled the room with his masculine presence. "You're so insufferably conscientious! Didn't you know I was waiting?"

Yes, he knew she was waiting. That was part of the man's problem. He enjoyed the woman's company beyond anything he'd care to admit, but he also knew the more time spent with her, the more he was becoming trapped, charmed, and committed.

In an attempt to maintain some semblance of self-control, he reviewed a mental promise made onboard Captain Stewart's ship, homebound, so many years before. "Surviving this tragedy, I shall never, willingly, expose myself to that kind of hurt again!"

Willingly? Recognizing the word for what it was, the man knew by his mere presence here an unanticipated precondition had already been met.

Not being a man to run from his fears, the captain simply set a new course for himself straight into the heart of the storm, and dared the fates to have their way. Aside from a short pause, which allowed their embrace to linger, the poor man's ongoing, emotional turmoil never reached the surface.

"Well, m'lady, there are two ways of looking at my delay. I could say anything worth having is worth waiting for, or if you'd prefer, I'll give you my explanation as to why it's the forbidden fruit that's always the sweetest!" Smiling as he spoke, the man pushed her out to arms length to watch her reaction, and admire this handsome woman once more.

With a "Phfff!" she pushed away from him, but turning her back she smiled over her shoulder. Her body language told him he was right on the first count, and she could barely wait for the second.

Captivated, his mind told him things he already knew. *Damn, this woman has a depth, grace, and beauty beyond those of any mere mortal!*

After dinner, they celebrated his birthday by attending the Jubilee at the Coliseum, and what a celebration it was. The massive structure alone was awe inspiring. Particularly, when one considered it was a temporary building on the corners of Clarendon and Saint James, constructed for this one occasion.

A thousand musicians, ten-thousand singers, a drum corps, church-bell ringers, and a hundred firemen—armed with anvils and sledge-hammers—to beat out Verdi's *Anvil Chorus*, all for his entertainment. A cannon was fired from the stage for the dramatic climax, and poor Alex could never be sure if everything had transpired as he perceived it, or if it could be blamed on the magic Abigail was weaving through his senses.

A reception followed for a select few back on Beacon Hill, in the hall over the Crown and Comb. It was announced during the introduction of Mr. Gilmore and Mr. Zerrahn, two of the Jubilee's stellar conductors, that the hall they were now in was to be demolished forthwith. Explained as necessary to allow for the widening of Hancock Street, their guests were told to consider this the last function ever held here.

A popular place for the socially conscious to gather, the surprising news stirred heated conversations.

No shrinking violet, Mrs. Lowell made it a point to corner some of her legislative friends, and demand an explanation. Embarrassed, the woman's respondents gave her words and lip service instead of the facts she sought. "The times, Abigail, just the times. That, and progress! It's a booming city, and we have to make room for the future, don't we?"

Her rebuttal about the city having already doubled in size by their filling in of the Back Bay, fell on deaf ears.

Later, on the short walk home, she explained to Alex that progress seemed to be just another word for graft these days. Land in the city had value, and the changes indicated the winners and losers of the fight, or struggle, for political power, and which faction was getting paid off. "Progress, my foot!" she sputtered.

Alex smiled, and teased about the real reason for the woman's anger. He claimed it was rooted less in concerns about honesty than in her being miffed over not being consulted. "After all, this is Abigail Lowell's city!"

Knowing there was a spark of truth in the banter, she suggested his schooner would make a perfect dumping place for what they dug out of the livery stable next door, when that was torn down too.

The next morning, strolling down toward the dock on that beautiful, aforementioned birthday day, Alex was thoroughly engrossed. Talking animatedly, the man was re-hashing the previous night's topic, and adding his own thoughts about shrinking dock space, railroads, and the pressures being put on his trade by the worlds so-called progress.

So engrossed, his surprise was profoundly complete when he helped Abigail down the gangplank and then whirled her off the end in his arms. Holding her tightly for what was in truth only a split-second longer than necessary, he became aware of people watching. Suddenly, in his own guilt-ridden mind, that moment of innocent joy became a rather flagrant, public display.

Alex spun angrily to confront these unexpected, not to mention uninvited, intruders onboard his ship. To the man's amazement, he found standing there waiting to greet him, the entire, rather haughty, contingent of ladies from his church in Yarmouth.

The women were visibly shocked by these actions of a well-respected, and quite possibly personally-coveted, member of their congregation. Standing there in disapproving silence, they looked down collective, condemning noses, and waited for the man to speak.

Stunned beyond words, a rather rare occasion for Alex, he stepped back as if from a blow. His neck began to redden, with the color progressing rapidly upwards.

Abigail, intuitively sensing exactly what was driving his discomfort, began to snicker quietly behind a discrete lace hanky. Alerted by the noise, Alex caught a mischievous glint of humor in her eyes. Sobering immediately, the man regained his composure in the process.

Following the philosophy of the best defense being a good offense, Alex put on an imitation of genuine pleasure when he boomed out, "Ladies? What a wonderful surprise to have you aboard! Let me introduce you to one of my business associates, Mrs. Abigail Lowell. She happens to be the agent who handles the Boston end of my transactions."

Behind the facade, his mind raced in three directions at once. *Damn! Someone in my crew is going to pay dearly for this! They should have gotten word to me of the presence of these women! Let's see, this was Eben's watch, and the only one on deck is John Cahoon trying to make himself invisible by splicing some chafing lines out on the bowsprit. Where the hell is everyone else?*

Although it was a cool morning for the season, the man was perspiring visibly. This unexpected visit had to be important, for it was totally out of line for 'proper' women to be found in this part of the city unescorted. Even at this early hour. Something in the shadows of his mind teased him, but refused to give up what it knew. Stalling, he introduced the women to Abby individually, with the hope time would come to his rescue.

Listing their relationship to each other, where in the village they lived, those who still had husbands—their occupation, the official positions they held in the church, and any other information he could think of, the man prayed

Abby would understand the precarious position of his reputation, and not betray his trust. His own handkerchief came out. Trickling into his eyes, he daubed at the river's source.

The obligatory social concerns out of the way, and his demeanor back to near normal, he gave up on trying to recall what, if anything he should remember. All he could think of was that these women had missed connections, or somehow run out of money, and found themselves in need of transportation back to the Cape. Other than trouble, they had no reason to be here, and it was becoming obvious something was on their minds. Thinking he'd spare them further embarrassment, he asked kindly if their visit were merely of a social nature, or if he could provide them with some necessary service.

Now it was the ladies turn to show discomfort and confusion. Still smarting personally from watching 'her Captain' waltz another woman down his gangway, Prudence stepped forward and asked in a rather contemptuous manner, "Is your memory failing you, Captain? You do remember the arrangements Sarah made, don't you? It was my understanding you had volunteered to host a breakfast for us this morning!"

"This morning?" Alex was puzzled. "Oh, Prudence, that's right! You ladies are singing as part of the Chorus! The Peace Jubilee! Of course, how could I forget such a thing?

Last night, you were wonderful, ladies, absolutely wonderful!"

Stupid! He'd just admitted attendance, and the 'With whom?' was bound to follow in natural order.

The obvious flattery was another thinly disguised fight for time, but things were starting to gel. He was silent for a moment longer, while the dawn finally broke on a severely overtaxed mind. With no warning or forethought, his voice came to life. "Damn! 'Sarah's Justice!'"

Hearing the curse word spill out of his own mouth, Alex realized he'd committed another social *faux pas*, and a second troublesome thought began to tickle the back of his mind. *Had he somehow been doomed to pursue some sort of personal agony forever—as in Dante's Inferno—or was this just a Calvinistic punishment for the new joy he was discovering with Abby?* His ears burned. A well respected captain should not find himself in such a position.

Recognizing this as an inappropriate time for procrastination, he blundered on. "Oops! Sorry, Ladies! Didn't mean to offend any of you by my coarse language.

As for the other, yes! I do have to admit I vaguely remember my sister mentioning something of this nature in passing. No specifics were mentioned, and I'm afraid I took it as an idle request should the occasion arise. Well now, how careless of me not to follow the matter up. What was that, back a month ago, or maybe even two? Humph? Never heard another word, and that's unlike Sarah not to set up a definite itinerary! Guess she was busy, and it slipped her mind."

Conveniently! It was a silent interjection, but he knew his sister.

"Well, no harm done, Ladies! Hope we haven't kept you waiting too long, is all. I know just the place, and we'd love to host a breakfast for every one of you. This 'is' my birthday you know, and what a wonderful way to celebrate. Eleven beautiful women to grace my table. The King should be so lucky!"

One thing at a time!, was his thought, as he returned Abby's frown with a smile. Dragging her along as co-host should get even with this woman for laughing at his discomfort, but Sarah's reward for her ingenious endeavors would require a more detailed and thought consuming effort. After all, it had been back in November when the first nervous feelings had begun to haunt him. Sarah had acquiesced to his match-making with Christopher so easily, warning flags went up, but then nothing happened. Over time, the captain forgot, let his guard down, and now he was paying the price.

A breathless Eben came thundering up to the gangway from the direction of the city. "Oh Captain, I see the ladies have found you!" After a few more puffs he added, "I hope they haven't interrupted your business dealings!" The twinkle in his eye suggested a double-meaning, but Alex was so relieved to see he'd misjudged the man's loyalty, the innuendo was overlooked.

"Thank you Eben! Negotiations went easier than expected, so I returned early to find the ladies waiting for us. Most fortunate indeed, because I certainly would not wish to have disappointed them. Can you imagine what people would say if I'd left these sweet and gracious young women to sing on empty stomachs?" *Oh yes indeed! Especially since it's these very—not so young—women who would do the talking.* He also wondered what delicious things they'd have to say about Mrs. Lowell, and what interesting rumors might start once they got back to Yarmouth.

"Ladies. . . ." Alex waved his guests up the gangway, shepherding them back in the direction Eben had come from.

Later, he explained Sarah's warped sense of humor to Abby, and how her sense of fair play, along with her elephantine memory, tended more toward revenge than charity. On his monthly visits over the course of the winter, he'd gone into minute detail about his sister and her children. How they'd come to live with him dominated a good part of their conversations, so Mrs. Lowell was well aware of the difficulties Captain Matthews faced in adapting to his new life-style.

Somehow, 'Sarah's Justice' had never come up . . . until now.

Not only did it meet with Abby's approval, but was something she empathized with completely. "A fact," she told Alex, "that all by itself, is reason enough to meet your sister whenever it should become mutually convenient!

We seem to have so many common interests."

This thought gave the man pause. He wondered what in the world Abby and Sarah could have in common, coming from such diverse backgrounds. But then a discomforting feeling swept through him when he realized it was he himself who provided the common thread, and that thought passed on to questions of whether or not he could live with two such headstrong females in his life.

During the winter, Alex had also mentioned his continued conflicts with his nephew, Andrew. These discussions held such a curious blend of pride and complaint they left Abby with a thoroughly confused understanding as to his true feelings for the boy. Wisely, the woman decided she'd have to judge young Mr. Sears for herself later, after he'd joined the crew of the *Yarmouth.*

Eben, an attentive spectator to all the goings on, declared to anyone within earshot, "If this particular trip is any indication, the summer of 1870 should turn out to be a very interesting sailing season indeed."

Chapter 24

Mal de Mer and Sea Chantys

Nature has a habit of balancing her accounts, so maybe this long, hot summer was her pay-off in exchange for the preceding, cold, storm-filled winter.

Haunted by nightmares of endless waves, and cold, dark water, Sarah felt lonely every time she thought of her boy about to face tempest and gale out there somewhere. Contrary to her wishes, the mild weather seemed to confound her fear of the elements, and her basic instincts bought no sympathy from this family. Out of arguments, and under pressure from all three of her menfolk, she finally relented and agreed to let Andy work as a crewman for both Alex and Christopher.

Alex needed her son most when he was booked to carry passengers. Signed on for a week at a time, the young man was at first hurt and surprised that he didn't get to sleep or eat at home when the *Yarmouth* was dockside, only a mile away. The Captain, however, knew what hc was doing. Aside from needing people on board to watch the ship against natural or human disaster, he had no intent of letting his sister get involved with the way he ran either his ship or crew.

In another calculated move, he gave Andy the job title of steward, with the intent of making him feel proud of his duties.

Stolen from the steamship lines, Alex felt it might motivate the young man a little more than just calling him a cabin boy, although the work and pay would be the same. He also had an ulterior motive, in that his nephew could be demoted from this position if he didn't produce his share of work, whereas cabin-boy was as low as a fellow could get.

In this capacity, aside from his deck duties and pulling a regular watch, Andrew was expected to wait on table, help cook the shipboard meals, make up bunks if the trip became an overnighter, and clean up after their guest's occasional indiscretions.

A learning, but rather humbling experience. Especially when he found he had to wait upon, and treat some of his land-bound classmates and peers like royalty when they accompanied their parents to Boston.

The first minor rebellion brought his uncle down on him like a hatch cover.

Andy complained about his so-called friends calling him a scullery maid, and treating him worse, so he'd refused to serve them.

The Captain would have none of that. He explained to his young charge how the customers were paying a dollar apiece for the trip, with meals twenty-five cents extra. For this amount of money, it mattered little who they were, or what he thought, he was to bite his tongue and serve them one and all alike.

The chastisement was harsh, but it was explained in a way he understood, and accepted as a type of conspiracy among the entire crew. The point was to please their customers. That way, if the payees felt the money well spent, they'd be back. Repeat business would benefit the ship, while her crew, Andy included, stayed employed.

If the Captain was prone to one fault, it was his lack of ability to sense when he'd won his point. He heaved one last bucketful into this discussion, and it almost sank Andy's boat. Finishing up his harangue, the captain issued a loaded warning. "Master Sears, if I hear so much as one more complaint from our guests, you will notice the price of that meal—multiplied by the number of passengers—missing from your pay at the end of the voyage!

Now, return to your duties!"

Control by intimidation was not the way to endear Andrew to any cause. Ask him to do something, and it got done. Order him to do it, or threaten him, and you had a very stubborn boy on your hands. Neither this subject, nor the tone, set too well with 'Master' Sears.

Alex didn't win much favor this day, but considering Andrew's temper was almost as quick as his uncle's, something must be said for the minor miracle of no following explosion. Their position being ten-miles at sea, the decision was no doubt a wise one. Obviously the captain would never allow himself to be driven to the point of throwing the lad overboard, but just the fact neither had a place to get away from the other to cool off, magnified their every conflict.

Andy swallowed his pride, and did as he was told. His emotion was channeled to the original source of contention, and produced a vow to get even with the boys who'd been guilty of the teasing. With this thought, his black anger faded to a dark cloud, but it still got dragged around for a day or two.

These same, so-called friends, ended up on the return leg. Picking up the needling right where they'd left off, they planted a seed of sullen resentment which came back to haunt them rather quickly.

Andy's job wasn't too bad when the weather was fair, and the normal summer southerlies were blowing. A one-way ticket would often get its owner right to the Boston dock in seven or eight easy hours. Under these circumstances, the boy would serve one main meal in the middle of the day, followed by snacks on demand.

Weather can be fickle. Sometimes the wind would howl from a direction at odds with their heading, and the same distance could take two, or even three days. Rain, and a cold, wind-driven fog could make life aboard ship pure misery. Andy's solace then was that with the ship pounding in the heavy seas, none of his passengers had much interest in the greasy, fried, codfish cakes; rancid, corned beef; stewed seafowl; milk-based chowder, or any of their other usual fare. Instead, those became the salted, soda biscuit, and hard-tack days, with slop-pails lashed beside every bunk.

As luck would have it, this very return trip ran into some foul conditions. Master Sears was quite seaworthy by now, and he seized upon the opportunity. What better time to get even with a certain friend or two for his earlier difficulties than when it was fresh in all minds.

With mischief aforethought, he sidled up to them at the rail. Waiting for a pause between heaves, he made a big show of munching on a piece of fried chicken, then generously offered his friends some from a pail loaded with the fumes of its heavy cooking grease. The poor fellows took on an added shade of green, and did their best to turn themselves inside out. Completely unsympathetic, a grinning Andy brought into question their Cape Cod heritage, and suggested they might think of taking up less adventurous professions than sailing, should they live long enough to make landfall again.

This did not go un-noticed by his uncle, as little on board ever escaped the man's attention, but it brought no rebuke. The captain may not have approved of the act, but he understood.

Alex was exceptionally busy this season, plying his packet trade around the shores of Massachusetts and Cape Cod Bays. Every year it seemed fewer sailing vessels put to sea, and even less tried to keep to a schedule. Bulk cargoes were about all that remained to these aging, silent hulks. With no fuel to burn, they could haul lumber, coal, and ice for three or four cents a ton cheaper than the railroads, and often get it to the point of use without a second trans-shipment.

To Alex, coal and lumber represented dirty work, and once undertaken, fouled or crippled a ship beyond any other use. Proud, stubborn, and more fond of his schooner than circumstance might dictate, the man preferred to take his chances with his schedule, and what little the Cape produced. Faced with a near-empty ship come sailing day, and profits that marched in lock-step, he clung to traditions others had long since abandoned.

Lately, rumors were flying of another local industry, the salt works, giving up due to competition from newly opened mines in New York. Made right in Yarmouth, by dehydration in large wooden pans set along the edges of the marshes, it was a labor intensive business, and very weather dependent. The apparatus itself always seemed to be in need of repair. The pans had to be watertight, their covers raised or lowered to accommodate atmospheric conditions, and the pumps tended constantly to assure proper filtering and filling occurred. Cleanliness was difficult to maintain, and once dried, the salt had to be raked, screened and placed in barrels for shipment. Shrinking profits and a cloudy future had come together to change yet another way of life, and in the process threaten Alex's own.

Sea salt made up the bulk of his summer freight, while his own existence provided a vital interdependent link in the survival of the few active works left. Worried about the future as much as the past he was guarding, Alex continued to haul their product to Boston at a cut-rate. He was one of the few Captains who owned his own vessel, and this gave him an advantage when dealing on close margins. Ten cents a bushel covered the expense of an entire round trip, so whatever the man could carry beyond that provided the edge to carry him through another winter.

Heads up, into the wind at anchor

Seasonally, he moved whole households to the Cape, which allowed those wealthy enough to afford his freight the luxury of escaping Boston's summer heat.

Come fall, and back they'd go again to be near the social life, general court, state government sessions, schools, and businesses only the city had to offer.

A smattering of fish products and local produce such as the eggs, mixed up his cargo occasionally. Paying passengers and return haulage, if he could find it, were pure gravy. On the return trip, his cargo manifest might include anything from furniture and hardware, to kegs of rum, or dry goods for the local retail trade.

To be profitable, one man to a mast was the recommended crew size for a coasting-schooner, plus the Master. The exception of course was a passenger vessel. Alex was not one to be bound by the suggestions of others. He made such short hauls, he thought it more economical to carry an extra man or two along to cover the watches, and help with the stray voyager. With a schedule to keep, he also felt better about not being at the mercy of any local labor force in Boston to help him unload, plus it avoided questions about the honesty, or work ethics of strangers.

With one or the other of the Hallet boys as his first mate and cook, the rest of the crew came from a pool of men who, as they had time, had been sailing with Alex for years.

For a boy, the work was hard, and his uncle, although a fair man, was a demanding master. Andy didn't mind. Besides the feeling of accomplishment a hard day's work could bring, it was the atmosphere and order of a sailing ship, and the camaraderie with his shipmates that fascinated and drew the boy back to every voyage.

Just because the Captain happened to be his uncle, made no difference in the way he was treated. Andy's bunk was in the forecastle with the rest of the crew, and he pulled his watch with no special significance or favoritism attached.

To make sure he wasn't being taken advantage of, he did ask around the docks, and discovered that his wage, at four dollars a month, was the equal of any other boy at sea. This pleased him, but he felt a pang of guilt afterwards to think that he'd questioned the fact.

The boy seemed to draw pleasure from everything around him. It was a slightly different mix of men each trip, and depending on who made up the crew, decided which instrument or voice was on board for his harmonica to accompany.

The music was varied, but chanteys were the most common pieces. Work songs, which reflected a sailor's life and commentary on things as varied as a Captain's popularity, to the spicy habits of certain easy women. He learned short-haul types, used to coordinate quick easy work, but the longer pull-and-rest rhythms of sail hoisting were more to his liking, because everyone seemed to know a different verse, and they went on and on forever.

Shake 'er up, was one they often used on the *Yarmouth*.

Oh shake 'er up and away we go,

so handy, my girls, so handy.

Up aloft from down below,

so handy, my girls, so handy.

His all time favorites became the windlass, or capstan songs. Intended to synchronize footsteps, the rhythm was easy and he already knew many of them. *Shenandoah,* and *A-Roving* had been popular for years.

On the off-watch, or waiting at the dock, he learned other songs of the sea, like *Reuben Ranzo.*

He learnt to write on Wednesday.

He learnt to fight on Thursday.

On Friday he beat the master.

On Saturday, we lost Reuben,

and where do you think we found him?

Why, down in yonder valley,

conversing with a sailor.

Ranzo, boys, a'Ranzo!
Belay there, lads, belay.

He shipped aboard a whaler;
he shipped as able seamen do;
oh pity Reuben Ranzo.
The Captain was a bad man,
he took him to the gangway
and gave him five and forty.
Oh pity Reuben Ranzo.

Ranzo, boys, a'Ranzo!
Belay there, lads, belay.

The mate he was a good man,
and taught him navigation;
now he's Captain of a whaler,
married a Captain's daughter,
and they both are happy too.
Don't pity Reuben Ranzo, lads,
this ends my little ditty.

Ranzo, boys, a'Ranzo!
Belay there, lads, belay.

Sailors the world over were a superstitious lot, often refusing to sail on a Friday, or on the thirteenth whether a Friday or not. If a shirt or other garment were put on inside out, it stayed that way until the next wearing for fear of a change for the worse.

Music too, was chosen with caution. One of the best known hoisting chanteys, *Blow the Man Down* was never taken lightly, for who in his right mind would dare tempt the fates to deliver such a wind.

Occasionally an officer might whistle to call up a breeze on purpose, but should a lessor individual forget and do so on deck by mistake, he stood in very real danger of being throttled or thrown overboard by his shipmates. Every man who'd ever put to sea knew a careless bird shrill would surely bring on a gale, with bad luck to follow.

Even on the *Yarmouth*, an obligatory chorus of *Stormy* would be sung after a squall or strong wind, just to be sure it was ended proper.

When stormy died, I dug his grave.

I dug his grave with a silver spade.

I hove him up with an iron crane

and lowered him down with a golden chain.

Old storm along is dead and gone.

Ay! Ay! Ay! Ay! Mister Storm Along.

A touch of nostalgia from the 30's, 40's, and 50's, when there were so many packets plying the waters between the Cape and Boston that they challenged each other to friendly races, was the basis of another favorite. The Yarmouth vessels were usually the fastest along the north shore of the Cape. Strange, but even when they were sold to their neighbors across the harbor in Barnstable, their replacements could then outsail the ones just sold. Naturally, it was the general feeling in Yarmouth that the truth of the matter lay more in the excellent seamanship and handling of the craft by their crews. In frustration, a Barnstable wag put a race to music that in truth had the exact opposite results.

The Commodore Hull she sails so dull

she makes her crew look sour.

The Eagle Flight she's out of sight

in less than half an hour.

But the bold old Emerald takes delight

to beat the Commodore and the Flight

and rule the ocean's bower.

These were grand times for a boy of Andy's age. Impressionable, his world was expanded a little further by each individual crewman's knowledge and background. He learned of local heroes such as John 'Mad Jack' Percival. Born and buried in West Barnstable, the man had Captained *The Constitution,* or *Old Ironsides* as she was more fondly known, on a round the world trip back in '46. 'Mad Jack' earned his nickname during the war of 1812. Deciding to celebrate Independence Day, July 4, 1813, in a proper manner, he sailed out and captured the British ship *Beagle* which was blockading the Port of New York at the time.

Andy found to his surprise that he knew other great men personally, or went to school with their children and grandchildren. A second West Barnstable native, James Otis, rose to fame as one of the Revolutionary War patriots. Right from home, in Yarmouth Port, Asa Eldridge was another. He'd Captained *The Red Jacket* in 1854, on her record setting run of thirteen days, one hour and twenty-five minutes from New York to Liverpool.

The boy also found it hard to believe that the clippers *Belle of the West, Christopher Hall, Hippogriffe, Kit Carson,*

Webfoot, Revenue, and *Wild Hunter* were all built a few miles from home at the Shiverick Brothers' shipyard in East Dennis.

Andy's crewmates had sailed on these and other ships, with heroes as well known or better. As a result, the men had many wild stories of strange ports visited, and distant seas crossed. Andrew was sure there was a grain or two of truth in the yarns, but the way he hung on every word of each tale, then asked for repeat performances when he wanted to hear a particular part again, ensured that he also got his full share of tall ones too.

The lad was well aware of this, but he loved them all just the same. His attention flattered the story-tellers, and endeared the boy to them. In a closed cycle, this encouraged the men to further embellish their tales, and dig up even more engrossing ones about sea serpents, pirates, and ghost ships.

Having time to gossip on easy days, the captain and Abigail were often choice topics of conversation among the crew. They were, after all, a captive audience to Alex's comings and goings in the Port of Boston, not to mention the fact that to a man, they secretly envied his good fortune in finding a woman of such distinction, intellect, and beauty.

The boy was particularly amused when he heard of the trick his mother had pulled on Alex a few trips back. He knew it had something to do with the Peace Jubilee, and the ladies who'd gone to Boston to be a part of it, but just what happened he wasn't sure. Only a few rumors had trickled around the village thus far, so finding out the real truth of the captain's embarrassment was news indeed. He wished he'd been there. Catching his uncle in tight-spots had gotten to be quite a sport around home.

Yes Sir, he thought, *my mother is sure clever all right!*

This admiration triggered a question he knew only one man aboard was qualified to answer. Selecting a private moment, out of earshot from his fellow shipmates, Andrew asked his uncle if this incident had been an example of 'Sarah's Justice'.

The captain's answer was accompanied by a flush of remembered social agony; a raised eyebrow which questioned the source of his nephew's information; and a simple, "Aye!" accompanied by much pipe smoke and a nodding head.

One thing about the now confirmed incident really peaked Andy's curiosity. Alex's ladyfriend was described by the man telling the tale as a Brahmin. The boy thought at first it might be her maiden name, or possibly a country of origin, as he'd heard her married name was Lowell.

Eben explained that in India, the Brahmins were members of the highest social level, or what they called 'caste' in the Hindu religion. The caste system was strictly observed in their faith, and they were forbidden to mingle with lesser individuals. To acquire an even higher plane of existence, these people were required to live a life of dharma, or virtue, and part of that was doing good for others. Spare time being one of the curses of the idle rich, these individuals spent much of it on noble causes. Ergo, in Boston, when a person was said to be a 'Brahmin' it could be a compliment, but it was also a tongue-in-cheek way of saying that they too were members of the non-mingling, upper crust in the city's social strata.

If Eben had stopped right there everything would have been fine, but the man had a habit of talking too much. He added, "Not only is the Captain's lady a member of Boston Society, but she's a real beauty too!

Now, you tell me, boy, with all her money and intelligence, what in hell does she see in a mere Coastal Captain?"

His audience of one suddenly got all red around the collar, and a bit stand-offish.

Andy found the statement offensive, even though he knew it had been meant in jest. To him, a Sea Captain was about as high as a person could get. And besides, now that he thought about it, he also had to grudgingly admit that his uncle was about the smartest man he had ever known too.

The boy decided Eben might just be blowing off steam to hide a little jealousy, but the remark left him feeling perturbed.

Eben must have known he'd hit a tender spot by the color that came to Andy's cheeks, and the way his back had stiffened. Anyway, he didn't bother pursuing the topic, and instead spoke of a passing paddle steamer.

In an act especially noteworthy when compared to his normal behavior, and showing judgment beyond his years, Andy bit his tongue rather than get involved in a squabble over something he wasn't too sure about. Unable to do the same with his mind, it played with some interesting possibilities. Tired of the mental confusion, he turned away from Eben and mumbled, "This must be some woman!"

Fully aware the boy's curiosity was killing him, Alex kept him uncompromisingly busy the first few times they made port in Boston. Poor Andy spent hours coiling, or flaking, miles of rope in big, flat, concentric circles. The rough hemp built blisters to match, and when they broke and bled Nathaniel had him plunge his hands into a bucket of brine from the corned-beef barrel. Unsuspecting, the sudden shock took the young man's breath away.

Grimacing almost as much as Andy, Nathaniel held the writhing boy's hands in place until the pain began to fade. Andy'd been too busy struggling to cry, and the clean cloths which bound his hands afterwards became badges of courage when the 'doctor' vouched for that fact.

The masts came next. Sluiced with galley grease to make it easier to raise and lower sail, the *Yarmouth* got such a liberal dose it's a wonder she didn't leave an oil slick all the way home. Andy spent this whole day riding up and down in a bosun's chair slung from the topmast rigging. The insides of his legs got chafed raw, but he didn't dare tell Nathaniel for fear he'd end up 'standing' in the corned beef barrel.

The following trip meant cleaning up the drippings, so the deck got holy-stoned and swabbed 'til it shone white in the summer sun, and the brass would have done any Naval vessel proud.

Eventually it had to happen. Bright and early one morning, after an all night sail down the coast in light airs, Mrs. Lowell met the ship as it was being warped into its place at the dock.

Andy was up in the rigging at the time. Not needed on deck until the ship was secure, he was perched on the crosstrees of the foretop, where—lacking a real tree—he'd climbed for the view. Spotting her from a distance, and knowing instinctively who this individual must be in spite of the early hour, the young man appraised his uncle's taste and decided a closer inspection was in order. He made up his mind on the instant that come Alex, hell, or high-water, somehow he was going to meet this woman today. Risking rope burns by sliding down a halyard, Andy joined the crew making ready the gangway.

An obvious attempt by Alex to divert the boy's labors elsewhere, came close to producing a mutiny. Knowing smiles passed amongst the crew. Placing bets on the outcome, they good humoredly waited for one or the other to explode.

Not privy to their mischief, but aware something was in the wind, Alex faced the usual churning-cauldron-within. The heat of the man's anger could not be disguised.

The intent of Andy's quest may have been innocent, but the result was an awkward confrontation for the Captain. Here they stood, nose to nose in a battle of wills, while Abigail, his passengers, and the entire crew stood watching.

Realizing he had no gracious way of diffusing the situation, Alex took a couple of deep breaths to calm himself. Defeat was something he seldom faced, and therefore difficult to accept gracefully.

Restraint of manner mirrored in his reluctant stiffness, Alex made the formal introduction. It was short, far from sweet, and immediately followed by a direct order for Andrew to go below and break out the luggage for their two paying passengers.

For no apparent reason, this whole episode, a simple introduction, had turned into another major embarrassment for the man.

From Abigail's viewpoint, she wondered if Alex's obvious reticence wasn't due in part because he feared Andrew might not approve of her, but that didn't seem right in light of his previously voiced opinion. He claimed the boy didn't like 'him', and found objection to most of the things he held dear because of it. Put in perspective, the man also cast forth the idea he didn't care much for the boy either, when in spite of his denials it was quite plain he cared very much.

Could it be the captain was afraid Andrew might carry stories home? Tales he'd rather not hear repeated around the village? Alex didn't appear to fear much, but something of that sort might get him in further trouble with those straight-laced ladies from his church!

Abby smiled at the memory of his concern over their reactions. Sarah had proved her intelligence, to conceive of such an elaborate surprise and have it all come off as planned.

Thinking a few devious thoughts of her own, Abigail considered the benefits a few tales from the big city might do for her personal crusade. *Possibly keep Captain Matthews faithful, and the competition off balance, but . . . would that be fair to Andrew? If I get him into more trouble, he'd be justified in not liking me, and then what?* She smiled inwardly, still intrigued by the idea.

Unable to pin down a specific reason for the captain's behavior, Abigail became a little apprehensive at this sudden crossing of swords. Always hearing the insinuations about men not being able to figure out how women thought, she posed the obverse philosophical question to herself as to why it was that males of every specie and age should be so unreasonably driven to protect pride and territory.

The next question was thrust upon her when she pondered rather indignantly whether Alex actually considered her as part of his territory, and if so, 'who' had given him that right? This brought an unexpected, but pleasantly-warm flush. Puzzled, she resolved to look up Darwin's new theories and see if they held an explanation.

Mrs. Lowell needn't have worried about Andy's approval. The boy was captivated in that first instant. In fact, he was so completely infatuated, that on future trips instead of just being put to work, he was confined to the ship as the only possible way to keep him out of his uncle's hair. This, of course, gave the older man even more stew to chew on.

Not only has that damned, little worm invaded my home, my ship, and my freedom, but now he's trying to take over my social life as well!

Finally seeing the interaction between the two for what it was, Abigail found herself both amused and relieved. That big, rough-tough, self-confident sea captain of hers was jealous of the boy. A child, one-fourth his own age!

If these two males weren't taking it so seriously, she could have laughed at the absurdity.

Chapter 25

High Society

During a short layover to exchange their load of salt for a return shipment of sailcloth and molasses, Andy was underfoot, so Mrs. Lowell requested permission from the Captain to take his steward on a personal tour of the city. Alex harumped and grumped, but all within earshot knew it was just for show. The woman had demonstrated often she could have anything within his power to grant.

Her motive was simple enough. She hoped to make amends to the poor, young man for what had become an enforced imprisonment, and maybe at the same time tease Alex a little for his heavy-handedness in this regard.

Andy was instructed to dress in the best he could muster. A simple request, but one which forced the boy to run a gauntlet of cat calls and friendly barbs from his fellow crewmates before he regained daylight. The flustered young man who appeared before her left the woman wondering what had gotten him so upset. Taking him in tow, she gave Alex an accusing glance, but the man had been on deck the whole time Andy was below.

If her intent had been to impress the lad, it certainly succeeded. One of their first stops was at the Statehouse on

Beacon Hill. There, he was introduced to Governor William Claflin from Medford. A close personal friend, Abigail tried to explain the Governor's favorable position on Woman's Suffrage. Mrs. Lowell devoted a goodly portion of energy to this cause, the results of which by reflection gave her a certain amount of recognition and political power.

A governor's aide took them on a short tour of the building, and because Mrs. Lowell was a familiar figure, they were received with a bit more than just idle curiosity by the press. The attention was a surprise to Andy, but Abby got rid of these pests by stating tongue-in-cheek she was not going to run for Governor again this year.

Abandoning their guide to the jackals, the two of them ducked into the visitor's gallery. A shouting match was taking place on the floor of the legislature, which seemed to be nothing more than posturing and bombast to Andy. Suggesting as much to Abigail brought a rewarding smile for his naive honesty.

Not wanting to bore the lad with an overdose of civics, she led him away to lunch at the Parker House. It was no mistake. Awed to the point of open-mouthed wonder at the palace-like, marble lobby, he found it hard to believe this was a mere hotel. Starting off with a touch of indignity and embarrassment at the fuss made over their arrival, Andy's outlook on the world was soon changed forever.

Everyone there was dressed so elegantly, the management provided the boy with a coat and collar tie so, as they put it, he wouldn't feel out of place! The garment was too long and generally ill-fitted, but the man who made the selection suggested it was because no one anticipated such a manly shape on a boy of his age. Andrew saw through the flattery, but he agreed with the premise that it was better to be properly attired than feel singled out.

Regrettably, the boy noticed the exchanged winks with Mrs. Lowell, and suddenly understood the real purpose. This charade was not to protect his feelings, but to ensure that the sensibilities of the other diners wouldn't be offended by his common dress, and questionable heritage.

Before he could become too uppity, an embarrassing distraction made him forget the whole thing. Abigail's perfume was nothing like the lavender-sachet smells that accompanied his mother. Young as he was, he still sensed it was more than just this woman's tropical essence that made him feel giddy when she stood so close, fussing with his collar, and tying the ribbon around his neck. How he could be so attracted to a woman this much older he didn't know, but there was no denying the fact. Mortified at his body's unbidden response, he buttoned the poorly fitted dinner jacket quickly, suddenly thankful for its comical length.

Many of the other diners seemed to know Mrs. Lowell, and the gentlemen rose from their chairs as she passed, to exchange greetings and small talk. Their women smiled and joined in, being very polite to Andrew as he was introduced. They all spoke to him as an adult, and the men inquired about which boarding school he might be attending, with each suggesting their own alma-mater as the best if he hoped to get into the University of his choice. They even offered help in getting him accepted, should he so decide.

Andy realized the offers were more to impress Abigail than for his own benefit, and did his best not to embarrass her. By keeping his own mouth shut, the boy felt sure no one would know what an uncultured lout she'd dragged in off the street.

Once seated, their meal and the service provided was so far above anything he'd ever been exposed to before, it was almost beyond comprehension. Seven whole courses, and this was only lunch! Trying to keep his mind busy, and in particular off the woman seated across from him, the boy watched the waiters work with studied intent. Dressed alike in meticulous black suits, white starched shirts, and matching ribbon ties, Andy tried, but could not find a single speck of food or dirt on their clothing anywhere.

Never still for a minute, there was a certain rhythm about the work of these earnest men. It amazed him how they seemed to anticipate their customer's every need. They served from the right, removed soiled dishes from the left, and topped off his water glass every time he took a sip. All this, while he noticed they spoke only when spoken to, and displayed an air of polite, distant, elegant indifference. It had never really occurred to the boy that something as menial as serving food to other people could be elevated to such a level of professionalism. Now, from a different perspective, his shipboard chores didn't look quite so demeaning.

How they could work so hard, and yet remain so cheerful was also baffling. The entire management was very friendly, for that matter. Particularly to Abigail, whom they referred to as Mrs. Lowell. Surprising him, after he was once introduced to the *maitre d'*, his name was also known to all. He became Mister Sears again, but to the boy's ears it now sounded much different than when his uncle called him that. More like royalty, or at the least someone important.

He tucked away a few of these nuggets-of-wisdom for use aboard ship. It was just possible that someday he might want to impress someone special with his own worldliness.

Unbidden, Temperance flashed into his thoughts. The girl had been known to sail aboard the *Yarmouth* with her family on occasion, though yet to grace her decks so far this season. The fact that Tempy seemed to have taken a back seat to Abigail never came to mind, but he chose not to dwell on thoughts of her either, for fear it might stimulate another of those unpropitious events beyond his control.

All through their meal, Andy silently thanked Elijah for teaching him proper table manners, and which fork to use. At least these lessons kept him from making a complete spectacle of himself in front of this woman he was so agog over. He was also amazed that he could remember enough of what he'd been exposed to over the course of the winter to carry on what he considered an intelligent conversation about current events and modern authors.

This tickled Abigail as well, but she thoughtfully and discreetly hid her amusement behind her dinner napkin. To her, this young man was a source of energetic delight. His awareness of the world around him, along with his curiosity and appetite for knowledge, was something she privately intended to reward if given the opportunity.

Studying him, the thought occurred that Alex must have resembled this lad in his own youth. The similar mannerisms and body movements betrayed the relationship. Recognizing this fact, she wondered if it had any bearing on the captain's harsh treatment of the boy. Did he see things in the lad he'd change in himself?

It was quiet during Andy's watch that evening. The fog rolled in to muffle sound and light alike. Eben shared the duty with him, but the man was trying to clean the jets on a carbide reading lantern, so he was too busy to talk for a change. Thankful for the peace, the boy had plenty of time to wonder about the events of the day just past. Still docked at Long Wharf, the *Yarmouth* waited for first light, and her Captain to return from his evening on the town before she'd spread her wings.

It had been a busy day. Andy perched on the main hatch cover, where he could challenge any would-be thieves slipping down the gangway. Sitting there, the boy could hardly believe how everything had fallen into place so neatly. *Could there be 'that' much coincidence in the world? Was it possible Uncle Alex had enough foresight to begin 'stacking-the-deck' in his personal favor against such a day as this? How could any man have possibly known, way back when he signed me up for those classes he made Mr. Gardner pay for, that someday his nephew would be standing on Beacon Hill, in the presence of Society, and the Governor?*

Andy shook his head. There was no question in his own mind, but that 'he' had no business being there, however the boy could also see how his uncle might fit. In spite of the rough edges shown in his regular, everyday living, the man could be quite charming if he so chose.

What was that other saying Alex was so fond of quoting? "When in Rome. . . ."

The Captain gained a point or two of respect that day.

It was evening before Abigail met with Alex, and gave him her own glowing report. She seemed quite impressed with his nephew's conduct and degree of polish.

This both pleased, and somehow annoyed the man, but he never let either emotion show. *No matter what the little beast did, it gave him no rights to share my woman!*

Well into the sailing season, the number of scheduled passengers began to drop, and therefore Alex needed less crew. They'd already moved most of the households which fled the city every year before summer's heat invaded, so now it was the Cape that was bustling with her seasonal newcomers.

Andy missed seeing Mrs. Lowell, and the time spent with his fellow shipmates on the *Yarmouth*, but the change was not without its pleasures. His mother's cooking was better than anything the Hallets put together, and now he got to help on Mr. Gardner's work boat.

The boy loved the fishing, but getting up day after day, so they could be on the water at first-light, was a bit of a strain. Now that it was early summer, and the sun came up well before five, eight bells—or four o'clock—was the latest he could sleep and make it to the dock on time.

Life aboard the packet had its routine and the regimen of duty, but here every day held a new adventure. The work was equally as hard, but no one could ever call it tedious.

All this freedom led Andy to wonder how other people could live and work in an office, or within the confined, monotonous structure of a mill existence such as his family had left behind. This world had so much more to offer.

With the spring planting and work season over, school was back in session, but Andrew was happily excused to continue his sailing duties. Only a short session of six weeks, it ended in mid-August so the children could return to the fields and aid in the harvest.

The gospel, according to Alex? "Hardly worth the interruption!"

Independence Day fireworks were spectacular when viewed from the water. Accounts from every town, concerning their parades of horribles and antiquities, were in all the papers, even though the weather did dampen things a bit this year.

Alex and Christopher both took some time off when the County Agricultural Society convened its fair in Barnstable, in August. A welcome break in the routine, it gave Andy a chance to become reacquainted with his land-bound friends.

Busy as he was, the boy always seemed to find a few minutes, or sometimes an hour, to share with Sammy and Ulysses at the shore.

Tempy got a little miffed when Andy seemed to prefer just laying on a dock in the sun, or fishing for minnows and crabs with his buddies, rather than spend the time with her. She thought listening to her piano recitals, or joining in a picnic on the lawn, would have been a much nicer pastime.

Fascinated by the boy, she couldn't help but notice he was growing into a man. A scrawny waif, when he first came to the Cape, he'd filled out and grown half a head in the few short months since. Tanned, with muscles from hauling sail beginning to show, he got more handsome with every trip.

As part of a proper upbringing, the girl had been taught wisdom and patience by her mother. She knew that fall would come sooner or later, and her sailor would be home then. Winters could be long, and time would be on her side. Andy had developed the wide, sea-leg stance of a sailing man, but a week ashore would cure his gait, and the dancing lessons promised for this winter might give him the social confidence to start courting.

Such thoughts made waiting difficult, but delicious. She dreamed of his strong arms holding her as they waltzed, to the envy of all others.

Andrew knew she was there, but the one time he walked her home from a band concert proved embarrassing. His sister and one of the Hallet girls followed them, and just as he was working up his courage to take Tempy by the hand, they began a teasing song about some sailor come a-courtin'.

Later, Nathan mentioned something about him having a girl in every port, and Andy spent the rest of the summer denying his romantic prowess. To the boy, she was as bad as poison ivy. The itch was there, but to scratch meant more pain than satisfaction.

Waiting became easier for Tempy once she found how handily she could tie the focus of her interest into jealous knots. The mere mention of another boy's name would do, but it became especially effective when she insinuated the gentlemen so-named pestered her endlessly while Andy was away at sea. Such power was heady indeed, and fun too.

White organdy and lace filled Andy's summer memories of Tempy. Hazy days, with blue ribbons to match her eyes, and the sweetness of that one kiss. . . .

Chapter 26

A Fishing Trip

Drifting by as quietly as a log on an oily tide, August was slipping away. With its heavy-air and dog-day heat, few regretted the passing.

The scheduled sailing day for his uncle's schooner was Thursday, which always made them special for Andy. Today's trip didn't involve him directly, a disappointing but expected happenstance, and yet the excitement was still there.

Traditionally, shipping was light at this time of year. It had Alex scratching, but he'd managed to put together enough freight for a paying trip this week. With no passengers, and his pool of part-time sailors waiting for their farming crops to ripen in the fields, it meant an overabundance of willing hands to crew the ship.

Relegated to fishing with Christopher again, Andy kept one eye on the activity around his uncle's craft as she shipped the last of her food and water for the journey. Setting heavy in the water, it'd be mid-morning before the tide rose enough to let the old gal slip over the bar today.

It was barely light when he and Chris made their first run. Mr. Gardner was always bragging how his work boat could float in a puddle with her centerboard up, so this morning's low-tide did not factor into his business.

Requiring daily attention, the lobster pots came first. Smelly, hard work, it was usually a relief to get these done. Baited with totally repulsive fish heads, or oily menhaden—always a week or so beyond when they should have been buried just to relieve those around them from the smell—the boy couldn't understand why a lobster would come anywhere near that carrion. Mr. Gardner's answer was simple. The worse the smell, the further away the lobsters would be attracted to their last meal. This left a few questions in the boy's mind as to why something that ate such terrible stuff could taste so good, but he figured it had something to do with God's will, and he wasn't about to mention religion around Mr. Gardner. One sermon, on Sunday, was more than enough per week, thank you.

Few lobsters came aboard in the heat of summer, and today's short harvest left the fisherman in a rather sour mood.

Chris kept the lobsters in a holding car attached to his mooring line, until he had enough to market. Convenient to watch against pilferage, the floating cage back in the harbor was a long sail from the end of their string of pots.

On the run in, Chris baited up some feathered hooks with tough strips of skin from an unlucky dogfish, in a poor attempt to salvage some of the wasted morning. To his eye they resembled eels, but to Andy they were still just pieces of the little shark that had bumbled its way into one of their pots.

The boy would never tell Mr. Gardner what he thought, but he figured any fish that bit those tough things had to be real dumb, or hungry enough to eat the boat too.

Trimmed out to the man's satisfaction, he threw the finished product overboard with what he called short lines. Everything being relative to its application, about fifty yards of heavy, tarred, cod line separated hook from boat. After the third or fourth bluefish, these mini ropes could seem pretty long to Andy.

In their normal routine, Mr. Gardner handed one to the boy while he took the other.

Dancing on the tail of a cat

A brisk sou'wester had risen with the sun this morning. Being as tight with time as he was with a dollar, the man was trying to make up for some of that lost while hauling empty pots and picking their way down through the channel at dead low water. Chris had the sail close-hauled, and as a result they were practically skipping along, the boat heeled way over, salt spray coming aboard at will.

Out behind, the trolled baits danced from wave top to wave top in their wake.

After this mad dash back to the basin to unload their meager catch, Christopher announced they might as well take advantage of the break, and layover long enough to eat their main meal of the day now. Leaving the work boat tied next to the *Yarmouth* on Central wharf, and thus avoiding the confusion around the fish dock due to the returning trap boats at this time of day, he told Andy to be back in an hour. As they parted, the man explained his intent was to sail around nine, which would put them in position to jig for mackerel on the slack tide at high water.

Arriving back at the boat at the appointed hour, Andy showed up with Ulysses in tow.

Provided they weren't lobstering, Christopher didn't mind the dog aboard. He'd long since proven himself a good sailor.

For the dog's part, he considered the aforementioned crustaceans a particularly interesting challenge. A fact which explained his lack of an invitation for these trips.

Each and every lobster that came aboard greeted him with the same, instinctive, wide-spread, open-clawed threat. Never one to back down from a confrontation, the resulting melee usually left Ulysses with a bloody nose, and poor Christopher with a mangled, unsaleable product.

Greeting the hairy creature today, the man once more made note of how aptly he'd been named in light of the many escapades he was rumored to be a part of. Especially now that he had a compatriot to share the blame. This, a not so subtle jab at Andy, considering the two had been caught raiding Mr. Gorham's apple tree recently. Ulysses, the identifiable link, had been waiting patiently below.

Alex was in the process of getting ready to cast off. The captain and his crew had just finished stowing an unexpected fifty barrels of potatoes aboard, and wedging these in atop a full load of salt already there took some doing. Now only an hour before high-tide, they had plenty of water to maneuver the heavily laden hull, so they were off to Boston.

The Captain and Christopher exchanged friendly barbs, insults, and idle chit chat over their respective rails. As they parted, Alex eyed the sky, and remarked that the air had a queer feel to it today. That is, in addition to the sultriness piling in with the smoky sou'wester.

Chris nodded, checked the cloudless, brassy expanse overhead for himself, then added that he'd noted the barometer seemed to be falling just a dight.

In spite of the brisk wind, the two of them came to the conclusion that it felt like a weather-breeder. "Not proper, mind you, but something's not quite right with this!"

Alex brought up the folklore, how more than the wind had been known to change direction during these strange periods.

Calling his faith into the conversation in hopes of warding off any twist of fate which might be tempted by the subject under discussion, Christopher agreed by saying, "Aye! Even the course of men's souls have been known to shift, through no fault of their own, on days such as this!"

Somewhat somber, and stating the obvious, with a pause for thought between each connected deduction, the man went on to suggest, "We'd both best keep a weather-eye out today. . . . Probably be a shift of wind later, with a sea change to follow . . . most likely be a little squally when she comes around too. . . . Wouldn't be surprised iffen we might be forced to reef the sail down hard, and run for safe harbor!"

Alex, puffing deeply on his pipe, nodded in agreement.

Pulled by the jib Nathaniel had just set, the bow of the schooner drifted away from the dock and started a neat little pirouette designed to reverse the vessel's direction.

Deep in thought, Alex knocked the spent tobacco out of his pipe by tapping it on the taffrail. Next, he turned toward Andy, and stood there watching him. With no verbal guidance, his crew hauled first the foresail and then the mains'l aloft.

Ignoring his crew's efforts, the man seemed to heave a sigh of indecision, and tugged absentmindedly at the main sheetline trailing by his face.

Mr. Cahoon relieved him of the rope, made it fast, then watching their progress against the sky, tended the ship's stern line and wheel.

Activity amidship indicated someone was busy cranking down the centerboard in pace with their motion.

Just as the sails started to grab the wind, Nathaniel's order came drifting back and Mr. Cahoon cast off, then turned to make the main boomtackle taut.

This whole, rather intricate, and impressive maneuver was a well choreographed and rehearsed number. A dance, or more precisely a ballet, the men had performed so often as to need little formal command.

Seeing the routine displayed from this point of view, Andy could sense what had to be done next, and measured the rhythm of the operation with pride in his fellow shipmate's work. He could feel the calluses left on his palms, earned while learning the procedure himself, and for a moment wished he were aboard to take part.

It was obviously deliberate, when the Captain called across the widening gap. "You take care today, Andrew!"

Something seemed to catch in the boy's throat.

This was the first time he could ever remember his uncle using his Christian name. That, and the apparent serious expression on Alex's face, sent a chill down his spine strong enough to raise goose bumps in its wake.

The routine, ingrained reply was automatic by now. "Aye, Cap'n!" Then, not knowing why, he added, "You too!" and raised his hand in a parting wave.

He watched Alex and his ship drift away. Gaining headway, she began to respond to the wheel. Suddenly the wind filled her sails and brought the old schooner alive. She heaved over on a starboard tack, which in turn produced another rush of activity onboard as the men trimmed her big lowers and set her stay sails.

Straight as a ramrod at the wheel, Alex drove her for the point at the end of Sandy Neck.

God she's pretty!, was Andrew's thought.

Christopher brought the boy back to this world with a start. "C'mon boy, fish are bite'n! Won't catch any here on the dock."

Buckets of fresh porgies greeted him. An oily fish similar to herring, or the menhaden lobster bait, Chris had put them onboard while he'd been gawking. Big ships had mechanical grinders to do the work, but here it was the boy's job to chop the hundreds of carcasses into a fine, bloody, smelly, slimy soup called chum. Later, they'd spoon it overboard a dipperfull at a time, to attract mackerel to the vicinity of their little red and white spoons.

No one could tell him why, but it was the shiny, unbaited hooks attached to these that the fish would actually end up biting, so to a mackerel there must have been something appetizing about the soup that got them hungry. Andy couldn't imagine chum attracting anything but flies, and was glad he had a constitution strong enough to keep his stomach from adding to its volume.

The wind had eased off slightly, but they still made good time. Working their way through the harbor-bound small craft scattered by the packet, they got out beyond the bell-buoy marking the end of the channel smartly.

The *Yarmouth*, her lee rail buried and water boiling around her stern, was pulling away from them rapidly now. Carrying as much sail as he comfortably dared, Alex drove the old girl hard toward Boston. With the wind in this quarter, and blowing like she was, Andy knew it'd be a fast, wet run today.

The boy enjoyed watching the dozens of sailing craft visible at any given time. He and Christopher would play a sort of game, and try to identify the boat approaching them by the rig she carried. Often they'd throw in the name of the helmsman too, by the way she was handled. An acquired skill, similar to the ability of a landside individual who can identify certain people at a distance by the way they walk.

Although many coal-fired, steam driven craft were often in view, to the sailors they were just smelly, smoky, impersonal lumps, and usually referred to derogatorily as stink-pots. Able to travel in any direction, in any wind or none, they were perceived as requiring little skill to operate, and therefore commanded a similar amount of respect.

The sea conditions this morning appeared to have discouraged those with little fortitude, and only the few hardy souls bound to their missions by reasons other than choice seemed to be venturing forth.

The pair of Yarmouth men agreed on a spot to try fishing, luffed up into the wind, dropped sail, and Chris threw out his usual, small trawl, sea anchor. He claimed it was to slow the boat's drift down the wind, and keep her head into it so she not only rode easier, but the waves didn't break aboard.

Andy suspected the truth lay closer to the fact that every so often a wriggling, live bonus would show up in the dragging, sock-shaped net.

Christopher's work boat, now renamed *The Sarah* for some unknown reason, was a broad-beamed cat. Like most local catboats, instead of a fixed keel she was equipped with a centerboard like the *Yarmouth's*. This could be raised so she'd slip over the bar at low tide, or lowered to handle the leeward, sideways push of the wind.

The man had built it himself as the useful showcase of a trade. In his off-season, he made a goodly portion of the prams, dinghies, and skiffs found along the Yarmouth shore.

This boat had a large, working, open cockpit, a small foredeck, and a cabin where two people could get in under cover if they absolutely had to. True to style, the one mast was stepped well forward in the foredeck, just short of the bow. He'd opted for a lighter weight than the tree trunk usually stepped in these craft, and as a result had to rely on stays for added support.

Sporting one sail, she was gaff-rigged. A squarish type of sail, it had a large spar called a boom along the bottom, and another smaller spar, known as a gaff, at the top edge. This top-gaff was where the lifting tackle fastened, running from there through blocks at the top of the mast and then down to where the crew could haul on the lines to raise, lower, or trim the sail. It was an attractive rig, and very efficient. Meant to be worked single-handed if need be, it gave the sailor infinite control over his boat.

Built more for practical reasons and ease of handling, rather than speed, or beauty, *The Sarah* fulfilled all four possibilities admirably.

Today their craft faced rolling waves, and pounded rather badly. It didn't take long for Andy, Ulysses, and Chris to get thoroughly drenched in this slop. In the meantime, the boy was doing his duty of ladling out chum, and both of them, Chris using two lines, were hand-jigging. A method of fishing whereby they moved the lines up and down in short, jerky motions to attract fish to the flashing spoons.

Once a school of mackerel had been located they'd anchor the boat, and it was quite possible for two men to pull in a couple of barrels full in half a day. An amount of fish that could add up to three or four dollars, if the market was fair.

Today, the conditions were brutal. The sea was just too rough to maintain this position very long. The wind, shifty and unpredictable, seemed to be picking up once more.

Poor Ulysses, usually happy to be with his buddy at any cost, wandered and staggered around the boat, while he panted to show his displeasure at its motion.

They'd hardly made a dent in the first bucket of chum when Chris decided it was just not worth the aggravation to sit here any longer. The man told Andy to haul in his jig-line and the trawl, then he'd see if they could find a little more shelter in the lee of Sandy Neck.

Eyeing what they had for wind, Chris instructed the boy which cringle to tie off at the jaws of the boom, while he did the same on the leach end. Now working towards each other, they finished securing the surplus sail to the boom with its gaskets and hoisted this much-shortened, or reefed version, aloft to grab the breeze.

The wind had freshened so much Andy could detect little difference in their forward speed from the outbound run under full sail, but the results of the reefing seemed to satisfy Mr. Gardner, so he kept his mouth shut.

They worked their way around a long lead net from one of the fish traps set on the sand bars off Dennis, and picked up a course intended to place them a half-mile or so to the nor'west of Barnstable's Sandy Neck light when they neared shore again.

Settling in, Chris tossed the baited hooks from their lobster run overboard once more, and handed one line to Andy. The boy took it, tied it off to a cleat on the gunnel as instructed, then hauled in a few feet to hold, so he could tell if he got a bite.

This was standard procedure with Christopher. He never wanted to waste a minute out here. Running from fishing spot to fishing spot they would catch a few blues, or the more elusive striped bass this way, and anything that came aboard the man figured was another few cents in the pot.

Suddenly a fish struck Andy's feathered bait. With the speed of the boat, he'd felt no timid, first nibbles here. No splash, no warning. Just, BANG, and the thing was hooked solid.

The boy quickly discovered he'd made a mistake.

Instead of holding the line lightly, to detect a bite, he'd taken a couple of wraps around his hand. The price paid was to have his arm yanked so hard it brought back painful memories of Brant and ice cakes. An old hand at hauling in blues, bass, and whale cod by now, Andy knew instantly he had more fish on the other end of this finger cutting, eighth-inch, cod line than he ever believed possible.

Thinking shark, or even whale, he was glad now that at least he'd done one thing right. As Christopher instructed, the line was tied off.

Surprised, he'd squawked in a mixture of pain and alarm when the fish first hit. This alerted Chris to the strike, and he eased off on the sheets to take some of the pressure away from Andy's straining efforts.

Laughing, he watched the boy attempt to haul in on the fish, then heard it die in his throat when Andy started to lose ground. It wasn't long before the line was pulled tight as a bow string between the cleat and their hidden treasure. Afraid the line would break, the man eased off the wind even further, bringing the head of the boat around.

Under control of a different helmsman now, the fish pulled the stern in the direction it preferred. The boat pointed back up into the wind all by itself, and the line twanged tight again.

Impressed, Christopher dropped the sail this time. They had lost way quickly anyway, from the sheer weight of whatever had taken the bait. About to help the boy pull the boat down to the fish, considering the reverse didn't seem possible, a slam on Chris's own line brought him into the fray directly. Wondering what they'd stumbled onto, the two of them began yelling and hollering to each other excitedly.

Andy's fish broke the surface with as much warning it gave when taking the bait. The creature came boiling out of a wave top with a leap that gave both observers the feeling its intent had been to reach the sky.

There, a four-foot, torpedo-shaped fish—blue black on the back and bright silver on its belly-side— flashed and twisted in the bright sunlight.

As the sparkling spray and fish began their slow, tumbling return to the ocean's surface, Christopher's excited voice came through clearly. "Tuna! Schoolies!

Hot-damn, we're in the middle of it now, Andy! These fish'll run from fifty pounds to a couple hundred, and if we can stay on top of 'em we can fill the boat. They only come this close to shore once or twice in a lifetime, so mark it well, boy!"

Calming down a little, he cautioned, "Don't get yourself worn out over the first fish! Wait 'til they tire against the pull of the boat, son, then we can haul them in easy.

Ya know, if it was your dog that brought us this luck, with no way for him to leave the boat an' take it with him, we just might see us a long and profitable afternoon."

He'd heard of a 'Jonah' scaring fish away, but Andy couldn't make any connection between Ulysses and tuna, unless to Christopher's mind it was the type of adventure the dog's namesake might have pursued. Looking down at his sore, line-burned fingers, he had a more immediate thought. *Wow, and we're going to fill the boat?*

Sensing the excitement, the dog was getting under foot, and doing what he considered his part to help by growling at the splashing dark shapes.

The men teased the fish up to the boat one at a time, then Chris hauled the tuna aboard with a big, barbless hook he'd mounted on a short gaff. As they came in, Andy marveled at their size. Ulysses apparently agreed, because even though it was his luck that was getting credit for finding them, he wanted no part of the fish. Retreating away from their thrashing tails to the foredeck, he stood there barking, adding his din to the mounting confusion.

Straddling these heaving bodies, Andy swung a short, weighted club to stun them much as he did bluefish, with a few quick blows just above and behind the eyes, then removed the hooks as quickly as he could. In the meantime, Chris hauled the boat around on a new tack, trying to figure which way the school might be heading. Bare hooks in hand, Andy paused to re-bait them, then over they went again to tempt anew their finny suitors.

While Chris was settling the boat down to its new course, Andy passed a short line through the dog's collar and tied the other end off to a nearby cleat. Forethought beat taking chances on losing his best friend overboard in the heat of battle.

Now heading nor'nor'east, almost directly offshore and down the wind, they were really flying, and the fish couldn't seem to wait. Like a cat chasing a mouse, the faster the boat went, the more eagerly the fish seemed to pursue. They went through their dogfish quickly, and turned to some of the smaller tuna for additional bait. It was more bloody, and not as tough, which obviously meant replacment more often, but seemed to work just as well.

After a couple of hours of mad, repetitious confusion on this same course, Christopher remarked that the whole of Cape Cod Bay must be full of fish, and the boy agreed. They were twelve to fifteen miles off-shore, maybe two-thirds of the way to Provincetown, and the school hadn't thinned out a bit.

For Andy, the fun had pretty much gone out of the trip. In his mind, as he helped Chris roll another flapping creature into the boat, it had long since turned into just plain work. He straightened up after retrieving the hook, knee-deep in blood and fish, then rubbed his back.

As the boy looked around to see what landmarks he could spot from so far out in this part of the bay, he stopped, frowned, then squinted. Next, he scrubbled his eyes with a couple of fishy knuckles. This only seemed to make matters worse, so he tried to dry these on his wet pants. After wiping his eyes again, he stared off to the west nor'west and decided the problem wasn't with his eyes.

Christopher turned to follow the boy's gaze and froze, half-crouched, mouth open. A strip of bait slipped through his fingers, back into its bucket.

Letting the sail out to spill the wind, he yelled to Andy to grab the tiller and haul in the fishing lines. In the midst of issuing these orders, the man scrambled to the cleat at the base of the mast where he started to undo the halyards that held their sail aloft.

Nervously glancing over his shoulder at the sky, Chris was about to lower-away when he had an apparent change of mind. His voice overly loud with excitement, he now instructed Andy to bring *The Sarah's* head up into the wind, and start releasing the reef they'd put in her sail earlier.

There was deliberate urgency in their motions, but no confusion.

Andy wasn't quite sure what it was all about, but by Christopher's actions he surmised they must be at risk to some degree, and knew this wasn't the time to question.

After the reef had been shaken out, the man hauled the sail to her full extension, including the peak halyard, and flipped a couple of half-hitches over the respective cleats to secure the lines. At the proper stage in his actions, he bellowed to Andy to let the head fall off again and haul the sheets tight to get them back under way.

Wading through knee-deep fish and gore to the centerboard well, Chris set the pin which locked the movable keel in the down position. In a rough sea, it was possible for the board to work its way back up, resulting in a complete loss of steerage and control. After checking all the lines to make sure they were set properly, the man hurried back toward the stern, scattering his fishy carnage in every direction in the process.

Christopher, somewhat out of breath, flumped his tail onto the bench and took the tiller from Andy. He explained, "Was going to reef the sail down a dight more, but then I figured if we can keep her running hard, down-wind like this, we've got a 50-50 chance of making Wood End off P-town afore the weather catches us. Might even make the harbor!"

With a full sail driving her, *The Sarah* was practically lifting off every wave top, but only too quickly the weight of boat and fish brought her sickeningly down the back side again.

It was insanely exhilarating, this repeated dive from crest to trough, and back to crest again. Aware they must be pushing the boat to extremes, Andy felt concern something vital might let go, but the excitement of the moment overshadowed any real fear, and he found himself more intent on swallowing hard to keep his stomach where it belonged.

They sat in a bloody mess. The dead tuna slid forward with every downward plunge, their weight driving the catboat headfirst, deep into the trough between each wave.

The Sarah, tough old girl that she was, took green water right into her cockpit.

When the next wave lifted her head, water and fish slid backward, where they threatened to bury the sailors and dog under the fruits of their own labors, and driving the men to perch on the edge of the combing, the dog to a barely tenable patch of rear deck.

Adding volume to the gore, the buckets of chum had long since been smashed by thrashing tails of dying tuna, or tipped over by sliding bodies. Andy, crotch deep in slop, used one of the empty receptacles in a futile attempt to help the scuppers take care of their flooded cockpit.

Curious about the radical departure from their work day, Andy asked, "What is it, clouds or a fog bank, Mister Gardner?"

"It's a damn change of wind coming down on us, Andy! Lookit the squall line, with all that rain streaming down! God, its got a heart blacker'n the bilge of a coal scow!"

The sudden change in Christopher's attitude made Andy uneasy. His immediate reaction was to become talkative, and full of questions. Pointing a finger up beyond the weather pennant at the head of the mast, the boy remarked, "Lookit them clouds up there! Shinin' in the sun, they look like Ma's cauliflower, with someone blowin' snow off the top!

How come if it's gonna storm, the sun's still out?

Is that the new light at Wood End up ahead, with Race Point beyond?

Highland must be off to the east'ard there somewhere, but can't see it for haze today!

S'pose it'll rain 'fore we make shore?"

"Most likely!" was the singular answer Andy got for his string of inquiries. This piqued the boy's curiosity even more. Accepting this as an answer to his last question only, he thought a minute before resuming his chatter. It was a strange day indeed when Christopher would stop in the middle of the best catch Andy had ever heard of, just because of a little rain and a shift in wind.

The boy suddenly noticed there were no other sails in sight, and not a single stink-pot around to smudge the sky either. Nervously he babbled on. "How come the sky goes from kinda greeny-black on this side of the clouds, to a pinky-purple on the other, and yellar in between?"

Chris's voice had a tinge of strain to it. "Toldja, gonna be a wind change when that line squall gets here, and a helluva lotta weather to go with it! Must be a real cold norther pushing all this hot, sticky stuff out to sea. Near as I can figure it, the hot stuff is green and the cold is pink. That part's a guess, but one thing I can tell you for sure, where they mix it ain't gonna be no rainbow. You think you seen weather? You ain't seen nothin' 'til you get caught in the middle of what we're facin'! Might even have to throw the catch overboard, just so's we can bail to stay afloat."

These words silenced Andy for awhile. For Christopher to even joke about throwing a fish over the side, they must be about to endure something real serious.

Having given up on bailing as a useless exercise, the boy sat there crouching at the high rail, holding Ulysses' collar in his hand. Absentmindedly patting the dog's head, he looked first at all the fish they might have to throw overboard, and then at the now ominous clouds which, in spite of their pounding dash toward shelter, were stealing closer by the minute.

Andy shivered, but not because he was cold. Sparkling and snapping like fireworks, he could see brilliant bolts of lightning coming one right on top of the next. Muffled by the distance, their accompanying cacophony of rumbling crashes rolled into one, long, uninterrupted roar.

"Do you suppose Uncle Alex made it to Boston before the squall line caught his schooner?" Then answering his own question, he continued, "Naw, only been maybe four, five hours since we lost sight of him!

Maybe he put in at Plymouth, or Cohassett! Or, would he just haul everything in and ride it out under bare poles, Mister Gardner?"

"Don't know what he'd do, boy. Never sailed with him enough to know his druthers. He's an ocean skipper though, so probably won't even shorten sail for this little blow.

No point to worryin' about him anyway, my friend, when we got all this ourselves. You wait, in a few minutes we're gonna have a week's worth of weather jammed into a space the size of Barnstable harbor, and no place to turn!"

Suddenly as if to emphasize the man's point, it got so dark Andy wondered if they'd be able to find 'any' land, let alone the harbor at Provincetown.

Christopher's voice held no nonsense in it when he ordered, "Go forward, and stand by at the ready to drop sail when I tell you! We're about two, three miles out now, and if we can weather the first squall, maybe we can sneak in before the real heavy stuff hits us."

Andy told his dog to stay put, and crawled along the high rail of their heaving, pounding little boat. Reaching the foredeck, the boy locked his short, leather, sea boots into the stays that held the mast in place. Stretched across the deck in the cold, blinding spray, and actual water coming aboard, was far from comfortable, but at least this way he could hold on and reach the cleats at the base of the mast at the same time.

Looking up to check the sail, he noticed the sky above was as twisted and tormented as the ocean beneath, and it required a conscious effort to bring his eyes back to the task at hand. Undoing the first couple of locked hitches, he loosened the last and lay there fighting each sea as it tried to pry him loose, watching Christopher for the signal.

Without warning, the wind stopped blowing completely.

Braced for anything, Andy and Christopher stood up slowly. With *The Sarah* still rolling heavily in the steep seas, the sail, hanging limp, flapped and waved to the motion. Even the thunder and lightning seemed to pause for breath, while the two men eyed a breathtaking wall of cloud that stretched up, and up, forever. Hanging over them like a giant, breaking comber, the mass didn't instill fear so much as it made them aware of their own insignificance. Their boat, a mere toy, to be crushed at the whim of God.

Now with the wind-created turmoil ended, the waves stopped breaking, and instead marched silently by. Ominous for their size, lack of a voice did little to make them less threatening.

Christopher, in the sudden silence, spoke quietly as if not to disturb anything. "You'd better lower away, Andy! No telling what's coming next, and the sail ain't doin' us no good with no wind in it."

Andy began undoing the lines when, startled, he looked up. There was a new sound. A low, moaning noise, so powerful as to be almost visceral.

Chris cupped a hand to his ear, and frowning, turned to locate the source. "Got to be behind this rain squall abearing down on us! Get that sail down quick, boy! She's probably the new wind, and from the sound, she's gonna be a real howler!"

Holding against the expected weight of the sail, Andy released the last loop of rope.

Nothing happened.

Glancing at Chris who was watching him, he yanked down on the peak halyard to clear it.

Nothing moved.

Now looking up at the rigging, he had no need to trace the various lines to find trouble. There, in one of the blocks at the top of the twenty some-odd foot mast, the rope was kinked and jammed in its pulley.

It may have occurred when the sail was luffed to lower it earlier, but more likely it happened during one of the many times their boat heeled over from a breaking wave. When the sail spilled her wind, the sudden release of pressure had allowed the line to slack and twist. Strain was re-applied as the sail filled again, and pulled the resulting loop into the block, jamming it harder than any human could ever hope to release.

Time was running out. The roar sounded like it was almost on top of them. Mixed with rain, a torrential wall of marble-sized hail engulfed the boat. Beating them down, and soaking the fishermen like the fire hose Andy had seen demonstrated at the fair, it stung like a swarm of bees.

Poor Ulysses whimpered, humped his back, and tucked his tail out of harm's way between his legs.

Knowing what had to be done without being told, the boy used the sail's mast hoops like rungs of a ladder. Pitching and swaying to the beat of the waves, it was a difficult climb, but he reached the stay-spreader and fought his way to a standing position. Wedging himself between masthead and upper stay, the boy reached back and hauled out his beloved sheath knife. Just beginning to saw on the jammed line, he was interrupted by a warning shout from Chris. "Hang fast, boy!"

With no time to react, Andy found himself suspended in mid-air. The mast had been snatched right out from under him like a tablecloth from under a dish, and he was falling. A wall of cloud and water in motion crossed his line of vision, but the turbulent sea buried him before he could twist and focus.

Starting the dive from twenty feet, he went deep. The water was cold. Currents imbedded in the rolling waves tumbled him over and over, and it seemed like forever before he reached the surface again. Looking about from a wave-top, he saw *The Sarah* nearby, belly-up and naked, Christopher and Ulysses splashing by her side.

Out of breath, Andy sheathed his knife and happily thanked his lucky stars he hadn't lost it again. By the time he'd swum to the boat, Chris was aboard and the dog was scratching and sliding in a similar attempt.

He boosted the worried creature onto the overturned hull, and with Chris' help, clambered out himself.

This was brutal. Wiping the water out of his eyes, he staggered to his feet on the rocking platform, puzzled as to what had hit them so hard.

"Don't know, son! Might have been a waterspout, or more likely a powerful wind gust. She's gone now though, and we got us a nice brisk little westerly asettin' in."

"What do we do now?"

"Don't do nothin', 'cept hang onto the centerboard here so's you don't fall back in. Got two, three hours a'daylight left, and I 'spect a sail or two will be showin' up 'fore the sun goes down. Now the squall line's past, things should be gettin' back to normal pretty quick."

Andy scooched down to pat and hug his wet dog, then his eyes widened, and he stood up slowly, staring intently at a spot just behind the boat.

Half whispering, he said, "Look at the shark, Mister Gardner."

Chris's head whipped around, following Andy's gaze.

There, cruising almost within touching distance, was a dorsal fin of impressive proportions.

Not just behind now, but all around the boat, fins began to appear.

Without realizing the significance of his actions, and aided somewhat by the self-bailing features of the cockpit, Andy had left a bloody chum-line behind the boat the entire trip. While he'd been bailing, trying to stay ahead of the waves coming aboard, the tuna had smashed the buckets of chopped porgies, then added their own blood to his knee-deep cauldron. Working as it should, this trail of blood and tattered fish remnants attracted predators from miles down their wake.

Hot on the trail across Cape Cod Bay, and right behind *The Sarah* when she flipped, they were delighted with this sudden turn of events. A whole boatload of blood, chum, and now the dead tuna, it was like a pot of gold at rainbow's end, and worth the chase. Called to dinner, and offered a spread of these proportions, the creatures massed to sate their voracious appetites.

More and more kept arriving, until the water fairly boiled around the tiny wooden craft.

Fascinated by this raw life being exhibited on all sides, the men chattered excitedly and pointed out the more spectacular events to each other.

It needed no mentioning that in their powerful silence, and sliding by close enough to spit on, the larger shadows commanded an unspoken degree of uneasiness and respect.

During the melee, a rather sizable specimen drove its head out of the water while holding a whole tuna in its smiling jaws. The action was probably an attempt to keep it's prize away from the competition, but the fishermen took it as a direct, taunting affront to their loss. Especially when the creature shook the fish violently, and they got splattered with the blood, spray, and guts as it came apart.

Andy wiped the slimy mess from his face, and tried to spit the taste from a mouth suddenly gone dry.

The gesture was not lost on Christopher. His attitude became sullen. He sputtered about their hard day's labor gone to waste, and the time and money lost at natures whim. But then a thought must have occurred to the man, and curiously he began to apologize.

Confusing Andy by his mid-stream change of course, the boy finally realized the fisherman's plea was now more to God than the one person of flesh and blood close enough to either accept or deny his supplication.

"I'm sorry! S'pose I shouldn't have been so greedy. Then maybe we'da seen the weather comin' in time to make safe harbor!"

Christopher's face tilted upward, and his voice rose, acquiring an edge of anger to it. "Don't think it's right for your messengers to flaunt their good luck at my expense though! It's my feeling 'twas punishment enough they reclaimed your bounty, without throwing it back in my face!"

Running out of tuna, sharks began striking other sharks in the thrashing, bloody confusion. Suddenly, a surging bump was felt as a misguided denizen bit at the dark mass of boat, tearing away pieces of wood and leaving a few teeth behind in exchange.

Feeling the splintering action right through their feet, Christopher became extremely agitated. He could picture the long hours spent building this wooden creation of love with his own bare hands and sweat. Becoming more vociferous in his anger, he screamed, "Stop attacking my boat, you abomination of Christ's genius! It's me that's going to have to put it back together again! 'ME'! Do you hear? Jesus Christ, isn't it enough that I bought you your dinner today? What makes you sons-of-bitches think you need the boat to pick your teeth with? Bastards from hell, leave it alone!"

Instantly, almost as if it were in retaliation—slap for slap—to Christopher's spoken grievances, the vulnerability of their own position was brought home in heart rending fashion.

A medium-sized shark spotted the moving shapes on their floating haven. Arriving too late for the feast, but agitated by the scent of blood, the predator sought whatever compensation it could find for its long swim.

Apparently mistaking the men for its more normal fare of seals, the creature followed instinct. Helped by the sloshing waves, its body slid up onto the hull quietly.

Terrified, Andy leaped out of reach, the gnashing teeth missing his leg by a scant inch or two.

One, blank, expressionless eye rolled toward him. Locking stares, the boy knew in that instant he was staring into an uncaring, bottomless pit of death. He froze. An icy fist in his throat choked the breath from his body.

Devoted Ulysses, forever on guard against any harm coming to his beloved, young master counterattacked with equal ferocity.

Before Andy had time to think or stop him, the dog sprang forward, and by nature drove his teeth into the throat area of the offending monster. This being the gill portion, it was the one spot his teeth could seemingly penetrate the tough hide. Sliding into the gill slots, they locked into the heavy cartilage. A spray of blood rewarded his effort.

The shark reacted to the pain, and thrashed, rolling back into the water with the dog still attached.

Panic-stricken, Andy felt in his mind he'd become a spectator. Not really a part of the drama unfolding before his very eyes. A bad dream! A nightmare . . . for horror such as this gripping him could never be real!

The rope that still tied Ulysses' collar to the boat dragged across his leg. In a frustrated scream of anger, exertion, and fear he made a desperate grab. Heaving with all his strength, a splashing explosion erupted next to the hull and his heroic dog flew back onboard.

The boy had been fast, but not fast enough. Another shark, its teeth already buried in the dogs hindquarters, came aboard too. With one flip of its tail, the cold beast acquired enough leverage to complete its intended purpose. Sliding back into the pink, frothy water, the lower half of the dog, feet askew, hung from its grinning, blood-filled jaws.

Andy held Ulysses in his embrace, tears streaming down his cheeks in unashamed anguish.

The dog raised his head wearing that same, worried, apologetic look he always got when he was in trouble. More plainly than words, the expression begged forgiveness.

Both men read into it, "Please don't cry!" And, "I know I did something wrong, but you watch, I'll do a better job next time!"

Ulysses lapped at Andy's tears with his big wet tongue, coughed, and let out a long sigh. His head sank back down slowly. He died as Andy gathered him in his arms.

Christopher, his heart in his throat, choked back tears of his own. Turning, he cursed, scrambled, and just in time, kicked at another of those silent, toothy, messengers of death.

Following the other's lead, this shark too had been reaching for the boy, and what remained of his faithful dog.

Chapter 27

A Day to be Blessed

Only a parent could know the anguish of Alex's despair. The frantic hunt took him back and forth across Cape Cod Bay in the long, slow reaches of a man determined not to miss a single wave. Keeping all hands aloft, the captain left the dock before daylight, and remained out until well after dusk.

No matter that hope faded as each day passed, the man met every morning with the determination and resolve that he'd not give up until Christopher and Andrew's fate had been solved to his own satisfaction.

A sail never passed without a hail from the *Yarmouth*, inquiring if wreckage, bodies, or anything out of the ordinary had been spotted. It didn't take long before the local Harbor Masters and Pilots, recognizing his ship, would sail out to meet him as he approached their port.

The water was full of flotsam. Investigating every reportage became a tedious job, but a life without knowing if that one piece might have been the clue they sought, was unimaginable.

The squall line had been violent when it passed over the *Yarmouth* that afternoon. Alex had seen it coming in plenty of time. He lowered all sail, and set a storm jib to maintain headway.

The old girl had made a good run before the weather caught them. Southeast of the entrance to Boston harbor, she was passing the new light on Minot's Ledge off Cohasset just after three o'clock.

Under a gusty, thunderous, hail shower, the jib blew out almost as soon as it was raised.

Riding heavy, these were dangerous waters not to have some way to keep the ship stabilized. Less than twenty years ago, a wild April night in 1851 generated a wave which destroyed the first Minot's Ledge light tower with one blow. According to witnesses, the light, a hundred feet tall, disappeared in the blink of an eye, with all hands.

To Alex, these summer squalls could be almost as nasty. With this load aboard, his schooner'd founder in a minute if he didn't keep her head into the wind. Rather than waste time bending on a new sail, he played another hand. The man directed his crew to take a couple of barrels from the deck load, and bash in their heads. After the potatoes were dumped out, they were slung in rope harnesses and attached to long heavy lines. Thrown overboard to drag, the schooner played out behind like the tail of a kite.

Snugged up and battened down as best they could, the captain monitored seas and wind to gauge his next move, and watched the clouds lower almost to his masthead. Busy, he found little time to concern himself with others, except to feel thankful *The Sarah* had been fishing inshore today. At least she could run for shelter.

Leaving an inch of hail in its wake, the weather swept eastward to the relief of all. A freshening westerly stirred up a choppy cross sea.

Hoisting rain-washed sail under a sparkling sun, the old schooner was a sight to behold against that dark squall-line behind her. With her full top, white spray and foam piling up under the bow, she spanked smartly past the islands of Boston's outer harbor.

Proud of their vessel and pleased with the trip, every man aboard felt this was indeed a day to be blessed.

Chapter 28

Salvage Rights

It was a lazy Sunday. Alex had held his shipboard services just after sun up. The men, making ready for a late afternoon sail, were storing the last of a mixed load of dry-goods when they got the word. Close to noon, an urgent telegram was delivered to their ship at dockside.

To: Capt A Matthews : c/o Schnr Yarmouth

Long Wharf : Boston : Mass

The Sarah 3 days overdue : stop :

Presumed lost at sea : stop :

S. Sears : stop :

Terse and cryptic, as all such messages, it none the less spurred intense activity onboard.

Alex tried to tell Abigail and the crew his pressing need to get home was not based on any concern for the safety of *The Sarah*, nor those she carried. The man expressed complete faith in both the boat's seaworthiness and Christopher's ability to sail her. He took the position that his sister and Amy were home alone, and worried, and he merely wished to ally their fears. The lie, however, was written all over their captain's face.

By Herculean efforts, they sailed within the hour.

On the fifth, depressing, and so far fruitless day, the *Yarmouth* extended her search to limits thought impossible for *The Sarah.* As she sailed into Provincetown harbor, easing by the new lighthouse under construction at Wood End, a lone fisherman passed them on his way out.

Using a speaking trumpet, Eben hailed the man in a manner which by now had become routine. "Haloooo there the boat! We're in search of a catboat, missing since Thursday last. Rigged out for fishing, she was *The Sarah* by name, out of Yarmouth. Have ye hailed or seen anything o' the likes o' her, or might ye have knowledge o' her crew?"

The man came about on a parallel tack, and at the end of an agonizingly long pause, he answered Eben's inquiry in the affirmative. Finally, Alex's forlorn, despairing quest brought the response he sought, yet feared more than anything in memory.

The fisherman explained how, on the day before, he'd spotted an overturned hull on the near edge of Stellwagen Bank. One, he agreed, that might answer the general description of a catboat. The location had been about five miles to the north, off Race Point. The man went on to explain that he'd fastened a line to the craft with the intention of towing it in for salvage, but she wouldn't budge.

He speculated the tide and current had dragged her there, and the only reason she stopped was 'cause with mebbe ten to fifteen feet of water over the bank, she'd found a spot shallow enough just short of the shoal for her rigging or gear to snag something on the bottom.

Getting late in the day, and with a heavy sea running, the man had abandoned his efforts until conditions improved.

If it was still there, he thought the heavier gear he'd brought along today would help him claim his treasure.

With both helmsmen distracted, the two vessels drifted closer on their shared course and almost touched. Old John Silva grabbed a boat hook, but before he could push them apart, the fisherman veered off sharply. Somewhat suspicious of their motives, it was obvious no one was going to snare him that easily. Now even more alert, the fellow told them they could follow along if they'd like, but he'd already registered the wreck and put his mark on it, so by law it belonged to him.

Alex, sensing the man's distrust, explained that one of the missing people they were seeking was his nephew. The one who'd saved the Provincetown boy, Captain Manny Victorine's son, from the wreck of the schooner *Electric Light*.

The man's taciturn attitude changed on the instant. He let go the sheet rope, and so ignored, his sail began to luff immediately. All excited now, the man requested permission to come aboard, and began clambering up the side of their schooner before he got an answer. With a painter from his own vessel in hand, the fisherman had no intention of waiting for such amenities as a boarding ladder. He swung over the rail, tied the line off, and began talking, all as one fluid motion.

Rough enough in appearance so the *Yarmouth's* crew might question his own scruples more than he had theirs, he left no question that he now trusted these strangers fully. From that moment forward, the fellow couldn't be more helpful.

He explained how the dead boy had been his brother's God-child, and if the Captain would be kind enough to accept his offer, the family would do anything in their power to repay the tremendous debt they felt they owed him for the hospitality he'd shown.

Alex looked gaunt from lack of proper food and sleep over the past week. He sighed, thanked the man for his offer and concern, and then went on to tell the fellow how they'd been searching since three days after the squall line passed through, and had just about given up hope.

While this was going on, the Captain wondered to himself how *The Sarah* could have possibly gotten way out here. And, under the circumstances of a boat long turned turtle, could he be sure if he even wanted this to be the wreck they sought? It might be better if this was just another derelict. An abandoned hull, given up to the mercy of the sea.

Fully cooperative, the fisherman seemed to be a little agitated and uneasy about matters. He finally blurted out how the wreck he'd spotted was a little unusual. Then seemed reluctant to part with the 'Why' of the matter, and it took some persistent prodding on Eben's part to get the man's troubling information out.

Clearing his throat, the fellow lowered his voice to almost a whisper. "Aye, she's belly-up, but when I found her she had signs of being chewed on pretty bad too!"

Eben didn't catch the significance of what he was being told. Not bothering to lower his own tone any, he asked, "What do you mean, chewed on? You mean she's been on the rocks somewhere, or pounding against a wharf? A collision! Some ship rammed, and rolled her over?"

Shaking his head, the man's whisper was barely audible. "None o' them! Nah. . . . Nahh . . . . Had to be sharks!"

The bile surging in his throat was so bitter Alex could hardly swallow. The captain attempted to speak a couple of times, but nothing audible reached the other's ears.

The man's mind had no trouble verbalizing. Out of control, it began to play games with itself. Evil games. *What in hell would make sharks attack an empty boat? Nothing!*

Therefore, the boat was not empty when those hellish denizens arrived!

Always the one looked up to—the man in charge—he himself had few places to turn. With no other choice, the captain hung his hat on faith, blind hope, and denial. *Twenty, twenty-five nautical miles from Yarmouth, this wreck is too far at sea! Aye, it can't possibly be the one we seek! Dear God, let it not be! Ohhh, God!*

Deeper in the man's subconscious, a voice started to whisper things. Shutting it out, he refused to listen.

To the others watching, his face took on a strange mottled appearance. Alex, suddenly becoming aware of their stares, realized that although he was holding the bowl of his familiar pipe in his hand, what remained of its stem lay crushed between his teeth.

Turning back to the fisherman, Eben asked if he'd been able to make out a name on his wreck. Wrapping his whiskered chin in a grimy hand, the P-towner thought about it for a minute. "Her quarterboards were pretty well chafed from the attached floating gear and wreckage banging against 'em, but I somehow gets the feelin' she mebbe started with the letter 'S'!"

Scrambling over the rail, the fellow leaped back down onto his own boat where he fumbled around in a bucket of trash sitting next to the rail. Frustrated by the result he was getting from what was obviously a search, he dumped the remaining contents across an already well-cluttered deck. Now able to pick and choose at will, he straightened up with a dog's collar in hand. The man tossed it up to Alex, and said, "Found this attached to a line tied off to the boat."

Even in mid-air, Alex knew without question who it belonged to. He'd made it himself from the same leather Amy used on that Christmas belt. Recognition gave his spirits a slight respite. A short-lived instant of hope.

Collar in hand, the exact opposite took place. Examining it more closely, euphoria turned to despair, and he felt sure his heart would explode. The buckle was still done up. Carved diagonally across the thick leather, more plain to him than if words had been written there in explanation, a series of slashes cut it almost through.

Alex found a chip of tooth embedded in one of the deep grooves. An unnecessary signature, for he already knew the tragic end his faithful dog had met.

Struggling for breath now, he tried to hold back the wall of despair and grief which seemed determined to bury him. The man might as well have been trying to hold back the tide, for all the good it did. He coughed, gagged, then swallowed hard. Anxiety, concerning the fate of the others aboard that boat drove this first wave like a storm surge.

Nodding to the fisherman to indicate his familiarity with the object, the captain unhitched the fellow's painter from the rail to allow the boats to separate. He then waved him out of the harbor towards the bay, not quite daring the strength of his voice to make an attempt at speech.

As if forgetting the man had been standing there all along, Alex beckoned to Eben, confirmed quietly what had just taken place, then suggested he pass the word along to the crew. Oblivious to his immediate surroundings, the last command was another waste of breath. To a man, all those aboard had been hanging on every gesture, every word spoken.

Still absentmindedly fingering the gashes in the worn leather collar, the captain instructed his good friend to follow their fisherman at a safe distance.

With a face as pale as the sails of his ship, Alex didn't bother to wait for the confirming nod. Turning his back on a world too cruel to cope with, the man retired to the privacy of his cabin. Somehow he had to come to grips with emotions that had almost buried him once, and now threatened to do so again.

Surprising many, the captain took the deck again as soon as he'd heard the command for their sails to be lowered and the anchor set.

With one exception, he'd regained his composure. Inside the man, a gnawing rage was beginning to build. A match struck, a spark dropped, a small fire growing . . . in a hay barn.

Alex felt its presence, but for the moment it supplanted the inevitable, overwhelming sorrow yet to come, so he let it burn. Leaving his ship in Eben's capable hands, Alex took a couple of the crew in the service boat.

Aware he'd never be able to face the family at home unless he examined the belly-up hull for himself, it was done with great reluctance.

One glance, and the man felt his heart palpitating and his knees getting weak. Bloodstains were visible all over and around the centerboard. What must have been copious amounts were sunbaked right into the paint and wood. A few tufts of black hair remained snagged on barnacles, but he no longer noticed the little details.

Numb to the men around him; beyond feeling or caring; he'd just spotted the most disheartening fact of all. Almost hidden by an abundance of splinters, a large, semicircular row of marks. Marks left by teeth. Very sharp teeth.

Just as the fisherman had described, up on the crown of this little island sanctuary, actual pieces of shattered, wooden centerboard were missing. Obviously not content to pursue their quarry in the water, the sharks had come aboard to leave a few calling cards as proof of their visit.

The why of the attack still eluded the captain, but the presence of the blood; the white, triangular teeth imbedded in the wood; the damaged collar; all spoke of its ultimate success.

So evidenced, it left little room for hope. The man could only give up a silent prayer that they had died quickly, without pain, and yet even that gruesome wish seemed to be ruled out by what lay before him. Exerting all of the will he could muster, Alex fought with his eyes to keep them on the macabre scene as his devoted crew rowed him slowly around the hull.

It was as if he were blaming himself for their demise, and consequently had to bear the penalty of this detailed inspection. In reality, the man actually hoped against hope that he might somehow spot something to change that which he already knew.

Below the surface of the water, a strip of the combing which edged *The Sarah's* cockpit had been torn loose. Even there he could see a haunting, circular, bite mark. His mind took off. *Damn! Fully aware they were doomed from the start, this must have been a long, hopeless, torturous struggle.*

Unable to shut the pictures out of his head, he imagined Andy and Christopher dodging the relentless beasts from one side of the centerboard to the other, until slowly, inevitably, and literally piece by piece, their grasp on life faded. Finally, when the two men and their dog no longer had the conscious ability to survive, nothing would remain but this boat and the empty sea.

Sliding by the farside now, something caught his eye. There, on the upper portion of the centerboard, a hand print. A print of such proportion it could only have been Andy's. Alex motioned the service boat in closer, and placing one foot on *The Sarah's* hull, he stretched out and placed his own hand over the bloody print. The touch proved to be almost too much. His mind turned the sun heated wood beneath the handprint into the warmth of life. Reacting to the sensation of Andy reaching out and touching him from beyond the grave, the man yanked his hand away as if he'd been burned, lost his balance and fell backwards, crashing over the gunwale back into the service boat.

Stone faced and on the verge of apoplexy, Alex dragged himself onto a seat. By a wave of that still-tingling hand, he directed their return to his schooner.

The rage inside had become a conflagration barely contained.

Aside from the normal, monotonous creak of the boomjaws keeping pace with the swells, a slap of ropes against mast, and the flapping loose mains'l set to keep her head into the wind, the ship was quiet. The captain sat on her taffrail staring out to sea, and away from *The Sarah*.

Eben had taken the others back over to help the fisherman right his salvaged claim, and bail her out.

The man, touched by their loss, tried to give the boat back, but his offer was politely declined. The *Yarmouth's* crew felt the idea of towing that mangled craft back to Yarmouth, and exposing her final moments for all to see, as bordering on the obscene. In exchange for their help, they settled instead on the rights to any personal effects which might still be found onboard.

That was one mournful journey toward home. Their course leading them through banks of fittingly dreary fog, a gentle, but stubborn southerly forced many long reaches between tacks. Progress this slow did nothing to raise the spirits onboard. Better to get something this painful out of the way quickly. Over and done with, so one could get on with the living, albeit a less rich and rewarding experience now.

These two individuals and their dog, gone forever, were more than just personal friends and loved ones. They were a part of the sailing family and fraternity of their close-knit little village.

Sorrowfully, their devastating, horrible demise had to be brought home. Home to those who still waited. . . .

Chapter 29

Shades of Black

Sarah, Amy, or both, had manned the widow's walk every daylight hour since *The Sarah* was listed as overdue. In happier times, Alex had mounted one of his spyglasses on a swivel post up there. Done so the women could watch the harbor's activities, and *The Sarah* and the *Yarmouth's* scheduled comings and goings, now they employed it to study each inbound sail with hopes of spotting a familiar face aboard.

After the *Yarmouth* sailed off in search, they watched her partings and returns with heartened anticipation, but with the days dragging into a second week, and still no results, their spirits and growing apprehension had turned into that stalwart despair only a seafaring family can know.

It was late afternoon when the *Yarmouth* returned from this trip, the black signal-flags of mourning flying from her masthead.

With the ship still well offshore, recognition drove Sarah from the rooftop. Too full of emotion, she refused to go down to the docks to meet the vessel.

The Howes girls, hearing the news through the village grapevine almost as soon as Sarah had seen the flags with her own eyes, arrived carrying a basket of baked goods. Prudence wasn't far behind, coming to lend comfort and a shoulder to cry on.

Amy, removed from the others by years of both age and grief, wandered down to the docks on her own. She met Alex as he stepped off the schooner. They embraced quietly, in shared sorrow. Not a word had passed between them, just looks that told her the search was over.

Alex handed his niece the worn collar with its graphic lacerations, and they turned away from the sea, walking side by side up the lane toward home.

Bearing his own cross of emotion, the captain did his best to tell the girl what had been found. Trying to be gentle but truthful, while at the same time leaving out the gory details, he just kept repeating that the wreck had been found at sea, and all evidence pointed to the loss of her crew.

Amy wasn't that easily convinced. With questioning as insistent as her brother's, she wanted to know exactly why Alex seemed so sure of their demise. The Captain, looking years older than the man who waved goodbye to Andrew on that festering, summer morning, paused. They were in the semi-privacy of a heavily leafed portion of the little lane, where it led up to Hallet Street.

He took a deep breath, retrieved the dog's collar from her hand, and bent it at a specific gash. The broken tooth gleamed white against the dark leather. Triangular, with little serrations along the edge, it left no question as to its original owner.

The girl shuddered involuntarily, followed by silence in the sudden realization of what the man was trying to tell her by his wordless disclosure. The nauseating implication sank in, her face flushed, and the leafy lane began to spin.

Alert as ever, Alex caught Amy's crumpling body with those same rope-hardened hands that had reached out to help her brother so often.

Over the initial shock, and now wanting to run from this world and the knowledge she had gained, Amy found her course denied. Her uncle gathered her up effortlessly, like so much fluff. Never a parent, somehow the man knew instinctively this girl should not be left to face her sorrows alone. Holding her protectively in his arms, he let the youngster sob out the bitter fruition of long held fears against the security of his strong shoulder.

The well of despair took many long minutes to spill its overflow and for Amy to regain sufficient control that he dared ease her back to the ground. Hanging on her uncle's arm for support, the two continued on to the house at an even slower pace.

Conversation was difficult, with bared feelings and raw emotion leaking out here and there, but they did manage to come to terms about how much of their knowledge should be passed on to Sarah.

Knowing her temperament, and how she felt about the sea, both shared the belief that some things might be too much for her to bear. Unspoken, they understood too who would ultimately pay the price. When wronged, Sarah was not one to hold her feelings in, so why feed the fire if they themselves were the offerings to be burnt.

Their concern was wasted. Sarah already had all the fuel she'd ever need.

The woman greeted her brother with a look of pure hatred. Never saying a word of greeting, nor asking a single detail, her stony continence and silence were the only punishment she had within her grasp at the moment. Saddling him thusly was but a small token of her true feelings, but she knew if it took until her dying day, somewhere, somehow down the road, Alex would pay for this double fault.

Against her wishes, this man, this evil incarnate, had taken her only son away to sea. There, the boy died a sacrifice on the altar the captain held most dear.

Inconceivably, this same hated individual had found a way to compound the torture. Not only did he take away Andrew, but he introduced Christopher Gardner into her life. A man she could truly love. A love, that now would never be. . . .

HIS fault? As if it could be anyone else's! HE tempted my son! They were HIS damned ships, and HIS damned ocean! My men could not have been killed any more surely had the devil himself used his own bare hands!

Hate? No, Sarah's feelings went much deeper.

Chapter 30

Heaven's Reward

The memorial service for Andrew and Christopher was held three weeks to the day from that fateful morning they'd set sail on their journey to eternity.

Sitting there forlornly, her gear bleaching in the sun, the *Yarmouth* remained warped into the dock. The day Amy met him at the foot of the gangplank, Alex had walked away from the sea and his ship. This inanimate beauty, which had been such a part of his life, carried too many memories for him to ever set foot on her deck again.

Brokenhearted and brooding, the Captain now spent all of his days alone in self-imposed exile. Buried in the solitude of his second-floor bedroom, the drapes were pulled so no glimpse of the ocean would intrude to remind and punish him further. The window sash was closed and locked to keep even the sound of gulls, and that tangy, fresh, salt smell out of his most private world.

Visitors who came to share the family's grief, thought it strange they never caught sight of the poor man. Those who came specifically to see the Captain, were turned away by Sarah. She claimed not to know of his whereabouts.

This action gave birth to rumors of dire illness, and in truth, if it hadn't been for Amy, the man most likely would have died of starvation. It was she who insisted on bringing her uncle sustenance, then stayed with him to make sure he ate what was brought. She, who sat with him in the dark, and by her conversation attempted to bring a little light to his world.

Congregational Church on Zion Hill, Yarmouth. 1870

The house, in its deathly silence, did nothing to help his mood. It too seemed in mourning.

Gone were the friendly arguments of children filtering up the stairs. No shrieks of laughter, which had at one time upset him so. With no wind to ruffle her skirts, even Aunt Sophie's ghost lay quiet.

The ride to the church that afternoon was traveled in complete silence. Sarah and Alex sat on the same seat in the buggy for appearances sake, but only because Amy sat between them. Sarah had not spoken to the man since he'd returned that doleful day, nor did she ever intend to do so again.

Alex's continence was black and white. He appeared to have stepped out of a daguerreotype, and it matched his mood completely. The day was hot and sultry. A brassy sun beat down much like on the start of that other, which had ended so horribly. Thunder rumbled in the distance. Dressed in his tightly fit, formal attire of mourning, the captain ignored the small rivulets of sweat trickling down his forehead. He felt, more than actually thought, *Close, thick air. Going to be another weather-breeder for sure!*

As such, even this reminded him of his loss. Recalling the last conversation held with Christopher on that fatal morning, he asked himself in the latter's terminology, *Wonder how this one will change the course men have plotted for their souls?*

In his mind's eye, he saw Andy and Chris standing on the dock as the *Yarmouth* pulled away. He remembered the admiration and pride in the boy's eyes as the old girl's sails had filled. The boy's love for the new life he'd found was obvious. Almost as a reflection from the lad's eyes the captain realized he harbored the same feelings, and suddenly understood in that instant he had been on a false journey. A self-imposed sabbatical, contrary to his self-stated purpose in life. *If God has a purpose for me, I must follow my heart.*

And now I understand, what little remains of that organ can only be found at sea.

If for no other reason, he vowed on the instant a return to his ship, her white sails, and the endless oceans . . . to keep the boy's memory alive, at least unto himself.

Grasping at anything to deter him from the destination of this current, dreaded journey, he found himself fighting the urge to turn the buggy from its funereal course, and head for the dock where his ship had lain so long neglected.

Eyeing the sky now as if to take in its measure for a day's sail, he acknowledged the weather to be a little different than that other. *Today she's a proper weather-breeder! Aye, no wind a'tal to slide away from this trouble what's comin'!*

In fact, there didn't seem to be enough air moving to breathe. The man made a conscious attempt to draw in a deep breath to relieve his discomfort, but the weight sitting on his chest had a mind of its own, and brought him back to the inevitable reality of the present.

Fighting it with all his will, in desperation he forced his mind to the remembered sadness which, until this instance, had charted the course of his life. A somewhat lesser evil at the moment, if such a thing were possible, than today's source of grief. For reasons beyond his immediate comprehension, that other cataclysm seemed so long ago. Almost as if it had never really happened in his lifetime.

Pouncing on the idea, hopefully as a way to distance his feelings from the horrible climax of this other day just three weeks past, he tried to put things into a frame of mind which made 'it' too seem like something he'd read about.

It? Yes, IT! Keep IT at arms length. Put a name on IT! Don't dwell on the sickening details, just wrap everything in a package with a big warning label, DO NOT OPEN! The locks? The locks should have an impossible combination. However, unlike the Pandora's Box of Greek mythology, this one's secrets should never be released to torment the world again.

Tricks of the mind! Has it actually been three weeks? Or, just yesterday?

The sermon and eulogy thundered on in the cavernous, new Congregational Church up on top of Zion Hill. Built to hold five-hundred seated, and not yet dedicated, today it was packed to capacity. The overflow stood along the walls and blocked what little relief was offered by the open, shutter-shaded windows. The heat was becoming brutal.

People had come from as far as Boston and Provincetown to attend. The mother of the Portuguese boy Andrew had saved was there to share her grief, reborn anew with Sarah's.

Abigail, shedding convention as was her usual wont, arrived from Boston as the only female member of a sizable contingent. It represented everyone, from Alex's brotherhood of Sea Captains, to the State House.

Alex was so troubled and immersed in his own thoughts and emotions, he barely knew they were there. The man never even missed poor Sam, kept away from this most solemn occasion by his own accursed affliction.

He didn't catch the title, but a piece of poetry was read as part of the church service. It whispered uninvited into the captain's mind.

Under foot, patience tried.

Charted course, far to slide.

Hated questions, youthful pride.

Envied truth, others sighed.

Blind men all . . . love to hide.

One to follow, one to guide.

Shore life chafed, never tied.

Oceans called, sails to ride.

Empty promise, seabirds cried.

Never missed . . . until he died.

Since that day off Provincetown, when they'd found the shark violated hull, the man's anger had been smoldering. Battening his emotional hatches with every ploy he could muster to keep it confined, the captain had done his best to twist its compass. Diverting it time after time, he'd sent it down endless, empty headings, hoping to sap its strength.

Now, in this moment of grief, it caught him with no watch posted, defenses down. Truly a monster risen from the deep, the anger burst its gaskets and ballooned to fill his mind like a sail filling with wind.

"Until he died!" The words echoed in his subconscious like a marble spinning around in a house of cards. Cascading down, cards knocked loose, feelings beyond human control tumbling every which way, order gone, chaos reigning.

Why Lord? Why? he railed. *How could You have opened up my heart like this again? What purpose or reason does it serve, unless your intent is to crush my immortal soul?*

A touch of sarcastic contempt began to creep into his thoughts. *You, who are supposed to be so 'Just'! If it is Your decision that I must be persecuted, why must others have to suffer too? Punish me if you will, dear Lord, but let me bear the weight of my guilt alone!*

Andrew? He was only a boy, Most Holy Father. A dear boy! A boy I had come to love as my own lost child! Did You have to be so cruel? Make him hurt that badly? Die so hard, for whatever possible transgressions he could have committed in his naiveté?

My sister! Has she been so evil as to be denied all happiness? Her only son? You should know that pain beyond any of us poor mortals!

And what of Christopher? He was Your devoted servant, oh King of Kings! Always putting Your church above his own base needs, and never stopping to question. This was a good man, Lord! Where is it written, that You should be so miserly with him in death?

As for myself, all this time I thought I was laboring under Your personal direction! Swept away and pointed up on new headings, I felt secure in the knowledge I was being guided by divine inspiration. You, showing me where to go, and how to interlock these parts sent into the life given me.

Hah! Is this my reward? Did I do so badly that You had to rip out my heart, and crumple all of these other, innocent lives around me? What is the need of all this hurt, pain and sorrow? So that You, in all of Your wisdom, can teach one poor soul a lesson? Well if that is the case, You have failed, for I have never learned a lesson worth even one life!

Speak! Give a sign! What am I to learn from this?

I am listening Lord, and yet I hear nothing! Tell me now, or by all that is Holy, take me from this accursed earth!

It began quietly. A whisper, twisting into a plaintiff cry. The cry built slowly, powerfully, expanding, until in the end it became an angry, confrontational roar. Danger! Storm Tossed Surf Pounding On The Rocks! WIND SCREAMING IN THE RIGGING!

AN/ENDLESS/REVERBERATING/THUNDER, RINGING/IN/HIS/EARS!

The noise woke him, suddenly, like a shout in the silence of a dream. Heart pounding and stunned, Alex looked at the people around him.

Unbelievably, he found himself standing in his, the front pew of the church.

Everyone else in the congregation was sitting in their own ascribed family pews.

As one, they returned his stare in shocked silence.

The captain knew from the feeling in his throat, it had indeed been his own voice which awakened him. His own thunder.

Have I bared my entire soul to the whole world? the man wondered. *Is this embarrassment yet one more punishment I must endure? What do You consider enough, Lord?*

The anger within, burned in all its glory.

Drawing in a deep breath, he stood up straighter and turning, continued aloud to the entire congregation. "So be it! If I have offended anyone, I am sorry. If others have peered deeper into another man's heart than they ever could have wished, so be that too! Maybe you've all learned something about the condition of your own souls, and your lives will be richer for that fact!"

Sarah reached out, and took his hand. She seemed to be smiling through tears as she looked up to him standing there so solidly beside her. In her own sorrow, she had never realized how much the loss had been shared, or how she had miss-judged her brother.

This heart-broken man smiled back, then nodded to his minister. The Reverend Dodge had come down from his pulpit, and was standing there, his arms stretched out to the Captain in empathy.

At last, without saying another word, Alex turned again and with unashamed tears streaming down his cheeks, walked up the aisle of the church. His wake was marked by the noise of footsteps echoing back in the silence, as, typically, he stomped out his emotion down the winding stairs to the narthex, then marched out through those arched, open doors into the late-summer sunshine.

In more ways than one, Alex stepped out from the darkness within . . . into a light so bright he was almost blinded. The man had to squint, to see at all.

A wagon had just pulled to a stop in front of him. Blocking his path, it looked like Sammy was driving. In fact, he was bouncing up and down on the seat, grinning from ear to ear.

Looking toward motion in the wagon bed, Alex was almost knocked to the ground as a body hurtled into his arms.

"Uncle Alex! Oh boy, am I glad to see you!"

There was no question in Alex's mind, but that his recent request had been granted. *The Lord has taken me. I am dead, and gone to heaven!*

This was Andrew he held in his arms! Hugging the boy as he now knew he'd so desperately feared would never happen, the man blurted out, "Oh thank you, God! Thank you for my reward."

Looking at the boy, he ruffled the youngster's hair and said, "Andrew, there are no words to express how you've been missed!" The fire was gone from the man's heart. He felt a peace and contentment settling in.

The boy's reaction to this particular show of affection was no different than it had ever been. He frowned and ducked the coarse hand.

Not anticipating any such actions in 'his' heaven, the first few cat's paws of doubt began to ruffle the surface of the

Captain's mind. "Andy? Andy, you're dead aren't you? Am I? What's Sammy doing here?" Now thoroughly confused, Alex suddenly felt weak. Losing the ability to stand, he sat down abruptly on the granite curb edging the drive.

Andy bounced around the man, as excited and noisy as Ulysses used to get when he knew they were going hunting.

Next, Christopher slid off the back of the wagon with a grin bigger than Sammy's, and offered Alex his hand. "We're back home, Captain!" A redundant statement of fact from a man of few words.

"Where's Sarah?" A second flow of words he need not have bothered with.

After a stunned moment to fully comprehend the meaning of Alex's unannounced, emotional outburst, Sarah had followed her brother out of the church in haste, concerned suddenly for his well-being.

Bursting out through the open door, and equally blinded by the bright sun, she half-fainted into Christopher's arms almost as the words came out of his mouth. Lowering the woman to the curb beside her brother, he kissed her cheek. Then, as she responded in ecstatic joy to the conscious awareness of her men's return, he kissed her full on the mouth in front of the whole congregation spilling out of the church around them.

"Will you marry me?" The man was full of talk today.

"Yes! Oh, yes!" Came Sarah's instant, breathless reply. This man was not about to sneak off again without her along. *Who was it,* she wondered, *that Alex quoted? "Tis better to have loved and lost, than never to have loved at all. . . ."*

Not only was that man a damned fool, he had no concept of the true meaning of love!

Then she grabbed her bouncing son, and hugged him so tightly it hurt them both. Through the tears of joy blurring her world, she began to sputter, "Where? Where have you two been all this time?"

Mixed in with similar questions and shouts from Amy and the other people milling around them, it began to sound like a gleeful chorus.

By now Alex had become convinced he was not dead. Regaining his feet, he added his voice to the volume of questions.

Carried along by this delirious throng, they traveled to the Crowell's home where it had been planned that sedate refreshments would be served after the memorial service. Instead, a grand celebration honoring their return would now be held, with people pouring out their own joy by bringing along to share whatever their larders held.

After everyone regathered, and things had settled down somewhat, Christopher stood up and related the tale of his and Andy's disappearance.

He told of the wild fishing orgy that had carried them so far out from shore, filled their boat, and, he sheepishly admitted, preoccupied them so he'd completely missed the approaching change in weather.

Next, he related the precarious predicament they found themselves in after the squall capsized their boat, and the day's catch spilled.

The audience, and he himself once more, were reduced to tears when he told of Ulysses' heroics, and the price the poor dog had paid. Regaining his composure, Christopher went on to explain how Andy had been determined not to let those beasts get what little he had left of his brave dog.

Balancing the body on the centerboard, the men danced back and forth, and kicked at the accursed, relentless scavengers as they tried to come aboard. The sea was still rough, which only aided the hunters efforts. Attracted by Ulysses' fresh blood running down onto the hull, as well as the activity of the men so tantalizingly close, the fiendish creatures had small reason to leave.

After such an early start, followed by the strenuous day of fishing on lean rations, the men tired quickly. Darkness was approaching, and the two of them began to despair when a, "Halooo there the wreck! Could you use a hand?" echoed around them.

A Grand Banks schooner, delaying its departure until the squall-line passed, had put out from Provincetown on the ebbing tide. Just by luck, they happened upon *The Sarah* out by Stellwagen Bank before nightfall buried the men from Yarmouth forever.

Taking them aboard, the captain refused their request to turn back, feeling that a second delay on top of a storm-postponed sailing, might hold him up until Friday. A sailing day that would surely put the curse of bad luck on a fishing trip he was already beginning to have doubts about. That meant Saturday at the earliest before the ship could get underway again, which would put him two days behind schedule, with two days less provisions before he even left port.

The man softened his decision by promising to 'speak' the next inbound vessel they met, and transfer his new passengers to their care.

At Andy's request, the crew gingerly took what was left of Ulysses, and put him in a keg. There they salted him down to prevent spoilage, so he could be transferred along with his friends.

On the edge of the shipping lane to Boston already, and it being almost dark, the fishing schooner had crossed the main travel lanes before light brought them an empty sea on the following morn. The first couple of days, every ship they hailed seemed to be bound for Canada, New York, or points further away. It took the best part of a week to reach the Banks, some one-thousand miles down wind. After having spent a number of days on the fishing grounds, a schooner so full of fish her scuppers were awash, passed inbound to Portland, and agreed to take them aboard.

Six days of fighting the usual southerly head winds, brought them into the Gulf of Maine at daybreak, where they found themselves in the middle of a mackerel fishing fleet. A thousand ships lay all around, so closely packed the Grand Banks Master found it almost impossible to pick his way through to the other side. A task which took most of another whole day.

The fish were biting, and Andy found it amazing to see a dozen men on each side of every ship, pulling the fish out of the water so fast it looked like a cascade in reverse. His and Christopher's best day at the same task looked so puny by comparison, it now seemed hardly worth the fish bait.

At the entrance to Portland harbor, they spoke a tubby little bark departing for Boston. In turn, this vessel was overtaken the following morning by a Provincetown owned and bound schooner off Salem harbor.

Christopher poked a little fun at Andy, telling his audience how nice it was to travel in such important company.

It seems that these people, upon finding out it was Andy, the hero of the *Electric Light* rescue they were transporting; and under what circumstances the survivors came to be where they were; elected to deliver the two men and their pickled dog right to the dock in Yarmouth Port.

Fate had her own timetable.

Frustrating their joy, the wind failed within sight of the church steeple. Admittedly, this was still twenty some odd miles at sea, but it took another whole day for the light airs to bring them in closer. Figuring their cargo of fruit would spoil if they wasted any more time on this errand of mercy, the schooner's crew finally rowed the men the last ten miles to shore in their ship's tender.

To their surprise, the only person around when the two disembarked was a totally delirious Sam. The rest of the town, it seemed, was at a memorial service for a couple of poor sailors lost at sea.

After Chris and Andy calmed the man down, they'd borrowed the delivery wagon from Taylor's General store on the end of the wharf.

At this point, Chris interjected a, "Thank you for the use of the wagon, Mr. Taylor!" to laughter and applause.

Sam didn't just grin, he beamed. He was so happy he didn't care how many people were around today.

Alex stood there with one arm—*social mores be damned*—around Abigail, and the other around his nephew, basking in the glory of the moment.

Their friend, the farmer Zachary Gray, sidled up to them. Putting down a large box, he congratulated the boy on his safe return. Next, he asked Alex and Andy if they had been aware of their dog's wandering nature.

He got hesitant, confirming nods. With a solemn look on his face, the man stated, "In that case, I have some very disturbing news for you. It seems, a few months back, your dog took it upon himself to consider my farm his own private port-of-opportunity!"

Andy looked at him questioningly, wondering if poor Ulysses had gotten into the man's chicken coop or something.

The boy knew his dog's weird perception of fun, but he thought, now—right after the poor creature's reported death—was a strange time for the man to complain.

The Captain understood a little more quickly. Alex scratched his head, and then started to grin. Finally he sputtered, "Why that scoundrel! You do mean to say that . . . well! He took his sailor's reputation to heart, and apparently did his namesake proud too?"

Mister Gray nodded his head. His sly grin and the twinkle in his eye a match for the Captain's own. Opening the large box he'd been carrying, the man said, "Yep! Got 'em right here!"

Under the man's gentle hands, four, eager, black noses pushed up through the folded cardboard. Balls of fuzzy fur, and unsteady on their feet, the six-week old pups showed their appreciation for this sudden freedom by wrestling each other for the privilege of being first into the boy's arms.

"As luck would have it, I brought 'em along to the party afore I even knew about the fate of their father!"

Speaking a little more softly, he added, "Thought the two of you might each like a pick of the litter."

Andy had become a man in his own eyes, but there are some tears which are too strong for anyone to hold back.

Glossary:

beam - The widest part of a ship. i.e. at right angles to the keel.

belay - To make figure-eight loops with a rope around a pin or cleat in order to hold secure.

boom - A long pole, or spar, attached to and used to extend the foot or bottom of a sail.

cat's paws – The first, brushing ripples of a coming wind on a calm sea.

cleat - A wooden or metal fitting w/two projecting horns around which a rope may be made fast.

close hauled – Sailing as nearly against the wind as the vessel will go, and still maintain forward motion.

counter down – Overloaded. The counter of a vessel is that portion of the stern from the water-line to the extreme outward swell.

flotsam – Wreckage of a ship or cargo found floating on the sea.

forecastle – That part of a ship forward of the foremast, usually containing the cabin where the common seamen live.

freeboard – The distance between the water-line and the deck.

gaff – The spar upon which the upper edge, or head of a fore and aft rigged sail is attached and extended.

gasket – A line or band used to lash a furled sail securely.

head – The bow and adjacent parts of a vessel. Because of its down-wind position on a sailing vessel, it is also where crewmen go to relieve themselves.

jam – To exchange news and gossip with another vessel at sea.

jaws – An attachment on the mast end of a boom. It partially encircles the mast, and carries the sail's thrust.

jetsam – Goods cast overboard to lighten a vessel in distress.

kedge – To move a vessel by carrying an anchor out in a boat, dropping it overboard, then hauling the vessel to it.

luff – To turn the head of a vessel into the wind, ending forward motion, and causing the sail to flap.

mumbley-peg – A game played by tossing a knife into the air. Each point-first hit divides a marked out area into smaller portions, with each miss eliminating the thrower.

painter – A small line or rope used to tow, or secure a boat.

port – The left side of a vessel.

reach – To extend, or stretch out. A course of sailing with the wind forward of the beam.

rip – A body of water made rough by the meeting of opposing currents, tides, or wind.

saleratus – Archaic term for baking soda.

starboard – The right side of a vessel.

sheet – A rope which regulates the angle at which a sail is set in relation to the wind.

sounding – Testing the water's depth with a weighted line.

tack – To change the direction of a vessel when sailing close hauled. i.e. a zig-zag course.

taff-rail – Railing around a ship's stern.

tarpaulin – Waterproofed canvas. Done by treating with diluted tar, hence the name. Often used to cover the hatches of a vessel.

try-out – To render, or melt fat/blubber as from a whale.

watch – An allotted portion of time, usually four hours, during which one is on deck, ready for duty.

HUMANE SOCIETY OF MASSACHUSETTS.

Wreck Report from Station No. 33 Barnstable

DATE OF WRECK, November 25 1888

NOTE.—Captains of Station will fill out this report with care and as fully as possible, and mail it at once to the Secretary of the Standing Committee.

Name of Vessel, Richard S Green formely the Riberia Engly

NATIONALITY, Rig and Tonnage, American Brigentine about 300 Tons

Cargo, Sand Ballas

Master's Name and Address, Andrew J. Patrick Barnstable Mass

Port of hail,

Where from, Boston

Where bound, Wilmington N. C.

Number and names of Officers and Crew,

Number of Passengers,

Exact spot of Wreck, One & Half Miles West of Sandy Neck Light H

Cause of Wreck, Heavy Gale from the N. E. & Storm & Rain

Hour of same, and state of weather, verry thick & raining

Time of discovery of Wreck, 8 A M Monday 26th Nov

Station Crew began work at

Returned home at

Number of trips of Life-boat,

Number of shots fired,

Number of trips of Breeches-buoy,

Number and names of lives saved,

Number and names of lives lost,

Was Vessel saved or lost? Vessel all right on the Beach Capt on Shore at Barnstable Crew on Board the Brig

Number of persons resuscitated from apparent death by drowning or cold,

By whom and to what extent assistance was rendered;

(Give name of Coxswain and crew, and if more than one trip was made with the life-boat state any change in the crew.)

REMARKS.—(All particulars not included in the foregoing will be here stated.)

verry thick Weather Could not Sea Sandy Neck untill Late on Monday Morning 26th inst the Capt Was on Shore in Barnstable Village at the time the Vessel Was dicovered

Thomas Harris KEEPER.

Until He Died: Catboat Nomenclature.

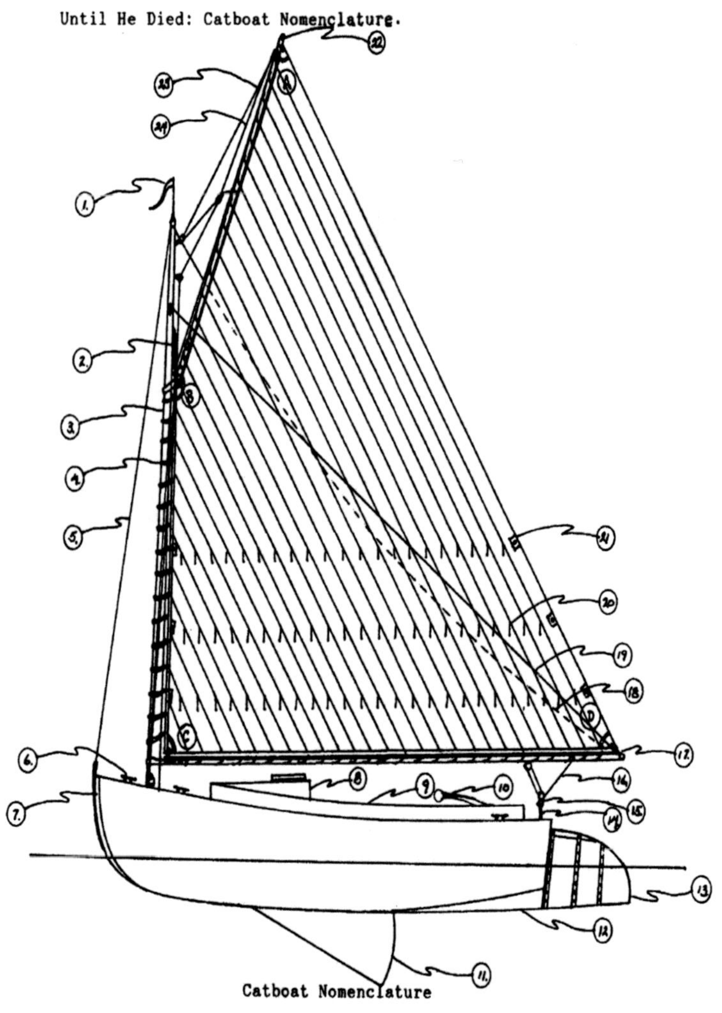

Catboat Nomenclature

1.Weather Pennant. 2.Throat-halyard & Lifting Blocks.
3.Mainmast. 4.Mast-hoops. 5.Bobstay, or Forestay. 6.Cleat.
7.Cutwater. 8.Cabin. 9.Coaming. 10.Tiller. 11.Centerboard.
12.Skag. 13.Rudder. 14.Traveler. 15.Traveler Block.
16.Sheetrope. 17.Boom. 18.Clewline. 19.Toppinglift.
20.Reefnettles. 21.Cringle. 22.Gaff. 23.Peak-halyard &
Blocks. 24.Bridle. A.Peak. B.Head. C.Luff. D.Leach.

Until He Died:

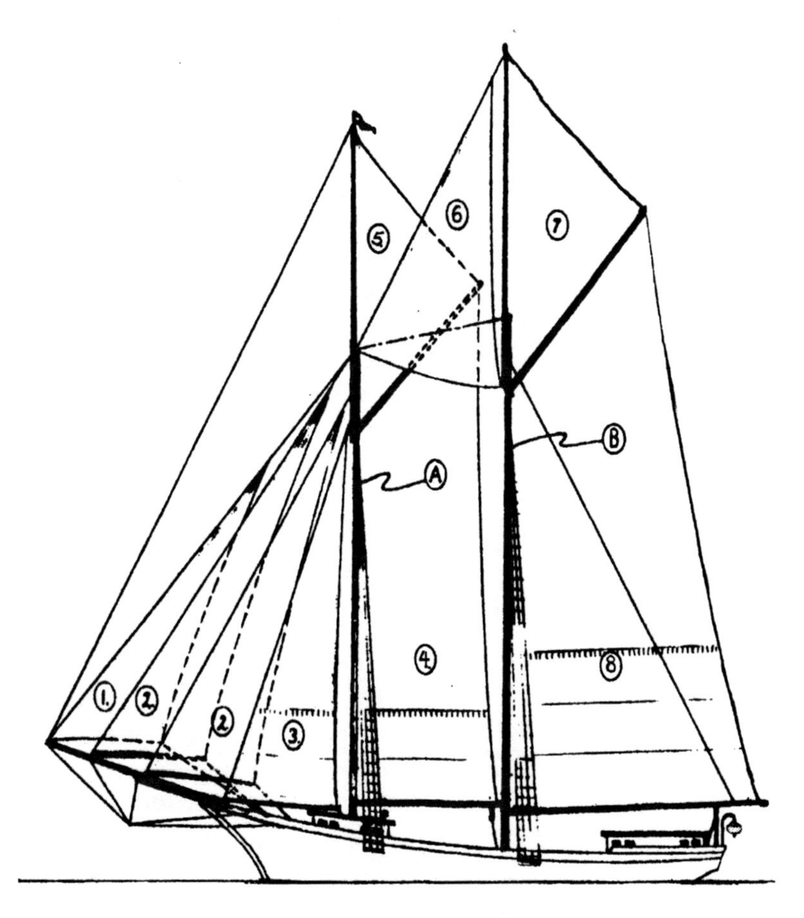

Typical Schooner Sail Schedule

1. Flying jib 2. Inner & outer jibs 3. Fore staysail 4. Foresail 5. Fore-gaff topsail 6. Main-topmast staysail 7.Main-gaff topsail 8. Mainsail

A. Foremast w/fore-topmast B. Mainmast w/main-topmast

Bibliography

Baker, (Capt.) Archelaus. *Account Book, Schooner Cohasset, 1873-1876.* (Original Document) Reprinted w/permission Cape Cod History Room, Cape Cod Community College, W. Barnstable, MA.

Beard, D. C.: *The American Boy's Handy Book.* Orig. published by Scribner (1890). Republished by David R. Godine (1953).

Bray, Mary Matthews: *A Sea Trip in Clipper Ship Days.* Richard G. Badger, The Gorham press (1920).

Brewer, John Peter, Edit.: *The Catboat Association. Bulletin #84,* Peter T. Vermilya, The Catboat Association (1987).

Daniel, Clifton, Ed. Dir.: *Chronicle of America.* Jacques Legrand, Chronicle Publications (1988).

Deyo, Simeon L.: *History of Barnstable County, Massachusetts.* H. W. Blake & Co. (1890).

Eastman, Ralph M.: *Pilots and Pilot Boats of Boston Harbor.* State Street Trust, private printing, Rand Press (1956).

Freeman, Frederick: *History of Cape Cod/Annals of Barnstable County.* George Rand & Avery S. Cornhill (1858).

Harlow, Frank P.: *Young Salt on an Old Schooner/Life Under Sail.* Frank P. Snyder, Edit. Macmillan, New York (1964).

Harris, C. E.: *Hyannis Sea Captains* . The Register Press (1939).

Mahoney, Haynes R.: *Yarmouth's Proud Packets.* The Historical Society of Old Yarmouth, Inc. (1986).

Otis, Amos: *Genealogical Notes of Barnstable Families.* Amos Otis Papers. The Barnstable Patriot (1888).

Perry, E. G.: *A Trip Around Cape Cod.* Chas. S. Binner Co., Boston (1898).

Quinn, William P.: *Shipwrecks Around Cape Cod.* Knowlton & Mcleary Co. (1973).

Russell, Patrick: *Scollay Square/Gone But Not Forgotten.* Boston Globe (1987).

Sloane, Eric: *Eric Sloane's America.* Galahad (1982).

Smith, Laura Alexandrine: *Music of the Waters.* lst prnt. Kegan Paul, Trench & Co., London (1888). Reissued, Detroit Singing Tree Press, Booktower (1969)

Snow, Edward Rowe: *The Islands of Boston Harbor.* Dodd, Mead & Co., New York (1936-1971).

Summerscape 1987: A Voyage Into the Past With the Cape's Courageous Men of the Sea. (Supplement to *The Barnstable Patriot*). Drawn from the Archives of *The Barnstable Patriot* Wkly. Newspaper. 1st pub, 26 June 1830. Barbara Williams, Edit. (1987).

Swift, Charles: *History of Old Yarmouth.* Pub. by Author (1884).

The Yarmouth Register. Wkly Newspaper. lst pub. 15 Dec. 1836. N. S. Simpkins. Archives, Sturgis Library, Barnstable, MA.

Thwing, Annie Haven: *The Crooked and Narrow Streets of Boston.* Charles E. Lauriat Co. (1925).

USCGS Coast Chart No.10: Cape Cod Bay. (1872, rev. 1880)

Villiers, Alan: *Men Ships and the Sea.* National Geographic Society (1962)

All photos from personal collection, or used w/permission of owners.

LaVergne, TN USA
16 September 2009

158116LV00006B/1/A